Praise

"A trip across America from a view point you would never expect." Steve, New Mexico

"I will never view homelessness the same way again." Ann, Washington

"Riveting from beginning to end" Karen, Montana

"So many stories stitched seamlessly together…" Chris, Georgia

Enjoy the journey.

Leigh Lincoln

ROAD HOME

LEIGH LINCOLN

Chapter 1

Freedom. Why was everyone always striving to achieve freedom? You know, after so many years of searching, I finally thought I knew what freedom was. But I couldn't understand why so many people claimed it was so wonderful. The whole idea of chasing after that dream no longer made any sense to me. Dreams, as a whole, didn't make sense to me.

Since quitting my job, well, more like running away from it, I'd wandered across the country, from one coast to the other. Didn't matter where I went, things still looked the same—bleak, miserable, lonely. Not being bound to any clock or responsibility would've been liberating to most. But nothing could satisfy my deep longing within.

You know that feeling? When you know you're empty, but nothing seems to fill the void? That was always my constant companion. To be honest, freedom wasn't all that it should've been. In fact, sometimes I seemed more chained than I ever had been before. For me, sitting and crying made more sense than running because I didn't know what I was longing for. How could I ever hope to find something I couldn't even name?

Darn, the coffee was cold. Feeling the iciness of the ceramic mug against my skin as I cradled it in my hands matched my mood. How long had I been sitting here stirring it, without even once bringing it to my lips to take a sip? *Doesn't matter, Cindy. The coffee was the price of admission.*

I sat there in my almost-clean, best-patched jeans, my not-so-holey blouse, my never-make-the-cover-of-Cosmo shaggy long haircut, and my ragged, chewed manicure. I could only imagine what those around me must've been thinking.

"Look at that odd ball."

"Why doesn't someone tell the poor fool that homeless people are not wanted?"

"Find a job!"

In the past few years, I'd heard all of that plenty of times and so much worse. If only they knew me, if only they knew my story—but, even then, it wouldn't change their opinion of me. No, it would only make me even lower in someone's eyes. If they could see beneath the homeless exterior I'd shown the world for so long now, it would be their turn to run. That was a mask that was now fused onto me, a part of me, and I had no plans to ever take it off again.

I looked around the mom and pop cafe, in that small town in eastern Pennsylvania. On yet another cold spring evening, I could spy only a few customers. These good folks had been looking at me in curiosity off and on, trying not to stare but failing. I could feel their eyes on me every second. You learn to ignore it when you're in my position, but it still sometimes makes your skin crawl. It makes you want to climb into the nearest hole. You must fight that feeling and go on. Those people may give you a slice of bread when you need it the most. Then again, they more than likely wouldn't.

The tables in the café: dingy. The padded benches: patched. The flowered wallpaper: faded from the sun. The food served: generous portions. Was that why customers kept coming back?

When your stomach gurgles at the mere thought of food, you know you need to keep your mind on something else.

Before the hunger overwhelmed me, I put my chin in my hands, my elbows resting on the table. Trying to imagine why there was a lack of customers here today in this nice little spot, I peeped around again. My guess was that it had more it do with the downpour, which had continued all day, than anything else. Everything outside was soggy and wet. The packed dirt parking lot was fast becoming a swamp. Yet in here was cozy.

Returning the stares of those around me, I got a good look at my fellow diners. Most of those huddled at the tables around me were middle class. Dressed in button-down shirts and ties or slacks and blouses. Singles whether for dinner or in life, I couldn't say. Those were the people who mostly looked down on the homeless. They knew they were only one paycheck away from being there themselves.

You hear so many sob stories over the years from people like them. You become almost immune to the horrors of it all after a while. They all swore that they never thought homelessness could happen to them. Yet they'd slipped through the cracks onto the streets with such ease.

For me, there was no slipping—I'd jumped head first into this life, fully believing that this was better than anything else I'd lived through. Hard to say if I was right or wrong on that score.

Forget the people; forget the stares—back to daydreaming.

When was life better for you, Cindy? I thought. *When were things sort of okay?*

College—now those were the good days. Barely working, barely studying, enjoying those last few years before officially becoming an adult. I was sort of out from under the heavy hand of my father, but not yet under the thumb of my husband. Funny how so many of my classmates stated that they'd love to go back to the era of the sixties. You know, drop out of life, become hippies, and hang out. Forever living like kids who never would have to grow up. They all only wanted to be free.

When you're eighteen, nothing seems out of reach. Nothing's impossible. The whole world is a glorious unknown just waiting to be explored. My classmates wanted to know what it was like not to be bound to the rat race forever. Their poor, unfortunate parents were slaves to their jobs. Their mortgages. Their car payments. Their social standings. We didn't want to be like that. It would've been nice to stay in that simple, pre-adult state forever, when life was happy, carefree, unburdened.

College encouraged that sense of freedom. So many professors never caring if you showed up. Nobody watching to see when you finally got to bed or even if you ever did. Usually, someone else was paying the bills. There were parties to attend. Games to be played. Dances to be danced. Boys to be kissed. Games to cheer at. Movies to go to dressed in costume. Nights where you'd lay out in the grass of the quad watching the stars with fifty other people.

Life to be lived with wild abandon, never caring what happened next. You were there to enjoy every moment as if it was your last. That was life at eighteen.

But it all was an illusion, nothing but a lie. Those kids didn't understand what a heavy burden living life was. I'd already lived more life by college than most people did in a lifetime, and none of it was good. And now I'd seen so much more, gone further than I ever should've gone, and couldn't go back even if I wanted to.

What were the words to that old song? Yes, I remember now: "Freedom's just another word for nothing left to lose."

Yes, that was what freedom was. I'd found that out the hard way. Over the course of many wasted years and many miles of wasted traveling with no purpose, I'd learned so much. A lesson that no one should ever learn. Freedom...

"Honey?" The rather large, plump older waitress stood by my table. Dull, dirty blonde hair was pulled back haphazardly in a loose bun. Her brown uniform was stained with grease and grime. She wore a tan apron, with pens and pads sticking out from the pockets at odd angles. Still, she looked better than I did, though that wasn't saying much.

I guessed I'd overstayed my welcome. Should've seen that coming since I was enjoying the comfy, albeit worn bench for so long. The warmth of being indoors was so nice, so much so that it'd been easy to not notice the time.

"What?" My loud, rather curt voice shot back as I gripped the table so tightly my knuckles turned white. I almost wanted a scene. Letting everyone know I was more than a homeless person seemed important at that instant. Someone with feelings and needs that had to be met. Someone who honestly knew that she didn't have anything left to lose, including the dignity and pride that she sometimes felt she'd never had in the first place.

"Ever'thin' okay? You'se been hunkered over that cup o' joe for hours now, but as far as I can tell, you ain't hardly touched it. I'm a real good listener, if'n you'se wanna talk." She kept nodding her head like a bobblehead doll and wringing her hands.

Huh, wonder if she was afraid to approach me? She seemed nervous enough, despite her warm words.

"Trust me, you don't want to hear my story—too long and uninteresting. How much do I owe you for the coffee?" Hoping it wasn't much, since I only had about a dollar in my pocket, I had to ask anyway. You can never take anything for granted in this life. I should know.

"Oh, not'in' honey, she's on the house. If'n you'se wanna come back and talk, I'm here til nine, not like we'se really busy here." She cocked her head, giving me a concerned smile as she waved her hand around to show the lack of customers in the room.

"Thank you for the coffee." Gathering up my rather dirty, worn coat and tattered umbrella, I stood up. With her hands now firmly planted on her ample hips, she'd become a wall standing in my way. I was tempted to climb over the back of the bench, make a bigger scene than I already had. Careful not to bump into her since she was standing so close to the small table, I did a little sidestep instead.

The look on her lined face was priceless. A sad, puppy dog face, like she cared what my problems could be.

You shouldn't care about strangers. You don't know what kind of can of worms you might be opening. You might be getting the worst surprise of your life. You might be getting me. I'm no angel.

I looked outside. It was still raining and getting dark fast. However, that wasn't half as depressing as the look on that waitress' face. I couldn't explain why it bothered me so much; usually I didn't care what others thought about me. It just did. It was like I was walking out on the only true friend I'd ever had. Would ever have. Which was ridiculous because I knew nothing about her and wasn't sure I wanted to. And besides, she knew nothing about me. Once anyone ever did, well, they would never want to be my friend or even be around me for long. After all these years, the freak image was still intact—the unlovable freak, that's me. I'd learned long ago who I was, and it wasn't a pretty sight. Ugly ain't only on the outside. You know it's true.

As my hand hit the door handle, I heard her whisper, "God, bless you, honey. He cares, He truly does." Then I stepped out into the rainy evening, shivering as the sudden burst of cold hit me. Pulling on my coat and picking up my well-used pack I'd left just outside the door, I began to wish I still had my car.

When I'd begun this never-ending, seemingly pointless journey, I had an old Toyota. But it had long since died at this stage. That car was a tribute to its manufacturers. It had almost 300,000 miles on it, with few repairs done before it gave up the ghost. Finally, the transmission had given out—no way I could've afforded to repair something so major. Even at that point so early in my wanderings, I was having a hard time finding enough odd jobs to pay for gas as well as food. You know, some things are more important than others, and food has to be at the top of that list. So I'd sold the car somewhere in Oklahoma, I think, although I wasn't exactly sure when and where. The days had become so blurred together. Especially lately. I couldn't seem to remember even the simplest things. Those details were in my journals, like many other now-pointless facts. Did anyone care if I'd been to Tulsa? Or Tacoma? Or Tallahassee? Did I?

Most days, I didn't mind the endless walking I often did, or camping out for days without end. But when the weather was bad, I missed having shelter. Any shelter. When you have no home, you look at things in a much different light. Sure hail could dent a car, but it could also kill you. You learned to seek shelter in the oddest of places. A car provided adequate protection from the elements, so it was ideal. A car was much safer and warmer than a tent. But what if you didn't have a car? Well, then you had to be thankful for a tent, if you had one, or thankful for a tree if that's all you got. Or you snuggle up to a dryer vent if that's the best you can do, grateful if it pumps out hot air once in the night. Anything to keep going one more day.

Today was one of those bad days, damp and dreary. Finding a campsite before I became soaked and it got to be pitch black needed to be a priority. I almost turned around to re-enter the cafe to ask for directions. But that would mean facing that waitress again. *And you're not doing that, Cindy. She'd want your life story.*

It was never fun to pitch a tent in an unfamiliar place in the dark. Being wet to the bone on top of it, well, that just meant setting myself up for one uncomfortable night. My nights were miserable enough with my morbid thoughts as company. No point in making things worse by being foolish.

Shaking off my thoughts with an all-over body shudder, I began to walk up the road as I always did. Placing one foot in front of the other, splash, splash, splash, I walked through the puddles. Too bad there were no dry socks waiting for me at the end of this march. Or a heater.

Want to know an ideal way to spend your rainy spring evening? Walk for about a half an hour with an umbrella that leaks. Scout for possible campsites while water is running down your back. Curse your rotten luck that you ended up exiling yourself to a life like this. Bring a date, a bottle of wine, try to light a candle—you'll have a grand time. I should know; I did all those things often enough, and tonight was no exception. Freedom was so wonderful sometimes. You'll see; give it a try. Or better yet, stay chained to your mortgage in your snug, dry house.

The place I found was about a half mile off the highway. In the dim light, it was hard to make out, and I'd almost missed it. I'd learned to never camp too close to the road where I could be spotted easily by cops. You couldn't be too careful around cops. Some were good and would give you help. Others would escort you across the county line and ask you to never return. No, cops weren't people to be trusted unless there wasn't another option. But I also didn't want to be too far from the road that I couldn't get help if I needed it—just one of the many little rules of survival that had served me well.

The ground was almost dry under the shelter of the trees. Setting up my pup tent was easy; it's not like I hadn't done it a million times before. My hands could put that tent up without me even looking at what I was doing. The tent was my closest ally, but even it would let me down someday. My last one had, and I'd replaced it without a thought. Well, some thought was involved. It wasn't like I walked around with a lot of spare change and could replace a tent at the drop of a hat. No, a great deal of hard work had been involved before I could move on with a new tent, and I'd hated every moment that it'd cost me.

Yet another meager dinner of stale bread and the last square of an old chocolate bar that had turned white. Someone had given me the bread a few days ago after I did some yard work for them. It was stale the moment they'd handed it to me. Those are the days when you should fight back, when you should say you are worth more than a worthless scrap that they were going to throw away anyways. But you don't because you know you won't have anything to eat if you say anything. Something is better than nothing is your motto. So there I sat in my tent, in my wet clothes, eating garbage in my misery. Again.

With a sigh, I settled down with my current notebook to record the day's events. Most days, I simply wrote a word or two about where I was and who I'd met. Lately not even that—yet another failure in my life. My mind began to wander again. Over the many years and miles this trek had taken me. Pictures began to form. Tears came unbidden and flowed down my cheeks, staining the front of my shirt.

How many homeless shelters and soup kitchens have you seen? How many times have you picked up odd jobs from nice people along the way for a meal or a little cash? Or even the not so nice for a few rude remarks? How often have you slept in a bed without sheets because it was the only bed available? How many times have you pitched this tiny pup tent, or for that matter just slept under the stars? But Cindy, you have freedom...

My most valued possessions were my notebooks, my journals; I had one for each of my ten years on the road. They were small, and I wrote in tiny script. Space in my pack was at a premium, so many things were more important than these small mementos. At times, I'd read them to try to justify those years. I was never successful; the years seemed like such a waste of my few talents and of my last remaining years of youth.

Tonight though, I couldn't concentrate on what I wanted to write. I couldn't do anything more than flip through the well-worn pages. I wasn't seeing the words, my vision fuzzy because of the tears I couldn't stop. For some reason, what that waitress said stuck in my mind: "He cares." Why should this god care about me? I hadn't stopped to give much thought to who or what a god might be, but I was sure that if there was one, he wouldn't care about me. There was way too much water under that bridge...

When I was younger, I remember only going to church at Christmas. To go to midnight mass with my very elderly grandmother was like a treat. It was the only time she would come anywhere near our house. I'd sit and wait by the front window, my small nose pressed against the glass, waiting with eager anticipation to see her old car pull up out front because she wouldn't come in. I had to run out to her; she wouldn't even leave her car. In fact, that was the only time I ever saw her, those trips to mass, until the year I sat and waited but she never came.

Finally, my father said she wasn't going to be coming again because she had died months earlier. Without a word, I went to my room and changed out of my dress. Feeling nothing for this woman who'd left me without a word of goodbye didn't seem out of place in my strange world. Odd that my father had said nothing earlier, but I guess it was another way for him to torment me.

In those years that my grandmother and I went to midnight mass, I'd follow behind her, heavy thumps echoing as she hobbled into the church, leaning hard on her cane. It was where I'd enter a special magical world for one brief enchanted moment in time. Too bad it couldn't have lasted more than that one night a year. I never understood a word that was said at the service. But you didn't need words to understand what was special in a child's mind. You simply needed to view the place as only a child could.

The way the candlelight danced around that darkened cathedral made the trip worthwhile. All the gold and silver trinkets placed in niches sparkled. The gigantic crystal chandelier hanging in the center of the room came alive. The faces of the porcelain statues softened and became real. If you were a child, it was a fantasy world come true.

Magically everything there understood it was Christmas and a time for happiness, joy, other- worldliness. There, for a few moments, I'd forget the tortures of life. Abuse was an everyday occurrence with my alcoholic parents. My first suicide attempt was at the age of ten. But here at this special mass, I'd get lost in the fantasy world of warmth and light. It gave me the energy to get through a few more days of anguish.

But that wasn't god. That was just warm fuzzies, a feeling that faded as soon as Christmas was over and real life came crashing back in. Now that I was an adult, I'd put aside silly fantasies like midnight mass. I knew better than to believe that there's a god. I knew there was no savior in this world.

Shaking off these thoughts, I realized how long of a day it had been and how bone weary I was. Time to get some sleep, because somehow things always seemed to look brighter in the morning. As usual, I tried my best to snuggle into my thread worn blanket; warmth was a luxury I was used to not having. You know you've gone too far from normal when being warm is rare. When one word from a stranger brings back a grandmother who'd been dead for almost thirty years. When your days were all filled with nothing because that was all you had.

Sleep, for me, was usually elusive when I was in this kind of pensive mood. Yet, somehow, that night, a deep sweet slumber overcame me as soon as I lay down. I don't even think my spot was what most people would call comfortable. But somehow I was beyond noticing, beyond caring. In my heart, I knew I'd come to the end of everything. Life was wasted on me. I knew that I'd only make one last journey. Back to where it had all began, though I wasn't sure why I felt the need to finally go home. I hadn't been home since I'd started this journey. But now, I knew I had to. Tomorrow, I would begin my long journey home.

Waking with the dawn was usually my habit, the sun coming up acting as my alarm clock. This was always the case when I slept in my pup tent. As the sun began its climb, the tiny space lit up with an explosion of light. From the moment I opened my eyes in the morning, I'd see every mote of dust dancing around the tent. You should see it sometime; it was the best way to be awakened, ever. Often, I'd lay there watching the light show for a while. Not like I had anywhere to go or any breakfast to eat most of the time, so what was the rush?

However, that morning, I had a plan nudging me from the back of my mind, urging me to move from my curled-up state and begin my day. Cautiously, I unzipped the door of the tent, taking a look outside.

You never know what's behind a closed door, or, in this case, a tent flap. Settling in the opening to get a good look at the grassy field that was between me and the highway, I took a deep breath. Mornings were always my favorite time of day—new beginnings, clean slates, freshness. This gorgeous one began with crisp, clean air left over from the rain the day before. One thing I'd learned was to enjoy simple and just be. If you scrunched up your eyes to look, you'd see each drop of dew on the grass. If you tuned out everything else, you'd hear the birds in the distance and identify the distinct calls. Or you could be a jerk and stomp around, noisy and loud, missing everything. Most people do, but I don't think it's right.

Pennsylvania wasn't as wonderful as the Arizona desert after a rainstorm. Not that anything could top that. *Now when was the last time you were in Arizona, Cindy? Think, think, think,* but I couldn't seem to remember. Why was everything so unclear lately? It was like my brain was completely fogged over. Nothing could penetrate through the dense haze I was in.

Vivid pictures of Arizona came to my mind. Even if I couldn't place myself there at a particular moment in time, it was still like I was there. Arizona, well, the whole southwest, was by far my favorite place to go—warm in the winter and as desolate as I always felt. There was a bond between the prickly cactus and me. We were the untouchables, the unlovables, yet strong enough to outlast everything no matter how little care we were given. We could wait for the sweet rain, when and if it ever came. But my life never seemed to have rain anymore. I never blossomed, never became something worth showing off. All too soon, I was becoming one of the cactus skeletons left to decay out in the hot desert sun.

Ah, but there, in the Arizona desert, you could smell the rain, that oh so sweet, sweet rain in an area that was always so very parched and dry. With sand blowing in the wind, everything felt gritty. The rare feeling of wetness was extraordinary: the sweet rain that could bring life or deny it if it never came; the simplest, purest source of life in the world.

Before any storm, the smell of dust hung in the air, the electricity so strong it could make your skin prickle. The heat sometimes seemed oppressive, like a weight bearing down on your shoulders, trying to grind you into the hard, thirsty ground. The grit whipped around in the wind or formed the mini tornadoes called dust devils.

The smell of the rain was there long before it ever arrived. The anticipation hung in the air, and you'd feel cheated if it never came to pass. Then after the storm had swept by, the sweet smell of clean air and water. There was the knowledge that life had been renewed. You could see it on every plant as water dripped to the dry desert floor. The desert would bloom and flourish, if but for a short time.

Why couldn't people have the experience of rain like the desert flowers? The flowers are smart enough to reach up as if to grab each raindrop as it falls. Was everyone like me? The prickly cactus that had dried under the hot sun? A withered shell clinging to life in a parched land? Yet still able to hurt others with the sharp barbs that were left? No, most people were soft and good. Flowers, not cacti. You know I'm right.

A bird's loud caw startled me out of my wandering musings, which was a good thing. I would've sat there all day otherwise. *Well, Cindy, so even the beauty of this day couldn't clear your dark thoughts.* Knowing I needed to find a way out of the deep funk I'd been in for the last several weeks, I had to do something different—anything different. This was by no means new for me to be holding onto such morbid thoughts and feelings. But this time felt unusual, somehow. I might've been wrong last night. Maybe my journey wasn't over. Maybe I should try to hold out a little while longer. Maybe, I was like a desert rose that must wait years for the right conditions to bloom. Maybe today I'd get a real answer as to why I should continue to live—why I should continue to go on, find a way to rejoin the human race, if in fact I'd ever been part of it to begin with...

Nodding my head, I said out loud with as much gusto as I could muster, "Time to hit the road."

After my last half piece of stale bread, I did my quick morning toilette. Knowing it was best not to smell bad, I always carried a few wet wipes to clean up each day. Then I broke camp, loaded up my pack, and headed again into the unknown. Well, the almost unknown. Most of this territory I'd crossed and recrossed before.

As I headed across the damp grassy field towards the road, I noticed a car was stopped along the side. Stopped cars always made my heartbeat quicken and often made me a little bit queasy. Of course, that was ridiculous; I was always hitching a ride somewhere. But being alone while hitchhiking made it more dangerous. I'd gotten into my fair share of scrapes over the years, so I'd gotten plenty of firsthand bad experience. Yet, I still continued on my crazy quest for whatever it was I was searching for.

Seeing someone climbing out of the small red sports car and waving, I squinted to get a better look but gave up. Even as he rounded the car, I couldn't get a clear view because the sun was in my eyes. As I drew nearer, he started shouting at me as he leaned against the car. One arm was draped on the top, one foot propped on the side. But his voice was carried away in the mild breeze.

Finally, I got near enough to understand, "Hey, I wanna help!" It was a strong voice—a cop maybe? I'd been arrested before and actually enjoyed it some of the time. Good hot food, usually. A dry bed, sometimes with an almost-comfortable, albeit thin mattress. A warmer blanket—no holes, unlike mine. Protection from the elements, or I should say better protection than a tent provides. Price of admission, you might ask? Well, all that can be yours for stealing a loaf of bread when you hadn't eaten in days. All in all, usually not a bad deal as long as you were in a small town with a jail that only had room for a half dozen or so inmates. Any more than that, and the experience could turn scary fast.

"What do you want?" I said as I slipped my pack off to climb the wire fence beside the road, careful not to snag my pants. Not like anyone would notice a fresh hole among all the others, but I would. All the while, I was trying to study the stranger as best I could. I had a general rule against riding with a single guy, but sometimes I broke it if he seemed like milk toast. You know the type—the kind of guy that couldn't hurt a fly. One who opens the door for you, gives you the last candy in the box, and always says 'Ma'am'. But even they can end up punching you in the gut sometimes.

He was the tall, dark, and handsome type in a suit, oddly enough. "My sister met you yesterday at the café; my name's Robert. We both thought you might want a lift. I'm going out to the west coast. It's quite a drive, but I can drop you off anywhere between here and there."

By this time, I was over the fence and only a few feet away from him. There was something different about him that I couldn't place. Although he seemed to be in his thirties, there was a childlike innocence and peace within him. Yet he seemed somehow old and wise as well. I'd met so many people over the years, but none quite like him. "Name's Cindy. Oregon sounds good to me this time of year, as good as anywhere else I guess. You going that way?" It wasn't where I wanted to go, where I felt I needed to go, but he didn't need to know that.

"Sure." He nodded his head and smiled. He seemed so warm and accepting of me. But he shouldn't have been; I was a homeless stranger—someone you help but only because you have to or feel you should.

"Your sister must be that interesting waitress who spoke with me yesterday. I was rather rude to her. I'm surprised she sent you out. How'd you find me?" Curiosity was getting the best of me; I almost smiled back at him.

He laughed, and it was almost mystical. "Oh, that's easy. This is the only decent camping spot for miles. We can talk more on the drive. Hop in." He opened the passenger door with a flourish and took my pack from my hands, but still I hesitated. "It's all right, you can trust me."

I wasn't good at split-second decisions, never have been. This one seemed to be one of those decisions where either way you choose you'd be wrong. I mean, really, I'd just happened to talk to this guy's sister at a café yesterday. Then today, he just happens to be going exactly where I say I want to go? Yeah, right. And everyone who wanders into a soup kitchen gets handed a gourmet meal and a hundred bucks. I was nobody's fool. Okay, I was a huge fool, but I couldn't be fooled by something that obvious.

Opening the trunk, he placed my pack inside, and I decided, what the heck, I might as well get into the car as well. After all, everything I owned was in that pack, and I wasn't about to lose all my worldly possessions. Few and meager though they were, I'd lost enough already.

Why do you care about those few things, Cindy, I chided myself, *you know that everything can be replaced.* The only things of any real value in that pack were my journals, and they held value only to me. Everything else was worthless junk, most of which I'd dumpster-dived for. But those journals, I needed those—they held me together more days than not. Or at least, I'd led myself to believe that.

"There are coffee and pastries for you since I'm sure you didn't have much of a breakfast yet." He pointed to a cup and a bag that were in the middle console.

After putting on my seatbelt, I reached into the bag and pulled out a danish. Glad for something fresh to eat for a change, I sank my teeth into the sweetness of my treat. Much of my diet consisted of scraps. Things people gave me from their leftovers. Expired food from typical soup kitchens. Stuff in dumpsters behind grocery stores. Very rarely, fresh food from good soup kitchens. Exceedingly rarely, things I purchased with my own money when I had some. I ate a lot of processed foods, junk food, and pastries. For some reason, these were things that everyone gave to homeless people. But fresh vegetables and fruit were never high on the list. Needless to say, any nutritionist would've had a fit trying to figure out a way to get me to eat a balanced diet. Well, even one balanced meal would've been a stretch.

As we pulled onto the highway, it hit me: he'd said he was going several thousand miles from here. Why was he driving in a suit? As far as I could tell, there wasn't any reason to drive three or four days in a suit. It would be wrinkled beyond recognition in a short time, so why bother?

I looked over at him, trying to get a better sense of who this man was that had given me a ride, but I was coming up with nothing—a total blank. His hands were rough like those of someone who performed manual labor, yet his face wasn't tanned and lined as it should be for someone who spent all day out in the sun. The suit he wore wasn't new and didn't fit him well, but his shoes were custom-made leather, shined to a high-gloss polish, and must've fit like a glove. His dark hair was closely cropped, with a hint of lines shorn into the sides so he kept up with modern styles.

"I have a short meeting in a town just over the border in Maryland. That's why I'm in the suit," he said, returning my gaze. It was creepy, like he'd read my mind. "Arrangements have been made for motel rooms in that town, and I'll drop you off before my meeting." He smiled at me again. I felt warm inside, not sure if it was him or the coffee.

"Well, thank you, but how could you be so sure I'd go with you?" I mumbled through a bite of danish, not quite believing this bit of good luck was true.

He laughed that laugh again. "God said all I needed to do was make the offer."

The god thing again. I had no reply but, "He cares," half under my breath. Why was I making such a big deal out of this? What I'd learned about religion in college wasn't flattering. It was nothing but a silly superstition handed down for centuries, something for peasants and the illiterate masses. It was a crutch to help weak people get through their horrible lives and a complete waste of time. It's not like it was a big help to me with my miserable life as a child. No, I'm sure, what little help that was there had more to do with my grandmother than anything else.

Trying to steer the conversation away from religion, I decided to switch the subject. "So what do you do for a living that earns you enough to drive a cool car and wear suits?"

"I do this and that, mostly point people to God," he replied with a giant smile.

I almost choked on my pastry. Then, I almost gagged on the hot coffee I gulped to get a grip on myself. Great, that was the wrong subject to switch to. From the crazy grin plastered on his face, he loved his job. Give him half a chance, and I was sure he'd be only too happy to tell me all about it. Boy, I was in trouble now.

"Serious?" Sure, he wasn't going hurt me, or at least the odds were in my favor. But he could definitely mess with my head, and I was already in a kinda weird place mentally. Plus, I was more or less happy with my established anti-religious stance. Well, as far as it went or as happy as I was about anything.

"And this car was given to me by a guy who knew I needed it. My job is lots of fun, but I tend to travel a lot, hence I needed a reliable set of wheels." The huge smile was still on his face, like he was proud of the fact that he was too poor to buy his own car. Trust me, that wasn't something to be elated about.

"Oh. So, I'm sorry about being rude to your sister yesterday. Do you live in the same town, or were you visiting?" That was the best I could do to steer the conversation away from touchy subjects. I reached for my second pastry, this time a bear claw.

He erupted with that laugh again. "She's my sister in Christ, not my real sister, and I was visiting that town as part of my job."

Ugh, this was going downhill fast. It was now obvious that I wasn't going to be able to get this conversation on safe ground. I needed a way out and quick. "Maybe this wasn't such a good idea, I mean me accepting your ride." I frowned. Having heard this kind of talk before, I knew it only came from those that were crazy into religion. You know, those people who stand on street corners with the signs saying 'Repent, the end is near.' Or those that handed out tracts to everyone they met. I didn't need this today of all days.

"Relax," he said.

Like that was possible. I was in the proverbial snake pit with no hope of escape until he stopped the car. Or I could jump out while he was driving down the highway at seventy miles an hour. Right now, that wasn't looking like such a bad option.

He was silent for a few moments, staring straight ahead at the road speeding by. Unhappily I munched on my pastry; at least I'd leave this car well fed.

"So, when did you begin your journey?" He began tapping his fingers on the steering wheel. It was kind of annoying — making my heart race faster like it was trying to outpace his fingers.

Oh good, a nice safe question, so to speak, and unless he asked why I decided to become a bum, I was okay. "About ten years ago."

"Oh my goodness, that's a lot longer than I would've thought! How have you lived? I mean, have you been camping the whole time?" His face was now lit up like I was the most fascinating person he'd spoken to in a long time. But I knew how far from the truth that was. I'm a nobody, nothing more than another nameless, faceless homeless person. You don't walk up to a bum on the street and start a conversation. Or at least you shouldn't.

"No. I've slept in shelters, barns, parks, cars, you name it." I looked down at my feet. I suddenly felt ashamed but not for being homeless — for being me. Knowing who I hid from the world, I was concerned that somehow Robert could see a little piece of the real me. I knew that was impossible and irrational. But you know that feeling you get when you've eaten a cookie before dinner? You're hiding it from your mother because you know you'll get in trouble? I was beginning to sweat under his scrutiny even though he wasn't looking at me as he drove.

"Tell me a story." That voice of his had such a calming effect on me, and my feeling of unease began to melt away. It was like he really cared about what I'd seen and experienced, like the waitress from yesterday, his sort-of sister, had. But why?

"About what?" I asked as I reached for my third pastry, another danish, and took a few more sips of coffee. I needed a few moments to compose myself. To try to put my mask back on since it must've been slipping. To reinforce the walls around my heart so no one's care could affect me. So nothing could reach me. Isolation was better than being hurt again. Or hurting others again.

"Anything you think was important in those years of wandering." Thankfully, his fingers stopped their cadence, and the car fell into silence.

That left the door wide open. I had to stop and think for a few minutes. Was anything truly important in all those years? The silence of the car came back to me as if to answer a resounding 'no'. But so much had happened, so much had gone wrong; this journey wasn't what I thought it was going to be. I'd gone everywhere but in fact had gone nowhere. Yet the one sound in the car was the steady, but faint, in and out of our collective breaths, and my heartbeat in my ears. That was in itself an answer. I was still here. That had to mean something. Right?

But why would he even care about any of that? About who I was? Where I'd been? Who I'd meet? What I'd done? But he was giving me a ride, so maybe I should break my rule of never sharing and indulge him with one quick story...

"Well, a few winters I've stayed in the Southwest. The winters are great down there with lots of sunshine, plenty of warmth, and no snow if you go far enough south. I was thinking about Arizona, the desert part, this morning. The smells from yesterday's storm brought it all back. You know the clean scent after it rains?"

Pausing for a minute, I could see a page from one of my journals. Might as well be holding it in my hand: *Oct, Arizona, Crazy college kids, Soup kitchen.* Okay, so the finer points were missing, but what was important was there.

"Anyway, I remember going to this little soup kitchen and lunch my first day there. It was down on the south side of this town in far southern Arizona. The people were wonderful..."

An added bonus about telling a story—I wouldn't have to think about what would happen when I finally got home. Or if I really wanted to go home after all. What if I'd been incorrect the night before and this wasn't the end of my journey? What if home wasn't where the answer lay, or there wasn't an answer at all? Confusion seemed to be my stock in trade.

Chapter 2

It was late October when I arrived in that dusty, desert Arizona town. The sun had set moments before, and the temperature was dropping fast. Not like that's unusual in the desert. My ride had dropped me off a few blocks from a park where they'd claimed I could stay the night. I hoped they were right, as the area didn't seem to be a good one. But then again, when did I ever end up in a nice neighborhood anymore? Homeless people weren't exactly welcome in places where Mercedes were parked. Where the McMansions were. Where the ladies who lunched lived. My world had gotten grittier the longer I'd been on the streets. But like a lobster in a slowly heating pot, I don't think I noticed how bad it had become most of the time. It simply was my life now.

Walking the couple of short blocks, I noticed how few people were out on this nice night. Sweating a little despite the growing chill, I passed rundown and abandoned commercial buildings. You know that feeling like you're being watched? Not likely you are, but your spine tingles anyway? That night, I was sure someone was following my every move. Being ambushed in the dark was one of my biggest fears; what would they do when they realized I had no money to steal? I never wanted to find out.

I wished I'd stopped at a different town earlier in the day when it was still light out. But I'd so wanted to be as far south as possible. When I started out that morning, I was determined that today was going to be my last day of traveling this year. I'd been hitching rides for almost a month to land somewhere I could make a nice warm winter home. Enough traveling for a while; it was time for this snowbird to find a place to land and finally rest. So this town was it, almost to Mexico; but now it was dark — not a way to start life in a new town.

As I entered the small city park, I saw several still forms huddled around. Some were under blankets, while others were only under several layers of clothing. Thus, I knew my ride had been correct with their information. My tension flowed out of me as I slowly unclenched my hands that I now realized I'd balled into fists. Not like I could've fought off an attacker with a twenty-pound pack on my back. Not with me weighing slightly over a hundred pounds soaking wet.

But in this park, all was secure. My brethren homeless were here, so everything was fine; there's safety in numbers. Some were on benches, some on the grass, but each had found a comfortable place for the night — as comfortable as one could be sleeping in a park, at any rate. This was their home, and mine also for at least this one evening. I knew that in the morning, they could guide me around and help me get the lay of the land from a homeless perspective. Where a soup kitchen was. The cheapest laundromats. The best convenience store bathrooms. Maybe a place with free clothes. Maybe a shelter.

And what was most important: where to avoid. There were places where homeless people would always be kicked out. You'd be yelled at and told in no uncertain terms that you were trash. No point in being shamed if you could help it. There's no printed tourist map with information like that. You gotta seek it out from those who live on the streets and understand the needs of the homeless. Because we walk in the same shoes, so to speak, we can help each other. Some will and some won't, but it never hurt to ask. Sooner or later, someone would give you the info that was needed.

As I found a place to sit under a tree, I settled in to watch the stars and city lights. As they twinkled in some kind of insane, competing light show, I began to cry. Maybe it was because it was beautiful, or maybe it was one of those days. Who knows? You ever feel like that? Where everything makes you sad? Where you've got to cry even if for no reason at all? I have days like that a lot. I try to hide it; people think I'm crazy enough because I'm homeless. I'm not crazy—well, I don't think I am. Confused, sad, sure that I'm not worth much—those things are true, but crazy? No, not so much.

Without warning, someone was shaking me. Nice and slow, I opened my eyes, crusted from the salt of my tears. Seeing a rather large black cop dressed in a blue uniform standing over me, I almost started to cry again. I hadn't even realized I'd fallen asleep still propped up against that tree, half slumped over my pack. My neck and back were screaming in protest over the awkward position I'd slept in, but my body should be used to it by now. I slept in strange places and positions all the time; beds were a luxury, not a necessity.

Birds were chirping their tunes. Cars were buzzing by in the nearby street. Life was going on as usual for the rest of the world.

"Miss, you can't stay here," the cop said in a deep, firm voice. It was morning already, the sky turning pink at the edges, signifying that my wakeup call had arrived. You know, every so often a traditional alarm clock would be nice. The beep, beep, beep would almost be comforting.

"Sorry," I muttered as I rubbed the gunk from my eyes. Gathering up my pack, I knew better than to argue with a cop.

There wouldn't be time for my usual morning ritual cleanup, ick. I may be homeless, but I still have enough pride to try to stay clean. Which, I might add, isn't the easiest thing to do in my present situation. Unable to help the others, I stood and watched. Everyone was being awakened by the small band of cops wandering the park. I wondered what the problem was. After all, we'd been there all night. Surely there must've been a better use of these officers' time than to round us up. It wasn't a crime to be homeless, nor was it a crime to beg for money, but I knew most people wished both were.

Good grief, how many times have I heard someone ask a policeman to arrest someone for being homeless? Now if that homeless person was drunk, that's an entirely different problem all together. But most of the men in the park with me that morning didn't have open containers. Yet here we all were, being rousted without a viable reason. How would you feel if a cop entered your home and did this to you? Helpless? Hopeless? Ashamed? Confused? That's what I felt at that moment.

"They do this every morning."

Turning, I saw the speaker—a weather-beaten, tall, lanky man whose face looked like worn leather. His hair was such a pale blonde it was almost white. He wore tattered brown shorts and a black T-shirt. His torn sneakers showed his toes sticking out, sockless. He was holding a small satchel that didn't close, and his belongings were trying to escape out the top. He could've been anywhere from twenty to a hundred years old. I was leaning towards a hundred because he smelled like death warmed over.

"Why?" I asked, completely bewildered. I'd slept in so many parks that I don't think I could even remember half of them, and this hadn't happened before.

"We're hard to see at night. But during the day we're real obvious, and that's not the kind of landscaping they want." As he said this, his mouth widened into a smile. The lines on his face melted, fading away most of the years of hard living he'd done. He rolled a fat cigarette between his stained fingers and lit it. "You can come with us; we go down to the kitchen and talk 'til lunch."

"All right," I said. It was always good to know that there would be at least one meal on any given day.

There'd been so many days over the years where there wasn't a meal at all, either for myself or for the other homeless I so often found myself surrounded by. Despite my many attempts at being alone, I never seemed to be. Shouldering my pack, I followed the motley bunch who were slow to gather their belongings and leave. I was the only woman in the group of about thirty people. Most were resigned to their fate of being driven out so early in the morning, yet a few pushed against the officers who were only doing their jobs as we left the park.

Old. Young. Fat. Skinny. Drunk. Sober. Almost clean. Crusty dirty. White. Brown. Black. Red. Yellow. You name it, it was in that bunch of men rousted from that park. If you looked, that was usually the case in a crowd of homeless people. But no one ever thinks to give a closer look. Everyone thinks we're all the same, but nothing could be further from the truth. Homeless people are like any other social group — mixed.

I once looked down on homeless people from my third floor office and didn't want to know anything about them. I kept thinking they were all the same — drunk, mentally ill, minorities. I now know the truth. Anyone can end up here for any reason, and the stories I'd heard would've broken my heart if I still had one. If I ever had one. No, my reason for being in this crowd was one of the more stupid ones, if not the stupidest. But no one would ever know my story; it was locked in my memory vault forever.

"Unusual to see a fresh face in the crowd, especially female. Where'd you drift in from?" the stranger asked, blowing smoke high into the air above my head.

"Here and there," I answered, moving a little further from him. Smoke makes me cough, and I didn't want to seem rude by suddenly breaking into a bout of hacking up a lung.

"Been out here a while and ain't found a way out yet. Be forewarned, there is none. Once you're out here, you can't go back." He pointed his thumb over his shoulder as he said this, like normal was so far away it could only be hinted at. He was more than likely right in that. What was normal anyways?

"I have a master's degree; I could get a job any time I want," I bit back at him, huffing as I glared at him. What right did he have to question my choices? It was evident that his choices weren't any better than mine; he was out here living on the streets same as me. From the looks of him, there was no way that this was a one-time thing for him any more than it was for me.

"As if anyone would take you with years of blank space on your resume." He chuckled, then broke into the raspy cough of a lifelong smoker.

"Oh." I didn't want to look at him, and I didn't want him to see me. I switched my glare to my feet and walked with my head down. My battered hiking boots clomped on the pavement. It was as if they were sealing my old life into a coffin six feet underground. Darn him for reminding me that I was stuck with this choice I'd made. I switched my gaze to the houses around us.

This was an impossible conversation to have; this guy had a one-track mind. Who said I wanted to stop living like I did anyway? At least for now, I needed to be out here searching, looking, discovering. Being in one place wasn't going to solve anything. Not that moving around seemed to be solving anything either. But someday, somehow, I'd find what I was looking for. I had to believe that; it was the only thing keeping me going.

How did that song put it? Oh, yeah, *The answer, my friend, is blowin' in the wind*—that's it. I needed to keep following the wind wherever it may blow. Who cared if I was beginning to look like a tumbleweed in addition to acting like one?

"How long you been out here?" I asked in desperation, trying to turn the focus on him.

"Almost twenty years," he said with what sounded like pride.

Well, he had a big blank space on his resume, much bigger than mine at that stage of my travels. Out of the corner of my eye, I could see his arm begin to rise, and I followed it with my gaze.

Pointing to a small shack at the end of the street, he declared, "That's the kitchen." He dropped what was left of his cigarette and ground it beneath the heel of his tattered shoe.

As we walked from the park, I'd gotten a good look around the area. Calling it a neighborhood, not a garbage pile, would've been a stretch. The place consisted of many small houses crowded close together. There seemed to be some sort of ongoing contest to see who could let their home decay the fastest. Or maybe it was who had the most colorful or artistic display of junk. On those houses that had paint, the paint was peeling. Chunks were missing from those that were stucco. The houses were, for the most part, earth-tone colors. My guess was that the original plan was to blend in with the desert landscape. However, that had failed in a spectacular fashion thanks to what the residents had added.

Many homes needed roof repairs; you could see where clay tiles or shingles were missing. The few porches were unusable because they were piled with junk—not your typical junk, mind you, but broken furniture placed in almost-artistic heaps. Small objects such as toys, toasters, and broken pottery were crammed in every free inch of space between table or chair legs. Almost every house had a hulk of a car in the front yard that was at least thirty years old. Broken down and rusted hunks of metal, most were on blocks with kids playing in and around them. It was like they were the world's greatest jungle gyms. Since the park that we'd slept in had nothing for the kids to play on, I guess it made sense in a twisted, dangerous sort of way.

There were refrigerators, washers, and other appliances in many yards. There were also plastic lawn decorations and ceramic Catholic saints, but no grass— only sand and dirt to run across. Every few houses, there was a tall, stately cactus, and these were standing like sentries over the whole place. Who or what they were guarding would be hard to say. Most houses had ropes attached to anything upright. Brightly colored laundry had already been hung for the day. The sheets and clothing were snapping in the breeze, whack, whack, whack. I had no clue how they were going to stay clean for long with children running between each piece, kicking up dust as they went, sun dancing on the sand as it was carried in the wind. Dogs were yapping. Some were chained to a stake in a particular yard, but most were just running free chasing the children.

Harsh smells of soaps and cleaners mixed with the smells of breakfasts being prepared. Spicy foods with the rich, tangy aromas of onions, sausages, and chili peppers. Smells so good you could taste them on the air. My mouth began to water, and I swallowed hard to keep from drooling, kicking myself that I didn't have anything to eat. Feeling angry when you have no right to be isn't a good thing.

It's not your food. You didn't work for it. Get over it, Cindy; ignore your hunger.

None of the people who'd given me a ride yesterday had been kind enough to also give me even a snack, much less a meal. That was all too often the case. Yet, my stomach reminded me that it still had needs and didn't care if people were kind or not.

The people I saw were Hispanic. Children of all ages were running everywhere—yards, alleys, streets. These kids were little more than naked since it was already quite hot. Even though the sun had burst over the horizon only moments ago, their skin shined with sweat. Their cute, chubby little faces would pop up in unexpected places. Then others would shout with glee at the surprise. The children's laughter echoed around the neighborhood. It bounced off the walls of each house and the junk in the yard. Laughter was everywhere at once—such a pleasant sound mixed in with the usual harsher sounds of life in a city. The beep of a horn, the whir of a motor, the rumble of a truck—the whole place was a chaotic world of odors, noise, and color.

At a chained link fence, my guide opened the gate to the kitchen yard. Little did I know this would lead to the place that would contain my greatest few months ever. Funny how I waited to be homeless to have a few months that weren't quite so horrible. Not quite so miserable. Not my childhood, when I was being beaten up by my father and put down by my mother. Not college, when other students thought I was weird. Not my marriage, when my husband thought I was cold and unfeeling. To be honest, my life had only been good when things were simple, and that was too much to ask for most of the time.

Life isn't simple; it's complex and hard. We demand too much of ourselves and others. Circumstances dictate that we be placed in situations over which we have so little control. We allow ourselves to be concerned with what we want, not what we need. Simple is as rare as a day without pain and as pure as a heartfelt cry. But simple is good, and simple is what I need the most but is the one thing that I can't seem to find easily. Maybe someday I'll find simple again. Like what I found there at a tiny kitchen on the wrong side of town where most people wouldn't be willing to go.

The yard was small for the purpose it served, earth hard packed from so many feet walking across it day in and day out. Unlike the others around it, it was clean and tidy. Milk and vegetable crates were being used as chairs and footstools by both old and young men. But not only those few from the park. I hadn't any idea where the rest of them came from. There must've been about a hundred people milling about. Almost all of the ground was being used by someone. Several people sat on the sidewalk in front of the house. Several more sat on cars parked along the street. The shack itself had been recently painted a bright pink, blue, and purple. Maybe someone's leftover paint? But it didn't quite hide the fact that the building was in desperate need of repair. Yet, the shack did stand out for being painted as a shiny beacon of newness in a sea of decay and despair.

Somehow, day-old donuts had arrived, so we were treated to breakfast. That would seldom happen over the rest of my stay, but I didn't know it at the time.

I only had a few cents rattling around in the pocket of my worn jeans, not enough to even buy a piece of penny candy. Just one look and you would know that this neighborhood wasn't a good location to find loose change on the street. If there ever was a penny to fall, all those kids would've been there to pick it up in two seconds flat. They needed the money as bad as any of the men already gathered here at the soup kitchen. Maybe more so, since they were impoverished by birth and not by their own choosing or making. Then again, maybe not, since they hadn't known anything different than gut-wrenching poverty. Why would they expect anything more than nothing? Would they even know that there was a better life out there somewhere? Not unless you took the time to tell them there was something more—something beyond the invisible wall around their world.

Pulling a crate out of the stack by the door, I found a spot to sit and began to munch on a chocolate-covered doughnut. I decided to introduce myself to the man who'd led me to this haven, who was hovering nearby. "By the way, name's Cindy."

"I'd shake your hand, but with the sugar factor involved..." He wiggled his powdered sugar-covered fingers in the air. He grabbed another doughnut and a crate, and sat down as well. "You understand, I'm sure. I'm Sam." He turned a bit to wave to a tall, skinny, long-haired, unkempt young man. The newcomer wore cut-off jean shorts, a ratty T-shirt with the faded logo of some band, and sandals. "Philip, come join us!" Turning back to me, he explained, "He runs the kitchen."

This new person also pulled up a crate and grabbed a doughnut. "So who's the new face?" Philip asked, giving me a casual once over.

"Cindy. Pretty, isn't she?" Sam replied.

"Won't last long in this environment—it's too harsh on the ladies," Philip said, as he pointed to the sun with his chin. They laughed.

I felt self-conscious. I knew that I wasn't good-looking, but I wasn't entirely sure why they were laughing at me. Then again, they could have been simply thinking how much uglier I could get. Leather looks good on a woman when it's hugging her curves. Not when her skin has been dried into it by long exposure to the sun.

"How's the petition going?" Sam asked.

"Not well. The neighbors don't agree that a soup kitchen is a vital community service. Everyone claims that you guys lower their property values. The city may shut us down if we can't get enough of the neighbors to sign the petition for the variance. It's stupid; we've been operating long enough that we should be grandfathered in. We shouldn't have to meet the zoning codes simply because we need to update and expand." Philip frowned, licking the frosting off his fingers.

Another thing you rarely see in soup kitchens—napkins. Sometimes you crave dignity even though you know you shouldn't. You want to scream until someone listens, but you don't. You quietly lick your fingers, wipe your hands on your dirty pants, and go on.

The conversation between Sam and Philip was interesting. The neighborhood didn't seem to have any value. The nicest property was the kitchen's, which wasn't saying much. What in the world could the other residents have a problem with? Some of the children we'd seen here looked worse off than the homeless children I'd seen in my travels. My guess was that many of the meals served at the kitchen went to the neighbors. The homeless men now enjoying the doughnuts on this beautiful morning would eat too. That went without saying. Yet, would you want to wake up to a trail of homeless bums walking up your street each morning? But then again, maybe the neighbors had no say because they didn't own the property they lived on.

"Another one was found dead this morning during the wakeup call," Sam said as he grabbed his third doughnut. I was on my second, this time a cinnamon sugar one.

I was wishing, yet again, that I could've had the much heartier breakfast that I'd smelled on the walk. Seemed like it must've been breakfast burritos or something similar. So much better then these hard doughnuts. All this sugar was making me feel a little bit nauseous on an empty stomach, but food was food.

"I heard. No one cares. The cops haul the body to the morgue, and tomorrow he'll be buried without even a marker. Half the time I wonder if they even try to find the family or the guy's real name for that matter." The faraway look in Philip's eyes as he said this seemed to show he cared, like each of these lives was precious to him.

Foolish of him; I was sure he had a home to go to each night. There was no reason for him to be so concerned about a bunch of homeless guys. It was enough for him to be down here running this kitchen; no one would expect anything more from him.

"Enough business, Sam. Today's Saturday; those college kids will be down."

"Ah yes, Steve and his harem!" Sam laughed, wiping his face free from doughnut crumbs with his hand. "They're enough to brighten anyone's day."

Abruptly, Philip turned and seemed to truly notice me for the first time. "How about you come inside and help me a bit?"

"Sure," I said as I gathered up my pack once again and followed him into the building.

Unlike the outside, the inside was dingy, lit with dim, bare bulbs. The walls were painted an institutional green color, stained with goodness only knows what. I peeped into the kitchen area, and it appeared that the kitchen was twice the size it should've been. The space went well beyond the entryway, creating a vast cavern. My guess was that one of the walls had been knocked down; thus the kitchen was also one of the original bedrooms. There were several stoves and refrigerators, but only one small sink and no counter space.

The building was cooler than outside, but by a small fraction, and humid enough for my dirty shirt to stick to my skin. The whole place reeked of rotting vegetables and celery. Without thinking, I wrinkled my nose in disgust. I was sure that I didn't smell much better, so then who was I to judge?

Cindy, a meal is a meal. You've eaten out of garbage cans, for goodness sakes!

Still, what would you have thought walking in there? You wouldn't have made it past the threshold before you turned and ran. Top Ramen is as low as you'll go? Fine. I'm kinda with you on that one.

"You can put your pack in the back room and wash up a bit in the bathroom," he said as he pointed to a door at the other end of the main room.

Rather blunt, but I didn't care, I needed to use the toilet in the worst way. In the rush out of the park, there'd been no time for the niceties that normal people get when they wake up. What I wouldn't give sometimes for a day when I could lounge in bed and get up at my leisure, not having to rush to ensure that I'd get the basics of the day taken care of. It was sometimes tough for me to remember a time when going to a bathroom any time I wanted to wasn't a luxury. Now, I was lucky to be able to use a bathroom half the time I needed one. Most of the time I had to make do with finding a semi-private spot behind a bush or trashcan. You have no idea how hard that can be sometimes.

When I came back out, I was put to work washing vegetables, in the bathtub of all places. That had to be some kind of health code violation—food prep in a smelly bathroom. Not like anyone was going to care—this place fed the people most tried to ignore on a daily basis. The vegetables weren't what you'd call garden fresh: limp carrots, a ton of wimpy celery, a few onions with black spots, mushy potatoes with eyes all over...typical soup kitchen fare—food thrown away by someone else.

I started my task with a sigh, wondering yet again why people felt it was kind to give something worthless to people with no value. Sometimes, I think it's better for us to go without than to be reminded of what our true worth in society is. Really, those of us out here on the streets know where we belong in the social hierarchy. Most of us know that most of you think pond scum is higher. But you're wrong. So very wrong. You see yourselves in us; that's why you're always looking down on us. I get it—it's a pretty quick slide to get where I'm at.

"Hi! I'm Patty."

Turning my head to look up from where I was sitting on the cold tile floor by the tub, I saw a short girl. She wore old gray sweats and a faded red T-shirt, grinning from ear to ear. Her long black hair was tied back in a ponytail. She wasn't much younger than me.

"I was told you might need some help back here." She bounced on her toes, way too happy to be here. This wasn't a place to be cheerful unless you were homeless and hungry. Even then, that was debatable.

"I'm almost finished," I said, not giving her more than a quick glance or two.

She seemed to hesitate, biting her lower lip. It was almost as if she was searching her mind for some common ground to open a conversation with. "So, what's your name?" She started to gather up the clean vegetables from the bin I'd placed them in. Not that the bin was what you'd call clean.

"Cindy." I tried to stare at only at the vegetables; they were easier to concentrate on since they couldn't talk back.

Feeling uncomfortable, I shifted my position. *When was my last shower? Who was this college kid?* She must've had plenty of money from somewhere to not have to work on weekends. Actually, we might've had more in common than she could've ever imagined. I was raised in a solid middle-class family, for what that was worth. Sure my dad was a functioning alcoholic, but I, for the most part, had everything money could buy and nothing it couldn't. No love, no acceptance, no comfort of knowing someone was there for me no matter what. I wondered if she ever felt the same. Not likely — she seemed much too full of bliss to have skeletons and demons hiding in her closet.

"Well, welcome, Cindy. I'm glad you're here." She patted my shoulder, and I recoiled at her touch. You don't touch the unlovable; it might rub off and destroy you too. You don't want to end up in my shoes. Trust me.

"I'm only here for lunch; I'm leaving town soon." Not exactly true. I was planning on finding a good camping spot to winter in, so no point in making any kind of attachments. Plus, getting to know people caused problems I didn't need. I'd learned that lesson the hard way. So many lessons learned, and I never seemed to learn them any way other than hard.

"Sorry to hear that; Philip was hoping you'd stick around and help him." She smiled at me again.

What was she talking about? Why would he want me? Nobody ever wanted me. "He never mentioned anything to me about that," I mumbled.

"Well, he's still working out the details. He does this for all the women who show up at the kitchen. This town's not a safe place at night. None of us want to see any harm done that could be avoided." The confidence in Patty's voice was almost reassuring.

"You must come here a lot to know so much about the way this program works."

"Every Saturday since I started grad school two years ago."

"Really," I said as I stood up and stretched. The vegetables were done, and I was a bit stiff from sitting on the hard floor for so long. We both loaded up our arms with the vegetables and carried them back into the main room.

"The food processor's all set up, girls," a young man's voice came around the corner from the far kitchen area.

"Okay, Steve," Patty responded. "Don't mind him. On Saturdays he thinks he runs this place."

We began to chop up the vegetables in the world's oldest food processor. It'd been set up on a rather beat-up table in what would've been the living room if this was still a house. The poor machine was forever getting jammed. Also, it made so much noise that conversation was impossible, but the radio they turned on was even louder.

Altogether, five college students were there that day: Steve, Patty, Amy, Sarah, and Meredith. They laughed, sang, danced, and cooked, completely acting like none of them had a care in the world, and I'm sure they didn't.

I began to wonder about these kids. They seemed so unconcerned about everything. Life was the here and now, nothing more. Did they ever feel the way I had felt in college — the need to drop out of life? It made me sad to think that I was once like them, as young, stupid, and innocent. But weren't stupidity and innocence the same thing? Now that I was a homeless bum chasing an ideal I couldn't name, did that make me any less stupid? No, less innocent, sure, so I guess maybe they weren't the same. But when I thought about it, I was never innocent. My father had taken that from me every time he got drunk and hit me. So no, I was only stupid. It was a given that I was going to continue to be so until I found whatever I was looking for, if I ever did. Which was kind of a big if. No, not kinda—it was a huge if. You know, like if the moon was going to break into a million pieces. Never gonna happen. My life was a wasted mess.

When the vegetables were chopped, they were thrown in the four immense soup pots. These were waiting on the stoves with stock in them that someone else had made, and then some pasta was added. The music was turned off—ah, quiet. I was glad for the silence because by that time, I'd gotten a pounding headache. From the sugar rush of the doughnuts or the noise? I don't know, it'd be hard to say.

Steve pulled chairs out of the back room, and we all sat down for a rest. After all the frenzied activities in that building, it'd gotten hotter as the morning wore on. Yet we slaved away, working so hard to get lunch ready for the crowd that was sure to come. After all, this was a free meal in a poor neighborhood. Homeless people come out of the woodwork whenever there's free food. Wouldn't you come running if you knew it would be your only meal of the day? I had a feeling that people were already lining up outside, but the windows were too dirty to see out of. Faint blobs of shadows weaving between the grime stains on the glass were all you could see. It could've been people, cars, or bugs.

As we sat and waited for the soup to finish, those college kids chatted about everything. From their schoolwork to the weather, no topic was off limits. Several times they tried to bait me into telling my story, but I never did. Why ruin their good time? Besides, I wondered if they'd ever stopped to listen to any of the stories of the homeless—the kind of listening when you open up your ears and really try to understand. When you try to feel the other person's pain. When it has touched your life in such a deep way that you'll never be the same. I knew how it had worked out for me, and well, let's just say I shouldn't be wishing that on anyone else. But could that be why they came to this dismal place? To listen?

Or were they here to make themselves feel better, having done their good deed for the week? That's why most people volunteer—to make themselves feel superior. *"Look at me, see what I've done."* That's what your puffed-out chests seem to say as you get into your fancy cars to drive home to your fancy houses. A little selfishness goes a long way. You make the most of it. We're glad, because then we get a meal.

But there's a wide gulf between a college experience and homelessness. I wasn't sure they'd understand even if they wanted to. I know even I sometimes couldn't believe what I went through as a homeless person. Well, as a person in general, I'd done so many things I now regretted. But there was no going back on this path I was on.

When it was time to serve the soup, one of the girls opened the door. Another pulled the table in front of it. Steve and Philip placed one of the soup pots on the table. The other girls placed disposable bowls, spoons, and loaves of breads there as well. Soon they were scooping up soup into a bowl, putting a slice of bread on top, adding a spoon, and handing it out the door.

I glanced out into the yard and the street beyond. There was indeed a long line, and I hoped that the four large pots would be enough. One small bowl of soup didn't seem like such a good meal. It almost seemed cruel. Yet no one complained; everyone simply accepted the soup and bread and said 'thank you.'

In silence, I watched as some sat on the crates in the yard to eat. Others wandered elsewhere, their homes in the neighborhood. Perhaps they had a favorite camping spot nearby, or they were like me and preferred peace and quiet. It didn't matter; there were too many to eat in the yard, and so some had to go elsewhere.

When the line was finished, Philip pulled the table away from the door. Closing it behind himself, he went back outside. Steve looked at what was left of the lunch, shaking his head.

"Sorry, girls, we get only bread today since there's enough for a bowl for Cindy and nothing more."

Shocked that they might've considered eating the food from that kitchen, I looked at them. Most people would've seen it for what it was — garbage.

We sat in silence as we ate. I the soup and what turned out to be stale, hard bread, they a half slice of bread each. I don't know how they choked down that bread plain. It was difficult enough with the broth from the soup to soften it up a bit.

When we were finished eating, Steve said, "Amy has an open space in her apartment. If you want, you can stay with her and work down here." It was clear he was indeed the boss of the kitchen and the leader of this crowd while he was there. Philip had been in and out the whole morning; he trusted Steve to do a good job. Either that or he liked being outside in the fresh air more.

Amy was a skinny, mousy redhead who'd said almost nothing the whole morning. She didn't look happy with what Steve was saying. I wondered how much say she'd had in this decision.

"Or we can help you get a permanent job around here and help you get established on your own. Philip has lots of contacts in the community."

"Why are you guys so willing to help me? You've only known me a few hours," I said. I wanted Amy to have an out if she was willing to leap on it, and I almost hoped she would. My plan of isolation was usually the best one; away from people, I couldn't do any harm — couldn't be harmed.

"Because we care about what happens to you. We believe God has called us to help those who are down on their luck. Besides, gangs are a real problem, especially in this area, and we don't want anyone to get hurt," Steve answered.

Amy stayed silent, looking at the ceiling, her face a blank mask showing nothing. So began my two-month stay. The space in Amy's apartment was just that—a tiny spot to rest my weary soul. Nothing more than an alcove with a futon, but it was a place to sleep. Better than my tent, which had been my original plan. I opted to work in the soup kitchen, so almost every day, I was down there. I tried to be at Amy's small apartment as little as possible since I wasn't exactly a welcome guest in her home. As the saying goes, fish and guests stink after a few days. So when I wasn't working, I was at the library, the park or an all-night diner, reading a book or people-watching.

I learned that Philip was a priest, even though he never dressed, talked, or acted like one. The priest from my childhood had been formal in his dress. Black slacks. Black shirt with a funny white ring under the collar. Black dress shoes. White and red robes over it all. When he spoke to my grandmother, he was stiff and cold, making it clear that he was better than us. Other priests I'd seen at soup kitchens or shelters were also formal in dress. All in black, minus the robes, and not willing to stoop to the level of speaking to the homeless. At least, not unless it was an absolute necessity. Yet, Philip sat with the unwashed masses every day, ate with them, and was as dirty as them. Something about it didn't seem quite right to me.

I worked with so much celery while in that kitchen that my hands smelled like celery much of the time. Even after I'd moved on, the scent lingered and was comforting in an odd sort of way. For days after I left, I would bring my hands to my nose without realizing I was even doing it. To breathe in deeply of the scent, to remind myself of the good people in that kitchen. To hear the noise of the food processor. To feel the heat and humidity in the kitchen because the swamp cooler didn't work quite right. To hear the gentle sounds of the children laughing as they played in the street. To hear the rough grunts of the guys lounging in the kitchen yard chewing the fat. To see the faces of everyone waiting for their meager lunch. Amazing that one whiff could flood me with all that. Like it was some kind of sweet perfume that was a reminder of your first love.

Saturdays were for the college kids. On the other six days each week, it was up to Philip, another priest, Andrew, and I to get the soup made. It was hard work but satisfying—no thinking required. Sometimes, I'd take bagged lunches to shut-ins first thing in the morning. Other days I'd work at a clothes closet at a nearby church late in the afternoon—simple work of sorting through the donations or handing out clothes. Some of these people had only recently gotten out of homelessness. Hanging onto their new lives by a thin thread that could break at any moment, it wasn't any way to live. Others were elderly, one tiny step away from losing their homes. When one has to choose between medicine, food, or shelter, what wins? Most were hard-working folks who were one paycheck away from homelessness. You know people like that in your own life. It might be a neighbor, a friend, or a relative. Or it might be you.

Those are the people that would always be at the bottom of the ladder. The war on poverty is never going to be anything more than a political game—a game played in Washington by people who hadn't ever lived in a shack on the wrong side of town. People who thought being poor was owning only two houses. People who'd always think they were superior when they're not. Those were the people that society should've looked down on, not us poor and homeless folks. But until you've lived at the bottom, you'd never understand.

Never once was I pushed to get a job beyond these basic tasks. Those were times of enjoyable work, because it was so simple. Here's your project for the day; now go do it. Why couldn't life, as a whole, be that simple? Why couldn't there be someone out there directing each and every step? Why must we be responsible for our actions? Why must we pay for the mistakes of others?

Soup kitchens are my favorite places. For the most part, you find honest people there — honestly bad or honestly good. There isn't much room for being in-between. These poor and homeless masses are the people that've been through the worst life has to offer. Yet they've somehow managed to survive, if for only this one more moment. Survival brings out either the best or the worst in people. That raw emotion is hidden beneath the surface, waiting to come alive again. In the microcosm of a soup kitchen, you'll see the result play out each day. The bad ones will steal your last crumb of stale bread, even though they've got a whole gourmet meal in front of them. The good ones will give you their dinner then the shirt off their back, and finally ask what else they can do for you. I feel at home in soup kitchens, more so than anywhere else I've ever been. I belong without having to do anything, be anything, or act a certain way. I just am when I'm there, and that is good.

However, those college kids were another matter. They continued to talk to me, to try to get me to see that they could care about me. They always asked me to go to church with them; I always refused because I knew church resulted in nothing. I never did figure out what their true motive was. Religion doesn't create caring people. It creates people trying to earn their way into the good graces of their imaginary god. Don't you see that too? Thus, it had to be something else.

After a while, it was hard for me to be around them. I was becoming more and more uncomfortable, like wearing a wool sweater that you can't find a way to take off. It itches like crazy, but you're stuck. I knew it wasn't good to have people care about you; in the end, all they would do was cause you pain, more and more pain. Just look at my father — he said he cared, and he beat me. My mother said she cared, and she ignored me. My grandmother said she cared, and she died. My husband said he cared, and he left me. No caring was never good.

The thing that finally forced me to leave was Amy giving me earrings because it happened to be Christmas. I knew she was getting too close to seeing who I really was. Not who I showed to the world. Not the mask I'd been making prettier and harder as the years progressed. But the real me behind the mask and the walls, and it signaled that it was time to move on.

I had no options. I couldn't stay since she was part of the soup kitchen world also, and so with a heavy heart, I left that night. I couldn't let my real face show or those walls come down. They were one of the few things in my life that I knew worked, that kept me safe because they kept people at a distance. But I kept those earrings; they've been the only jewelry I've carried besides my watch. Well, until that watch stopped keeping time and I threw it out. You can't keep worthless junk.

The earrings look like autumn leaves, and little did she know how much they represent my heart—dying fast, with only the cold ground to look forward to. Well, I don't know, I guess maybe she did, but if she didn't, it was a rather odd gift to give...

Shaking my head hard to bring me be back to the present, my teeth rattled. I knew I needed to switch stories before I shared too much of my private thoughts with Robert. I'd started to remember things I'd thought were buried too deep to ever be brought up again. That wasn't good.

Keep it simple, Cindy, tell the facts and nothing more. Don't reveal yourself, don't let him know who you are. Better yet, shut up!

Even so, for some stupid reason, I dove into another story before he could even utter a word...

"Well, soup kitchens aren't the same from one end of the country to the other. In the Southwest, they're low key with soup and bread. Maybe breakfasts or desserts, if you're lucky. Ah, but in the Northeast—now there's the place to go for free food! It's always hot and fresh, and there's plenty for everyone..."

I had to keep talking; it was like a faucet had been turned on and couldn't be turned off. Since I never felt the need to share anything with anyone, it was an odd feeling. The trick would be to not share too much, to not go too deep, to keep those walls in place, to never show the real me...

Chapter 3

After wintering in Florida, I'd hitchhiked around the Eastern Seaboard for several months. You know, vacationing. Seeing the sights. Getting yelled at by people in seven states. I'm sure your holidays are much the same.

My ride dropped me off on the outskirts of a coastal city in Maryland early one morning in late April. It was a little chilly, but not bad as I pulled my thin coat tighter to fend off the cold breeze blowing off the ocean. I could taste the salt in the air and hear gulls in the distance. Trying to block out the sound of cars, I closed my eyes for a moment. Their noise was ruining my illusion of being on the beach on a warm, sunny day. You know the feeling—digging your toes in the hot sand, the breeze just cool enough to keep you comfortable.

The blare of a horn snapped me back to the real world. I hate it when that happens. My fantasies were so much better than my reality.

As usual, I was almost out of money, so I decided that this was as good as anywhere to plant myself for a little while—maybe find some odd jobs or do some begging on a street corner.

Figuring that my best chance at finding a shelter or soup kitchen would be downtown, I looked around for a bus stop.

Delight—it's a wonderful feeling. When you reach into your pocket and feel something cold against your skin, that's when you know you've got a few cents left to your name. Or, on the flip side, there's anger. You reach in and feel nothing but lint. You've let things go too long, and your limited options are now gone. Today was delight, so I treated myself to a bus ride with the few coins I found in the pocket of my jeans.

In the early morning, it was obvious that everyone else on the bus was on their way to work, dressed in suits and ties or skirts and jackets; then there was me. I wore my best jeans that had a hole in only the one knee and two ragged shirts under my torn coat. None of it was what you'd call clean. Okay, filthy was putting too nice of a spin on it.

Added to that, my pack was acting as an awkward extra rider to the crammed bus. There was no good way to stow it out of the way as the people streamed off and on. Each time the bus stopped, I got bumped and had to readjust my pack. Not to mention the scowls and dirty looks that everyone was giving me. You would've thought this was their personal car and their personal space. Yeah, I was making everyone's day that much better and brighter, just like I always do. But they would have to live with it; after all, I'd paid my fare, so I had as much a right to be on that bus as they did. But the "Get out of my way!" and "Why are you on the bus?" comments were starting to get to me. My face was getting redder by the stop. You don't have to be rude to me because I'm homeless. People are people. Look past the exterior for once in your life.

When the bus stopped, we were at what looked like some kind of transfer center. I knew that would be the best time to ask the driver for some help since the bus now emptied out completely. Thankfully, I learned from the driver where a soup kitchen was and what time lunch was served. You never know;

sometime public servants can be helpful. Unfortunately, most of the time, bus drivers refuse to talk to homeless people. Or, they won't answer questions and tell you to go to hell instead. It was one more thing I'd learned to live with.

The simple fact is that it's much easier to ask for help from another homeless person. Anyone who worked for whatever city you happened to be in at the moment would more than likely ignore you. Deal with it. You don't pay taxes; thus you don't pay their salary. They know it and act like it. Yeah, kindness isn't in anyone's job description.

After transferring to another bus, I had to walk the last few blocks. Spotting the cross streets that I'd been told to look for, I knew from the number of people that it was the right place. I mean, why else would there be a clump of people there in the middle of the morning? For goodness sakes, the line for the free meal was already about a block and a half long. Even though lunch was over an hour away, people were snaking around the building as far as the eye could see. Well, you might've done that for concert tickets, I suppose. But here, there was a wide variety of homeless and poor people in the line.

Men, women, children, young, old, all races and nationalities, and all down on their luck. There were also quite a few women and children in the line who didn't appear to be the typical homeless or poor. Many were dressed well, some in work attire or uniforms, the children clean and neat. It didn't fit with my usual experience. I couldn't figure out why people would stand in line for free food who didn't appear to be in need of it. Maybe they thought a celebrity had been sighted.

After I'd joined the line, I slid my pack to my feet, glad to get a few moments of rest. You never realize how heavy a burden it is to carry everything you own with you every second of every day until you do it. There are times you want to chuck it all, say 'forget it, I can do without,' but you know you can't. How gross would it be to never be able to change your underwear at all, even if you now only change them once a week? No, but it feels good to lay that burden down every once in a great while. Even if it's for only a few fleeting moments. There are so many other burdens in life that you can't ever do that with. Like regrets.

Soon, a young black woman in some kind of uniform came over to me with a smile lighting up her face. Smiles like that can be contagious; this one made her even prettier than she was, which helped. Everyone she passed by smiled back.

"Hi! My name's Janice. I see you're carrying a pack; you must be new in town. Need a bed for the night?"

"Sure," I replied with a shrug. Rule number one of being homeless: Never turn down an offer of a bed or a meal, the simple reason being that you never know if or when they'll be offered again.

"Follow me; there's a place run by the nuns up the street. Your place in line will be saved 'til we get back," my new best friend Janice said. "Right, Henry?" She smiled at the short Hispanic guy behind me in line and patted his arm.

"Of course, anything for you, girlfriend," Henry said as he licked his lips suggestively with his tongue. As he slid his hand across Janice's backside, she was quick to slap it away like it was an insect. "Ah, girl, why you gots to treat me that way?"

She ignored him, turned, and started walking away—shaking her hips as she did so. Prompt to pick my pack up, I followed her, not wanting to miss out on my chance at shelter for the night. We walked up the street, which in a few blocks turned from a commercial area to a section of brick row homes. Janice pointed to two tall brick homes that were connected by a covered walkway on the second floor. This left a small flower garden on the ground floor only now beginning to bloom.

Pretty little crocuses—you know it's spring when you see them. All you think about is that summer is right around the corner. You plan BBQs, beach parties, and vacations. All I think about is trying not to have heat stroke if I'm not far enough north.

I plan a way to get to Maine or Wisconsin — anywhere that I can live outside without dropping dead. You don't have air conditioning in a tent, you know.

As we approached the nearer one, she walked up the steps, me trailing behind. Ringing the bell, she said into the speaker, "Hey, it's Janice here." She sat down on the steps, resting her chin on her fist. "I've got a key, but I can't bring in a visitor without askin'."

"Okay," I said as I joined her on the steps, setting my pack at my feet. We waited in silence for several minutes before someone answered.

"Ah, yes, Janice, what is it you require today?" A female voice, with a definite clipped English accent, answered from the speaker.

She stood up. "Sister Rita, I've got..." She hesitated.

"Cindy," I pitched in.

"...Cindy here, and she needs a bed."

"Very good." The door buzzed open. "Come in, and I will be with you in a moment. I will get you keys and assign a room."

We entered a darkened hallway and walked back into an equally dim office. It was hard to see the small woman in the corner of the room.

"Room number 203, front door key," she mumbled to herself as she looked through keys that were pegged on a board on the back wall. "Good, now let us take you upstairs."

She opened a door in the back wall, and the bright light was a shock in the hallway beyond. I was surprised to see that the small woman was Indian. She was wearing a red saree, had a dot on her forehead, and was probably in her sixties. We followed her up a flight of stairs and back another darkened hallway, where she opened a door.

"I hope this will be to your liking."

The room was nice, with a bed, dresser, and desk, all done in peach and cream.

"I see you have a pack, which you may leave here while you go get your lunch. These are your keys." She handed them to me. "We only serve dinner here, and that is promptly at six each evening. There is cold cereal and fruit, if you wish to have breakfast or a late-night snack in the dining hall. The dining hall is in the basement."

"Thank you," I said as I accepted the keys and put my pack on the bed; then I followed them back downstairs. This was the first shelter I'd stayed in where you got your own room and a key to the outside door. Usually, you had to share a room with at least one other person and never had keys. Plus, I was rather surprised that the woman had asked me no questions about who I was.

"We expect you to find a job, as after one month, rent will be due," the matron said as we exited the building.

So maybe it was some kind of a boarding house, not a shelter—but then, wouldn't she have asked for my last name and some ID? I was glad she hadn't asked for ID; I didn't have any, and there was no way I could get one if anyone ever demanded it. After my driver's license had expired years before, I had, like a fool, tried to renew it. But the state I was in at the time wanted me to have a permanent address. I didn't even have a temporary one, unless take a left at the oak tree, walk twenty paces, then take a right and look for the black/green pup tent counted as an address.

Needless to say, I was laughed out of the DMV. Like having an address somehow made you more of a real person. But, I knew that wasn't true—just because you seemed invisible on the streets, it didn't mean you were. Thus, that link to my past life was forever severed, as so many others had been along the way, which is why I now got jobs I could do under the table or took handouts from anyone and everyone. Maybe now you understand why homeless people are always begging on every street corner. Maybe now you'll look at us in a little different light.

"Don't mind Sister Rita; she won't throw you out if you can't make rent. As a nun, she can't—the church won't let her," Janice said as we headed back down the street to the soup kitchen.

"Thanks, that's nice to know," I replied. Okay, so maybe it was a shelter; they'd never throw you out of a shelter unless you were drunk or high. Well, if you got in a fight with another guest, they might, depending on the reason.

This was a weird turn of events. I was expected to find a job and not free load because I'd found a shelter where people paid rent—amazing. I always needed some money anyway, since I wasn't one of the homeless who tended to stay in one place or a small area. Rather, I wandered from coast to coast, and I'd found I couldn't always rely on the kindness of strangers. I often didn't know where to find soup kitchens or food banks in strange cities. Many small towns had no services that could help me. Besides, begging often got me no results, and asking to do odd jobs often got me only a few meager scraps. I'd have to think about how best to deal with this situation; it might be best to move on before the month was up.

Arriving back at the kitchen, I saw that our place in line had indeed been saved for us by Henry. He was only too happy to have Janice back. He gave her a huge smile and made some rather crude gestures. She ignored him again and wandered off to talk to others. Seemed to me she was the unofficial hostess of the soup kitchen line.

I also noticed that many men had joined the women in line. Most must've come from some type of manual labor work; they were dusty and dirty from a hard day on the job. Others continued to join the line next to someone who'd saved them a place. The line got longer and longer, wider and wider, and more crowded. No one seemed to mind whose place was whose; everyone was chatting with friends, old and new. The line seemed like it was more of a formality, there to keep people on the sidewalk and out of the street, not as a way to mark who was going to get fed first.

Standing there and taking it all in, I never cease to be amazed by how happy many poor people seem to be. People like me, with nothing, have no reason to be cheerful. I'm depressed almost all the time. Wouldn't you be? Yet here these people were. Cracking jokes. Laughing over what the children were doing. Talking about who did what to whom. Who was having a baby. Who was getting married. Who had a new job. Who was moving on to a better life. You would've thought it was a giant social club, not a soup kitchen line.

"Lunch will begin soon," Janice said, walking up behind me, breaking into my thoughts. "I've got to go back to work after this, but you go back to the house and relax after we eat."

"Where you work?" I asked to be polite, not caring even a little. I'd learned early in my journey that it was best not to care.

"At a fast food joint a few blocks away; I've got a split shift today," she answered, looking around at the crowd while smiling and waving at many of the new arrivals. They all smiled and waved back. Like it was old home week at a reunion.

"Like it?" I asked as I moved a few feet forward with the others in line, as it was now beginning to inch forward at a rapid pace. I was glad for that. My stomach was telling me it was well past time for something to fill it; it was always so demanding. My feet were getting tired of standing on the hard cement, my back aching from the pack it was no longer carrying.

"It's okay; I'm just getting enough cash to get to where my daughter is." She turned to look at me with yet another smile.

"I see." Rule number two of being homeless: Don't pry for more info than is freely given. We all have a sad story to tell, or else we wouldn't be homeless. However, most of us don't want to be asked by everybody and his brother what it is. If we wish to share, we will, simple as that.

We were silent the next few minutes until our turn came to enter the building. Turned out it was a warehouse, filled end to end with dozens of tables, some large and some small, half of which were now filled with the hungry masses from the line. We were ushered to a small table by a smiling teenage hostess who offered us juice, water, or tea after we were seated. It surprised me that a soup kitchen had tables for everyone to sit at, and we were given a choice of drinks. Not only that, but the tables had nice blue and white checkered tablecloths. Flowers in a crystal vase decorated each table. Also, the hostess had asked how she could 'serve' us today. Like she thought we'd walked into a nice restaurant and actually had the money to pay.

"You'll like the food here; they've got some of the best chefs in town!" Janice was helping herself to some bread and butter that sat in a wicker basket in the middle of the table. "Dig in!"

The other four people at our table were greedily stuffing their pockets with bread. Instinct told me that if I was to get any, I'd have to act in haste. He who hesitates around free food gets left out. No, Confucius didn't say that. At least, I don't think so.

I selected several slices of a whole grain bread that was fresh baked and hot—what a shock that was. Not stale store-bought white bread, which was the usual fare at the other soup kitchens I'd been in. As I began to eat, to my utter amazement, more bread was placed on our table. This was done by another smiling teenager, who whisked away the now-empty original basket. The drinks arrived with heaping plates of food: spaghetti with meatballs, mixed vegetables, and a cup of pudding on the side— all served by yet another smiling teenager. You know when you fall asleep hungry? Then all you could dream about is food? That was the state I was now in. It was hard to believe it was real.

Most of our meal was in silence because as more people came in, the noise level became almost deafening. The place was a complete madhouse— hundreds of people eating, with dozens milling around serving them and nothing to dampen the noise in the warehouse. The walls were bare bricks. The roof was bare metal, with steel beams exposed. Lights were hanging down from those beams by only the electrical wires. A swinging door gave a peek to the stainless steel industrial kitchen beyond the main dining hall. Each time someone brought out more food, you could see the wink of the metal. But the hot fresh bread kept coming to our table, unasked for. For the first time in months, I'd eaten so much I felt sick. It was a wonderland, despite the bare bones appearance — things are often not what they seem.

"What's up with the teenage waiters?" I asked as we were heading out the door.

"The kids are from some homeschool club; they're here every day," Janice said.

"Oh, that's interesting. Well, thanks for your help today. I'll see you later," I said as I headed up the street to the shelter house. In my experience, kids were often the best ones to work with the homeless. They're completely non-judgmental — or too scared stiff to show anything else. It's hard to tell the difference.

It'd only been a few days since my last stay at a shelter, but I still took a shower before I finished unpacking. Even now in my present state of living nowhere and everywhere, I liked the sensation of being clean. Even if it's no longer an easy task, you still should take the time to be presentable. You people who live for the weekends where you can be a couch potato in your dirty sweats wouldn't understand. Soap's intoxicating to me, and I steal little slivers of it from bathrooms when I can find some. Usually, I've got to make do with wet wipes that I take from convenience stores or fast food places. They work better for your skin but don't smell as good as soap. Washing your hair in a dirty gas station sink with that soap is almost impossible. Worse yet is that foaming stuff. So a real, honest-to-goodness shower is a treat.

As I combed out my hair, I thought about that last shelter that hadn't worked out. It was an old Army base, and the people who ran it somehow forgot that it was no longer part of the Army. They expected us to get up at the crack of dawn to exercise for an hour before a meager breakfast of oatmeal. Then, there was room inspection after breakfast. Yet another hour of exercise before a peanut butter and jelly sandwich for lunch. Lessons on discipline until dinner, and finally, more exercise after a poor dinner of soup. It wasn't for me; I got plenty of exercise walking as much as I did, and my normal diet was poor at best. Best guess, I was at least twenty pounds underweight before I got there. If I'd stayed at that shelter, they would've killed me in a week—I'd lasted a day and a half. Yet another example of you well-meaning people not understanding what homeless people needed. A little discipline would've been fine, but not to the point of trying to kill someone.

As I surveyed the room I was currently in, I thought that my luck may have turned a bit. This didn't seem like it was going to be a hard place to live at all.

Janice had told me where a TV lounge was so we could meet there later and hang out. I couldn't figure out why she was so desperate to be my friend. She'd seemed to know everyone at the soup kitchen earlier. I was sure any one of them would've made better company than me.

With nothing to do until dinner, I decided to kick back and relax in front of the TV. I couldn't remember when I'd last done that, since most shelters didn't have a TV. It was surreal to do something so normal. All I needed was bonbons, and I could've been the housewife I'd always dreamed I'd be someday. What a joke; I'd never once thought that my life would ever be that easy, that carefree. Do you have someone who can provide for your needs so it can be? Do you wish you could? Or are you like me and know how foolish that is? Because I always knew I had to protect myself, even as a child. When I failed, I knew there was no one there to save me.

No one bothered me all afternoon as I watched reruns of old comedy shows. A few shadows fluttered across the wall, as people wandered by in the hallway. I'm not sure if I laughed along with the canned laughter of the shows, but most of it didn't seem funny to me. My life was so far removed from what others considered average. I'd become too cynical to find humor in much anymore.

Soon, it was time for dinner, and I went downstairs to find I was the only lodger in the dining hall. Sister Rita and three other women were in the kitchen. They all seemed rather plain in their dark dresses against Sister Rita's red saree. I declined to say hi. Yeah, it was rude, but oh well. They looked busy.

"Welcome, Cindy. These are the other nuns that live here and help me run the house. Dinner will be served in a moment. Please have a seat; we will serve you shortly." Sister Rita popped her head out the opening for a moment. The smile on her face showed that she was glad to see me. Well, she didn't know me yet. Give her some time, and she'd change her tune.

Looking around for what might be a good spot, I picked a table in the corner. Far away from everyone else, if, by chance, someone else came. The plain wooden table had chipped edges, the top worn smooth. The soup kitchen I'd eaten lunch in earlier that day was nicer than this place. Here had horrible, dreary lighting and no decorations. There were about a half dozen tables in the room, each with four chairs. There was one long florescent light that was putting out a glow on only a thin strip on the floor below it. The walls were crumbling limestone foundation bricks—you know, the kind that would be damp every time it rained—and even now, on a sunny day, the place smelled vaguely of mildew. The room lacked any kind of vitality and charm.

Sister Rita came out and placed a simple meal of a hamburger and fries in front of me. She then seemed to glide to the other side of the room to join the other nuns who'd followed her out with their plates. She blessed the meal before beginning to eat, the other three never saying a word. We all ate in companionable silence, me wondering why everyone else who lived here was passing up a free meal. As Sister Rita picked up my plate when I was finished, she asked if I'd like to join them in prayer and Bible reading. Of course I refused. Now I understood why no one was there— everyone was avoiding the nuns. You got the meal, but you also got their religion as a side dish. Yuck. Way to leave a sour taste in your mouth.

Returning to the lounge after dinner, I sat and watched more reruns. It felt odd to be alone in a house and not in my tent; I was out of place like a fish out of water. The TV earlier had been at least somewhat enjoyable or at least tolerable. But now it had become grating, like a cricket stuck in a tent all night. I was starting to wish I was outside, in the fresh air. That was what seemed normal to me now, and my skin was beginning to itch like I'd gotten a rash.

Hmm, I wondered if I was allergic to furniture? Or people? Or both?

"Hey, would you like to see where I work?" Janice asked as she entered the lounge. She must've been back for a while since she was now wearing skin-tight jeans, plus a black tank top with the word "hot" blazoned across it in neon pink lettering. No bra. You might've mistaken her for a hooker. Who knows, you might've been right.

"Sure, I've been sitting here way too long." I laughed as I stood up, shaking my head and thinking how I almost regretted eating so much at both lunch and dinner. How often could any homeless person say that?

We headed out the door and up the street; a local fast food place appeared on the right as we turned the next corner. It was rather rundown, dingy and dirty; the owners were most likely using it as a tax write-off.

"You'll like these guys—they're great," Janice said as she opened the door.

As we entered, the thing that struck me was that I was the only white person in the building. Customers and crew alike were all black. However, unlike the outside, the store was neat and clean on the interior, despite how busy it was.

A good-looking, lighter-skinned, young black man wearing a uniform approached us. He laughed, his face warm and welcoming. "Hey, Janice, you know your shift's over, right? You live somewhere, but it's not here!"

"John, I just wanted you to meet Cindy," she said, pointing to me. "She's one of us." I assumed she meant homeless. Or broke.

"Oh, all right then. I'll get her a cup," John said as he went behind the counter, grabbed something, and returned to us with his hands behind his back. "I hereby welcome you into the drinking club." He bowed slightly as he extended a large, pink plastic cup out to me with a grand gesture. The words "Crazy Is" were printed on the side in gold lettering. He gave me a quick wink.

I wasn't sure what was going on, but I reached out and accepted the cup. "Uh, thank you," I said, giving John a weak smile.

Janice laughed. "If you bring that cup in here, you get free drinks from the soda fountain any time you want. Plus, when it's not as busy in here, we sit around and talk even though we're supposed to be working. Now you're welcome to join us."

So began my short stay in that city. I never did try to find a job, but I did hang out at that fast food place often. At first, the all black, mostly teenage crew was polite to me when Janice was there. They ignored me when she wasn't. But soon, I became a fixture. They came to include me as one of their own, even including me in white-bashing sessions. They felt that a poor, uneducated white man was trash, and became that way because he chose to be. Whereas, a poor, uneducated black man in the same situation was a victim of society.

Filled with young hopes and black pride, they felt that blacks could take over the world. If only whites would make the system fair towards all, that is. My comments about reverse discrimination went on deaf ears, but didn't get me ostracized at least. They didn't care that whites were losing scholarships, economic aid, and jobs. Nor did it matter that their personal high school history lessons were mostly about blacks. Martin Luther King was their hero, but most said violence was the only way to get attention. Power was what was needed, like Malcolm X.

Almost every day I ate lunch at the soup kitchen; the meals were always wonderful. Plenty to satisfy even the heartiest of appetites, which I was quickly developing. Which wasn't a good thing; all too soon, I'd be moving on and back to eating scraps. You just don't go from eating filet mignon one day to eating moldy cheese the next. Well, not easily, that is.

I learned that they did have the best chefs in town. Each day, various restaurants would lend a chef or two to cook the food and provide all the ingredients. So the down-and-out got the same gourmet food the rich and famous did. But one paid for the meal by waiting an hour or more in line — the other fifty dollars or more a plate. What a country we live in.

At night, I'd sometimes eat dinner with the nuns at the shelter. But after that first night, they tried to talk to me about religion each time. I was usually the only one there, which made it awkward. Almost all of the other lodgers ate dinner elsewhere or went without. I never did try to find out which. The religious talk made me uncomfortable, to say the least. Preferring to go hungry or filling up on free soda at the fast food place, I came to avoid the nuns as well.

You know, it's sad that you've got to get preached at to eat sometimes. Would you want that every time you ate? Maybe you would because you're one of those religious people. But you shouldn't force it on someone who doesn't.

The neighborhood the shelter was in was filled with bars, churches, and small shops. Along with block after block of row homes, everything was like soldiers all in a line. There were so many children running around in the streets, even late at night. They were so happy and seemed healthy enough, although I couldn't figure out when they had time to sleep. The houses were all brick row homes like the one I was staying in. So everyone lived on top of each other, and I guess that's why there was a strong sense of community. Everyone knew everyone, and everyone knew everyone's business.

People would sit outside on their steps or porches beginning in early evening. Even late at night, people were still talking to everyone and anyone who happened by. Everyone seemed so happy, like this was the best place in the world to live, and I guess maybe for them it was.

A few homes had been renovated and looked almost new; most, however, were run down. Many were crammed with several families living in tiny apartments. A few were single family homes. Some were only two stories high. Others, like the shelter I was in, were five stories high, a few even taller than that. Most were somewhere in between, making the skyline jagged and rough. The streets were always littered with trash. On occasion, a homeless person would sleep on the sidewalk or someone's front steps. No one ever shooed them away. All were welcome, no matter what rung on the social ladder they may have been on. You haven't ever seen as much of a melting pot of humanity.

As the days grew warmer, I loved to wander the city, looking at the unusual architecture and culture that made up this place. Gargoyles, statues, cornerstones, and steeples were hiding in various nooks and crannies. There were clowns, musicians, dancers, and other street performers to enjoy, if you but took the time to wander and explore to see where they may be on any given day. There was never any need to pay for entertainment or to sit and watch TV again. Take off in a random direction, and something will pop up that's sure to be an interesting surprise. But you so-called normal people never take the time to enjoy what is there around you every day. You let your busy lives control your every move and miss out on some of the best that life has to offer. Yet, I'm the one to be pitied.

One day, I found a park with a beautiful lake where I could sit and read, soaking in the sunshine, feeling nothing for a while but the heat of the sun on my face, the breeze on my skin. I'd often wander around in the grass without my shoes on to feel the wetness of the dew on my feet. Or I'd walk through a wooded area, listening to the birds whistling to each other. Or the squirrels chattering in their funny way. There is something about a connection with nature. You feel part of the earth, like you're meant to be. I guess that may be part of why I'd come to enjoy camping out so much, or maybe I was becoming a hermit. But even these wanderings in the city made me feel empty after a while. Renewed my feeling of always being alone even with millions of people around me.

Janice and I would sometimes wander around the city together on her weeknights off for an hour or two. On Sunday mornings, she'd go to mass with everyone else. The sisters preferred that we believed as they did and attended mass. But I always avoided them as much as I could. I knew what mass was like from my childhood. It hadn't done me any good then, and I had no desire to repeat that experience. This journey was about finding a new path, not repeating an old one that had already proven to be a failure.

But one Sunday night, I was surprised to find Janice knocking at my door. She'd never done that before. Normally, she was so tired from work and mass she didn't want to do anything but sleep on Sundays. That is, if she'd gotten the night off. But that night, she was restless, looking for something or upset. I wasn't sure which because I've never been much good at being able to figure people out.

Not long after we left the shelter, a homeless man asked us for money. To which Janice replied angrily, "Then do what I did, find a shelter and get a job!"

I'd never seen her be anything but upbeat, sickeningly sweet, and happy. She was now sounding like me—angry, upset, and slightly crazy. That wasn't a good thing. You never want to see the Jekyll and Hyde thing right before your eyes.

We walked to where she said she used to live, another shelter. She said it wasn't as nice but not run by a super strict nun, either. That's what finally opened the floodgates, and she told me about her daughter. She'd sent the girl to her grandmother because she couldn't bear to see her living in a shelter.

"I'm sure the state was going to put her in foster care. They kept snooping around this shelter when we lived here. They wouldn't stay out of our business; like they'd any right to say anything—I was a good mama to my baby!" Janice screamed in frustration and looked at me for reassurance.

"Uh, yeah." It was the best I could do; I had no idea how she was with her child, nor did I want to.

"I can't go live with my mother. She hasn't forgiven me for getting preggers as a teen then refusing to marry the boy that knocked me up. Like he gave a crap about me or my baby; it was us against the world from the get go. But I'm going to get my daughter back and never make the same mistakes that led to us living in a shelter again. I can tell you that for darn sure.

"I've been clean and sober for about a year. I've worked so hard for that, like everything else in my life. Now I've finally got enough money saved to work my plan for a new life. With my precious baby girl in an apartment all to ourselves. But, I'm afraid that my mama won't give my baby back to me when I'm ready. We had the worst fight we done ever had on the phone this afternoon. I don't know what to do. I need to get my baby back." She gave a piercing cry, and several people turned to look at us for a moment before continuing on their way.

Well, that explained her mood. Not like I cared—it wasn't good to care. "Well, um..." I couldn't even bring myself to say a few platitudes to her.

As we walked, I could smell the salt air from the ocean. Almost taste the faint hint of fish from the docks. Hear the seagulls scream overhead. The breeze was gentle on my skin. It was keeping me cool, as our pace had gotten quicker and quicker the more Janice talked.

I was slightly out of breath, not sure how long I could keep this up. I tried to ignore Janice's tears. I don't know why she felt like I'd care, or maybe she thought I'd help somehow. Since I couldn't help myself, that was foolishness.

Her pace slowed, and I could see that she was breathing harder than I was. I hoped her rage and energy was spent. I tried to focus on what was around us, what I was seeing. I've got enough problems of my own, and there was no need to get involved with someone else.

Had to look anywhere but the person beside me. There were so many people out in the middle of that Sunday night. White, black, Hispanic, Asian, Indian, homeless, couples, singles—you name it, we saw it. It was the first time I'd experienced a whole night of wandering around a city. We covered roughly ten miles, and I absorbed everything I saw.

The range from wealth to poverty will be what I'll always remember most about that night. All that separated million-dollar homes with rundown row houses was one block. One block of shopping centers, or one block of parking lots. There were prostitutes on many corners. Of course, the ever-present homeless were sleeping in many empty nooks and crannies.

Have you ever really looked at your town? Ever spent an entire night walking around? Or do you merely drive around in your car only seeing what you want to? No point in wondering about that; all of you who've got a place to live are blind. You don't need to face reality. But it's there, even when no one sees it.

The whole time, Janice poured her heart out to me, and I watched the city around me. Ignoring her pleas, her tears, her pain. I don't cry out to others, so there's no reason that anyone should ever do this to me. I don't want to know anyone else. I don't want to care about someone else. I don't want to feel for someone else. I don't want this to ever be directed towards me. Again. I know what it will lead to, and it isn't something good.

While her pace had slowed, her rant hadn't. People off and on would stare at the two of us walking by—one calm and one a raging lunatic. For once, the crazy one wasn't me.

That was one of my last nights in that city, it seemed that I'd now seen all it had to offer. I could no longer look Janice in the eye; she needed a friend, and I wasn't it—couldn't be it. A friend would never do what I'd done to someone else. I'd done enough harm before I'd ever met Janice, and I wasn't about to do that to anyone else. I got the itch to move on; my answer wasn't here, only more pain for myself and others. As I always did, I disappeared into the night. The emptiness couldn't be filled, could never be filled.

"Wow." Robert cut into my story and my many thoughts that I hadn't shared, or at least that I hoped I hadn't shared. "The motel is over there." He pointed vaguely with his chin to a building on the right side of the street.

"Good." I'd been so involved in my recollections that the time had flown by. Yesterday, my memory was so blurry, but today, these stories had come back so clear. Like I was seeing a movie of my life—it was odd. I hadn't even realized we'd left the highway and entered a town, I was so engrossed in watching that movie.

All of a sudden, I thought about how much I was looking forward to a nice hot bath and a real bed to spend the night in. I was sure I was going to be disappointed. *Cindy*, I thought, *you know better than to want even something as simple as that — you know you don't deserve it...*

Chapter 4

Robert got out of the car and went into the motel while I sat and waited outside for him. I had never thought even for a moment that he was serious about the offer of a motel when I'd gotten in his car that morning. Like any other hitchhiker since the invention of cars, I figured he'd tell me to find another ride. The second we got to the town where he had his meeting, the moment he got off the highway, he would've had enough of me. Would you want to spend several days with a homeless person riding shotgun in your car? Heck, would you want to spend several minutes with a dirty complete stranger? Much less one you found hitchhiking on the side of the road? The answer was no. Well, not unless you were a lonely trucker. Someone who was desperate for company to keep you awake during long hauls, then maybe. Which is why most of the time it's so hard for me to find a ride.

I was rather confused by Robert's behavior. He'd listened to me ramble on for over an hour as we drove, not interrupting me once. Now here we were at a motel, where he was actually in there paying for a room for me, if in fact that was what he was doing.

My life was odd, this day was weird, and Robert made no sense whatsoever. I wondered if he was going to tell the motel what kind of guest he had with him so they could hide all the valuables. Unlikely; Robert didn't seem to care that I was one of 'those' people. After all, he'd left me in his car, and I noticed the keys were still in the ignition, dangling there with the metal blinking in the sunlight coming in through the windows.

Why in the world would he trust me that much after such a short time? I could take off and leave him stranded, but no, that's one thing I don't do—steal. Well, not unless it's food, then that's fair game. Everyone has the right to eat a meal every once in a great while. Or was this some kind of a test? Was he expecting something in return for his trust, this ride, the breakfast, the motel room? It's not like he'd be the first guy to come on to me.

The silence was getting to me, so I cocked my head to look around. The motel was old but well maintained in a residential area. In fact, the motel seemed to be the only business in sight. The street was narrow, unmarked, with newer cars parked sporadically along the sides. The building had a pretty, red brick face with vines climbing the walls. Windows peeked out between the leaves. Flowers were planted along the sidewalk that coiled around the perimeter. There were no other cars in the parking lot of the motel. I guess we were the only ones to check in so early, and everyone from the night before had already checked out. The homes that I could see were small, but nice. They were also built with red brick and had neat little lawns and flower gardens. Tall, old trees with limbs reaching to the sky far above the rooflines.

Definitely not the kind of neighborhood that homeless people tend to hang out in, even to beg. *It's obvious, Cindy, you fit right in—not.* Maybe once I might've. In that other life when I had that house with the white picket fence. Before I gave up and stopped trying to do what was deemed acceptable by polite society. Before I realized that polite society was hiding evil in plain sight. That it wasn't any more acceptable than anything else, it only had a prettier face. Do you know what I mean? Have you seen that too?

I began tapping my fingers on the door handle. For some reason, the silence was bearing down on me like an oppressive weight. That was unusual, since I welcomed and relished being alone on a normal day. Thus, all the endless days and nights of camping when I could've been staying in a shelter instead. But this day wasn't what anyone could call normal. Not that you would call any day of mine normal.

When I finally saw Robert coming out of the lobby, I jumped out, thankful that my confinement in his tiny car-turned-cell was over. Holding up two card sleeves, numbers written on them in thick, black magic marker, Robert smiled. He handed me one, which held the plastic key to my room. With haste, I slipped it into my coat pocket—the left one because it's the one without the large hole. Giddy with delight, I tried not to show it. I felt like Charlie in Willie Wonka being handed the Golden Ticket. No way was I letting that key slip through my fingers or, in this case, fall out of the hole in my pocket. At least for this one night, I'd have the safety of sleeping alone in a locked motel room. No tent, no thin blanket to keep me warm, no peeing in the bushes. No, I'd have a real bed, a bathroom, a heater, walls, and a roof—a tiny slice of heaven.

"Your room's on the right side of the lobby. Also, Cindy, this is to buy some clothes and any other essentials you may need," he said as he gently picked up my hand and placed a thick, heavy manila envelope into it.

Feeling a slight jolt of electricity pass between us at his touch, I suddenly felt hot and a little bit faint. We stood there for what was only a second or two but seemed much longer. His gaze bored into me, making me want to sink under the pavement to hide from it.

"There's a mall two blocks that way." He pointed up the street after he'd finally released my hand. The odd sensations I was feeling began to fade. Whew.

How many times had these offers been made to me with the expectation of a sexual favor in return? No way was I ever going to accept money from some guy! That lesson didn't need to be learned; I'd never been that desperate and never would be. I could sleep hungry, wet, or cold. I couldn't ever even think about the possibility of making my situation even a tiny bit better by doing that. Never that. There were so many prostitutes out on the streets in every town I'd been to. Many old, haggard, used-up women wishing they'd never gone down that road. Sure I'd made plenty of mistakes, maybe wasn't the sanest person. But there was one hard and fast rule in my mixed-up life: Never take money from a man, any man, for any reason, because it only leads to one place.

"You seem kind, but I can't take your money," I said as I looked away from him, emotions rolling over me like a tidal wave. Willing myself not to cry as my chest tightened, making it almost impossible to breath.

I knew it was unlikely any kindness in him was what caused him to give this gift to me. I'd so wanted him to be kind, so needed him to be kind. Today was going to be different, but in the end nothing had changed. He was only another in a long line of wolves out to destroy me.

"I insist; many people donated this money for you, knowing how much you need it. You can't carry much in that pack of yours, and what you do have more than likely needs to be replaced. I'll be back at one so we can go to lunch together," he said as he handed me my pack he'd pulled out of the trunk. "I won't expect anything in return, ever. Not all men are alike; you should know that by now." He closed the trunk lid with a thunk.

With a sad shake of his head, he turned to get back in the car. "See you at one." He threw those words over his shoulder as he slid into the driver's seat.

"All right," I mumbled.

I was shaking so hard from head to toe it was difficult to get the words out. I'd disappointed him and it felt wrong somehow, but I couldn't put my finger on why, exactly. Then I realized that I actually still had that envelope in my hand. I hadn't dropped it, tried to give it back, or anything. I'd accepted his money, and now I was standing there cradling it in one hand like it was a lifeline. It was anchoring me to Robert in a way that I definitely didn't want to be. I felt more than a little sick to my stomach; at any moment I could hurl. At least I was in a separate room so I could deadbolt the door. I wasn't sure I could trust him, wasn't entirely sure I wanted to trust him. What right did he have to place me in this position?

As I stood there and watched him drive off, unwanted questions began to form in my mind. Who and why had he asked for money on my behalf? And what would he have done with the money if I hadn't accepted his offer of a ride? I'd only been in that town for the one day I'd spent in the café and the night I'd camped. Also, it's not like I'd tried to win friends at that café; in fact, I'd been downright surly.

As I headed through the lobby to my room, I looked at the time. A little before nine a.m. Good; it's early enough to get in a long, hot shower before heading out to shop. That'd help me feel better—the shower, not the shopping. Shuddering at the thought of having to go shopping, I completed the march down the hall to my assigned room. I paused for a moment when I reached the right room.

Placing my hand on the door, I felt how solid it was before finally sliding my key into the lock. You have no idea how good a door can feel—especially if it's keeping you in, not keeping you out. Protection is something I crave sometimes, a need almost as strong as my hunger. But it's so much harder to satisfy when danger is at your side every moment of every day. So, I zip up my tent flap and ignore it.

A motel room to myself was like entering a palace. You can't see a motel room the way I do. You would've seen this one as yet another cheap motel room in a small town, but I thought it was marvelous. It was a simple room, as was befitting the simple exterior: a bed with a flowered bedspread that matched the curtains; a small nightstand; a plain, brown, upholstered chair next to a small table; a TV hung on the wall over a small dresser.

I put my pack and the envelope on the dresser and got out my only other set of clothes. They were a little bit cleaner than what I was already wearing, which wasn't saying much. Having been rather lax lately, it'd been awhile since I'd found a place to wash my clothes. That'd been in a small pond about a week before, so they weren't much cleaner coming out than going in.

But this morning, I wanted to be clean as I stepped into the steamy shower and let the hot water pound on my skin. Something in me was awakened — a feeling of how good it was to feel alive, clean, secure. The scent of the cheap motel shampoo was exciting. The sting of the strong soap was exhilarating. The longing for something more was still there. Life had to be more than a few brief moments of feeling something, anything. Not feeling numb most of the time like I did...

Come on, Cindy, I thought to myself, *shake it off, snap out of it, you're giving maudlin a bad name.* I stepped out of the shower determined to get something accomplished with my morning — even if it was something as simple as going shopping. It felt strange to have a goal for the day other than the basics — finding food and shelter. When you're homeless, obtaining those two things can take you all day. Sometimes more than that, so there's seldom a need to think beyond those two things. Well, sometimes you need new clothes or other items, but it can take weeks to get those. Thus, it's an ordeal that's best left until you can't live without the item anymore.

Even when I decide to go somewhere else, I seldom have a place in mind. I stick out my thumb and hope for the best because I don't want to think about having to make a choice. Anywhere else is as good as where I was before. I'll still have to deal with finding food and shelter when I get there. These are things you never think about until you don't have easy access to them on a day-to-day basis. When you can't do something as simple as go to the grocery store on your way home from work and pick up the milk. Then you begin to see everything as a life-and-death struggle. It wears you down quick.

Now, shopping had never been one of my favorite activities. I'm not a princess or a diva, nor am I much of a girl for that matter, and I knew that it wasn't going to be easy. Even in my former life I hated to go shopping. When I was making a six-figure salary and had to wear skirt suits or pant suits to work, shopping was a necessity. Shopping was a chore, but never a pleasure, and I could've purchased anything I wanted to back then.

Well, I guess not, my husband kept me on a pretty tight leash. My paycheck was deposited into his bank account. Then he gave me an allowance to pay for all the stuff for the house, as well as anything I might need or want. It'd been his idea for me to keep my old car. He said we'd get a new one when we had our first child, but I never got pregnant no matter how hard I tried. He got a new car every year we were married and a new girlfriend as well. Truth be told, the girlfriends came a lot more often than yearly. Yeah, they were more like a flavor of the month. Guess no one was keeping him on a leash, but someone more than likely should've been. There were too many "should've beens" in my marriage. Heck, there were too many should've beens, could've beens, and would've beens in my life.

After I was dressed and ready to go, I picked up the heavy envelope to get an idea of how much I could purchase. Thinking it was all one-dollar bills, which was why the envelope was so thick, I felt the weight of it in my hand. Solid. My needs may be simple, but even the cost of the bare necessities could add up fast. I wanted to know how best to prioritize my needs today. You know, pants or underwear? Shirt or sweater? When I slid open the envelope's flap, I got the surprise of my life. I dropped the envelope on the floor like it was on fire. Poked at it a few times with the toe of my shoe to see if it was going to magically disappear.

There had to be more money in there than I'd seen in years. By that, I mean if you took everything I'd had and added it all together.

Shocked, I was feeling lightheaded and nauseous again. Maybe I shouldn't have eaten all three of those pastries in that bag Robert had in his car. But food was food when you're hungry all the time. You eat what you're given no matter if it's too much, bad for you, something you dislike, or rotten.

Finally, curiosity got the better of me. With great care, I retrieved the few bills that'd spilled out onto the carpet like a fan. Then I picked up the envelope itself, stuffed full even without the bills that had escaped.

Gingerly, I sat on the edge of the bed, where I counted the money over and over with trembling fingers, trying to be sure I was getting the total right because it seemed so unbelievable, impossible.

Almost two thousand dollars, what?! There were piles of cash all over the bed when I was finished. I had carefully counted out the money into piles of one hundred dollars—a habit leftover from my days as an accountant at the bank. Now the bedspread was more green than anything. A few of the flowers from the print were peeping out between the bills. Mostly tens and fives, but a few twenties and ones were in the mix. I couldn't stop staring at the whole lot of it for several minutes.

Thinking the money would disappear, I kept closing my eyes and opening them again. But every time I opened my eyes up wide again, there it all was looking back at me. You wouldn't have thought it was real either. Be honest now. No way—you would've been slightly freaked out too.

Laughing hysterically, I debated about rolling around in the money on the bed like they do in the movies. However, that caused me to sober up in a flash. This wasn't my money. This wasn't a sudden lottery windfall. I hadn't earned this money in any way. This money could only lead to trouble. I didn't understand Robert's motives at all, not even a little bit.

I wondered again about the mysterious people who'd given the money. Could they be real? For the most part, it was in small denominations; it didn't seem likely Robert had given it to me out of his own funds. Yet I now felt even more uneasy about accepting such a generous gift. It was hard enough to contemplate when I'd thought it might be only a few hundred. But this? This was crazy. Of course my hand had seemed to have a mind of its own when it took that darn envelope.

Come on, Cindy, what're you going to do? Leave it at the front desk for Robert and run? Don't spend any of it and stay? Yet, if you spend none of it, Robert will know when you show up still wearing nothing but your rags. What'll he think if you openly reject his gift but still want a ride? What to do, what to do, what to do?!

Many people wouldn't give money to a homeless person. The obvious reason is the assumption that the money would go to drugs and/or alcohol. Admit it, that where your mind went. Am I right, or am I right? Truth is, not all homeless people are drunken bums. There are a lot of homeless people that never use drugs or alcohol, ever. There are many that'd take even a small amount of money given and buy food or medicine. By that I mean real medicine, not illegal drugs. Most would then share these items with others within their group of fellow homeless. I'd benefited from that several times over the years, and I'd even done it a few times when I'd been given money.

The last time was on a snowy winter night a few months ago. A stranger gave me a hundred dollars when I was begging on a street corner. Without a second thought, I took that money and bought hot soup. Then I took the soup to a group of homeless men I'd seen an hour earlier at a local park. They were so thankful for the hot meal on such a cold night. Having nowhere to go, they were huddling over their makeshift fire barrel for warmth.

What would you do if someone gave you a hundred dollars? You, with your nice house, your nice car, would you share it? Or would you treat yourself to a fancy meal at your favorite restaurant? Never had to think about it, now, have you? But not everyone is selfish. Homelessness doesn't change that; we're still people just the same as you. We're poets. We're philosophers. We're singers. We're teachers. We're lawyers. We're CEOs. We're you if you fall. We're you if you slip up and make a royal mistake. That's a little hard to think about, isn't it?

Sure, there are the bad apples in the bunch that I'd never help, and I'm one of them. But many of us don't deserve the prejudice and the social stigma that go along with being homeless. We're trying to survive the best we can in a world that we don't fit into neatly. For whatever reason, we're different, but since when is that such a bad thing? Pilgrims were different and founded this country. Pioneers were different and settled the western part of this nation. Astronauts were different and landed on the moon. I'm different, and I ended up being homeless, thus I was protecting a lot of people from the harm I could do.

Somehow Robert must've seen something in me. He realized I didn't fit the image that everyone always has of homeless people. Either that or he didn't care if I used this money for alcohol or drugs. I shook my head, not knowing what to think or what to believe. I knew what I'd never do with the money – play into the stereotype and get drunk or high. I'd never tasted alcohol yet. The only illegal drugs I'd ever taken were in failed suicide attempts. No, I'd seen the devastating effects of alcohol in my father – not a road I was willing to go down.

Looking down at the money once again, I knew that this was a lot more than that gift I'd been given months ago. This gift could be setting me up for something dangerous if I accepted it. What exactly did Robert think he was buying with this money? Another thought hit me – was it a trap? What if I took off with the money? Would Robert report me to the police, saying I'd stolen his money? I had no way of knowing what I'd gotten myself into.

What're you going to do, Cindy? Think, think, think! There had to be a solution, a way out of this mess that was only partially of my own making. If only I'd dropped that darn envelope in the parking lot! But my life was filled with ifs and buts, and I only made more mistakes at every turn. *Make a choice, Cindy! You have to decide!*

I was almost screaming to myself by this time. This was turning into an even harder choice than the one I'd made earlier, deciding to get in his car or not. Going through the options over and over in my head, I felt that I needed to stay with Robert. For whatever reason, something was drawing me to him. It almost hurt me to think about not going with him in the morning, which was completely insane. He was up to something, and there was no way it was anything good. But until I knew what was going on, I was in this for the long haul. My whole life was dangerous, so it's not like this ride with Robert was any less so.

So you're going to be the proverbial stupid moth going towards the flame! Yep, I was. So that meant I needed to spend some of this money to get a few things. Mind you, it was only to keep up appearances, nothing more. I knew I couldn't keep the rest of the money.

That settled, I planned on slipping what was left of the money into the glove box of Robert's car. The trick would be to find a time before I told him he'd taken me far enough. I still wasn't sure where that would be exactly. However, if he made any kind of pass at me, that'd definitely be as far as I'd need to go with him. I knew for a fact that he could find some other poor soul to give the money too. It's not like I was the only needy person on the planet, or in this corner of Maryland, for that matter. If I changed my mind and didn't go with him in the morning, that was fine.

With great care, I gathered up each pile. Afraid they'd disintegrate with a touch, I hardly felt them. Relief filled me as I placed the money back into the envelope, only keeping out the few hundred dollars I felt I'd need today. The bills felt hot in my pocket as I shoved them in.

Stupid as it may sound, I hid most of the money in the motel room. Violent shaking struck my hands as I hung the "Do not disturb" sign on the door. A vain hope that someone from the motel wouldn't enter the room flew through my mind. I didn't want anyone to find, then steal the money, even if I didn't feel it was mine. Which was a rather childish fear, to be possessive of something that you don't own. Yet, I wanted to show Robert I was responsible even if I was homeless.

Feeling like I was a thief, I glanced around the corridor to see if anyone was watching me. Heading out to the lobby, I tried not to run until I was outside. Breathing in the fresh air where I could feel more like myself again, a brief sprint felt good. Normal for me, all was right with the world again because I was outside. But I missed my pack, almost feeling naked without it.

The mall was easy enough to find as I went up the street. Two blocks of houses, then voilà, a giant, out-of-place, glass-and-steel shopping center in a sea of black asphalt. I felt odd going in with the intent to buy items, rather than to panhandle or find a fountain to troll for coins. When I did have a few dollars to spend, I went to dollar stores, discount stores, thrift stores, or yard sales. Never malls, and most definitely never super nice malls where the rich people shop.

Much to my dismay, this mall was as upscale as they came. So my less-than-perfect outfit stuck out like a sore thumb as I wandered from store to store. Trying to figure out where the best place to make my purchases wasn't going to be easy. Here I was in my rather dirty second-best outfit: jeans that had holes so big in the knees I probably could've made cutoffs out of them without scissors; my T-shirt that was several sizes too large, plus had a huge bleach stain in the front; my worn coat so faded, who knew what the original color had been.

While all around me, women in designer outfits and high heels sparkled. The click-clacking on the tile floor echoing in the open space. If you listened closely, you could hear it calling out to me, "You're not worthy." Even the babies were dressed to impress as they lay in their strollers.

Wanting to cry and say, "Forget it," I knew that I couldn't. I had to complete this task and stick to my goal for once in my life. Failure wasn't an option, well, for today at least. Swallowing hard, I had to face the terror that was this mall.

Shop clerks kept an eagle eye on me to make sure I wasn't going to rob them blind, peppered with phrases like, "Please don't touch the merchandise" or "Maybe this isn't the best store for you." Like there's an ideal store for homeless people or something. Come to think of it, there is — the free clothes closets some churches have.

Rage was replacing shame, then regret replaced rage. Then shame crept back over me like the ever-present friend that it was, and I felt like I wanted to cry again. Do you know that feeling? Has anyone ever looked at you like a thief for simply being there? It wasn't like me to be so bothered like this. Yet today, I wanted to find the nearest dumpster and throw myself into it. Save these people the trouble of having to. Yeah, I know how foolish that sounds. Homeless people sleep beside the dumpster, not in it. Got it.

Children stared until their mothers pulled them aside— scolding them about not talking to strangers or getting too near homeless people. Like homelessness was some kind of contagious disease and not a pathetic commentary on the state of our society. I had a feeling that I was the first, only, and last homeless person most of these rich children would ever see. Thanks to their snobby, overly protective, uptight parents, their world was a bubble—a bubble of perfectly dressed people who ate at the country club and played golf. Or something equally horrid. Sad—some of the best helpers at soup kitchens were the kids that would come with their parents on holidays. They didn't care that we were different from each other.

The fountain in the middle of the mall was where many mothers and children were gathered. As I neared, one child dropped his toy, a bear, because he was swooped up so quickly by his mom. When I bent to pick it up, she yelled, "I'm calling security. Don't come any closer!"

Backing away from me, using her child as a shield, she glared at me. She tried to push her shopping bags out of the way with her foot and press buttons on her cell phone at the same time. I picked up the toy anyway, thinking she'd have to accept it if I offered it up to her with my now unsteady hands.

"I'm sorry," I said as I tried to give the toy to the now shrieking child. His face was beet red as he struggled to get free from his mother's clutches, and I understood his pain all too well. My mother hadn't put me first either. Good mothers should. Few mothers do.

She snatched it out of my outstretched hand. Stomping to the nearest garbage can, she threw it away with such force it made the can wobble. I felt bad for the boy and hoped it wasn't a favorite of his; he shouldn't have lost a toy because of me. She then grabbed her bags, and I watched her stride away in a huff. I then hurried to the trash can to fish the toy out. With joy, I saw that the stuffed bear was no worse for wear, and I brushed off its soft fur.

Wishing it was Christmas time so there'd be a toy drive bin to drop it into, I held it for a moment, relishing the way the soft fur felt against my rough skin. Spotting a discarded shopping bag, I shoved the toy into it, satisfied that I'd rescued it. Knowing I could leave it at a shelter later, I was going to have to take it along for the ride. Some homeless child would be grateful to have this toy. Most of them had none, and it'd be a happy surprise for some lucky child to be given the gift of this cute little bear. When you've got no clothes, a toy isn't a priority but is still a necessity. Ask any child; you'll see how true that is.

As I continued to wander the mall, most shoppers avoided me and gave me a wide berth. After the incident with the toy, I ignored those well-dressed people. Squared my shoulders, stuffed my emotions away. *I'm used to being treated this way; I've always been treated this way.* I know full well that I'm less than human. My parents told me often enough. Then my husband joined that chorus and started singing that tune as well. Someone has to be the bottom of the totem pole, and I'm okay with it being me. Well, most of the time. When I tried not being at the bottom I got slapped back down to my rightful place. Lesson learned; no need to repeat it.

As I looked at clothing items in several stores, I rubbed my fingers against them. Looking around, making sure no one saw me, I know I shouldn't have touched them. But I wanted to feel how soft they were. Those clothes hadn't ever been washed with hand soap in a dirty gas station sink or without soap at all in a creek.

Feeling my cheeks flush, I frowned as I remembered how nice it was to have fresh clothes to wear each day. Again, I debated if I should forget the whole thing. Forget Robert, walk out of that mall, and find another ride. Had I sunk this low that I was now afraid to even do something as normal and mundane as buying clothing?

No Cindy, I said to myself, *you can do this. It was shopping for clothes. Not finding food after going hungry for a week. Or taking three months to save up the money to replace your tent when the roof ended up with a hole in it so the rain leaked in.*

Looking around, I knew everyone was staring at me. I could feel their eyes crawling all over me, detesting every inch of me. Still, this was something I had to do.

In the end, I knew that any clothing items I purchased wouldn't stay nice for more than a few days. How I was going to carry extra clothes would be a problem later as well. So, I decided to only buy a few basic things. Besides, when it was all said and done, I was getting more and more uncomfortable. Like a bug was wriggling in my stomach. The idea of spending even a dollar of these unnamed faceless people's money was eating me alive. I couldn't figure out why I felt so bad about accepting it. It's not like I was above begging for money, food, clothing, or shelter. Maybe because it was so much. Maybe because deep down I believed it really was from Robert, who by any standard was rather odd. Or maybe because I knew I didn't deserve a gift, even a tiny one, and this gift was by no means small.

Hope was all but lost that this shopping trip would be a success. That's when I found a department store where a young, pretty salesgirl was helpful. She didn't seem to mind so much that I wear the mark of a homeless person. You have no idea how relieved I was to find her. You can walk into any store without a problem. I can't.

"How may I help you today?" she said politely as could be to me as I entered her area of the store. Like I was a real customer, which I guess for today only I was.

"I need a new outfit, but I'm not sure what exactly to get." Shuffling my feet on the floor, I was almost afraid to look at her. Afraid she would change her mind and not want to help me.

Afraid she would turn out like everyone else I'd run into so far in that darn mall.

"Let me show you some items that I think will work for you and fit your budget." She smiled at me. There was a creepy bald guy with a name tag that identified him as a manager lurking nearby. He'd been following me since I entered the store, my new shadow. He didn't seem thrilled that this salesgirl was willing to assist me but he kept silent. Yet his eyes never strayed; they were stuck on me.

"I think these colors will look quite good with your eyes," she told me as she held up several shirts. I almost laughed at that. Like the trees would care about something like that the next time I was camping.

So, Mr. Oak, do you think green or blue is my best color?

"Let's see about pants next, what size?" She looked me up and down, appraising my shape but not in a creepy way.

I had only a vague idea. The pants I was wearing were being held up by a belt made of a scrap of rope that I'd pulled out of a dumpster last year. That was shortly after I'd found the pants in a free bin at a shelter, where size wasn't a big concern—how many holes in each leg was.

"I don't know, maybe an 8." Sheepishly, I gave her a half smile. Honest, I wasn't trying to make her job any harder than it already was, but I was a bit of a lost cause when it came to all of this.

"That's okay, I can measure you real quick. Let's duck back here," she said as she nudged me behind a partition to give us some privacy. With quick efficiency, she measured me without any hesitation. Even though that required touching me and my less-than-clean clothing.

With a slight shiver at her touch, I decided to think about something else. "Um, I need a bra also." I looked up rather than down at her since she was on her knees still figuring out my pant size.

"Okay, should I measure for that as well?" She sounded way too cheerful, considering what she was having to deal with at the moment.

"Um, yes. I'm not wearing one so I've no idea at all." I took a quick peek at her to see her reaction at that. She didn't even blink, and I was glad I hadn't told her that in fact I hadn't owned one in several years.

I used a super tight tank top under my t-shirt or blouse. Most homeless women do; for some reason, bras never get donated to shelters or clothes closets. So we do without because bras were too expensive to purchase on our own. You have no clue how uncomfortable that is at first, but you get used to it after a while.

"No problem." She finished measuring me, stood up, and led me to an area where there were pants. The manager was still following, I wondered if he'd been able to see us behind the partition. If he had, then he'd seen quite the show. But he still hadn't said a word. "These pants will look great on you." She held up a few pairs for my inspection.

I looked over the items that she'd collected. A little shell-shocked at the prices, but you would be too if you hadn't been shopping like this in forever. At least she'd picked items that were on sale, and they seemed to be of good quality. I pointed to the shirt, sweater, and pants I wanted. She found the right size bra, and then she added panties and socks to my small pile without even asking me if I wanted them. I guess she figured if I wasn't wearing a bra than odds were I needed them as well. She was right, so I didn't say anything in protest.

"So let me show you to the fitting room." She smiled to me as she picked everything up, but there was no way I was going to do that. I was going to have to trust her measuring skills. The last thing this poor girl needed after being so nice was me changing in her dressing room. Or worse, something not fitting quite right and needing to be restocked. Because now it would be dirty for the simple reason that it had touched me. You wouldn't want to be the person who ended up buying that shirt would you? Of course not.

"No, it's fine. Just let me check out." Even a weak smile was beyond me at that stage, and I gaped at her, like the fish out of water that I was.

"Are you sure? Measuring is rarely good enough; you want to look your best, don't you?" She patted my arm like she was my sister and gave me another warm grin. Proud of myself, I didn't recoil at her touch like I almost always did.

"Um, really, it's okay. I've taken up more than enough of your time." Biting the inside of my cheek so she couldn't see, I tried not to cry. She was being too kind, and it almost hurt as much as my cheek did.

"Okay. Let's go over to this register." She walked to a counter where the manager was standing, watching us. "So, with the coupon we are running this week, that will be $104.95."

She didn't ask how I was going to pay. Simply told me the total and waited with the patience of a saint while I dug the money out of my coat pocket. I had no idea what coupon she was talking about. But I was thankful that the total was less than the running one I'd come up with from the price stickers. She was rather good at her job if she was able to get me a whole outfit, underwear included, for that price in this store.

Looking sideways, I could see the smirk on the manager's face. It was there right until the moment before I placed my money on the counter. He was sure I was up to something, that this was some kind of game or bad joke—until that second I tried to pay in cold, hard cash.

Then, he looked crestfallen for a moment, finally, with a look of triumph, he said. "Please check the money with the counterfeit pen."

I should've been humiliated. Most people would be, but this was normal for me, and frankly, I couldn't have cared less if the money was fake. I know that there are scammers out there who use homeless people to pass off fake money and checks. Businesses know this too. However, the items I purchased were not ones that would've fit that scenario. You know, things with high resale value — stereos, TVs, iPhones. Plus, none of these bills were large. It wouldn't have been worth the time of any crook to have been using me in a scheme.

"Um, yes sir." The salesgirl threw the guy a scowl; she liked me for whatever reason. She checked the money as quickly as she could, then started to finish the transaction when all the bills were fine.

"You're sure they were fine?!" The manager screamed at the poor girl, the veins in his neck popping out, he was so angry. This wasn't the ending he'd planned for me. No, he wanted me to be hauled out of the mall in chains to a nice, cozy jail cell where he could visit me — never.

"Yes sir." She handed me my change and smiled at me again. Then she placed my items in a black shopping bag. It had the store's logo branded on the side in bright gold lettering. "Good luck," she said as she handed me the bag.

I guess the salesgirl was hoping I was on my way to a job interview and that was why I was in need of some new clothes. Otherwise, "good luck" was an odd thing to say. I didn't have the heart to tell her why I was buying the outfit. That I was a hitchhiking homeless person. That I'd been lucky enough to get a ride with someone who wanted to take me all the way to the other side of the country. But he, for whatever reason, wanted me to be clean along the way.

In haste, I walked out of the store before the manager found a reason to hold me there. I wouldn't have put it past him to slip something in that bag and accuse me of shoplifting. I put the bear from earlier in the bottom of the larger bag. Not having a receipt for it might've been a problem while I finished my shopping. You never know, what with everyone keeping such a close eye on me.

Then I went into a home goods store and found a warmer wool blanket to replace mine, which was in tatters. My old blanket had been a thrift store find years before. It was a standard issue olive green wool blanket with US stamped on it. That blanket was worn and scratchy, hardly held together by a few stitches I'd placed in it over the years. But still, I wouldn't throw it away. Instead, I was planning to share my good fortune. By leaving that blanket where another homeless person would find it, I could help in my own small way. One man's trash truly was another man's treasure in the world of the homeless. My tattered blanket would make someone insanely happy indeed. Please, from now on, donate your used items rather than throwing them away. It's better when we don't have to dumpster dive.

Finally, I went to a drug store, where I purchased a few needed items. A new toothbrush to replace mine that was several years old and missing half its bristles. Aren't they supposed to be replaced every few months? Small folding scissors. So many uses for such a small item. Nail clippers. No more ragged manicure from biting my nails. Deodorant. Ah, for a few months I wouldn't smell like sweat most of the time. Chapstick. Yay, no more cracked and bleeding lips. Maxi pads. I can't remember the last time I'd had them—what a luxury not using wadded up paper towels would be. Band-Aids. How nice it would be to cover a cut and not end up with another bloodstain on my clothes. An extra comb. Mine was missing half its teeth. I also found a few boxes of crackers, cans of tuna, and granola bars. I wished their selection of food was larger, but what can one expect at an upscale mall! Then I splurged on a white hair bow and a tiny sample bottle of green apple bubble bath. Not much of a splurge when I thought about it, what with the pile of cash I now had stashed at the motel.

It all was so foolish. Most days I didn't have food to eat, yet here I was spending a dollar on bubble bath and two more on a hair bow. Maybe instead of slipping the money into the glove box of Robert's car, I'd keep all of it and buy food. Good food for other homeless people and maybe some other necessities. I'd know better than Robert, or anyone else for that matter, how best to spend that money. How to get the maximum benefit. It was something to ponder, but did I want the responsibility? But I should never have the power over anyone's life ever again. Even a little bit of control was a bad thing in my hands—it was yet another of the oh-so-many failures in my life.

Arriving back at the motel around noon, I took another quick shower. Ah, to be so clean. I needed to remove the dirt that'd gotten on me from the dirty clothes I'd put on after my first shower. Scrubbing both my old outfits and my coat in the bathtub, I hung them to dry so they'd be ready to wear later. Surveying the area, I felt a little bad for the maid who'd have to clean up after me—the bathroom was a mess. Dirt and grime was everywhere. White towels were now tan, and I'd used all but one of them between the showers and trying to clean up my mess. Nothing could be done about it though; I needed to be clean. My clothes needed to be clean. An opportunity like this doesn't get handed to me every day. Oh well, the room was paid for.

I then put on my new outfit so Robert could see what I'd selected. There was the added bonus that I was now clean while wearing clean clothes for the first time in I didn't know how long. Usually, if I found a place to clean up, I needed to do so in a hurry and had to decide which was more urgent—me or my clothing. Other times, I washed my clothes in a freezing cold creek. I wasn't about to go swimming in that to get clean and risk hypothermia.

Thinking practically when I was shopping had been my priority. With the help of that nice salesgirl, my new outfit was a pair of simple black jeans, plus a loose, dark green, cotton shirt and a dark blue cardigan to round out the ensemble. That salesgirl had been a wiz with her measuring tape. Everything fit me to a T, even though I hadn't tried it on in the store. Also, with the new scissors, I'd given myself a quick haircut. Then with the small white bow, I tied back my long, dark brown hair. It was now considerably straighter and a little bit shorter. You, in all likelihood, wouldn't be caught dead cutting your own hair. But to me, going to a salon felt more like a leap off a ten-story building than a walk in the park. I couldn't even bring myself to think about it, even though I'd passed one twice while at the mall.

Finally, in honor of one of the stories I'd told that morning, I dug the autumn leaf earrings out of my pack and put them on. It'd been years since I'd bothered to wear them; they felt odd banging against my neck. So much so, I almost changed my mind about wearing them but in the end, left them on.

Cindy, this is the best you've looked in a long time, I thought as I looked at myself in the mirror for several minutes. It almost seemed like another person was looking back at me. Someone that I didn't recognize, didn't know.

Are you who you think you are? Or is a stranger looking back at you when you look in the mirror, too? I was slimmer than I'd ever been. My face was creased from sun exposure, making me seem older than I was. My hairstyle was unlike how I'd ever worn it before. My posture was more hunched than ever from the pack.

While on the outside at least I was different, my heart was still as confused as ever. My soul still was empty. Even if I was clean and pretty-ish where others could see, nothing had changed. I alone knew the real me; I alone knew the truth. Masks can be made to look better, but they're still there to hide who you really are.

There was a knock at the door; it had to be Robert because there wouldn't be anyone else that'd even know I was here. Not like anyone would ever think to look for me anymore.

Opening it with sweaty, shaky hands, I saw him standing there in jeans and a gray sweatshirt. For once, I was overdressed.

"Hey, you look great, Cindy." His smile said it all.

"Thank you," I shyly replied.

Looking down at my feet, I wished I'd gotten some better shoes than my beat-up hiking boots. Nah, they'd never had fit in my pack later. But I'd gotten his approval. My heart gave a little flutter in my chest, my ears ringing with the whoosh of my blood pumping harder. The corners of my lips involuntarily turned upwards in a hesitant smile.

For the first time in a long time, I was all woman. Why was I trying so hard to please this man, when earlier I was so sure that this ride was a prelude to sex? For all I knew, it still could be what he was wanting. Just because he got two rooms today didn't mean he'd do that tomorrow. That is, if I was still on this trip with him to who-knows-where at that point. As I full well knew, a lot could happen in a short period of time...

Chapter 5

Leaving the hotel, we walked to a nice little restaurant. It was a few blocks in the opposite direction from where the mall had been. Again, all the buildings were houses right until this one block of businesses. Inside, the restaurant was filled with what looked like family photos. They were on every wall, the back of every booth, and even on the menus. Weddings, babies, graduations, birthdays, and families all looking back at you. Sad that I had no happy times like that in my family. There was nothing like that in my past that I'd ever want to remember. So, I tried with all my might to ignore all those happy, smiling faces and focus on the menu. But it wasn't easy; their eyes bore down on me from every angle. Mocking me. Haunting me.

I was glad when the waitress came. "Robert, so good to see you again." She was beaming at him.

"And you as well, Ruby. Do you know what you'd like, Cindy?" Robert looked at me, and I nodded.

We each said what we wanted to eat, and Ruby went with our orders, so I was able to close my eyes for a while. I was good at blocking things out. Well, I used to be good at doing that—it was getting harder and harder with each passing day. It's like trying to ignore the sun while it's blistering your skin. You know it's still there, still trying to destroy you. So you've got to move into the shade at some point, as much as you may hate to. Face facts; deal with the issue. Or, in my case, go home.

While we were waiting for our food, Robert said, "Have you read any of this book before?"

I heard a thump, and I opened my eyes a fraction to see that he'd placed a Bible on the table. I knew I had to at least look at him now since it was evident that he wanted to talk. Ugh. And now I also knew his game; he was going to preach to me. Double ugh. Yes, please show me what I was doing wrong. Give me the whole God speech—blind faith, fairy tales, myths, and magic. Then try to get this sinner to repent, turn around, start over, go and sin no more.

Well, I'd let him try—not like he'd be the first. That was one thing wrong with many soup kitchens; before you got your lunch, you got preached to. What if I told you what you were doing wrong before you could eat when you hadn't eaten for days? How would you feel? Most people were like me; they learned to tune it out—blah, blah, blah, whatever, amen, let's eat. You're foolish if you think otherwise.

"Some, when I was younger." I frowned.

"How old are you now?" He smiled at me.

I had to stop and think for a moment. I'd stopped celebrating birthdays years ago. Not like they mattered, just another reminder of my wasted life.

"Thirty-eight."

Where was this line of questioning going anyway? The conversation was making me nervous. He didn't seem to be approaching this like any of the others had. When they'd foolishly tried, they'd been much more straightforward. I think I'd heard someone call it "fire and brimstone" preaching. You know, all you can do is sin, so you're going to hell. Seemed I was already in hell and rightfully so. How much worse could things get?

"Did your parents go to church?"

"No, my grandmother did, at Christmas, for midnight mass." Funny, I had been thinking about that the day before. Remembering how naïve I'd been to believe in that magic as a child. I hadn't thought about that for years, and now here it was, twice in two days.

"Why does this conversation make you so uncomfortable?"

Oh great, how can he tell what you're feeling? I was trying hard not to squirm or show anything on my face after that first frown. Yet something must've clued him in. I hesitated a long time before answering, playing with my napkin on the table. Twisting it into a tight knot, then letting it uncurl. I didn't want to offend him — okay, maybe I did. Religious people are so blind to reality. Living in their world of sunshine and rainbows, there were no problems without answers.

"Well, this God you think you know is a myth and means nothing when you get right down to it. He doesn't care about what happens to us, nor does he help us or speak to us to give us direction."

Thankfully, the food arrived. "Live life for now, and you alone are your best friend and ally," I said as I picked up my fork, waving it around to accent my point. Or to scare him off. Take your pick.

"We'll discuss it more later." He bowed his head, and I knew that he was blessing his food in silence because I'd often seen others do this as well. At least he hadn't said his silly prayer out loud and made me wait to eat also.

Diving into the delicious, simple meal, I savored the roasted chicken, steamed mixed vegetables, and wild rice. Again I thought that maybe life on the road wasn't so great after all. How often in the last few years had I gotten a meal this satisfying? Was there something else out there that could fill me for more than a moment? And if there was, why hadn't I been able to find it yet?

I was well into my meal before Robert raised his head and began to eat also. Ha — his food was sure to be cold, which would serve him right for being so stupid to pray.

Conversation was nonexistent for the rest of the meal, which suited me fine. It seemed that my biggest threat from Robert might be his religious speeches. He seemed nice enough, but it was obvious that he was deceived by all the religious lies and nonsense. I'm sure you've met people like that. Stuck in the religious mire, unable to see anything else. Yet, I'm the crazy one.

"Do you mind if we sit and talk for a bit?" he asked when he'd finished eating his entree and I was almost done with my apple pie.

"Sure," I replied. It was his money; he called the shots up to a point. I still had no plans to ever go to bed with this man. However, talking was okay; if it got too weird and religious, I'd tune him out. If he was offended, so be it; if he wanted the rest of his money back, that was okay too. After all, my plan was to return it eventually anyway.

"Would you like a cup of coffee or tea?"

"Tea, please," I said as I looked around. The lunch rush was over, and the restaurant had all but cleared out.

He ordered my tea and a coffee for himself. When the drinks arrived, he sat for some time sipping his coffee. We watched the few remaining patrons. "You said the priest in Arizona didn't act like a priest. I take it to mean that he never spoke to you about God or the Bible."

"Right," I said as I sipped my tea real slow, savoring the sweetness on my tongue.

"But he was acting like the High Priest, Jesus. The Bible says that Jesus served His disciples by washing their dirty, dusty, sandal-clad feet. Jesus also says in the Bible that if we serve those who are less fortunate, we're actually serving Him. That priest didn't need to preach; he was living out what he believed in each step and action he took." His fingers began to tap on the Bible as he said this, a steady, quiet cadence, like a distant drum beat. "The nuns did as well, to a degree, but they still felt the need to push you to go to church with them. Plus, they'd talk to you at dinner time. Which one made you feel more comfortable?"

"Philip." I was quick to reply because that was easy to answer. I could forget that Philip was a religious nut who'd given his life up to a delusional faith. He, more often than not, acted like he was homeless like the rest of us at the kitchen.

"Because he was like you, a normal, everyday person. Nothing special."

"Yes."

Robert stopped the tapping and sat still for a few moments, sipping his coffee once more before asking, "Why'd you lie about where you wanted to go? I know you don't want to go to Oregon."

Great, how'd he know that? "I didn't want you to know where I was going."

"Why?"

"I'm not sure; I guess because I'm never sure what I want or where I want to go," I said. Or, at least every time I thought I knew, it turned out to be false, but I wasn't going to tell him that. In addition, I still wasn't convinced that I was ready to go home. Ready to face anyone there. Ready for my rather insane life to end, one way or another. This was all I'd known for so long now. Was it as bad as I made it out to be?

Oh, get real, Cindy! You're homeless, for crying out loud!

"I know what you want and where you need to be, but it's up to you to accept it." He smiled, a soft and gentle smile, like the kindly father of my dreams always had. Then he tapped his finger on the Bible once more, like the answer was in there or something. No way it could be, though.

"I don't want anything," I shot back as I gripped the chair seat so hard my knuckles turned white. I knew that kind fathers were as much a myth as God was, and I shifted my gaze out the window to the people walking by. I didn't need anyone to tell me what I wanted, especially some religious person. He didn't know me, couldn't know me or all I'd been through, what I'd done.

We sat in silence for who knows how long. I was staring out the window; he was staring at me, and I could feel it with every fiber of my being. He was giving me goose bumps, but I still wasn't going to give him the satisfaction of returning his glare.

"You know that isn't true. There is a longing deep within you that you can't explain; it eats at your heart, making you cry at times. It has more power than your sense of judgment, so you've followed the longing across many miles. But how can you find something you can't even name?" he finally said, at a level a hint above a whisper.

Somehow I got this feeling that only I could hear him, that he'd spoken those words directly into my brain. I'm not quite sure how to explain the feeling so you'd understand. But it was more like his voice was a mirror of my thoughts somehow. Terrifying and eerie.

My gaze snapped back to his face; how could he know what I'd thought only yesterday? *Don't panic, Cindy,* I thought, *stay together. Don't let him see how weak you are; no one should ever know that you aren't strong. Just keep breathing, in and out, in and out. Nice and slow, deep breaths now.*

My hands were beginning to hurt, so I peeled them off of the chair. I crossed my arms over my chest in defiance, with my hands curled into tight balls. Not a good idea; they still hurt, and that wasn't helping. But the pain felt good for some reason.

Does he hold the key to what you've spent years of your life searching for? No, that'd be too much to ask, too much to hope for.

"How do you know so much?" I said in a voice that was weak and shaky. My mask's cracks were showing, and I was seconds away from letting Robert see way too much of me. If he hadn't already. This was bad, really, really bad. *Get up and run. Do it now!* Yet, I remained glued to my seat. Paralyzed by his words.

"That answer you can't accept right now. You must forget the past and unlearn all you have knowledge about. You've been told so many lies, and I'm sorry for that. Truly sorry. Let the child in you come out and begin again to learn. Be hungry to learn only the truth; never give up. The answer's there for you to find.

"I put a card that I wrote verses out for you on in the Bible; please read that card. You can read the Bible itself if you'd like — I'd suggest the book of John," he said as he stood up, sliding the Bible across the table to be in front of me. Then, with a casual flip of his hand, he dropped some bills to pay for our meal. Just like that. Sermon over. Do with it what you will.

With some hesitation, I picked up the Bible, which felt like it weighed more than a car. Wanting to drop it, but knowing I couldn't. I felt like my arm might rip out of its socket from this new burden added to my life. Afraid to say anything for fear I might cry, I simply gave a faint smile and nod to him.

Why was I letting him, of all people, get to me? Or had the years on the road been way too long? Was it time to get back to a more normal life and stop looking in vain for the answer to my dreams? Was a normal life what I'd been dreaming of, or was it something more? What was a normal life anyway? Or was I right in thinking that I should give up and end everything?

"Thank you, Robert," I mumbled, fighting back the tears. Why did he seem to care so much anyway? Who am I that anyone would care about me?

The walk to the motel was in tense silence, neither of us looking at the other. We simply marched up the street side by side, combatants who'd merely reached a temporary truce. Unsure who was going to be the first to break it. Yet neither of us did.

Arriving back at my room, I threw the Bible on the bed and decided to take my long-awaited bubble bath. Robert had said he'd come by about seven for dinner after his afternoon meeting. Meaning, there were several hours to relax, if at this juncture that was even possible.

As I waited for the tub to fill and the bubbles to get fluffy, something drew me to the Bible Robert had given me. It was stupid, because I knew it was a fairy tale. Why read any of it? I'd seen and heard enough nonsense in my life. Did I really need anymore?

No, you don't need to read that stupid book, Cindy, enjoy your afternoon. Enjoy the peace and quiet. Enjoy your bath.

Sinking into the tub, I decided to ignore that book. It was, after all, just that—a book. I soaked in the tub, enjoying the delicious, fruity fragrance of the bubbles until the water was ice cold. My skin was as wrinkled as a prune, and the bubbles had all gone flat. After my bath, I lay on the bed, wrapped in the one clean towel left from earlier. As I stared at the white popcorn ceiling, the odd glittering seemed to wink back at me. Knowing I had to at least read the verses Robert had written out, I let out a low whistle. The simple reason was the same one that had led me to buy a few things with the money. Robert would know if I didn't, and I still wanted this ride with him to continue.

With a deep sigh, I blew out a deep breath, wondering how I'd ended up in a position of feeling the need to please someone again—yuck. I'd sworn to myself that I'd only please myself once I'd started out on this journey. Yet, I guess, it's not like anything else had worked out.

My feelings from the day before returned with a rush. I couldn't continue on the journey I was on, but I didn't know where else to go. Home now seemed like a mirage—something that wasn't there as an actual physical place.

Cindy, can you finally find the courage to end it all, or are you going to keep being such a coward? I never could end things before, and it wasn't like I hadn't tried...

Enough of this, Cindy, read the stupid card already! I grabbed that darn Bible. As I read the verses on the card that afternoon, I knew that everything for me had stopped. Something had shifted; things looked different. But I didn't want to admit it even to myself, and I'd never have told Robert that.

> "For this reason I say to you, do not be worried about your life, as to what you will eat or what you will drink; nor for your body, as to what you will put on. Is not life more than food, and the body more than clothing? Look at the birds of the air, that they do not sow, nor reap nor gather into barns, and yet your heavenly Father feeds them. Are you not worth much more than they? And who of you by being worried can add a single hour to his life? And why are you worried about clothing? Observe how the lilies of the field grow; they do not toil nor do they spin, yet I say to you that not even Solomon in all his glory clothed himself like one of these. But if God so clothes the grass of the field, which is alive today and tomorrow is thrown into the furnace, will He not much more clothe you?" -Matthew 6:25-30

But this God wasn't the one who'd fed and clothed me for the past ten years. Complete strangers had when I couldn't do it myself. Sure, most of them had been part of a church group of some kind, but that wasn't God. Or was it? Which brought me back to the "he cares" thing people were always saying about God. But why would He want to? To be specific, why would God want to care about me? I'm nothing, a nobody, unworthy of anything—nobody could say I was worth more than the beautiful birds. If life was more than food and clothing, then what else was there—what was I missing? Was it this God that I kept pushing away, so sure that he wasn't real? Why would this God be the one to help me? Did I even want to be helped? Did I deserve to be helped? Could I be helped after all I'd done?

And what was that nonsense about Philip being a priest by serving and not by preaching? The priest in the church when I was young never served anyone. Never helped me, even that year I went to midnight mass with the black eye so swollen it wouldn't even open. I guess what Robert had meant was that actions spoke louder than words. But how many people live like that? Do you know people like that? If I hadn't been told Philip was a priest, I would've never known, so it's not like he was pointing me to that God of his.

I read those verses over and over and over. My thoughts tumbled like rocks, around and around in my head. In the end, there were more questions than answers...

The next thing I knew, there was a knock on the door. I was still lying on the bed, looking up at that ugly ceiling, wrapped in only a towel. The hours had slipped by unnoticed. *Darn, Cindy, how could you be so foolish to get so wrapped up in this Bible stuff! Just a few words of it has you questioning anything and everything, getting you nowhere.*

"Just a minute!" I called. Hurriedly, I threw back on my new outfit from earlier and pinned back my still slightly damp hair. Finally answering the door, Robert looked at me and laughed. "What?" I spit out. It wasn't possible that I looked that bad! I was sure I was rather disheveled from my haste, but to laugh at me was rather rude.

"You got caught up in the Bible verses, didn't you?" he said, his face lit up with a gigantic smile. Like a little kid in a homeless shelter getting ice cream for the first time in six months. You would've thought I'd made his year.

"Back to the God conversation again, huh?" I said sarcastically, I wasn't going to admit how much those verses affected me. For the simple reason that I didn't understand why they did; my inner turmoil was greater than ever.

"All right, I'll back off for now." He held up his hands in a surrendering gesture and didn't even seem hurt by what I'd said. A goofy grin was still plastered on his face.

Why was I so uptight? Why did this silly myth bother me so? Rulers created religion to keep the illiterate masses happy and suppressed, a false sense of hope to keep them going when life sucked. I was educated— "unlearn all you have knowledge about" is what Robert had told me to do earlier. It made no sense; it was like the world had been turned upside down.

Dinner was a fog. My mind kept rehashing the events of the last two days, the last ten years, my whole miserable life. Back at the motel, I climbed into bed exhausted. Even the pleasure of sleeping in the relative comfort of a bed was lost in my jumbled thoughts. Why was I letting this eat at me? Unlike the night before, I couldn't relax, and sleep came super late. I kept tossing and turning until the wee hours.

In the morning, I was awoken by Robert's knock on my door at seven a.m., telling me to meet him in the lobby a half an hour later with my pack ready to head out. There seemed to be no time for another shower, so a quick wash-up had to suffice. Then I packed, or rather stuffed everything into my pack and rushed out the door. We ate a quick breakfast in the motel's lobby. You know, the cheap, free breakfast of doughnuts and coffee that so many budget motels offer. Not the best of meals before heading out the door for the day, yet so many people do it. Any other day, I would've been elated about even this simple meal, but today I only wanted to go back to sleep.

"Well, I'm not sure how far we will get today," Robert said as he finished loading the car with his small suitcase and my pack and I climbed in. "But you can take our minds off the miles by telling me more stories." He climbed in as well and headed out of the parking lot. "I'm sure you've got a million of them at this point."

"Sure." With as little sleep as I'd managed to get, I wanted to control the conversation as much as possible. That way I couldn't be caught off guard by any more religious talk from Robert—I was confused enough at this point. "I've met some rather odd people along the way."

And by that, I meant religious people—after all, those were the ones who were most likely to help out a stranger. Not like I was going to tell Robert that. No reason to keep offending this person giving me a ride any more than I probably already had. Especially given the fact that so far he'd kept his word about the motel and paid for all the meals. Also, he was still willing to give me a ride this morning. To be honest, I had no idea why I was even in his car at that moment. Because I was suddenly convinced that Robert was the oddest person by far I'd ever met...

Chapter 6

"Hmm, let me think. Well, Robert, I remember one March I was hitching a ride to California and..."

I'd gotten a ride quickly from where I'd started in eastern Texas early in the morning. I then bounced from ride to ride across Texas the rest of the day. So ridiculous and sometimes quite comical how long it can take to get from one place to another. If you don't get a decent ride first or second try, you could be at it a while. What would take only a few hours in a car you own could take a few days when you resort to hitchhiking. People would whiz right by you as you stood on the side of the road for hours, daydreaming or watching the clouds go by, waiting. Hoping for that one kind soul who'd be willing to take the chance to pick you up. You should always try to look your best on days you're hitching a ride. Looking scary will turn people off. But my best is still worse than most people would ever look, so yeah, they're taking a big chance on me.

That day I'd gotten lucky, to a degree. Every time I'd gotten out of one car, another car came along soon after. Each was willing to take me a few miles further up the road. The only way

I could've gotten luckier was if I'd found a single ride that would've taken me all the way across Texas. Or, better yet, all the way to the coast of California, but no such luck there—I was a human ping-pong ball for the day.

The other big problem I was having was that, as was often the case, I couldn't pick my route. The most direct route from point A to point B wasn't how I ended up going. Not like I worry about time or whether I ever end up where I set out to go—half the time I don't even have a plan of where to go. So that's not much of a problem. That day, my rides ended up taking me in a more northerly route than I would've liked. It was no skin off my nose. I simply rolled with the flow and went wherever my rides took me. As long as I was heading in a generally westward direction, it was all good. In fact, if I'd never gotten to California, that would've been fine too. But I was looking forward to the beaches for a while.

"Hey—wake up!" The guy I was currently riding with said as he roughly shook my arm. "We are just outside Amarillo. You need to find another ride." He'd stopped at the bottom of an exit ramp, and I groggily crawled out of his car, noticing on his dash that it was a little after six at night, not so good.

I took my pack out of the back seat and swung it on my shoulders. I started walking back up to the freeway on the other side of the exit. A light, steady rain was falling, and it was rather chilly. So I swung my pack back around to take out my light coat, not like I had a heavier one to choose from. A pack isn't a closet—you don't have room for endless options. You have only the bare essentials: one extra outfit, a coat, personal care items, camping stuff, and some food. Well, the food was optional.

After putting the coat on and pulling the hood up, I noticed the rain was turning into wet, slushy snow. "Oh man, I sure hope someone else picks me up!" I mumbled to myself as I looked around and realized that it wasn't a good place to be camping in.

There was almost nothing around. Flat prairie land with no trees. A few fences. No place to find some shelter or to set up a tent where it'd be partially hidden. The guy couldn't have dropped me off at a worse spot—well, maybe Mars or the moon would've been worse. But you can't drive there. I bet some of you wish you could just drop every homeless person off there, never to see them again. Yeah, out of sight, out of mind.

Since I'd begun shivering within moments of getting out of the warmth of the car, I needed heat. I decided to keep warm by walking. Heading up the road swinging my arms, I banged my bare hands on my arms and sides in a hugging motion for warmth. These are the kind of nights when the shelter of a car could've made a big difference in my life. So I kept walking. For the time being.

Unfortunately, it was about twenty minutes before another car even drove by. So much for freeways always being busy. They didn't stop or even slow down for that matter. Would you on such a horrible night? More than likely not. Why would you? Your car is warm and dry; best to keep it that way.

The snow was coming down in earnest by then. Big, hard ice crystals were starting to stick to the grass on the side of the road. My well-worn shoes and thin, well-used coat were no match for the frozen wonderland I found myself in. With each step, I stomped my feet to try to keep them a little warmer. Feeling the cold's slow climb up from the frozen pavement through my feet and up my legs, it was all I could do not to panic.

Seeing the lights of Amarillo in the distance, I figured I could at least walk that far. Maybe find a cheap hotel and spend my last few dollars on a room for the night. So much for food for the next few weeks, but it was better than freezing to death in a freak spring snow storm. You know, it's that priorities thing again. Being alive and hungry might've been better than frozen to death. Maybe not. What would you choose? Most likely, I should've sat down in the snow and given up. But I, for whatever reason, didn't. Stupid of me, I know.

As I walked and shivered, I decided to give up putting my thumb out if another car did happen by. No way was anyone stopping in this weather. I hunched deeper into my flimsy coat that was doing little to keep me warm or dry. However, a few minutes later, a semi-truck stopped a little way in front of me. I rejoiced, even though I'd admitted defeat moments earlier. I don't think I could've gone much farther. Beyond frozen, soaked to the bone, and I had no feeling in my fingers and toes by this point.

The guy in the truck got out when I was close and came around to me. I collapsed in his chubby arms. Funny, he looked a little like the classic Santa. White hair, long, white beard and mustache, big, round belly, and happy smile. All he was missing was the red suit, but instead he was wearing faded jeans and a blue flannel shirt.

"Hey, little lady! You okay? You shouldn't be out on a night like this, you're like an ice cube. I can feel you shivering from the top of your head to the tips of your toes. Where you walking to?" he said as he helped me get my pack off.

"I was trying to get a ride, but hardly anyone's out, so I was walking to Amarillo." It hurt to say, my teeth were chattering so hard, as he leaned me against his truck so he could get the cab door open.

"My goodness, that's got to be four or five more miles! You never would've made it. Here you go, let's get you in where it's nice and warm," he said as he half tossed me into the cab, then tossed my pack in behind the seat. He closed the door, walked around the truck, and got in as well. "Is Amarillo your final destination?"

"No, I'm trying to get to California. I want to spend some time on the beaches. After this, I'll need some time in the warm sun and sand to thaw out," I said with a half-hearted smile as I settled into the seat.

Putting my icy hands out towards the heater vents going at full blast, my fingers began to tingle. The pain became almost unbearable in only a few moments. Ruefully, I wished, yet again, that I had mittens or at least an extra pair of socks. On days like this, I needed to keep my fingers from getting so cold. Running the risk of frostbite was never a good idea for anyone. But for someone like me, with no access to healthcare, it could be a death sentence. Not that death was such a bad thing, but I didn't want to go in such a slow and painful way. One piece at a time.

"Well, you're in luck, little lady, so am I." He chuckled as he eased the truck back onto the freeway. "But they're saying on the radio that it's snowing pretty heavy in New Mexico. Don't know how fast we'll be able to go."

"That's all right, I'm in no hurry now that I'm somewhere warm and dry," I answered. There was no reason to rush to another spot. It's not like anything awaited me—now or ever. I'd burned my bridges to the real world long ago. Not like I was ever going to tell him that.

"My name's Dan." He looked at me intently. Was he suspicious about something? Not sure why I was hitchhiking? Or was he being a typical man and ogling me? "You look tired. That seat leans back a little, so how about you get a little shut eye."

"Sounds good, thanks. My name's Cindy, by the way," I said as I leaned the seat back and curled up.

Rubbing my legs and arms to speed up the warming process, I was beginning to feel all of me again. Yet I was afraid I'd never be dry until I could find a place to change my clothes. Every part of me was achy. I was sure I was going to end up with a doozy of a cold. Not like it would be the first time I'd been caught out in the weather and ended up sick. When you've got no home, things like this were to be expected.

It seemed like a few moments later that the truck stopped and I woke up with a start. Looking outside, I could see that the snow was still falling, soft and gentle. Big, wet flakes now lit only by the headlights of vehicles.

"Why'd you stop?" I asked as I sat up the seat to get a better look at what was going on outside.

"There's a major traffic jam because New Mexico state police are too stupid to plow this mess!" He hit his hand on the steering wheel hard; I almost jumped out of my seat. "Not like this whole freaking state owns more than two snowplows anyway—it's ridiculous!"

He reached over to play with a few knobs on the dashboard, slapping them around and not accomplishing anything. It was clear that he was agitated by the whole situation, needing to take it out on something. I was hoping that he wouldn't take it out on me or, worse yet, throw me out of his truck into the freezing-cold snowy night.

"You warm enough? You were a bit frozen when I picked you up six hours ago." His tone as he said this was now mellow; apparently, the angry episode had passed.

Nodding consent, I snuggled back into the seat and closed my eyes again. I'd gotten enough rides with truckers to know how important keeping to a schedule was for them. I was sure he was only upset about losing so much time, but I still didn't want him to take his anger and turn it towards me.

Having been an abused child, I still cringed whenever I was around someone who was angry. Especially a man. Now I showed it on the inside, not on the outside. The world no longer saw my reaction, but I did. I knew that the best thing was to make myself as small as possible, not say a word and hope that he'd forget I was still there. It was a trick that would sometimes work with my father, and I hoped it'd work now since I'd nowhere else to go. He was silent for a long time, and I almost fell asleep again, every once in a while cracking an eye open to take a peek at him.

"Bet ya anything those kids in that VW bug from the 70s in front of us will get cold soon. Then they'll come ask if they can sit in here," he said as he began to move around.

I popped my eyes all the way open to see what he was doing. I didn't want any surprises given his unpredictable mood.

"Want a soda?" he said, and I saw that he was reaching into a small cooler stashed behind his seat.

"No thanks," I said as I closed my eyes again.

About five minutes later, there was a knock on his door. I opened my eyes when he rolled down the window, letting in a cold blast of air and a puff of snow. I couldn't hear what the person outside said, but Dan replied, "Sure thing, son, go on around." Rolling the window back up, he turned to me and said, "Open the door and let that couple from the bug in."

After I unlatched the door, I moved to the floor space between the two seats. It seemed only fair that the newcomers should have the seat in front of the vents. I was plenty warm, my clothes were dry by now, and this couple couldn't be warm if they were asking for help.

"Thanks so much," a man's voice called as a young woman was pushed into the cab, soon followed by the young man climbing in. He sat on the seat and she sat on his lap before they managed to get the door closed. The frigid wind and snow was once again shut out of the truck. "We hate to intrude, but the bug's heat doesn't work unless you're going over forty."

"That's all right, I figured you guys'd be getting cold. I used to drive one of those little old pop cans. Too hot in the summer and too cold in the winter, and nothing you can do about it," Dan replied as he flipped on the CB radio. "I don't think the situation has changed, but we'll listen for a while and see."

"How far back in this chain are we?" The young woman was rubbing her hands to get warm; she had no mittens on and only a sweatshirt, no coat.

"About two hundred and fifty vehicles. There's some problem getting the trucks over this big hill a few miles up. So the freeway is officially closed until they get all of us up, over, and out of the way," Dan said.

"Honey, I don't think we're going to get back to Phoenix before class on Monday. Will your school think this is a good enough excuse to miss?" There was so much love in his eyes as he leaned closer to her; he began to rub her arms to help her warm up as well.

It was obvious they were both deceived — no one could be that much in love. More than likely newlyweds, with the bloom still on the rose. My marriage didn't even have a sweet honeymoon stage. I found out my husband had cheated on me on our wedding day. I should've left him then. You know those guys, the proverbial skirt chasers? The men who know every woman in town because they've been with them all? Well, my husband was one of those. Thus, it shouldn't have been a surprise when he cheated on me again later. But it was. Felt like I'd been slapped. Again, and again, and again. Yeah, love isn't a real thing.

"Hope so," she said as she snuggled against his chest and closed her eyes.

"Amber is a college student, and her school's rather strict about being absent. She'll drop from an A to a B for missing even a day," he said in way of explanation, like either Dan or I cared about a complete stranger's grades. I looked up at Dan; he was ignoring us completely.

Everyone became silent. I continued to watch this couple in the dim light from the instruments on the dash. Those lights were giving the whole cab an eerie glow. He was now stroking her long, auburn hair with one hand, and the other was wrapped around her waist. He was a ruggedly handsome blonde, she a slim, pretty ginger—I guess one could say an all American couple. But neither of them was dressed for the weather. Sweatshirts and jeans, no coats, hats, or gloves. They must've been caught unprepared. Married, because they both wore simple gold wedding bands on their left ring fingers. Yet she had no engagement ring, so maybe they didn't have a lot of money.

Well, that could've explained the clothes situation as well. Maybe they couldn't afford to buy a decent coat or were too proud to go to a charity office and ask for one. I'd been like that once—my father had made it clear that we never take handouts. After his fall from grace, when he was no longer functioning as an alcoholic. When he'd hit rock bottom as hard as he could. Now I couldn't live without handouts.

Without warning, the CB crackled to life. A male voice could be heard singing, "The foot bone's connected to the ankle bone..." as the snow continued to fall.

"If you kids live in Phoenix, where're you coming from?" Dan asked.

"Well, Vermont. It's Amber's spring break, so we went to see my parents. My mom's got cancer, and we wanted to see her one last time. She's got a few weeks left," the young man answered, stoic.

Man's man, can't cry over something like than in front of strangers. Or he'd already cried more than he could and had no more tears left. Or, he was too tired from driving to even realize the importance of his words. Either way, it seemed rather an odd reaction.

"You took a 70s VW bug all the way to Vermont?" I said, stunned, not picturing that at all. After all, my car had been much newer and it was now dead. How'd they keep a car that old running, much less take it on long trips?

"Sure. Why not?" Speaking with her eyes still closed, Amber's voice was muffled by her husband's chest. "Tom knows a lot about mechanics, and the engine is almost brand new."

"Looks like you've got a lot of stuff crammed in there, can you even see out the back window?" Dan said as he bumped into me getting himself another soda out of the cooler.

Pulling myself into a tighter ball in response, I shivered. That touch brought back an unwanted memory in a flash, and it was all I could do not to scream. *Keep it together, you don't want to end up out in the snow!*

"Well, when we left Vermont we could because we had a car carrier on top of the bug. However, car carriers are designed for cars with flat roofs, not domed ones," Tom said as he demonstrated the two shapes with his hands. "Anyway, the wind was quite bad in Virginia, and the carrier went flying off. Even hit someone's minivan. Luckily, there was no damage to the other driver's vehicle. So, after the policeman decided not to give us a ticket for reckless driving, we picked up what we could save. Jammed it all into the bug and kept going." Tom laughed and kissed the top of his wife's head. "We tried to rearrange it later so we could see out, but nothing seemed to help. If it wasn't things my mom wanted us to have, I think we would've left all of it in the middle of the interstate! Let it be scattered all over the East Coast by now."

"Our pregnant bug gave birth," Amber said, giggling, entwining her hands in her husband's. "And boy, what a mess it was!"

The CB crackled to life again. "Anybody know why this line ain't moving?"

Someone responded, "A stupid yellow double is stuck across both lanes at the top." That started a long conversation.

"And I betcha he didn't bring chains because it's March."

"Have the smokeys said if Albeq is open?"

"Not yet."

"Where're those damn snowplows?"

"I heard they couldn't get here because there're too many of us blocking the way."

"The leg bone's connected to the knee bone."

"Who's that singing?"

"I see a smokey!"

"Ho, ho, ho, help is on the way!"

"Anyone have some alcohol?"

"The knee bone's connected to the thigh bone."

"Now, now, no one needs to get drunk quite yet; we'll get unstuck sooner or later."

"No, you idiot!"

"Oh, your brakes freeze up?"

"Yup. Why else would I be asking? Have any?"

"I've got some rubbing alcohol that I'll give to this smokey sitting right beside me. I think it'll do the trick. Where are you?"

"Just about six miles back from the top."

"It's on its way."

"The hip bone's connected to the back bone."

"Someone shut up that horrible singer!"

"Anyone got some juice to trade for chips?"

"No, but I've got M&M's!"

We all sat in silence, mesmerized by the conversation on the CB, half asleep in the wee hours of the night. Watching the snow fall, only to land on the windshield in intricate patterns. The warmth of the heater made me want to pretend I was sitting before a beautiful stone fireplace. Maybe in a remote cabin, far away from the world. Watching the snow through a window with tiny icy webs creeping across it as the night wore on. A cozy blanket wrapped around me. A comfy armchair to snuggle in. Ooh, a steaming cup of hot chocolate to sip and fresh cookies to nibble on. You know, anywhere more comfortable than here.

The CB speech at times was clear, other times garbled. Yet it kept rambling on and on until finally we heard shouting.

"The line's moving!"

"The line's moving!"

"The line's moving!"

We all slowly became more awake and wound up, aware that the situation was changing. Our small world would soon be no more.

There was a knock at the door, and Dan turned off the CB as he rolled down his window. "Yeah, they're in here," he called out after a short pause. "That was a highway patrolman; the line's moving, so you kids better get back to your bug."

"Great!" Amber and Tom said in unison as they were already halfway out the door. Each scrambling to get back to their normal life, far away from this cab. Dan and I weren't part of their world. Only welcome for a moment when they'd needed some help. Well, Dan was at least. It's not like I was ever part of anyone's plan.

I looked at the clock on the dashboard. It was almost 5:00 a.m.—we'd been sitting there for over four hours. A little snow had blown into the cab while the door had been open. With my fingers, I swept off the seat then moved back into it as the door closed. I blew on my fingers for a minute—they were now chilled from the quick brush with the snow.

From my perch on the floor, I knew that it'd been snowing most of the last few hours. Now I could see outside and get a full picture of the result. No more New Mexico with cactus, scrub brush, scraggly pines, and rocks. I was now looking at a frozen tundra with the occasional tall cactus or tree sticking up through the snow. It must've snowed over a foot and a half in the course of the night. High drifts from the wind made it seem like more. Luckily, the snowfall had slowed to almost nothing at this point. The line of vehicles moved less than a mile before it stopped again.

The couple from the bug came back, so I slipped to the floor again. Tucking my feet under me, I rested my chin on my knees.

"Hello, again!" Amber announced with much more cheer than the situation called for. She sunk into her husband's lap again. "I guess God wants us to spend some more time together."

Needless to say, I was less than thrilled to find out that Amber was one of those crazy religious nuts. She was worse than most if she thought that God controlled every second of her life. Like the ones that think their car not starting is a good thing. Preventing them from getting in an accident. So stupid. How do you respond to that kind of delusional thinking? Play into it and agree? Ignore them and hope they will go away? I went with ignore for the moment. It seemed to be the easier of the options.

"Well, I'll turn the CB on again so we can hear what's going on out there. Doubt it's good news with how little progress we made," Dan growled as he flipped the switch again and the CB crackled to life.

"The neck bone's connected to the head bone."

"Ain't anybody figured out who that gosh awful singer is yet?"

"Yeah—whoever you are don't you think it's enough torture to be stuck? We're in a spring blizzard in the only state without any fudging snowplows, ya know."

"The hand bone's connected to the arm bone."

Dan decided to join the conversation for the first time all night. Grabbing the mike, he barked out, "Hey, why'd this darn line stop again so soon?"

"Cause another double is stuck."

"Another stupid idiot in a four wheeler is passing me on the shoulder."

"The shoulder bone's connected to the back bone."

"I see one too."

"Can someone stop them, block their path or something so they won't clog up the works even more?" Dan yelled into the mike, frustration lines all over his face. "I've got to get my load through, and I'm sure the rest of you do too!"

"I can swing out a little to the left."

"I can swing to the right."

"The neck bone's connected to the head bone."

"Just shut the heck up!"

"Bad news — this smokey thinks someone flipped, and if that's right, we're here for the long haul."

"Damn!" Dan yelled, throwing the mike at the CB.

With a loud crack, it hit against the dash before falling to the floor, missing my legs by an inch or two. I was too stunned to move or react. Then, with great force, he flipped the switch back to off and picked up the mike, now swinging by its tail. He set it haphazardly in its cradle, giving a loud grunt as he did.

"I can't get any sleep until Albeq when I pick up my relief driver, and if I never get there..."

We all were quiet for several minutes. I sat and watched first Dan, who looked like he might punch out the windows as he flexed his hands in and out of a fist. Then Amber, who looked like she wanted to cry. Real slow, I began to scoot backwards. Trying to get out of the line of fire, in case the situation got even more out of hand. If I'd thought for even a second that I would've been safer out in the storm, I would've left that truck in a heartbeat. Instead, I was trapped and trying not to pass out because I was starting to hyperventilate. My breath coming in quick pants, my head swimming, my stomach roiling.

"Everything'll work out." Amber's honeyed voice cut the tension, her words flowing like soothing water.

"Yeah, I know. Sorry, ma'am, for getting upset and swearing back there," Dan said as he hung his head in shame, looking first at the floor at his feet, then out the side window into the snowy night.

She only smiled in reply, oblivious to the fact that Dan wasn't looking at her. Tom, up to this point, had been sitting silent with his eyes closed. His head leaned back against the seat and his arms wrapped tight around his wife.

Now he added his two cents. "This hurts us as well. I'll lose a day or two of work. I've already shared how this will hurt Amber's grades. We understand the pressure of a time schedule."

Amber turned her gaze towards me for the first time all night and said, "You're the only one of us not in a hurry." A statement, not a question, as if she knew me all too well.

Looking up to her face again, I could see something bright shining in her hazel eyes. Her gaze was penetrating, and I wished she'd close her eyes like she'd done most of the last time they were in the cab. She was seeing right through me—like she was reading me somehow.

"So you're in college, huh? What's your major?" I asked because for some reason I needed, not wanted, to know more about this unusual young woman. Should've stuck with ignore. That would've been a much safer option.

"Psychology. I hope to be a youth counselor because Tom's a youth pastor," she answered. That explained the gaze—she was trained to read people, so there was no mystery to this. "You're not a truck driver, so you must be a hitchhiker. Where are you going?"

My mind reeled. How did she know that? No one could be that good. Then I remembered what Dan had said about his relief driver, so again, there was no secret here. "I'm supposed to meet a friend in California, but my car broke down. I decided to go there the cheapest way possible—hitchhiking," I lied.

The world narrowed down to the two of us. Everything else became dim and faded. "You can tell me the truth. I won't condemn you," she whispered as she took my hands in hers. My hand burned like it was touching hot coals, but somehow it didn't hurt.

"I have no friends," I said.

"You never have," she stated. "Where do you want to go?"

Did I ever know the answer to that question? Did it even matter? All of a sudden, I couldn't take her gaze anymore. It hurt in a way that I couldn't describe, like my heart was being pulled out, and I had to break the spell.

I yanked my hand away and looked up and out the windshield to see that the day was dawning. The snow, as it gently fell, seemed to be on fire. Finally, looking back into her eyes, all I could see was heartbreak and a deep pain, greater than my own. Somehow I instinctively knew that this was because of me. I'd let her down because I hadn't been able to answer her question. Simply put, I had no idea where to go to find the answer that I was seeking. Yet, she didn't have the answer either or surely she would've told me to ease both of our pain.

"The line's moving again," Dan said, startling me back into reality, not the limbo of my twisted thoughts.

"All right," Tom said as he gently patted Amber's back. I think he sensed that something had passed between his wife and me. But he had no idea what. "Dear, we've got to go." She didn't answer, simply left, with Tom right behind her. "Thanks again for keeping us warm," he called as he shut the door behind them.

As quickly as I could, I returned to the seat so I could watch as they got into their car. I never took my eyes off of them until, less than a mile further up, they followed a police car up an exit ramp and out of sight. I guess the officer had some back way into Albuquerque that they could take but the trucks couldn't.

Tears came to my eyes as their car disappeared into the morning light. Almost wishing they had to come back and sit with us again, my gut was in a tight knot. But it wasn't to be. She knew nothing, but I still wanted her near, the longing in me stronger than ever. Even you can see how foolish I was being about that.

Dan finished driving to where cat trucks were waiting to tow the semis over the top of the hill. The process was slow. Each semi was chained up, towed to the top, and released, then the cat would come back down for another one.

When it was finally Dan's turn and we were on our tow to the top, Dan, breathing a sigh of relief, said, "At least it's all downhill after this!" By now it was almost 10:00 a.m. and Dan was looking beyond exhausted.

I, on the other hand, was wired. How had Amber gotten so close to the truth about me when all I told her was lies? But her knowing me still didn't get me any closer to the answer I was seeking. It still didn't fill the void in me. The hunger for something was always there, and so the journey continued. I kept pushing on in the vain hope that I'd find my freedom, from myself, from my past, from my pain...

Coming back to the present with a start, I realized that I had tears streaming down my cheeks. Looking over at Robert, I hoped he hadn't noticed. Yet, he didn't seem to be paying any attention to me. He kept looking at the road.

Why'd you tell Robert that story, Cindy? I guess so he could see that I knew that religious people only cared when it suited them. When they had to do good works because this God of theirs demanded it. Or, in this case, when they knew that they had only a few minutes to spend with me before they never had to see me again. After all, Amber had had all night to talk to me. If she had wanted to find out my story, she could've tried a whole lot sooner.

I felt that it was best to press on with another story or two. Which was stupid on so many levels. I was completely in over my head, and I knew it. Robert was making me into something I wasn't without ever saying a word. Even so, I covertly wiped away my tears and fast as lightning launched into another tale...

Chapter 7

"I've camped at two national parks. Maybe I should tell you about those trips..."

I arrived at the Great Smokies National Park early in May one year. I wanted to spend at least a month or so there. Since I learned that it was completely free as long as one didn't use established camping areas, it seemed to be a must-see. If you're going to camp as much as I was doing, at least you could do it somewhere pretty. Not at the edge of towns like I usually did.

It was an amazing time of hiking around the backcountry. I had no idea so much wilderness could still exist in this overcrowded world. I was thrilled to find a place where I could be so alone most of the time; in solitude is a kind of rest that is seldom found. Do you understand what I mean? When you can't sleep in a city without some kind of white noise to drown out everything else? When an elevator by yourself is a blessing?

I grew up deep in the heart of a large city, where all the vicious animals were humans. Therefore, I was unsure if I could survive in the woods on my own with real animals. Yet, it didn't matter if I made it out alive or not. My life is worth little, so I plunged deep into the forest with almost no thought or planning.

Oh, I know, you're right. That's how I live my whole life. Now that I have no home, no rules, no keeper. The life of wild abandon I thought I had at eighteen had nothing on what I was now living. Definitely not a good thing. But you can keep your day planners; this is one thing I think I've gotten right. Spontaneity is wonderful. You should give it a try sometime; stop scheduling every minute of your day. Only don't overdo it like I've done.

As hard as being an unprepared pioneer was, I still found a kind of peace. Here in the wilderness was a freedom from people looking down on me: no one telling me that I wasn't living up to their expectations and no one telling me what I was doing wrong. There was no one to yell at me, no one to tell me their problems, and no one to tell me to leave. Yet even there, I still felt that something wasn't quite right, that there was something I was missing. But I was determined to enjoy it while it lasted before the itch to move on got to be too great.

In that vast forest, I'd often hike for days in the dense woods without seeing another person. Only animals. The shy deer, who would run away from me if I made any sudden moves or come close to me and eat right next to me if I sat still as a rock. The millions of salamanders that seemed to be everywhere at once—in the streams, under rocks, or in the logs lying on the forest floor. My favorites were the ones that looked like spotted fall leaves. But there were also red ones and black ones and green ones. I never knew what kind I'd spot next peeping out at me from the most unexpected of places.

The chipmunks and the squirrels that would chatter at me if I got too close. The birds singing their merry song in the trees. Once I even spotted a bear, thankfully from a great distance.

The few people I saw at first were happy to share a meal and stories of adventures. I must say that it was one-sided since I had nothing to offer in the way of either of those things. I'd entered the woods with little food, thinking I could forage for what I needed, and boy, was I wrong on that score. Even in the forest, I ended up begging for food the same as I did when I was out on the streets. But it was far harder with so few people around. As for telling people about myself, I never did that. So, I'd eat their food with the greed of a beggar because that is what I am. Listening to them tell me about their grand escapades on other hikes in other parks and other countries, I ate their meals, all the while knowing that it might be a few days before my next one.

Early on in my stay, I met several people who were trying to walk the entire way from Georgia to Maine on the Appalachian Trail. I didn't meet any later, so I guess that walk is so long that they had to start out early in the season. Many others I met were there for a few days or a week to enjoy the beauty of the park. One time, I met up with a group from a college who were doing some kind of a research project. Looking at the salamanders that I'd been finding so fascinating, I was glad others were enjoying them as well.

After I'd been there almost two months, I was ready to leave. Time to head someplace new. Now that the weather was warmer and summer was at hand, there were more and more people in the park. On one hand that was good because I was now getting food almost every day and sometimes even more than one meal a day. But what had been a wilderness was now like a park in the middle of a large city, filled to the brim with people who were noisy, and I couldn't be alone any longer. With a heavy heart, I realized that even here in this vast forest, I couldn't be lost completely. Someone always seemed to find me.

It was time to move on; my answer wasn't here. I think that even then I was beginning to realize that my answer might not be anywhere. You know, you can only look for so long before you become discouraged. Feel the need to give up. Feel the need to question your reason for being. Well, at least I did. I have off and on for years.

Thinking that my best plan of action would be to hitch a ride up to Gatlinburg, I began to break camp. You always try to find the largest place around to start a long hitchhiking trek. The bigger the place, the more strangers in town. Around there, that would be Gatlinburg.

With mixed emotions, I gazed around for the last time. The place had come to feel like a kind of home to me in such a short time. Not like I'd stayed in one place for long in my new life. No, I tried to keep moving as much as possible. Trying to catch one last glimpse of the birds and animals as I packed, each thing I saw became seared in my memory. A bright flash of orange here — maybe a salamander was nearby. A bright flash of red there — maybe a robin had flown by. But I was lingering and I knew it. I needed to get a move on before I'd wasted yet another day.

So I hiked most of the morning until I found a road and then changed into my best set of clothes that I'd washed the night before. Not that they were great. Jeans with a patch on the rear. T-shirt with a stain on the shoulder. Oh well, what you gonna do? Not like there's a free clothing bin in the wilderness to rummage through. I settled in to waited for any signs of a car. At least this was one of the few times that it wouldn't matter so much that I wasn't as clean as could be. It'd be plain to anyone in the area that I'd been camping, so that would lower any expectations.

I'd almost fallen asleep standing up leaning against a tree close to the road in the bright sunshine. Then, a group of people in a jeep with the top down came down the road, so I stuck my thumb out, but they drove on by. I turned my head to watch them go up the road, disappointed that I hadn't snagged the first car I'd seen. But then they stopped a little way ahead of me and backed the jeep to near where I was standing.

"Hey, Jenny! You know we told you not to hitchhike!" a young woman called as she stood up in the open cab and turned around to look at me.

"That's nice. Who's Jenny?" I replied with dripping sarcasm. It was clear that they'd mistaken me for someone else, but I hoped they'd still give me a ride. Even with my snarky response. It'd taken me far longer to find a road than I'd planned when I'd broken camp that morning, and it was now late afternoon.

A tall, dark-haired young man hopped out of the back, extending his hand. "Sorry, we thought you were a coworker of ours who's got this habit of disappearing for days. I'm Wayne." I shook his hand. "So you need a ride? Well, we're kinda crammed in here, but the more the merrier! Hop in."

The gang in the jeep cheered when I nodded agreement, picked up my pack, and moved to get in. Wayne helped me into the jeep, which already contained five people including him. Then he threw my pack into the already-jammed rear.

"I'm Mary," the young woman who'd thought I was their friend said as we all got settled into the small space. She had kinky, curly, short brown hair and an unmistakable twinkle in her eyes. "The driver is Shane." This young man had pale blond hair, and he waved as he pulled the jeep back onto the road. "Abbie and Jake are in the passenger seat." She had short flaming red hair and an odd crooked smile as she turned a bit to wave at me. He was a sandy blond who appeared to be a bit overweight. Mary had ended up on Wayne's lap in the back seat, as Abbie had on Jake's.

"I appreciate the ride, even if we are packed in like sardines. I need to get to Gatlinburg eventually for supplies." Not exactly the truth, but they didn't need to know that. Better they think I'm a tourist like them, not a wandering homeless person. "How far you going?" I asked as we picked up speed and the wind began to whip up my hair. Which I instantly regretted not putting up in a ponytail that morning.

"Well, we'll be going to Gatlinburg after we attend a supper cookout," Abbie said as she twisted around to see me better. "You're welcome to join us in all our evening activities."

"Well, I'd hate to intrude..." I started to say, trying to be polite, knowing that I hadn't had a decent meal in several days. I had been too busy avoiding people to worry about the fact that I needed them for food. With all the hiking I'd been doing, it wasn't a good thing that I hadn't been eating.

"Oh, it's no trouble at all. We bring guests all the time. Stan and Molly don't mind," Jake interjected.

"If you're sure..." I began to reply.

"Yes!" they all chimed in.

Shane leaned over, putting a tape into the player in the dash. Before I knew what was happening, music was blaring, making further discussion impossible.

They were familiar with the music, even though it was nothing I'd ever heard before. They even had movements they did in connection to the words as they sang along. Hands waving in the air, heads bobbing in time to the music. It was quite funny; they were a bunch of carefree kids out for an afternoon drive. Letting the wind whip their hair as the music played at a deafening level. Ah, to be that innocent again... Well, you know how I feel on that subject already. No need to repeat myself.

About a half an hour later, Shane pulled into a campground area. Parking next to a beat-up old Datsun and a brand new Mustang convertible with the top down, they all piled out.

"We're here!" Wayne announced as loudly as he could. They laughed and play fought as they walked the short way through the trees to the campsite. There were three people already gathered. With some hesitation, I followed behind, unsure exactly what was up with these rather boisterous young people. But, hey, they'd promised food. You know my feelings on food. I'll do a lot for a meal.

"Hi!" a short, perky, dark-haired woman called as we neared, "you're late."

Jake stooped to kiss her cheek and said, "So sorry, Molly, we picked up a hitchhiker."

"Not Jenny again!" Molly replied. The horror on her face was quite evident. You know, like that classic scream face. Kinda funny when you see it for real.

They all laughed. "No, but we thought she was," Abbie said as she flopped onto a picnic table bench. "I'm sorry, did we get your name, or should we call you Jenny the Second?" Everyone laughed again, but Abbie looked at me in a rather odd way, like she was a hostess who'd been rude.

"No, my name's Cindy," I replied.

"Well, I'm so glad you could join us tonight. I'm Molly." She drew near to me and took my hand. "That's my husband Stan over there by the BBQ." He gave a wave. "And that's Stevie over there laying out the food." She gave a wave. "Dinner's ready; we were just waiting for this gang. Stan, go ahead and say the blessing over the food."

I let go of her hand and stood off to the side until they were done bowing their heads. Talking to whomever or whatever they believed in. You know, I always seem to find these kinds of people. The praying kind. There must be more of them out there than I would've ever thought possible. Or, I'm a magnet for them and am somehow attracting them to me. Or, worse thought, they're some kind of magnet drawing me to them.

Everyone began to dig into hamburgers and tons of side dishes heaped onto a small folding table. I followed suit, glad for the free hot meal, heck, glad for food in general. After everyone sat down and began chowing down, another young woman wandered in. When I noticed her, I gave an involuntary shudder because she looked enough like me to be my twin. No wonder everyone had thought I was her. You've heard it said that everyone has a doppelganger—well, I'd just found mine. You know, you should never have to look in a mirror and find out that you have a better self out there. Not a pretty sight. Better clothes, better haircut, better person in general.

"Hey, it's Jenny!" Wayne called as he stood up and went over to her, scooping her up in a big bear hug. "How'd you get here?"

"How do I get anywhere?" she replied with a smile and a gentle shake of her head.

"You know we told you not to do that anymore. We'll give you a ride," Abbie said as she looked up from her plate of food.

"It's so much fun though. Tonight I met this super nice guy from Utah..." Jenny smiled as she said this.

"Oh, brother!" Mary smacked her hand on her forehead. "Not another man in your life!" Everyone laughed at that.

"Let's see, there was the guy from Brazil, and the guy from Washington, and the guy from Canada, and the guy from..." Wayne said as he counted on his fingers.

"Enough! We all know the stories," Molly cut in as she slapped her hand on the table hard enough to make the plates bounce. "Seriously, Jenny, you're going to get hurt."

"I know this isn't my place, especially since you gave me this wonderful meal, but..." I said. I know I should've stopped there, but I've never been one for tact. "I've been hitchhiking for several years, and nothing's happened to me. You should leave her alone and let her have her fun. Trust me, it's as safe now to hitchhike as it's ever been." At that point in my journey, that was true. I can't say that now with any honesty.

"She's right. God said He'll protect His followers," Jenny said as she sat down with her plate of food.

Well, I didn't know anything about this god protecting anyone, but I was quite sure I could protect myself. Little did I know then how wrong I was. Guess you shouldn't boast about things; it only comes back to haunt you later. Has that happened to you as well? You end up eating your words as a last bitter meal after you find out how very wrong you are?

"Jenny, the Bible also says to be as wise as serpents. We aren't supposed to place ourselves in harm's way simply to prove that He can protect us." Stan spoke up for the first time. He was older than everyone else there, including his wife; he even had a streak of gray in his black hair. "Now let's eat and enjoy this evening. Then we can discuss this later in private."

No one spoke much the rest of dinner, then Stan said they were going to start the entertainment. Everyone took off shouting to those in the campground to come for the show, and a few followed them back. No one in the group seemed to mind. Everyone took turns doing skits, singing songs, playing with puppets, and telling jokes. Soon, many people from around the campground came over to see what was going on. By the time they were done, there was quite a crowd gathered. Most of the subject matter had to do with their god, which seemed silly and contrived. I mean really, why ruin someone's vacation by making them go to a church service in the middle of a campground? It was definitely not my idea of entertainment.

I wandered around the campground for most of the performance. Looking at the trees. The kids playing. The birds singing in the trees as the sun gradually began to sink below the horizon. As I often do when I'm surrounded by nature like that, I got goosebumps. Why couldn't those religious nuts just enjoy the beauty around them like I was doing? The area of the campground that they were in was so noisy. I was sure that they'd scared off any wildlife that might've come close.

Beginning to absentmindedly kick some rocks around, I started throwing sticks in a stream. I watched them float lazily along, spinning this way and that. Metaphor for my life—no direction, no plan.

Cindy, maybe you should've tried to find another ride instead of waiting here so long, I chided myself. I had no idea where in the park I was nor how far it was to Gatlinburg; this was all such a waste of time. When the laughter died down, people began wandering back to their own sites. I returned to the group I'd come with, my hands behind my back, resigned to the fact that I might've wasted an evening for nothing. I might have to spend the night here and try again in the morning.

"Hey, Cindy, ready to go to Gatlinburg?" Shane asked as he started to load up the jeep with their props from the skits.

"Yeah," I said. It was rather late, and I was pretty tired. As late as it was, I was going to have to find a place for the night in the dark, in a place I'd never been. Ugh, I hated when that happened. You have no idea how hard it can be—you know where your home is. Try finding a cozy spot where you can be partially hidden in the dark. Worse yet, try doing it in the rain. Okay, I know it wasn't raining that night, but you get my point, right? No fun.

"How'd you like the show?" Abbie asked me as everyone else started to wander over.

"I'm not into religion, no offense." With my hand, I waved a bit. I didn't want to lose my ride this late in the evening. The odds of getting another ride now that it was after dark were slim to none.

"Too bad," Wayne said as he climbed into the jeep. "We hoped we'd be able to tell you more about Jesus on the way to Gatlinburg."

The jeep pulled out of the parking lot and onto the highway. Everyone had the same cramped seating arrangements as they'd had when they first picked me up.

"Where you going to stay tonight?" Mary asked as she wiggled to get more comfortable on Wayne's lap. "We always stay in the basement of the church Stan and Molly live in. There's plenty of room if you want to bunk with us."

There was no way I was going to spend any more time than absolutely necessary with these people. They'd given up way too easily on the religious talk, and I was sure it was only a matter of time before they tried again. Most religious people were pretty persistent when they wanted to get you to believe like they did. Been there, got that T-shirt.

"No thanks, I prefer to sleep under the stars," I replied with a frown, since in truth I would've loved to have a roof over my head. Maybe a nice warm shower after months of camping in the wilderness. But the price, in this case, was too high. Much, much too high. Yes, I could wait to find a shelter or a least someone's home later. I'd never stay in a church—that was asking for trouble. Shelters run by nuns or religious organizations were bad enough, what with all their yammering on about your sins and how you must repent. Thus, I avoided shelters when I could; camping was the life for me. No thank you to a church.

They must've figured at that point that I was a lost cause. They put the tape back in and sang at the top of their lungs the rest of the way. Kind of surprised me they never tried to tell me about this god of theirs again. But the more I thought about it, the more it made sense. It seemed that they felt that some people weren't worth the effort. Or weren't up to some standard they'd set for possible converts. I mean, I'm a hitchhiker. Not one of the campers with their fancy SUVs and expensive camping gear that'd been in the campground. Anyone could see that I wasn't their target audience. They were being nice because they'd stopped by accident thinking I was their friend. Not because they actually wanted to help someone.

When we got to Gatlinburg, I got lucky. They dropped me off at a grocery store—must've believed my lie about needing supplies. Having no money, I walked up and down the aisles looking for someone who looked like they might not be a local. I was able to easily find a ride that night from a trucker who was stocking up on energy drinks. I then proceeded to sleep in his truck on my way to who-knows-where. I'd forgotten to ask him where he was going, not like it mattered...

I stopped my story and looked over at Robert. He still hadn't interrupted me. The only way I knew for sure he hadn't fallen asleep was that he hadn't crashed the car. We were still speeding down the highway. Maybe he really was that interested in what I had to say and he was mesmerized. Maybe he'd tuned me out and was listening to his own script in his head.

I sat staring at him for a few minutes as I debated whether to launch into another story. I was getting tired, and not only physically. My brain was turning to mush from all of the thinking I was making it do, when normally I did very little—just floated along. You know, kinda like a couch potato without the couch or TV. Okay, maybe nothing like that.

"So what's the other trip in a park?" Robert asked quietly.

Okay, I guess he was listening after all...

Chapter 8

"Well, I always wanted to see Yellowstone Park as a child after I saw a movie on it in school. It seemed so far away, so exotic. Which is ridiculous, you know, since it's right there in the middle of the country, but it has all that crazy stuff in it. So, anyway, I hitched a ride there so I could see the place for myself..."

It was a lot easier to get into the park without paying than I'd thought it would be. The ranger at the entrance never asked the couple I was with who I was. He must've figured we were all in one group, never having any idea that my plan was to ditch those strangers as soon as we were a few miles into the park. After all, I wanted to head out on my own, be alone. Wanted to hike until I couldn't feel anything anymore; I didn't need a car.

This was the first summer I was a hitchhiker, though, thus I wasn't in good shape. Nothing like I am now that I've walked hundreds, if not thousands, of miles. Plus, Yellowstone turned out to be much bigger than I'd thought. So, I ended up hitchhiking around most of the time. However, I had to be careful to watch for official-looking vehicles. No point in having my stay being cut short by being caught. I'd become somewhat of an expert at dodging police when I needed to. Well, maybe not an expert—it's not like you'd call me a criminal mastermind or anything. But dodging park rangers didn't seem like it was gonna be all that much different.

During the day, over the several weeks that I stayed in the park, I wandered around seeing all the sights. At night, I found good places to hide while trying to get some sleep. Since I'd been in the park much longer than most people stay, I got to love the place like it was an old pair of jeans. Worn, yet comfortable. So I came up with an idea to make some money by giving private tours and asking for a "donation" at the end. That way, no one could say I was operating an illegal tour group in the park, in case anyone should ask. I figured the worse that'd happen would be that the park rangers would throw me out of the park. No big deal because I also guessed that if they caught me in the park, they'd throw me out for not paying to get in as well. Yeah, I know, my plans aren't always the best. You're getting to know me too well at this point.

However, my idea worked like a charm. It only took me a few days to earn more money than I'd had in the last few months. Before I'd arrived at the park, I'd tried my hand at various other odd jobs with limited success. This place was a gold mine, but I also knew it was unfair to keep it up—I was taking work from the real employees.

You may wonder about that, but I do have some scruples. I know you work hard to pay your bills and taxes and things. Okay, your hard work also gives me handouts sometimes, so my thinking on this is a little messed up. Anyways, I now had more than enough money to keep me going until I planned on leaving in a week or so. Therefore, I had no plans to push my luck by doing any more tours.

The day after my last impromptu tour, I decided to treat myself. You may ask what a wandering gypsy could think is a reward. A decent meal at one of the many restaurants or cafés in the park? Doing laundry at a laundromat? A candy bar? What? And waste my precious, hard-earned dollars? Oh no, my treat was my favorite hike, of course. Going to this special place I'd found since being in the park rather than seeing something new was a perfect plan. I loved the challenge of climbing Uncle Tom's Trail and wanted to take in the view one more time.

It actually isn't a trail in the truest sense. It's instead a flight of stairs leading down into The Grand Canyon of the Yellowstone. It ends up near the bottom of the beautiful Lower Falls. The hike down is easy. It took me only about an hour that morning because I stopped often to enjoy the views and let others pass me by.

Why anyone would want to rush on this amazing hike is an absolute mystery to me. The view is spectacular, one of those things that everyone should see once in their lifetime. You should go—honest, you must. But I, as usual, was the only one who was savoring the sounds of the water crashing against the rocks. The wind rustling through the trees. The birds singing. The chipmunks' shrill chirping echoing against the canyon walls. At least, I was enjoying it until a group of inconsiderate humans came along yelling and laughing, disturbing the world as it was intended to be.

Each time it happened on the climb down, it set my teeth on edge. I wished I'd come later in the day. The last time I'd hiked this trail was at night so I could see the moonlight bouncing against the water and the rocks. That was the only time I'd done this hike completely alone except for my animal friends. It was better that way. Being in solitude. With my thoughts and nobody else.

When I finally reached the bottom, I was disappointed. There was another person already there. I guess it could've been worse—it could've been a noisy crowd. He was tall, slim, about my age, with very pale skin and black hair. Wearing faded jeans and a worn, blue, button-down shirt, he seemed so relaxed. He was taking pictures with a beat-up, old, heavy camera—the kind that you've got to use real film with and change the lenses on. You know, the ones nobody bothers with anymore in this world of instant everything.

I watched for a few minutes as he seemed completely engrossed in getting a perfect shot of the rainbow. It arched across the falls as the sunlight bounced off the water. Yet, somehow I knew that he sensed I was there but it wasn't important in the moment, which made me feel good. He, like me, was enjoying the beauty around him. Taking it all in, not rushing, not making a sound to disrupt it, being a part of it for a little bit. It felt right to enjoy this moment together. Then the spell was broken as another loud group descended the stairs. Thudding footsteps so loud on the metal almost drowned out the sound of the waterfalls.

He knelt and began to put his camera away into a small, battered, tan leather case at his feet. "Beautiful, isn't it?" he said as he looked up at me and smiled. "My name's Dave." He extended his hand.

"Mine's Cindy. And yes, it is, which is why this is the sixth time I've climbed down here. The rainbow's what gets me the most, but I also climbed down here at night once. Boy, the ranger wasn't happy with me over that stunt!" I replied as I shook his outstretched hand. It was a joke—I'd gotten lucky and hadn't been caught that night. Obvious, since I was still here.

"So how long have you been in the park since you've done this hike so many times? Or has this been the only thing you've seen?" He chuckled. He raked his fingers through his hair and then let his hand drop to his side.

"No, I've seen lots of other things too. I've been here most of the summer." I smiled at him. I guess I shouldn't have told him how many times I'd been here already—it made me sound a little obsessive. Okay, a lot obsessive. But I was here for the views, nothing else.

"Well, I got here yesterday. My father always said if I ever got here to be sure to walk down this trail. He never told me where else was a must-see, so I'm not sure where to go after this, though, and I still have three more days here. Would you be able to show me around since you've been here so long? Or do you work in the park and this is your day off?" Dave said as he picked up his camera case and stood up.

"No, I don't work in the park. I'm a visitor like you." *That should've been obvious from the big pack I'm lugging around,* I thought. *Or maybe he's trying to be polite.* "Sure, I could show you around." I smiled at him.

Well, I thought to myself, *you haven't sought out any more tours. But you aren't going to ask for money this time.* He seemed nice enough. As an added plus, he wasn't as annoying as the other people I'd given tours to. It'd been clear that they hadn't wanted to slow down and enjoy the beauty around them. They were still in the rush, rush, rush mode of their everyday lives. No time to stop and smell the roses — well, in this case, the pine trees.

That was one of the few things I'd learned in my journey so far — to take my time. To notice what was around me and enjoy each and every moment, because that was all I had anymore. Do you do that? Notice the flowers that bloomed overnight on your usual route to work? Or are you one of those who rush? Never seeing anything as you go flying by? If you're a rusher, don't bother to visit Yellowstone or any other park. You'd only be wasting your time and ruining the visits of those who want to enjoy it at a slow pace. Stay home and miss what's next door instead.

"Thank you." His eyes smiled back at me; his face was warm and friendly.

"When was your father last here? I've been told that there was a major fire awhile back and some areas aren't really the same." There were plenty of areas I'd hiked that showed evidence of a fire. Scars as obvious as some of mine. I wonder if some of the scars were invisible, as most of mine were. Did the roots of trees burn too? Leaving the tree looking fine for a while but without anything to ground it? Do you know? Might have to look into that sometime. Because that's how my life seems to be. My roots had been destroyed by my father long before I reached adulthood. Not like anyone had noticed. Or if they had, they never bothered to try to help me.

"He never said anything about a fire, so I'd have to say before that. It was the year before I was born. He always said he wanted to come back some day but was in an accident soon after he was here and became a quadriplegic. So, when I was younger, he'd always tell me stories about the summer he worked here. I guess my vicarious memories may not match up with what I'm going to be seeing. That's if what you've heard about the fire is true," he said with a sad sigh and a slight shrug of his shoulders.

"Oh, I'm sorry. It's too bad you and he couldn't have hiked down here together," I said as I sat down on the bottom step. I didn't care, and I don't know why people were always sharing their problems and stories with me. That's how trouble started. I didn't need any more trouble in my life.

The latest noisy bunch had left, and we were alone again, so I pulled my meager lunch out of my pack. It was a simple peanut butter and jelly sandwich and a jug of water. Yet it'd be more than enough to give me the energy to get back up all those stairs. My plan was to take it slow and enjoy the view like I'd done on the way down.

Dave sat down next to me and pulled a small feast out of his small day pack. "How about we share?" he said as he passed me what turned out to be a roasted chicken sandwich on multi-grain bread, a bag of chips, and an apple. Keeping the same for himself, he grinned. "I've got more than enough for the both of us."

"Thanks," I mumbled between bites as I tore into his much better meal, only a wee bit curious as to why he happened to have two lunches with him. You don't question the lunch fairy. She doesn't magically appear often enough to keep a flea alive, much less a person.

We ate in silence, listening to the water and watching the rainbow dance in the bright sunshine. Every once in a while, a bird would fly across the canyon, its cry almost indiscernible over the noise of the waterfall. The water roared like thunder against the canyon walls, drowning out most other sounds. It felt good to be sitting here, with the warmth of the day and the beauty of the scene spread before us. My physical hunger was satisfied for the moment. My senses were filled by everything around me.

Yes, this most likely was as close to happiness as I was ever going to get. My dreams were now reduced to simply getting a better lunch and a good view while soaking in the sunshine. I hadn't been on the road much more than a year. Yet already I'd known even then that I'd lost everything. That I'd gone too far to go back. That I'd done something so horrible it could never be undone. You've got no idea how much I ached at that moment. Pain so deep it was never ending. You ever felt that? Like the water of the falls hitting the rocks over and over again, with no way to stop it. Pounding you, for all eternity. Beating you for what you've done...

"I hear the hardest part's the climb back up," Dave said, breaking into my thoughts. "Maybe we should be heading back." He looked concerned. I wondered if I'd said something as my thoughts had wandered back to that fateful night.

"Yup, going up's no picnic. Race you to the top!" I said with as much cheer as I could muster, giving him a half smile. I needed to stop thinking about that night, to stop thinking about what I'd done—it was over, and nothing could change the past. You may wish for a time machine to fix your mistakes, but it's never going to be a reality. Living with your mistakes is an unfortunate part of this ugly world. No way around it.

We definitely didn't race. We took our time, stopping at each bench so that he could take his camera back out to snap more pictures. Yeah, he must've wanted to share them with his dad— sweet in a sad way. I mean, way to rub the guy's face in the fact that he couldn't hike down here, or anywhere, ever again.

More than three hours later, we could finally see the last step. Sure, you can do the climb in fifteen minutes or less. But you'd never know what you're missing by running up those steps as fast as you could. We played hide and seek with a marmot who kept poking his head out of his hole while we sat on a bench and watched, laughing at his crazy antics. We got a chipmunk to sit on Dave's lap by putting a leftover chip on his leg. The chipmunk didn't seem to be interested in eating it but was curious about what it might be. We spotted an eagle, sitting proud and tall, watching us from his perch in a tree. Not wanting to dignify us with a response of any kind. Wouldn't you want to see those things too? All you've got to do is slow down. Relax. Breath. Just be for a moment, or two, or twenty.

"You've got a car here?" Dave asked as he strode to his car, a beat-up Chevy that was older than he was by a lot.

It seemed like a rather foolish question to me. If I had a car, I most definitely wouldn't have hiked those stairs with my heavy pack on. Just like if I worked here, I would've left it at home. I mean, let's be honest, my pack isn't small by any stretch of the imagination. No way would you mistake it for a day pack, good only for carrying a small lunch around. Everything I own is in the thing, tent to clothes. Over the years, it's weighed between twenty and forty pounds. You getting the idea yet? Yeah, I don't carry it for laughs.

"No, I hitched a ride up here this morning. I'll go wherever you're going, so it'll be easier for us to meet up tomorrow to start seeing the park. If that's fine by you," I replied, all business now that the hike was over.

"Alrighty then, where do you suggest we go for dinner? My treat," he said as he opened up the passenger side door and gestured for me to get in, grabbing my pack in the process.

"Depends on where you're staying," I said as I watched him stow my pack in the trunk. Of course, you know by now that I'm always keeping an eagle eye on it. I'm as possessive about it as you are about your house. After all, they're the same thing to me.

"Lake Lodge."

"Great. Let's go to the convenience store there, grab some sandwiches, and eat dinner down by the dock. The moon rising over the lake is fantastic," I said after we both climbed in the car and he began to head out of the parking lot.

"So are you sure you can take the time to show me around for the next few days? I don't want to take you away from your vacation here. I can pay you a little for the inconvenience since I'm sure you are going to show me things you've already seen. Plus, I'll throw in lunch and dinner each day. If that sounds like a good deal to you, that is." He smiled at me, looking over to make sure that I was going to be happy with the arrangement.

It was an amazing deal, more so if he ate that well every meal. Then my little bit of money could go even farther than I'd ever imagined it would. "Sounds good to me." I smiled back.

We saw geysers, hot pools, wildlife, stone monuments, and anything else I could think of. We visited all over the course of the next three rather busy days. We found bison, elk, deer, coyotes, big horn sheep, and even bears as we wandered around. Dave was happy with everything. But, what's not to love about Yellowstone? Yes, you're right, it's a giant volcano, but it's still awe inspiring.

We tried to take our time at each place. That meant we had to leave the lake area at sunrise each morning and not return until sunset each night. I don't know about Dave, but I fell into my sleeping bag exhausted each night and was slow to crawl out of it each morning. Yes, I had a sleeping bag back then. You know, I think I had it for maybe about a year more before it ended up being too trashed to be useful. So much better than a blanket, but so much harder to tote around everywhere. It took up too much space in my pack. Thus, I didn't replace it with another one, only a thinner blanket. It weighed less, took up less space. Not as warm, but better in the long run.

As we were returning to the lake area at the end of our last long day together, he asked me, "So what're you going to do next? I mean you've got no job, you aren't from around here, and you can't stay in the park forever. I hear it gets pretty cold in the winter."

"I know. In the next few weeks, I'll head south for the winter. I'm a snowbird, only not rich or retired like most of the other people who are," I snapped back. It was none of his darn business.

We sat in silence for a few minutes. "Don't you have a home or family who can help you out? Or is that what you're running from?" he asked in a quivering voice, and when I looked at him, I could see a tear in his eye.

Remember my rules? Rule two: be precise. Don't ask for info. Yeah, it's a major pet peeve of mine when you people feel it's your place to ask me this or to get upset at my lot in life. I've put myself in this position by my actions and poor choices. You've got no right to second guess what I've done. Stop thinking you do.

"Sure, everyone's got a home and family. Where's your home?" Snapping back, doing what I always did — going on the offensive.

"I live in Taiwan," he replied after he took a few moments to regain his composure. Trying to control his breathing, adjusting himself in his seat. "I'm continuing the work my father started at a church there. This is only my second visit to America in my entire life, even though I'm American. Funny, isn't it? I came here last year to bury my father, and now here I am to see the place he loved the best."

Feeling bad that I'd been rude, I didn't quite know what to say next. "Well, I'm glad you came to Yellowstone. I've found it to be one of the best places in America, and I've been all over in the past year or so. I know what I'm talking about," I said somewhat contritely. Here I'd thought he was taking all these pictures to show his crippled father, but in fact, his father was dead. *Way to go, Cindy, you assumed the worst of him because of how horrible you are.*

"It's beautiful, and now I understand why my dad loved it so much. God created the heavens and the earth, and it was good. That's what the Bible says, and you seem to understand it so well, unlike most people. Are you able to go to church often in your current situation? I mean, they could be your family, right? They'd provide what you need." He tried to give me a weak smile but failed and ended up looking like he might start crying in earnest.

Pathetic. Absolutely pathetic. You can't cry over me. When something isn't worth anything, you get rid of it. But you don't get upset about it. That's dumb.

"No, I never go to church. No offense, but I'd rather not discuss religion." Why in the world would he think that because I liked nature I'd go to church? That made no sense to me, a total non-sequitur. Like saying homelessness and wealth were the same. Or a cardboard box and a mansion were the same. You'd never think that, right?

He looked hurt and confused, like he'd read me all wrong and I wasn't who he thought I was at all. Well, I knew I wasn't what I showed to the world; true ugliness shouldn't ever be shown. That's what my father always said when he was beating me for being a bad girl.

Looking out the window at the trees that were growing so thick and close to the road, I sighed. They looked like they could reach out and grab me. Wishing they would, I felt awful that I'd hurt Dave. Up until now we'd been having a good time, with lots of laughs, which was a rarity for me. I, to this day, don't know why I felt so bad — it was his own stupid fault for making the leap from nature to church. Would you have made such a leap? Unlikely, I'm sure.

We finished the ride in silence, me watching the trees and him watching the road. He pulled into the parking lot nearest the lake where I'd been having him drop me off each night. I got out, determined not to say another word. *One of us being wounded was enough,* I thought as I slammed the car door closed. I began to walk away as fast as I could, breathing hard. Okay, so both of us were wounded.

"Wait!" Dave called after me as he jogged to catch up, waving a small package over his head. "Here's your payment for the tour. Thanks again for the last few days. I enjoyed getting to know you. My address is in there also. Please write to me and let me know what you're up to sometime."

I stopped and accepted the package. "Sure, no problem," I said over my shoulder as I began to walk away again, a little slower this time. No way would I ever send him a note, not in a million years. Not even if my life depended on it.

He'd said he was going to pay me, but instead he'd handed me whatever this was. I almost threw it away in the garbage can at the edge of the parking lot, but something stopped me. *Maybe there's cash in there with whatever else he felt compelled to give you,* I thought to myself.

Therefore, with great trepidation, I carried what felt like a bomb to the place I'd been camping, where I could open it in private. I'd been surprised to learn that he was a minister. He'd never brought up religion once in the entire three days. You know he couldn't have been a good one, never once doing anything to even give a hint about it. Until he dropped the news with a thud and ruined what had been a good time. Of course, if I'd known from that first moment, I never would've said yes to taking him around. Would've missed out on a lot of meals and a few laughs. My stomach thanked him for waiting until the very last moment to tell me. It's not good when your stomach rules your actions most of the time. Yet that was a big part of my life now.

"What was in the package?" Robert asked, bringing me back to the here and now. To this car, to this guy who was also more than likely a minister. Who, all these years later, I'd still taken a ride from, even after knowing that may be the case.

"What?" I asked. Breaking into my thoughts had been a bit confusing and disconcerting. I hadn't been ready to end my reminiscing about Dave quite yet. There was something I was forgetting about that encounter. I'm sure you understand what that's like. Like something's at the edge of your memory. Or on the tip of your tongue. Yet, you can't quite recall what it is. Something important was right there, but now it was gone. Poof.

"What was in the package?" He repeated his question, like it was of vital significance. The most important part of my story — without it, the telling of it had been a waste of time.

"Oh, a Bible, a card with his address, and three hundred dollars. Which was a bit of a shock — I had no idea he had that kind of money on him."

"What'd you do with the Bible?"

"Left it at the convenience store the next day as I left the park for good." I leaned my head against the window and closed my eyes. All of a sudden, a wave of absolute exhaustion came over me even though it wasn't even eleven in the morning.

"What about the card?" he said just above a whisper.

"I guess it was still in the Bible..." Yawning, it was hard to keep my eyes open. Telling all these stories was wearing me out, stretching me to my limits. I didn't know how much longer I could keep it up. Every part of me hurt, every part of me was tired. Body, soul, mind, and I only wanted to drop into a deep, soft pit and sleep forever.

"I think you've had enough for the day. There's a town up ahead. Let's stop and let you get some rest. Is that..." He began to say something and got no argument from me. At that moment, I fell asleep, dreaming of waterfalls, rainbows, and sunshine. Plus something hanging in the sky that I was so desperate to reach out and grab that my whole body ached. But I couldn't get it no matter how hard I tried because it kept slipping out of my fingers...

Chapter 9

"Cindy, wake up, we're at the motel." Robert was shaking my arm, and I half opened my eyes to see him standing beside the open car door. "I put your pack and your lunch in your room, which is right here in front of the car. Here, let me help you get in and lie down. I also put another card with a verse on the nightstand for you to read later."

I let him guide me the short distance from the car to the room but pushed him aside and closed the door hard when we got to the threshold. I wobbled to the bed, flopped onto it, and passed out again. I guess I was right about not getting enough sleep the night before. No surprise there.

The little alarm clock on the nightstand beside the bed said it was almost 3:00 p.m. when I woke up. Feeling only a bit more refreshed, I was still weary. Loud gurgling from my stomach in protest at not having been fed since breakfast was the only sound I heard. There was a vague memory of Robert saying something about my pack and lunch. Stretching, I rolled off of the bed to scout the surroundings. The room was almost identical to the one from the night before, but the bedspread and curtains were in a red and black stripe pattern, not flowers. The chair was black vinyl.

Next to my pack on the dresser was my room key and a small cooler—must be my lunch. I used the bathroom and debated about taking a shower before eating. But after all my attempts at getting clean yesterday, I figured I was clean enough. Bet you wouldn't agree with me on that—oh well. You can keep your daily showers. Horses get clean by rolling in the dirt. So there.

I turned on the TV and opened the cooler to discover several sandwiches, milk, juice, an apple, and a pudding cup. Eating the first sandwich, turkey and cranberry salad, I channel-surfed, trying to find something interesting, but everything seemed bland and tedious. The comedies weren't funny, the dramas were mundane, and the documentaries were unrealistic. So after a few minutes, I ended up flipping the TV off because it was getting on my nerves—silence truly is golden. Why must you people in homes always have noise all the time? I remember I always had the radio, TV, or fan on, but now, for the life of me, I don't know why.

The second sandwich was tuna and apple salad. I paced like a nervous cat around the room as I ate. That's when I spotted the card on the nightstand. It was written by Robert, as it had the same precise handwriting as the card he'd given me the day before. Yet, I was torn about whether I should read it or not. It had to be more from the Bible. I was so confused by the verses that I'd read the day before that I was unsure if I could handle another dose of that right now. Yesterday, I'd been correct in thinking that Robert could mess with my head. In fact, he was doing a splendid job.

It's a stupid book, for crying out loud! You know that. Don't let it bother you. Ugh, why are you letting this bother you?!

The third and final sandwich was a chicken and pecan salad. *Cindy, you shouldn't be eating so much,* I thought to myself. I was like a prisoner getting their last meal, or, in this case, last meals.

If you don't end your journey of your own free will, eating all this food will surely kill you!

Of course, there are worse ways to die. I'd seen homeless people freeze to death in the snow. You know that had to be a much more dreadful ending than overeating. Maybe not. Either way, I didn't want to find out right now. I drank the small container of milk in one gulp and took one more glance at the dreadful card before snatching it up.

Read it as quick as you can. Get it over with, Cindy. How much worse could this make things seem? Ha, famous last words.

> *'For I know the plans that I have for you,' declares the Lord, ' plans for welfare and not for calamity to give you a future and a hope. Then you will call upon Me and come and pray to Me, I will listen to you. You will seek Me and find Me when you search for Me with all your heart.' -Jeremiah 29:11-13*
>
> *Read your journals, you'll see this is true.*
> *Robert*

What!? So that's why my pack was already in the room before he woke me up in the car. How dare he look through my pack while I was sleeping! *Darn. Why'd you trust him enough to get back in that car this morning?*

I kicked the bed in frustration, not feeling most of the pain through the toe of my thick boot. I then stomped around the room in a blind rage for a few minutes, finally crushing the card in a ball before throwing it across the room. I was ready to scream, destroy the motel room, or beat my fists against the wall. All of the above at the same time would've been a good idea, too.

That's it, I thought, hurt, ashamed, and furious. *You're going no further with this man.* I was so glad that the night before I'd been in such turmoil that I hadn't pulled my notebooks out of my pack. Thus, no note could be found about him. I was right—this man wasn't as nice as he pretended he was. He was the punch-you-in-the-gut-when-you-least-expect-it type. Great, just great.

He'd been trying to manipulate you from the beginning, and he wanted something from you. This was all about sex, had to be. Yet, for some unknown reason, he needed this elaborate game beforehand. Predators come in some rather odd forms. Too bad there wasn't a "freaks are us" website you could look them up on. No, you had to find it out the hard way, like this. Trusting someone until they hurt you. Yeah, my plan of isolation was looking better and better all the time.

About that time, however, I got a good look at my pack. The lock on the zippers looked like it was still in place. Walking closer, I tilted my head in puzzlement. Realizing I was right, my heart skipped a few beats. The lock hadn't been tampered with. Years ago, I learned that most homeless people are trustworthy. But, you never knew, a rare bad apple could be in the bunch — one who'd steal you blind if you gave them the opportunity, never mind the fact that what a homeless person has is almost always someone else's trash. If it still could be used for something, someone who has nothing will want it. So, I've got a small combination lock on the zippers of my pack. Not foolproof by any means, you understand. But it was enough of a deterrent that I've never had anything removed from my pack without my consent. It was evident that this was the case now — no one had been in my pack since I'd closed it this morning.

But, if Robert hadn't been in my pack, how'd he know about my journals? I sank to the floor with a thump. My anger evaporated as quickly as it'd come upon me, now replaced with tears of disappointment at myself. That I'd gotten so worked up over something as stupid as my journals.

Who cares who reads them? The truth wasn't even there. I'd never written a word about what I'd done; there was no clue to my true self in them. The only way for Robert to know was if I told him; I was unsure if I could bring myself to do that. To be honest, there seemed no reason to.

Sitting there in stunned silence for I don't know how long, I massaged the rough carpet with my fingers. Then, I began to crawl around on the floor, looking for that darn card. Finally found it wedged behind the dresser. The card was now smudged from the dust and grime back there. Someone wasn't taking much pride in their work. Or the management never checked to see if the rooms were clean behind the furniture. Either way, it was something my father would never have tolerated.

When it was my turn to vacuum, I had to move the furniture and leave it out until he approved of the job. Or risk being smacked around for not doing it right. But I don't suppose you could do that to a paid employee. I doubt your boss has ever done anything worse to you than dock your pay. Too bad those rules don't apply to parents. No, behind closed doors, they could beat you senseless for any reason at all. At least mine had.

With great care, I opened my pack. It now seemed like there might be a landmine in there waiting to go off and destroy me. I dug to the bottom to remove my journals where they lay secure in their waterproof bag. As I removed all of them, I gave a gentle rub to each well-worn cover, thinking about which year each one represented, the hardships I'd endured.

I walked to the bed and propped myself up with the pillows. With great deliberation, I put the tiny notebooks at my side. These journals I'd managed to keep safe no matter what all those years had brought. No matter how rough I'd slept. No matter how little else I had. These were all that mattered. They were all the tiny free gifts some stores and banks give out. Each had only about twenty pages in it. Each was stamped with the name of a business and town that I must've visited at some point. Yet one notebook contained a year's worth of memories, a year of my life, and a slice of time that I'd never get back. These journals, in a way, had become a part of me. I would've been lost without them. Well, I was lost even with them. America had become a raging sea that I was drowning in, tossed to and fro in the waves.

I smoothed the card from Robert as flat as I could, trying not to damage it any more than it already was. Reading it again, I knew that what was written on it was wrong because my life was one calamity after another. There was no future and no hope. There never could be.

Sure, you're right—I'd brought most of it on myself. But if this god of Robert's had any kind of plan at all, it wasn't working out so well in my case. It was clear that his god was worse at planning than I was, and I was horrible at it. One look at my life for even a second and you'd see what kind of a disaster it was. You'd see that any plan had been thrown out the window years ago, long before I'd ever set my feet on this path of my so-called new life.

Setting the card aside, I pulled a journal out of the pile beside me and thumbed it open to a random page.

"June 11: Memphis, Best BBQ ever, Blues Man in alley"

There must've been fifty or so of us hanging out in an alley at 2:00 a.m. when the BBQ place closed. I don't remember now who'd told me to go there. It doesn't matter now. The night was hot and muggy, your clothes sticking to you like a second skin. If you've ever been to the South, you know what I'm talking about. The smell of garbage hung in the air from the dumpsters that most people were now using as furniture. Nobody seemed to mind that the ambiance wasn't the best; everyone was in a party mood.

Some guy called the Blues Man was keeping everyone entertained, strumming his old, beat-up guitar while we waited. Most of it was blues tunes, but there was some rockabilly and folk music too. Some were dancing to the music; others were tapping out the beat with fingers or feet. Tinny sounds from the dumpsters' drummers blended with the sweet sound of the guitar. Babies to people so old they could've been around during the Civil War, hanging around waiting. Swatting at the flies in time to the music. You'd have thought it was a hip, happening night club — not the dirty alley it was at other times.

Then, the waiters from the BBQ place came out the back door with enough ribs, slaw, and corn on the cob to feed a small army. All free for the taking for everyone there. Those ribs were to die for. That tangy, slightly bitter sauce was dripping down chins and arms as you kept reaching for more. The corn had so much butter on it, it tasted more like butter than corn. You were sure the corn would slide right out of your fingers like a greased pig as it was eaten. The slaw was so rich and thick, with a slight hint of sweetness, it was like dessert. Everyone was eating until they had their fill.

The music continued to echo in the alley as I walked away into the night, satisfied for a moment. My footsteps were lighter despite how much I'd eaten. My head was still replaying the music.

Okay, I thought, back in the present, *God, if you're there, you got lucky with that entry pick.* That does show my welfare being taken care of for one night, but great ribs once in my life isn't a pattern. I flipped the pages like a fan, allowing the journal to fall open once again.

"Nov 3: Houston, Heavy Rain, Night at the bus station"

It'd been raining hard all day; I was soaking wet. No real surprise there. Don't believe I'd had an umbrella then. Maybe. Hard to say. The only homeless shelter I'd been able to find had said they were full. A public bus stopped beside me, but it had an "Out of Service" notice in the window, so I didn't know what was going on. The driver opened the door and told me to get in. She then told me that her husband worked at Greyhound and I could sleep there for the night, in their break room. It was against the rules, but the manager had called in sick, so no one would ever know. They gave me a hot dinner, a soft couch to sleep on, and breakfast in the morning. Then I was out the door, ready to start hitchhiking to somewhere else. Dry, well rested, stomach filled.

This was ridiculous; this couldn't be a plan from some God. Sure, I got fortunate sometimes and was in the right place at the right time. But there was nothing more to it than that. Random chance is all. Nothing more, nothing less.

I tossed the journal aside, now angry at myself for giving in to this madness. There's no way that there's a God. There's no way if there was that he cares. There's no way if there was that he'd provide anything. There's no way religion had any of the answers for the very real problems and pain that life offered.

Banging my head against the headboard several times in frustration, I ended up with a bit of a headache. I should've taken the money and left Robert yesterday. No, I should've just left yesterday without the money. This whole situation was wrong, and I knew it with every bone in my body. Problem was I didn't know what was wrong with it.

Was it Robert? Was it the money? Was it this god of his? Was it me? Take your pick; maybe it was all of the above. It was yet another question that I didn't have an answer to.

My hand reached for another of my journals of its own accord. I had no control over it; it was no longer part of me. I watched dispassionately as it picked up a journal at random and then as both my hands flicked it opened to a page.

"Aug 28: Seattle, Fish Market, Lady and her house, Mute?"

I was down on the wharf hoping for some scraps from the fish market. Fish head soup would be so good to eat at a makeshift camp on the beach. Corny, you know? But, hey, you make do with what you got where you are. Anyways, there was this little Asian lady, so wizened and hunched from age it was almost sad. She came up to me and beckoned me to follow her. I asked her why, but she didn't reply—just started to walk away, so I followed. Several blocks later, she hailed a cab and handed the driver a card, which he read then handed back. We got in the cab. Drove to a house with odd characters painted on the orange front door. There was this amazing garden in the back. Big pond with big goldfish in it and a bridge over it. Beautiful trees trimmed into intricate shapes. Gorgeous flowers in full bloom.

We ate dinner in the garden—Japanese food, I think. I don't know exactly; I'm not into gourmet cooking, now, am I? We were sitting cross-legged on mats in an odd hut; later, I learned it was a tea house. Then she showed me to a room in the main house with only a thin mattress on the floor and no bedding. You can't complain about something like that; it was a bed, after all. In the morning, I couldn't find her in the house, but beside my pack was a large pile of food and a note bidding me good-bye. She'd never spoken a word. My fingers flipped the pages again.

"Jan 13: Baton Rouge, Baseball fun for the kids, Pizza party"

The shelter I was staying in wanted to have an outing for all the kids who lived there. A nice gesture for kids who've got nothing, but some of them didn't even have socks. Some local baseball team agree to host a clinic for the kids to teach them the basics of the game. I thought it'd be better to take them to a restaurant to get them a decent meal for a change. As usual, I kept my thoughts to myself. Why rock the boat? None of those kids were mine.

We all showed up at the park—adults to watch, the kids to play for hours. Everyone was getting hungry, but typical of homeless people, no one was going to say anything. Then some group arrived with pizza, soda, and ice cream for us. Some of the kids cried because it'd been so long since they'd been able to have such a normal day. Your kids ever cry over pizza? Not because they want it and you won't get it for them, but because they can't remember the last time they had it? Thought not. These kids did. Sad as anything you'll ever see.

Well, as you can see, that one wasn't for my benefit or welfare. However, those kids sure did get a boost from it. Those kids had only known poverty because their parents could never seem to make things work out. You've seen parents like that, I'm sure. They'll spend money on booze but not food. They'll spend money on a big TV but not rent. Those kids deserved so much more than what little they got.

I must admit, though, their happiness was infectious. A bit of it rubbed off on me; I got encouragement from their joy as well. So I guess you could say it was for my benefit a little bit. In addition, pizza sure had been good for a change.

Dropping the journal back into the pile, I leaned my head back on the headboard. It was sore from where I'd hit it a few minutes earlier. I shut my eyes because the whole room was spinning, and I wondered if I'd hit my head a bit too hard.

This proved nothing, I thought. *Providing a morsel for someone who's starving isn't providing welfare, and it isn't ensuring that anyone will have a future.* What kind of future did those kids in the shelter have? Absolutely none. What kind of future did I have? Not much of one — I'd thrown it all away to go on this crazy ten-year road trip. All because I couldn't deal with everyone telling me over and over that I was no good.

Well, my boss did say I was mediocre once — good enough to keep my job but not good enough to get a promotion or a raise. It may have been the nicest thing anyone ever said about me in that other life, before I stopped caring. Yeah, I know, yet another sad, pathetic thing I'm whining to you about. But you can't have a future without a past grounded in something good. Right? Plants can't grow in bleach. Kids can't grow where there's no love.

I had to stop and think for a moment; this thing with Robert, whatever it was, was making things seem different. It was like the world had been flat and in black and white but was now beginning to be in three dimensions with a few shades of color. Not vibrant colors so far, only earth tones. It was odd, disconcerting, disorienting, and yet somehow, in a strange way, comforting.

So the question is, Cindy, did you really stop caring? Or, for all these years, have you just been stuffing those feelings in a box? One which you keep trying without success to leave on the side of the road as you wander from town to town?

If I knew that, then I think I'd have part of the answer to what I was seeking. Then again, maybe not since I still didn't know the question. Or maybe this could work like Jeopardy — I'm given the answer and then can figure out the question later.

Okay, fine, that sounds crazy even to me, but I wanted to believe it was possible.

There was a knock on the door, which startled me, and I shrieked as I fell off the bed, landing hard on my hip. So lost in my inner world, I'd forgotten where I was or that Robert more than likely would be by at some point to go to dinner.

"I'll be right there." Picking myself up, I rubbed my hip — I was going to have quite the bruise in the morning. Grabbing the motel key, I stuffed my journals back into my pack, letting myself out the door as I hung the "Do Not Disturb" sign on the handle. You must know that I was regretting the fact that I didn't have time to hide the money again. It lay in my pack for anyone to find — not a wise move.

"Hey, you like your privacy, don't you — you did the same thing yesterday," he said, pointing to the sign. "Well, I thought you might like some dinner."

"Sure," I shrugged and shoved my hands in my back pockets. I'd polished off three sandwiches a short time ago, but I knew better than to pass up a free meal. You go with the flow when food is involved. Remember my rules? Rule one was to never pass on food. When you don't have much, you gotta stick with what works. My rules worked. Well, up to a certain point.

"You feeling better? You didn't look so good in the car earlier," he said as we started to walk away from the motel.

"Yeah, needed a nap is all. I'm fine now." I looked around.

The parking lot was full, and there were a few people milling around unloading their cars. Unlike at the motel the night before, you entered all the rooms here from outside in the lot, not from the lobby. Thus, this was where the hive of activity was. The motel had plain gray siding with white trim. No landscaping whatsoever, only the asphalt of the lot leading into the street. Across the street was a martini bar and another motel, similar to ours. As we walked, all I saw were more businesses — not a bad part of town, just a busy one. I had no clue where we were, not what state nor what town.

"Where are we?"

"Western Maryland, almost to West Virginia."

He looked at me kind of funny, like I should've known this. I guess I, in all likelihood, should've. There was no reason why I couldn't see what was around me when I was telling him stories in the car. Yet, for some reason, I could only see what was in my mind's eye as I was talking. But, then again, I had no idea how long I'd been asleep before he'd pulled into this town. So I guess I had an excuse for not having a clue. You can't expect me to see when I'm asleep, now, can you? No, that'd be silly.

"Oh." I decided to shut up before sounding any more stupid than I already did. Then again, my stories, I'm sure, had already led him to think that I'm not the brightest bulb.

It wasn't like he should've had any expectations of me. There was also the fact that I'd admitted to being homeless on a voluntary basis for ten years. Yeah, would've made you think I was an imbecile too, right? Of course it would. No sane person ups and puts themselves out on the streets. You just don't do that. Unless you think you've got no other options. Unless you're me and you know it's for the best.

We entered a small hamburger joint, the old-fashioned kind with waitresses in skirts. White button-down shirts. Hair in ponytails. Booths with red-checkered tablecloths and mini jukeboxes on each table. Old records hung from the ceiling, and posters from 50s rock stars and films were on the walls. You felt like you'd stepped back in time. Welcome to the sock hop. For a moment, it had an odd, comforting feeling to it. But, as all good things in my life, the feeling couldn't and didn't last long at all. Yeah, boo-hoo.

"Robert!" A waitress rushed over to us as we selected a booth and started to sit down. Her brightly dyed reddish-orange hair matched her skirt, lipstick, and fingernails. All were a shock to the eyes. "You haven't been here in ages. I've missed you so much." She leaned into the booth to give him a big hug and a kiss on the cheek, leaving a lipstick smudge. Eeww.

"I just knew you'd be here. How are you, Angela? Keeping up with everything?" Robert laughed as he replied.

"Of course! You were so right about what I needed to do. Church is great, my marriage is great, my son is so much better, my job is so much easier, and I have you to thank for it all." She beamed at him, patted his arm, and completely ignored me.

"Now, you know that isn't true." Robert frowned, taking her hand in his.

"I know, but without you, I don't know if I would've found my way to God." She shook her head then pulled her hand away and reached into her skirt pocket, pulling out a pad and pen. "Now what can I start you folks out with today?"

"Malted milkshakes. Sound good, Cindy?" Robert looked at me, I nodded agreement. As Angela turned her back and left, Robert grabbed a napkin to try to wipe the lipstick off. It didn't work—the orange only smeared more, leaving a bleeding slash across his cheek.

I wasn't sure what to make of this exchange. Here was one of his minions, and she seemed to be so very happy to see him. Robert seemed to not want any of the credit for this loon, so that was a mark in his favor at least. Yet, that kiss spoke volumes. But why'd he want us to meet? Was she one of his conquests?

Did he have a girl in every town? Was the other waitress whom he called his "sister" another one? What in the world had I gotten myself into? Ugh, this was worse than I'd ever imagined.

"Another one of your sisters?" I asked, my lips puckered like I was sucking a lemon.

"Yes, she and her husband were having a very hard time a few years ago and came to one of my meetings. I'm pleased to say that they both saw the Light, and things are much better for them now." He started to tap his fingers on the tabletop. I was beginning to think that the tapping thing was a nervous tick of his. "She now understands the verse I left for you earlier. She knows God has a plan for her life, and now she has hope where she once had none. I know you read the verse from how startled you were when I knocked. Are you ready to talk about the verses from yesterday and today yet?"

"No." I grabbed the menu card from where it was leaning against the napkin holder. I stared at it hard, like my life depended on it—it was hard to read. I had no idea what light this woman had seen, but I was pretty sure I didn't want to see it as well.

"That's fine," he said as he stopped tapping his fingers. "I haven't got any more meetings for some time, so you've got me all to yourself. But at some point you'll have to make a choice, and you'll have to tell me where you really want to go. You can't drift forever. So you'll have to tell me what you, in fact, want, and the sooner we start talking with honesty, the better. There's only one lifeline and I'm trying to help you find it."

"I want to be left alone," I whispered into the menu, unable to look up at him. I knew I needed to make a choice, had known for a while now. But he was making me too mixed up to make one. Either that, or it was another one of my excuses.

"But that doesn't end the pain." He reached out to take my hand, the menu sliding to the tabletop.

A feeling of warmth and peace washed over me, unlike anything I'd ever felt before.

"If it did, you would've found a way to go to the ends of the earth by now, to a place where no one would've found you. But you know you need human contact, that rare human touch that brings healing."

The waitress returned right at that moment, oblivious to what was going on at our table. She set the shakes down with a thunk, and the table rattled. "Here you guys go. You want your usual, Robert?" she said in her loud, brassy voice.

In a flash, I pulled my hands under the table, looking Robert in the eyes as he replied, while giving me a sad smile, "Yes, thank you, Angela. How about you, Cindy? What do you want?"

Our gazes were locked for a moment, and I was getting queasier by the minute. Yes, I was sure he didn't mean what kind of burger. But I wasn't going to answer that question. I still felt I couldn't, because I, to be truthful, didn't know.

"Just a cheeseburger and fries, please," I said as I switched my gaze to Angela, refusing to acknowledge Robert further. "And make mine to go, I've had a rather long day."

"Sure thing, honey." As she left, I stood and walked to the front of the shop to wait for my food. Robert never followed me.

Walking back to the motel after I got my order, I began to feel a little bit stupid for having a snit at the restaurant. One minute I felt safe with Robert, and the next I wasn't sure what he was up too. Yet, overall, I was fascinated enough by him that I felt I wanted to stay on this roller coaster ride as long as it lasted. But why now, after all these years, was I ready to listen to this religious nonsense? Why were these stories of mine making it seem like these religious people weren't so bad? Or as crazy as I'd always thought they were? That maybe there was something or someone out there guiding me? When I'd always thought I was simply floating along without a purpose? That maybe there was a greater plan that I wasn't seeing? That the problem had been me all along? That what I'd been running from all these years was myself, and that's why I'd never found my answer?

It's official, Cindy, if you weren't crazy before, you most definitely are now! Ugh.

Back at the motel, I let myself into my room and ate my dinner in the peace and quiet I'd asked for. Once again, I was alone, but Robert was right—it didn't feel good. I did need others. The four walls should've been a comfort yet felt like a prison, keeping me hidden from the world but not necessarily safe. After all these years on the road, I now realized that I'd camped because I didn't want to be rejected and hurt again. Not because I wanted to be alone like I'd always believed. But almost every person in my life I'd let get anywhere near me only wounded me, or I wounded them. Alone was better; it would always be better.

Only that isn't true, I thought. *Look at the stories you told Robert.* None of those people had hurt me, because I made sure to run away again before they could. But would they have if I'd stayed? I'm almost positive they would've. Maybe not on the same level that my parents or husband had, not all people were the same— everyone is different. Was it worth trying anymore? Could I find a way to connect with people while still keeping myself safe? But the bigger question was whether I could keep others safe from me.

I snuggled more deeply into the soft chair, pondering what this could mean. Each new day with Robert was making me question more and more things in my life, heck, in the whole world.

There was a knock on the door. I looked around, completely disoriented. The clock said 7:03, which meant it must be morning already. I was sure that I'd returned from the diner later than that the night before. I was still dressed, sitting in the chair and wishing I'd slept in the bed because my neck had a massive kink in it.

"What?" My voice was hoarse, my mouth dry, and I wasn't sure if I spoke loud enough to be heard.

"Be ready in ten minutes. We're eating in the car." Robert's voice was muffled through the thick door.

Crud, I'd have to take the world's fastest shower because I'd never taken one yesterday. Can't waste an opportunity at being clean, honest to goodness clean. At least my pack was ready to go — I'd never unpacked anything after returning to the motel the night before.

"Fine." What was the rush anyway? Yesterday he said that he had no more meetings and something about him being all mine. Not like that was a good thing given the present circumstances.

After my super quick shower, I put one of my old outfits on since I'd been wearing my new one for two days and had slept in it. The better one — the pants with the patches, my blouse with a few holes. It was more comfortable than the new outfit I'd bought with Robert's money. I felt a little more like myself now, a little less out of sorts. I looked around the room to make sure I wasn't forgetting anything and then headed out the door.

Twelve minutes after Robert's knock — not bad, Cindy. Strange, I thought, *you aren't even questioning leaving with Robert today. Cindy, are you now buying what Robert is selling, hook, line, and sinker?* Maybe I was.

Okay, so the clothes hadn't brought back all of the downtrodden, homeless me. Only some of it.

After I'd settled into the car with the coffee and doughnuts left on my seat, I tried to decide what story to tell next. It was time to push back on this religious nonsense. I could no longer sit back, passively letting Robert mess with my head. I needed to show him my side of things and how the real world works. After all, I knew that religious people didn't have any idea. Their platitudes of "If you only believe, everything will work out" and "Jesus is the answer" for apparently everything could only go so far.

Leaping off bridges was never a good idea, yet they seemed to advocate it with the expression, "Take a leap of faith." Please, you've got to be kidding if you think that will help anyone. At least Robert hadn't spouted any nonsense phrases, yet. But you know as well as I do that if I gave him enough time, he most likely would.

However, first I knew that there was one question still lingering in the back of my mind. "Robert, how did you know about my journals?" In my position, wouldn't you have been thinking that too? Was he Superman and could see through the material? Clairvoyant and could read minds?

"You seem like the type of person who'd want a record of their life," he said as he drove out of town.

"Why's that?" I picked at some lint clinging to the edge of one of the patched holes of my pants; it was better than looking at him.

"Because you're looking for an answer, therefore you wouldn't want to go to the same place twice. You'd want to know where you've been, to be reminded of that and to not repeat those steps." Tap, tap, tap—those darn fingers of his again.

Well, duh, I'd never thought about it before like that, but he was right. While I often went to the same area over and over again, I never went to the same cities or towns more than once.

"Um, I'm ready to talk about the verse from last night. I thought a lot about this god of yours giving people a plan for their welfare and a future and a hope. I'm going to tell you a story to show you why it's wrong..."

Chapter 10

It was a mild early October day, and I'd been in the parking lot of a grocery store in a small town in Alabama for over an hour, trying to find a ride out of the area with no luck. Everyone I met there was a local, no one feeling the need to stray far from home. As I looked around in vain again, I spotted a tiny old lady with her white hair in a neat bun. She was wearing what looked like her Sunday best dress—a pretty pink and white floral with a matching pink jacket. She was trying without success to get a huge brown paper bag of groceries into the trunk of her brand new white Cadillac. My concern was that she was going to hurt herself or at least lose her groceries. The bag must've weighed as much as she did.

"Ma'am, do you need some help?" I said as I approached her. I might as well do a good deed since I was going nowhere today. You never know, helping her might lead to a clue about an odd job or where a good place to stay might be. Stranger things happen; you see them every day. Well, maybe you don't, but I do.

"Well, of course, dear. Since these groceries are for you, you should have asked to help sooner. But never you mind, you are here now. So get to it," she said as she stepped back from the car, pushing the sack my way.

Obviously she had me confused with someone else. Did I look like someone she used to know? Your guess would've been as good as mine. Yet, I still felt I should try to help, so I put my pack on the ground and loaded her car with all the bags from her cart.

"Is there anything else I can help with, or is there someone I can call for you?" I asked, fake smile planted on my face.

When in the South, you've got to be polite. Smile, say your pleases, thank yous, Ma'ams and Sirs. If you don't, they'll think you're a damn fool Yankee rather than merely a damn Yankee. You get fewer "Bless your heart" comments that way. Oh, and in case you didn't know, that's not always meant as a nice thing to say to someone. Often, it's a pretty insult. Okay, most of the time, it's a major insult. Go figure. I sure never could understand that one.

Anyways, it's not like I'm a stranger to slightly addled people. There are lots of them that are homeless. For the most part, they're harmless as long as you try to stay calm and speak slowly and crystal clear to them. I was unsure if she should be driving or even be alone for that matter. However, since I'd been in that town for less than two hours, I had no idea where to turn to for help. No one in the parking lot seemed to be paying any attention to her. Even after I, an obviously homeless person, had approached her. So much for respecting and caring for our elders. And you think I'm the troublemaker in any given situation. Yet, here I was having a nice conversation with this old woman without anyone rushing to her aid.

"Do not be silly, dear, I am not crazy, just old. Older than dirt, if you must know. Now, when I pulled into the Piggly Wiggly this morning to do my shopping, I spotted you all sad as could be. Then God told me clear as day that I should get enough to feed you as well. It was an answer to a prayer, I tell you. I have been praying for some help around the house, and now there you were. So when God told me to shop for you, that is what I did. Stop blathering on like an idiot and get in the car before the ice cream melts," she said as she slapped me hard on the back, leaving my teeth to rattle from the assault. Then she turned and got behind the wheel of her car.

Well, that left me speechless, so I did as I was told. I was afraid of what she might do if I refused — it was clear that she was beyond a little bit confused to full-blown crazy. She drove out of town and turned onto a dirt road leading into a dense, wooded area. Soon we passed a small forgotten church, its steeple leaning to one side. Doors hung open so the kudzu could crawl right in. Then, we passed some run-down shacks. Most of their roofs had long since caved in, and all the doors and windows were long gone.

Weeds were growing out of the windows — must not have had any floors inside. Finally, the woods parted to show a beautiful, old, white mansion, on a small rise overlooking a sea of white cotton, standing proud and alone like an old soldier.

"So what do you think of The Old Home Place?" she asked as she parked the car in front of the porch with four towering, two-story-high columns. It looked like something out of *Gone with the Wind*, forgotten by time. The house wasn't exactly run down, but it was in need of some TLC, like a new coat of paint and some landscaping. "Oh, of course, my grandpappy who built it was a slave owner. So it was a plantation back then, but we must not say that anymore, now, can we?"

"No, ma'am," I replied. "But it's something, all right."

"Now you hurry up and get the groceries in," she said as she got out of the car, not exactly with a spring in her step, but she definitely still had a lot of get-up-and-go in her.

Grabbing the first couple of bags, I followed her into the house. The hallway inside was as impressive as the outside. There was a grand, sweeping wooden staircase leading upstairs in the main hall. All the doors on both sides of the hall were closed except the far one in the back. The doors were carved in an intricate flower and vine pattern. The light wood was polished to a brilliant sheen. The hardwood floors were so dark, they almost seemed like black marble, the seams invisible from years of polishing. There was light streaming in from a large, high window above the front door and one set high above the staircase. On the walls were old portraits and photographs. Some looked to be as old as the house based on the outfits the subjects were wearing. You could see the history of the house, for they must be this lady's family. I set the bags in the kitchen in the back and went out for the last few bags plus my pack, while she began to put things away.

The kitchen was all black and white, from the tile on the floor and countertops to the appliances and cabinets, pleasing to the eye. My hostess must've been a rather orderly lady, because her kitchen was spotless. Everything had its place. Helping her put the groceries away, I noticed that almost everything was labeled as well. We worked in companionable silence, passing items around the large kitchen.

When everything was put away, she said, "Come out to the porch and set a spell." She took a plate of sandwiches out of the refrigerator and filled two glasses with ice, then placed everything on a tray on the counter. "Bring that out with you." She pointed to the tray.

"Yes ma'am," I replied as I followed her out the kitchen door to the back porch lined with rocking chairs. You wouldn't think that me being such a puppy dog was normal behavior and you'd be right. I don't think I'd ever done this before. Simple obedience was something I'd do if a police officer told me to leave an area. And no, it didn't extend much beyond that.

Outside, it was warm but tolerable, all thanks to the mild breeze, shade from the roof, and several large oak trees. She sat in one of the chairs with a small table beside it, so I placed the tray on the table. A sea of cotton was spread out before the house until it was broken at the horizon by a line of fuzzy green. It was most likely trees but hard to tell in the afternoon haze. Buzzing of some kind of bugs. Chirping of birds. If this was your house, wouldn't you want to sit out here to eat your lunch too? Lazing away the afternoon?

"There is a pitcher of sun tea in the corner over there," she pointed to the far left, "so fill up our glasses. It is fine for you to have some. I have not had the time to turn it into my special tea yet. I prefer it with some whiskey in it; it fixes what ails these old bones. But I do not figure you would want that, you do not seem like the type that drinks." She had an impish grin on her wrinkled face, making it seem much younger than it was.

"Yes, ma'am," I replied, as I again did as I was told. I pulled another rocker nearer to the other side of the small table and sat down as well. "Oh, and no, ma'am, I don't drink alcohol."

"Those cotton fields used to be mine," she said after she'd taken a bite or two of a sandwich. "Had to sell them off years ago to keep the house; cotton's not worth what it used to be. I do not know how those boys that own it now make a go of it."

The chair clacked against the porch as she rocked slowly in time to the rhythm of the branches beating on the roof. As she finished her sandwich and most of her glass of tea, she was looking around, surveying what was once her kingdom. As for me, I'd eaten several of her good chicken salad sandwiches and drunk my glass of tea. I seemed to always be hungry, but by now you know that's because I often only eat one meal a day.

"By the way, my name is Miss Oliver. You may call me Minnie. Leastways, that is what my friends do, and I consider you a friend since you will be staying here and all." She reached over to pat my hand with her wizened one. It felt like crumpled paper, dry and a little bit rough.

"My name's Cindy." I almost smiled at her but thought better of it. She might think I was being condescending.

Somehow, I wasn't in the least bit bothered by the fact that she'd commanded, not offered, to have me stay with her. I'd somehow accepted it as a forgone conclusion as soon as I'd gotten in her car, which was unlike me. Minnie had an odd calming effect on me. She was unlike my own grandmother, who'd never seemed to want to have anything to do with me. Well, except for one day a year for midnight mass.

Somehow, Minnie being crazy wasn't a problem. I often ended up talking to the homeless guys who were. Like the guy who I'd met years ago who thought he was a general in WWI. Never mind the fact that he was only in his thirties at the time and so was born years after the war had ended. So what if she talked to this imaginary God of hers and followed his instructions? She definitely seemed harmless, and she was a good deal smaller than me. If I needed to defend myself, it'd be easy enough — not like I could see her getting violent. But she did say she drank, which wasn't a good sign. From plenty of firsthand experience, I knew that even small people could be mean drunks. I'm sure you've met people like that or at least seen them. Right? Little bitty things who turn into alley cats after a few beers. Not a pretty picture.

"Now that I have had lunch, I most likely will rock myself to sleep for a while, usually do. One of the joys of getting old. You may explore the house if you want. The upstairs only gets used when my son brings his ill-tempered brood, so it is a mite dusty. There are two unused rooms downstairs that you may choose from, but we have to share a bathroom. Or, if you prefer God's living room, you can camp anywhere on the lawn." She smiled at me, a twinkle in her eye at her joke. You know, old people can be such spitfires sometimes.

"Thank you, but I think I've had enough camping for a while." I smiled back. "I think I might join you in a nap here on the porch, the view and the sunshine are so pleasant."

"Good enough." The chair's slow rocking motion continued. But her head began drooping after a while as she nodded off, the rocking coming to a gradual halt. The thuds wound down to a gentle squeak then nothing.

All of a sudden, I was awakened by a loud crash. What had been a gentle breeze earlier was now strong gusts. As I opened my eyes, I could see lightning flashes streaking across the sky. Then, seconds later, another loud crack of thunder. The sun was now hidden behind dark clouds. The pleasant afternoon had turned gray and menacing.

"Looks like a storms a-brewing," Minnie said as she stood up. "We best be getting in and seeing to fixin' some supper."

"Yes, ma'am," I replied as I gathered up the tray and the jug of tea.

That day was a metaphor for what happened in my short stay with Minnie—pleasant, then all heck broke loose. Everything was fine for about a week. I did all the chores around the house. Minnie, for the most part, sat out on the back porch in her rocking chair, watching the cotton grow, as she put it. We made a fine pair. She needed the help, and I, as always, needed a place to crash and some decent food. It was odd that she never left the house once. I guess she was happy where she was. Or else all her friends had already passed away. She'd tell me stories about growing up on the farm, her marriage, and her son. Some funny, some sad, most somewhere in between. You ever listen to older people ramble on about the past? Interesting, isn't it?

In this case, Minnie hadn't wandered far from the patch of dirt she was still on. She'd been married at the abandoned church we'd passed—it'd been part of her family's land. She talked a lot about that church; many of her memories were tied to it. That was one of the last pieces of land she'd sold, with the understanding that the church would be maintained. However, it hadn't been. She seemed saddest about that over everything else. Sometimes, she'd begin to sing hymns and ask me if I knew what they meant.

The only thing I'd had to say was, "No, ma'am. I don't know anything about religion." Wasn't the nicest thing to lie to this sweet woman, but religion was a conversation I didn't want to have. No point in ruining her happiness this late in life.

But she'd let it pass and go back to rocking back and forth, muttering to herself. I was perplexed as to why she wanted to spend this time with a complete stranger rather than family. Yet, based on what she'd shared with me, she, in all likelihood, had her reasons. Only, it was sad, she should never have been left here in this big house to rattle around alone. I wonder if my grandmother lived alone at the end? I never knew. What I do know is that taking care of elders doesn't extend to those who were abusers. There isn't even an ounce of me wondering if anyone would take care of my parents when they were older. Would you take care of your parents if they'd beat you or neglected you as a child? Well, would you? Don't be judging me if you can't understand my feelings on that point. But Minnie was one of the kindest, gentlest women I'd ever met. No way did she deserve to be abandoned. Even if her family was horrid, there had to be someone other than me. Anyone was better than me.

Well, her son, John, arrived, and poor Minnie lost all her peace and quiet. He blew in like a hurricane one day, his six-and-a-half-feet-high frame fitting in the doorway with an inch to spare. He had auburn hair, pale skin, and lots of freckles. I now understood why his mother had described him as being madder than a white speckled hen under a red wagon. That's what she'd said most of the time, anyways, when she'd talked about him. Southerners have such a funny way of saying things sometimes, but that hit the nail on the head. He was wearing a pinstriped suit, flashy red tie, and shiny black dress shoes. Such an odd thing to wear to visit your mother at home. Who was he trying to impress? His mother? Me? Himself?

"She can't stay here!" Anger was dripping from every word John spoke. He hadn't even crossed the threshold of the house before he'd made this pronouncement.

Yeah, he's one of you who thinks homelessness is a disease that you need to avoid at all costs. Gotta love those people. Wish it was; that'd be easy to fix. You know I'm right. If it was a disease, someone would've taken the time to find the pill to cure it faster than anything.

"You are the one who was always saying I needed help and that at my age I cannot be living alone." She reached up to pat his arm; he was a giant compared to her. "So I prayed hard, and the Good Lord sent me a helper in my time of need. God is so good; you should never forget that." She wagged a finger at him, trying to shame him.

He roughly brushed her hand away. "Seriously, Mother. The man from the grocery store who called me said she was homeless and had shoplifted a few things. Then the next thing he knew, she was getting in your car, which is the only reason he didn't call the sheriff." His frown was so big, I wondered if it hurt.

"I was never..." I started to say.

"Cindy, this is not your fight," Minnie interrupted me. Like heck it wasn't. "She was never in the store. I was in the parking lot before she was. I watched her for some time before I went into the store to shop, and she was still outside when I came out. That is when I asked her to come with me because God told me to. She has been such a blessing to me this week and has been no bother at all. I cannot say the same about you." She had such a look of peace on her face, it didn't seem like she was in a war of words at all. More like she was sitting on the porch watching her beloved cotton grow.

"Mother, this is the last straw. I've already called and made arrangements for you to move to that nice nursing home we talked about. You know, the one up near where we live. It's clear that you can no longer live alone; you've lost all sense of good judgment." He looked like he was about to pick her up and haul her out of there by force.

"Over my dead body." She stamped her foot and put her hands on her hips, as if that could've stopped him from doing anything he wanted to. Yet her face still had that sense of calm, like she knew how this would end, and she'd be the winner. "As I have said many times before, you will have to get a court order to remove me from my home. My home that I was born in, raised you in, lost a husband in, and will die in. If you want to visit, you may stay, but if you want to argue, you must leave." She pushed him hard in the middle of his barrel of a chest, but it was like an ant pushing a mountain—he didn't even flinch.

"Fine, I'll see an attorney. Good day, Mother." He spun on his fancy heels and left, muttering to himself. I wondered if he might be a touch crazy like his mother. It runs in families, you know.

"Well, that was a fine how-do-you-do." Minnie closed the door with great care, like she was afraid she might break it. "He never even said hello."

"I should leave. I don't want to cause any further problems between you and your son." Tears in my eyes, I shook my head. She was too nice of a lady to have this much trouble because of me. It's not like I was ever going to stay there long, and if she didn't know that, she should've—gypsy was stamped all over me.

Have you ever met someone who screamed wanderlust without saying a word? Someone who'd never settle down? Well you ain't seen nothing 'til you've seen me. Very seldom was I in the same state for more than a few weeks. Well, a month or two at most. No, my feet knew how to move. No moss there.

"Now, there is no need to be silly, child. He will never win in court. I have God on my side." She patted my hand. She seemed to think those words were enough to settle the matter, but I knew lawyers always won. I'd been married to one. Look how well that had turned out. He slept with anything that moved. I tried to kill myself. We divorced. Now I'm in permanent exile. Yeah, Shakespeare was right. Kill all the lawyers.

The next morning, we were awakened by someone pounding on the front door well before the sun was up.

"Oh, dear. Who could that be?" Minnie's sleepy voice wafted into my equally sleepy brain from the next room.

"Don't get out of bed, Minnie," I called as I rushed to answer the door, pulling on my jeans first, then my coat over the ratty T-shirt I was wearing as a nightshirt.

"Morning, miss," a young sheriff's deputy said as I opened the door rather slowly, afraid of what might be on the other side.

"If you're here to arrest me, don't bother. I didn't steal anything from the store. In fact, I never even entered it. I'm sure there's a surveillance video to prove that." Crossing my arms in defiance, I glared at him.

"Uh, okay. I don't know what that's about. We got a call about a domestic disturbance at this location, and I was sent out to do a welfare check." I couldn't get a good look at his face to see how serious he was about this; the porch light was rather dim.

"You must be misinformed. There's only me and an elderly woman here. We were both sound asleep. I'm sure if anything was amiss, one of us would've heard it and woken up. Which is what we did when you had the nerve to pound on the door." If looks could kill, yeah, I know that dumb cliché is meaningless. Too bad you can't shoot the sheriff or, in this case, the deputy.

"Well, miss, I still need to come in and check everything out." His stare was more hateful than mine.

"You must be joking, right? All the lights in the house are off. You must've noticed that when you pulled up. Minnie needs her rest. If it was just me, it'd be fine." For some reason, I felt that I needed to protect Minnie from this man. On a normal day, I'd never say anything back to a cop. Obey his orders without question, yes. Not have this staring contest, yes. Wouldn't you have tried to protect this elderly woman too? Maybe, I was just mad because I'd been woken up too early in the morning. For a rather stupid reason. By a cop, no less. And not for the first time in my life.

"It's the law, miss. If you don't let me in, I'll have to arrest you." He pushed me aside roughly. Turning on his flashlight, he scanned up and down the wall until he spotted the light switch and flipped it on. The hall lit up with a blaze of light. Marching down it, opening doors, he shined his flashlight in each room before moving on.

"What in the world are you doing, young man?" Without warning, Minnie appeared at the end of the hall. Her long, white hair usually so neat in a bun or a braid was now wild around her, giving her the look of a mad scientist with her long, white robe billowing around her. "Is that you, Caleb?" She squinted in the bright light to get a closer look at the deputy.

"Um, yes, ma'am." He stood with his hand on a doorknob, looking for all the world like a child with his hand caught in the cookie jar.

"Just wait 'til I tell your momma what you have been up to. She will never believe that you now wake old ladies up in the middle of the night just to ransack their houses." Putting her hands on her hips, she shook her head. "Now go on out of here, git." She pointed to the door, stomping one foot hard on the wooden floor, the sound echoing in the hall.

"Yes, ma'am, but I had to check after the call we had." He started to slink for the door, his head hung as he went. The flashlight now dangled from his hand, sending the light bouncing around the room.

"That is plain foolishness. You knew full well who lives in this house and that there would be nothing wrong." She waved an accusing finger at him, and his gulp of shame was audible in the ensuing silence.

He didn't say another word as he brushed against me and exited out the front door. I closed it with a loud slam as soon as he was through it. I looked at Minnie; she looked deflated now that the intruder was gone, like a balloon with the air leaking out, fast. She looked older than she'd ever looked in the short time I'd known her.

"Let's go back to bed." I headed down the hall towards her, with every intention of guiding her towards the bedrooms.

"No point in that—the sun will be up in less than an hour. We might as well start breakfast." She turned, entering the kitchen. Beginning to pull things out of the cupboards in a wild frenzy of activity, she was almost panting.

"Here, let me do that," I said as I saw her start to climb on the stepladder. She must've been wanting to get something out of the top cupboards reaching up to the ten-foot-high ceilings. You know, those high ceilings sure look beautiful, but boy, are they impractical. You've got to get stuff stored on those top shelves somehow. But it's like making an ascent up a mountain for an old woman. Not a good idea.

"Now you think I am old and feeble too?" With a fierce wave, she continued to climb. I watched in horror as she swayed in slow motion then lost her grip on the counter. I tried to catch her as she fell, but we both landed in a heap on the hard tile floor with a heavy thump.

"Oh, Minnie! I'm so sorry, are you hurt?" As I began to give her a light frisk, I bit my lip to keep from screaming, I was so angry at myself for letting this happen. I was as careful as I could be, but she still groaned when I touched her right hip.

"I am just fine; help me back to bed now. Then, you go ahead and make me some breakfast. I think I want to be pampered with breakfast in bed this fine morning." She gave me a half-hearted smile, trying not to show her pain as she patted my hand on her hip.

"I think I should call for an ambulance." Frowning, I felt more tears begin to form but knew they wouldn't help matters.

"No, I am not leaving my house. If there is anything wrong with me, my God will heal me and make me whole. He knows I want to stay here in my house. He will protect me." She patted my hand again, giving me another wan smile.

With as much caution as I could, I picked her up from the floor. She weighed much less than I thought she would. My heart was racing, my thoughts going a mile a minute. If I didn't call for help, her son would blame me if something serious was wrong with Minnie. However, if she only had a bad bruise from the fall and was fine, she'd hate me for calling after she told me not to.

I laid her down on her bed. She smiled at me and began to mutter in what sounded like a foreign language. I went to fix breakfast for us, still unsure what to do. Her muttering had me even more concerned. Had she hit her head as well as her hip? It wasn't like her mental state had been very great on an ordinary day. Or at least in my mind, it wasn't. In the middle of scrambling some eggs, someone began pounding on the door again. Crud.

"If it's that darn fool Caleb again, I'm going to hit him with something. I don't care if he's a sheriff's deputy," I grumbled as I walked up the hall to answer the door for the second time in less than half an hour.

It's not even six-thirty in the morning yet. When I opened the door, I was even more upset to see that it was John and not Caleb standing there. "What do you think you're doing waking people up so early in the morning?"

"I know I didn't wake you up. The sheriff's deputy was already out here. Let me see my mother," he barked.

"Did you seriously call the sheriff in the middle of the night?" Exactly how much did this guy hate his mother? She seemed like she'd been the type to have been a great mother, not like mine, but someone who cared. Yet, here her son was being such a bully.

Okay, I'll be the first one to admit that Minnie was crazy. You know, the full-blown loony bin type. Talks to herself — there's no God, so who else's she been talking to? Invites strangers into her home because the voices told her to. Likes to watch plants grow. I could go on, but you get my point, I'm sure. However, there were so many better ways to handle this situation than what John was doing right now. Like he was a spoiled brat who had to get his way or else.

"It's none of your business. Now excuse me." He pushed past me, and I watched him go into his mother's room. There was nothing I could do at that point. So, I returned to the kitchen and attended to my eggs that I could smell burning. Stuck to the pan, unsalvageable like this day was. Yet, I still ate them as quickly as I could. Last meal and all, something for the road.

I never did see Minnie again. A short time later, an ambulance came to take her to the hospital. I packed up my things, walked to the road, hitched a ride, and left. I felt guilty about everything, so after a few hours, I backtracked to that town again. I found the hospital and was going to ask to speak to her, but I never got the chance.

"Phyllis, can you believe what happened to Miss Minnie?"

I was walking beside the hospital where there was a garden area. Several people dressed in scrubs and business attire were sitting around smoking. I stopped. Could they be talking about my Minnie? No one was paying any attention to me, as usual, so it was easy to eavesdrop in on most of the conversation. Sometimes it's nice when you people ignore me. Pretend I'm invisible. I hear things I need to know and would never find out otherwise. So thanks for that.

"No, Lynn, I was as shocked as anyone when I heard. I mean, I know she was over ninety, but there was nothing wrong with her. The x-ray came back clean."

"I bet John scared her to death. He was mean even when we were in high school."

"Maybe, but I've heard of other patients that have given up. They think something's wrong with them. and then that's it."

"You think she died because she thought her hip was broken?"

"Not exactly. Yesterday, John filed papers to become her guardian, and I think she knew about it. If her hip was broken, she would've lost the case for sure. Then she would've had to give up her home, been forced to move to Atlanta with John, and that's what killed her. Of course, she probably would've lost the case regardless."

"Oh, what about..." I couldn't hear any more because they'd been moving away from where I was standing. Their voices were getting softer as they did so.

Tears streamed down my face, my fists clenched. I almost threw up in the bushes as I sank to my knees. That sweet lady was dead, and I might've had a share of the blame. No, I had a rather large role in the whole affair. I hadn't done enough for her, and by being in her house I had started the series of events that ended in her death. Yet another failure on my part...

"So you see, Robert, Minnie loved her life, but your God didn't have a real good plan for it. She could've continued to live for quite a while longer. Happy in her home, watching the cotton grow and rocking in her chair all day. But instead, she died in a few hours because she fell off a stupid stepladder. That doesn't seem like your God had much of a plan for her welfare. If your God was real, her son wouldn't have disrupted her life; he would've left her in peace, wouldn't he? Or, if your God was real, wouldn't there have been someone there who could've caught her? Or better yet, stopped her from getting on the ladder in the first place?" My finger punched out each of these points. I almost hit Robert's chest in the small, confined space of the car.

"Didn't you try to protect her when she fell?" Robert tapped his fingers on the steering wheel. That habit of his was driving me nuts. It felt like he was trying to drive a nail into something that was going to take forever.

Each tap echoed in my head, saying "failure" over and over. Do you ever feel like everything in your life is trying to remind you of what you've done wrong? Lately, everything seems to. Yeah, I was definitely headed into full-blown crazy territory myself. You don't need to say it. Robert was pushing me over the edge. Well, at least his finger tapping was.

"I told you I did, but I failed." I frowned.

"We're human. Sometimes we fail. But if we try, the blame isn't with us or with God. He uses us as best he can, but we're not always capable of succeeding."

"But I can't be part of your God's plan. I don't believe he's real, so he can't *use* me." I felt enough guilt over this incident. Robert didn't need to add more.

"In the Bible, God used a donkey to speak to a man to save his life. So, if God could use a donkey, God could certainly have used you if it was part of His plan." He turned to me with a kind smile, but in that moment it just felt like he was mocking me.

And is he equating you to a donkey right now? Really, if he is, that's pretty rude. You need to push back even harder, Cindy — set him straight, enough of this game.

This all was giving me a whopper of a headache. You know, the kind with the little tiny guy inside your head with a jackhammer, trying to kill you. You see stars, you're queasy, and every noise feels like you're being beaten. Yes, I was having so much fun at the moment, thanks for asking.

I had another story that made my point in an even stronger way, but it was a pretty big gamble to tell it. This next story would begin to reveal a side of me that I wasn't sure I wanted anyone to ever see. Including Robert, or maybe, especially Robert.

I sighed. Looking out the window, I couldn't see anything. Everything was a blur, like we were driving too fast. Must've been the killer headache. *Go ahead, Cindy, make your point, it's not like you've got anything to lose here.* Well, I had a lot to lose, but I didn't want to admit it. The only reason I was pushing this so hard was because this God might be real. If he was, and I pushed too hard, I'd lose everything. If I believed what all the religious people had said to me over the years. But, no, I wasn't going there. Not yet, maybe not ever.

"Yes, I've got another story that shows how little your God gives to people. How little he provides for their welfare." Well, here goes nothing, breathing as if it was going to be my last time. Sucking in a huge gulp of air before letting it out real slow.

At least this will only show him you're a little bit crazy. It's not like what happened in Oklahoma — now that would show him you're really evil...

Chapter 11

A tiny strip mall, weaving off the left side of the highway in a remote area of the mountains of West Virginia. One warm evening in early May, people busy shopping on their way home. As I was leaving the small grocery store, I breathed in a slow, deep breath of the fresh mountain air. Once again, I'd found myself somewhere I was hoping I'd get a ride out of soon. Camping in a parking lot is never fun. You can't set up your tent in your favorite parking spot and think no one is going to notice. No, that was only asking for trouble. Sure, you could camp there if you had an RV, maybe if you had a car. But a tent? No way. Parking lots had some standards, some class. Tents were only for the unwanted riff-raff.

Spotting several people gathered around in a clump, I wondered what all the excitement was. At the center of the bunch was an old white Ford four-door sedan and a young, frazzled woman. She was slender, dressed in worn jeans and a faded, oversized red shirt. Her blonde hair was pulled up in a ponytail, but much of it'd come loose, now wild about her face.

She appeared to be changing her baby's diaper on the trunk lid. Getting closer, I tried to figure out why this was such an interesting event that so many people felt the need to observe. I mean, let's get real here. Who wants to see a diaper being changed? Would you? You've gotta admit, it's rather gross, even when it's your own kid. Am I right?

"I tell you, lady, you can't do that. It's got to be some kind of child abuse or something. I've already said I'd buy you some diapers," Mr. Large and in Charge, the biggest and quite likely the loudest in the bunch said. His beefy finger was being shaken at the poor woman so hard, I thought it might go flying off.

"So did I." An elderly lady off to the side was so quiet she was not heard by most. But as she pounded her cane on the asphalt of the parking lot, thud, thud, heads turned in her direction. "So did I," she repeated. As several heads nodded assent with that, everyone looked at each other for encouragement.

"I've already called the cops," a skinny, pimply faced kid with a green apron from the grocery store said.

"All done, Timmy, let's get you back in your car seat and get out of here," the mother said to what I could now see was a toddler, ignoring the crowd around her. She only had eyes for her son, as it should be.

"We ain't going to let you do that, lady." This was from Mr. Large and in Charge again.

You know the type. Proud in his shiny-from-use suit, with its frayed cuffs and tie with a stain on it. Important only in his mind. Every mob must have a bully as a leader, and he was it for this group. He was now gripping his lapels with his thumbs and forefingers, bobbing up and down on his heels in his well-worn loafers—trying to look significant but failing. Best guess—he's the manager from the tiny bank branch I'd spotted at the end of the mall. Small fish in an even smaller pond who thought he was a gigantic fish. By that, you know I'm not talking about his large girth but rather his ego.

About then, a police cruiser pulled up beside the crowd, and the officer rolled down his window. "What's up, Jake?"

Jake, aka Mr. Large and in Charge, said, "This lady pulled off the highway, sat on the trunk of her car, and breastfed her baby without covering up. Then changed him with strips of what looked like rags. She said he's almost two, and it just ain't right."

"What exactly isn't right? Her breastfeeding in public, or her using unconventional diapers?" the officer replied. His contempt was under control by the thinnest of margins at being called out for such a trivial matter. Exasperation at the whole situation was written all over his face, from his grimace to his eye roll.

"Both."

"Everything."

"You name it."

Everyone spoke at once, trying to get their two cents in, like this was the most important thing that had ever happened around here. Maybe it was. If you live in a small town, you might think so too. Well, in this case, a bump on the highway would be a better description of the place. No houses were visible from where I was standing, only this strip mall and trees.

"Okay, folks, the law says that moms can breastfeed anywhere and says nothing about what diapers have to be. So here's what's going to happen. Miss, what's your name?"

"Annie," the mother said, so quietly that everyone was straining to hear.

"Annie's going to get in her car and go wherever she was going. Meanwhile, the rest of you are going to leave her alone and forget this ever happened. Everybody wins because I leave happy. Get it?" There were a few nods from the crowd in response to the officer's pronouncement. Yet from the frowns on everyone's faces, no one was happy about how this was working out. "Good."

Annie picked up her baby and opened the trunk to her car. As fast as she could, she stowed away the items she'd used to change the diaper. I decided to approach her and ask her for a ride since she wasn't from here. "Where you headed?"

"You heard the officer, leave me alone," she snapped as she was now strapping her son into his car seat in the rear of the car.

"I'm not with that bunch, honest. I just need a ride. I've got a bad feeling they may turn on me next. I'm not exactly the poster child for normal. I doubt they'll take kindly to me trying to hitch a ride from their nice little parking lot. My name's Cindy, by the way. Your son sure is cute. I love kids. I always wanted to have one, but it wasn't to be." I said it all with a rush, winded with the effort.

"Okay, fine, get in." She closed the back door and opened the front door, blowing her blond bangs up with her sigh as she slid behind the wheel.

"Thanks." In a hurry, I walked around to the passenger side and got in before she had a chance to change her mind and leave without me. I placed my pack between my knees and started to buckle up.

"Wait. That's silly. Put your pack on the floor of the backseat. You might as well be comfortable," she said as she looked over at me as she was starting to put the key in the ignition.

"Okay, thanks," I mumbled as I got back out, stowed my pack, and got back in. She turned the car onto the highway, heading towards Kentucky, which was only a few miles away. "How far you going?"

"Just to a holler over the state line. If you're wanting to go the other way, I'm sorry. I know a place you can stay if you need to, and we can see about getting you another ride tomorrow." She smiled at me as she said this.

"No, wherever you're going is fine by me. So what's the deal about the breastfeeding and diaper mob back there? I'm not judging or anything, it's just I don't understand why everyone was so mad at you," I asked, curious since I'd missed the first part of the quarrel.

"Timmy has a lot of health issues and is allergic to many foods. Therefore, I'm still breastfeeding as a supplement even though he is almost two. I don't bother to cover up because he only pulls it off. He's old enough to think it's a crazy hide-and-seek or peek-a-boo game, so we end up in a tug of war. Plus, he's allergic to bleach, so he can't use disposable or cloth diapers. I make my own diapers for him from rags I've washed in a neutral soap, but they can only be used once. Those rags are too hard to clean without bleach once they've been on Timmy's stinky butt, so I have to throw them away. I've tried to potty-train him, but so far no luck. Those good folks back there didn't understand that what I was doing was for the health and well-being of my child. No matter what I did to try to make them understand. Not like it was any of their business anyway." With a laugh, she shook her head. "But everyone seems to think raising a child takes a village."

"Sorry, I guess I shouldn't have asked." I raised my hands in surrender. I felt bad I'd said anything. Pretty clear this was a sore spot for her and not the first time she'd been confronted about the matter.

"No, it's fine. It's been a very long trip. I'm tired and ready to be home. My grandmother passed away, and we went to her funeral in Bangor, Maine. I debated about going. I haven't been more than a few miles from our holler since Timmy was born. In the end, though, I needed to say goodbye to my grandmother no matter how hard the trip would be. So, enough about us, what's your story?" she asked, taking her eyes off the road for a moment to get a good look at me.

"Needed a change of scenery," I replied. This was one of my stock answers when anyone asked. I thought it made me seem less crazy than the truth. Maybe it did, maybe it didn't—I don't know since I never told anyone the truth anymore. You ever do that? Give a half-truth to make yourself seem better? I bet you do. It's one more thing we've got in common, you and I.

"Hmm, now I know there is more to this than that. It's as plain as the nose on your face." She crinkled her nose and tapped her fingers as light as a feather on the steering wheel as she said this. "But I guess you aren't going to share what that might be."

We fell silent, and I watched the trees on the side of the road. Since it was spring and everything was starting to turn green, new life was everywhere. Buds were on the trees, and tiny flowers were starting to bloom. I think I preferred it when it was fall and death seemed to be everywhere. Flowers fading, leaves falling, snow coming around the corner. Not like she needed to know that; she'd freak out and throw me out of her car.

We crossed the state line and drove several miles more, up and over the rolling hillsides. She pulled off the highway onto a small road for a few miles, then finally onto a dirt road that was little more than a rutted track through the thick forest.

"We're almost to our home," she said. "We only have two rooms, so you can't stay with us, but up behind our place, there's an old pole barn. The roof leaks in places, but I'm guessing you've got a tent in your pack you can set up in the barn and stay nice and cozy. Right?"

"Yes. Thank you," I replied, surprised she was offering to let me stay with her. She had no wedding band. With a small child, she should've had the good sense to know not to let a stranger into her life. Mothers should protect their children at all costs. You know that too. Heck, even animals in the wild know this.

"Sure, I wish I could offer you something better than that..." She seemed to choke up for a moment. "Oh well, sorry. But if you help around the property, you can eat meals with us and wash up in the house when you want. We ain't got much, but what we've got is yours," she said as she stopped the car in front of what looked like a rundown, forgotten cabin in the woods. It looked downright sinister in the fading daylight. You could've filmed a horror movie there without changing a thing. Yeah, she wasn't kidding about not having much — I might've had more than she did, and I was a wandering hobo.

Outside, the cabin was a wreck, if you wanted to say something downright generous about it. I doubt it'd ever been painted or even whitewashed. It was plain gray, with weather-beaten boards. The front porch leaned to one side, and part of its roof was only a gaping hole. I hoped the main roof of the house was intact for Annie and Timmy's sakes. But based on what I was seeing, you know that was a rather vain wish.

Shutters hung lopsided over the windows. Well, at least I wanted there to be glass behind the battered wood. For all I knew, it was paper. You know, depression era windows. Weeds almost as tall as me were right up to the cabin, and vines crawled around the porch posts and onto the roof. Trees leaned into the cabin on three sides, their limbs resting on the roof and creating a canopy over it. You got the feeling that if something wasn't done soon, the forest would win. The cabin would've been swallowed whole — nothing but a long-forgotten memory. That might not have been a bad thing. Then Annie would've been forced to move some place nicer. Like anywhere else in the world. Like Calcutta.

Getting out of the car, I grabbed my pack. She gathered up her now sleeping son, kissing his forehead as she nestled him in her arms. She stood for a moment looking over her property, cradling her son and smiling at all she surveyed. It was clear that she was glad to be home again, goodness only knows why. Most homeless shelters are better than this dump. Most of you would be well aware of that if you've worked in them even once, or if you've bothered to take a peek in one as you've dropped off a donation to make yourself feel good.

She entered her house without using a key because there was no knob on the door. Pull a string hung through a hole in the door, and voilà, you're inside. When you live this far out in the woods, you don't worry a whole lot about someone breaking in — especially in a cabin that looks like it's about to fall down. What would be the point? What would anyone, besides a homeless person, want to steal? A homeless person would only want to move in. So much better than a cardboard box. So much better than nothing.

The interior was clean and neat as a pin. Annie had taken great pains to make this place a true home, not just a roof over their heads. A small main room acted as a combo living room/kitchen area with a couch and a coffee table. Spying a single bedroom through an open door, I could see two twin beds. The bathroom, if there was indoor plumbing in this place, must've been in the bedroom area. The couch was old and worn and had a handmade afghan on it in a dazzling array of colors — likely made with love from scrap yarns. There was a basket on the mantle above the fireplace with knitting needles sticking out of it at odd angles — maybe a work in progress?

The coffee table had been made with rough-hewn logs. The countertops in the tiny kitchen alcove area were wooden as well. There was a small stove and a refrigerator that both looked to be from the 50s. There's no way that they should still be working, but the noisy hum from the fridge told me that it was at least trying to. The quick glimpse of the bedroom showed patchwork quilts on the beds. I wondered if she'd made them or if they were hand-me-downs because they were faded and the patterns were indistinguishable. Or, she could be washing her laundry in a creek like a homeless person does. That wears your stuff out in a real hurry. Trust me on that one.

"Your home's very nice," I said, trying to be polite. It was beyond shabby chic, all the way down to third-world hand-me-downs.

This was a first for me — someone helping me who, it was real clear, needed as much help as I did, if not more so. How she could raise a child in this much poverty and then invite a stranger to share even a small part of it was beyond me. Deciding that I should try and find a way to repay this woman's kindness, my heart sank at the thought. Not something I, on a normal day, did or even felt I needed to do. But, helping around her property wasn't going to be enough payment for her generosity. Unfortunately, though, I'd spent my last cent at the grocery store for my meager snack before she'd picked me up. Even if I hadn't, it's unlikely that I would've handed her every penny I had. It's that food being the king need of them all thing again. You understand, I'm sure.

"Thank you," she said, beaming with pride. Someone being proud of this seemed a rather ridiculous notion. Like me being proud of the tree I'd slept under last week. "Let's have some supper, and then I'll help you find the barn," she said as she laid her sleeping child on one of the beds. She then closed the bedroom door as quietly as its squeak would allow.

As quickly as she could, she made up a cold supper of crackers, cheese, and fruit, and placed it on the coffee table. She sat beside me on the couch, bowed her head, and said, "Thank you, Lord, for guiding us to our new friend today. Thank you for all you've given us. Bless us, oh Lord, for these gifts we're about to receive. Amen."

Well, you could've knocked me over with a feather at that moment. What exactly had her god given her? And why would she thank her god for any more gifts it was plain she wasn't about to receive? Good grief, look at the abject poverty she was living in! This was blind faith at its absolute worst. She was happy to be living with what little her god had given her — it made no sense. Or was this a show for me?

After our fast supper, I was glad to get settled into the barn — even if it meant sleeping in my pup tent again. To be honest, the barn turned out to be only a little bit worse off than the cabin. We'd waded through weeds most of the way from the cabin to the barn, our way being lit only by the light of a kerosene lantern now that darkness had settled into the holler. However, the barn itself seemed in decent shape given its apparent age.

Looking like it was made of giant Lincoln Logs tightly placed together, the barn had no cracks in the walls. It was no joke about the roof though — you could look up and have a great view of the starry night sky in quite a few places. My own private skylight — too bad there was no glass in the holes.

The next morning, Annie gave me a tour of the rest of the property after we ate a simple breakfast of scrambled eggs and fruit. She had a small greenhouse where she grew most of the food she and Timmy ate. Apple trees grew everywhere. There were a few laying hens for eggs, most of which, she said, she sold at a local market. There was a stream where she could catch fish when she wanted a change of pace. It was peaceful, not another soul for miles. Well, maybe it just seemed that way because Annie's cabin was at the end of a dirt road and at the bottom of a holler. Thus, all you could see were trees, grass, vines, and sky.

"So why do you live out here in the woods?" I asked when we finished the tour.

Timmy sat on one of the few patches of grass that Annie had bothered to mow with an old push reel mower. He was playing with twigs, happy as could be, laughing to himself as he moved his sticks around. Not seeing any real toys anywhere, I wondered if he had any. I came to the conclusion that he more than likely didn't. They would've been a luxury Annie couldn't afford — something I understood all too well. Something kids in shelters understand all too well. But when you're two, you shouldn't have to play with sticks because there aren't any toys. When you're ten, you shouldn't have to play with bottles because there's nothing else. We're supposed to be the richest nation in the world, for pity's sake. Every child should have at least one real toy.

Annie began gathering eggs from the chicken coop, in disrepair like everything else. "After my husband, Ron, was killed in a car accident, I found out that he owned this property, and I'd had no idea. I learned that it'd belonged to his family for generations. I up and decided to move here, sight unseen, so I'd always have a daily reminder of his legacy. I was pregnant with Timmy at the time. I wasn't thinking real clear, but I fell in love with the cabin at first sight. Someday, I hope to have the money to fix it up, but until then, we make do. It's kind of hard in the winter — the power line goes down a lot. We have to light the house with lanterns and heat the house with the fireplace rather than the electric heaters. But the cabin has generations of love and faith instilled in its walls."

She stopped what she was doing and smiled before she continued on. "Ron's granddaddy was a preacher who roamed these hills, going into each and every house in each and every holler to tell them about the love of God. Even after his pregnant daughter ran away with a blues singer, he never gave up his faith. He preached to anyone who'd listen almost until the day he died. Ron only found out about his granddaddy a few months before we were married. Even then, it was only because the county nursing home tracked him down as the last living relative. Ron was able to meet his granddaddy just the once before they both passed away."

There was nothing I could say to that; the woman had run away from life same as I had. The only difference was she'd chosen to land in the middle of the woods hiding herself away. If she wasn't disillusioned by the whole god thing, I might've found a kindred soul. But it was obvious that she was crazy from grief, and two years or so wasn't enough time to heal that wound.

You ever feel that kind of pain? That kind of loss? Did it make you crazy? Did you run? Did you hide? Or did you continue on in your life, pretending that nothing had happened? Takes all kinds in this world. It's okay if you handled things differently than Annie and I. It's too bad if you get sucked into the god lie though. Not having an answer is better than being lied to. At least, I thought so—I could be wrong on that. It's highly probable that I'm wrong on that; after all, I'm never right about anything. Don't go listening to me; I'm as mixed up as they come.

We spent the rest of the morning working around the property doing various chores. It seemed like she'd been doing the bare minimum to keep the place from not falling down on her head and nothing more. It was real clear to me that she didn't have the money, the time, or the energy to do anything else. Sad—it was such a lovely piece of land. So much could've been done with it.

She talked on and on as we worked, I listened with my ears half opened most of the time. She told me about how blessed she was because her god had given her so much. She told me how she was trying to carry on her husband's family tradition of preaching. Going into the hollers to talk to her neighbors was rather foolish, if you ask me. She told me how she was helping her community by providing meals to the sick. Timmy's hand-me-downs were given to whoever needed them. There were so many other little things she thought she could help others out with. Helping me was par for the course in her life.

It shouldn't have been. She was so happy with nothing, it was insane. Could you be in this situation? Or are you living the American Dream, as materialistic as they come? Always wanting more and more things? Piling on the stuff you don't need. Hmm, now why does that not sound any better to me? Okay, so needs need to be met, but nothing more. Well, maybe a few wants are okay too.

After a lunch of peanut butter and jelly sandwiches, I thought I'd work all afternoon. Annie said that Timmy would be taking a nap. Whacking down weeds with an ancient-looking scythe I'd seen in the barn, I figured I could do some good. Sometimes, instead of feeling the need to cry, I feel the need to ruin everything in my path. I get so angry at a world that has allowed so many bad things to happen to me and others. Yes, it then seems like destruction is the only answer. You know that feeling? When punching the nearest wall would be the best thing to do, even if it leaves a giant hole? But you want to do it anyway? You just don't care? However, the occasions when you can act on anger as strong as that without getting in serious trouble are few and far between. But, for me, this was one of them. Watch out weeds, here I come!

All morning, working side by side with Annie, I'd gotten angrier and angrier. It seemed so unfair. Here was such a nice woman, with a nice kid. It sounded like her husband had been nice, too. Look what life had given her—nothing but a dead husband, a sick kid, and a dump in the middle of the woods. I'd gotten what I'd deserved; in fact, I'd gotten more than I deserved. I knew I deserved nothing, and I'd given it all up. Well, what little I had left at that point, because I knew it wasn't what I wanted, what I needed, or what I deserved.

After I'd cleaned and sharpened the scythe, I decided I'd clear as large of an area around the cabin as I could. Thus, it'd be easy to mow it later. You know how it is; you can't mow grass if it's thigh high, at least not with a push reel mower; an industrial powered one, maybe. But, if I could get a large area cleared and mowed, the grass could grow in better. That way, Timmy would have a larger area to play in; the kid deserved at least that much.

As I worked on the weeds, beating them with all my might, my anger didn't subside. Instead, it kept building and building, like waves ahead of a storm. Life didn't make any sense; nothing made sense; nothing had ever made sense. Talking with Annie had made everything nonsense. How could she have nothing and still give so much to others? To me? How could she think her life was so good? How could she be so happy? Or, was she only better at putting on her mask each day than I was? There was no way that could be true. Nobody could be so good at faking life!

My skin began to prickle, like someone was watching me, and I stopped thrashing. I glanced over my shoulder to see Annie standing at the corner of the cabin. She had her hands over her mouth. Tears were streaming down her face, and the look of horror in her eyes was so intense, I panicked. Afraid for her and for Timmy, my heart fell into my shoes. I dropped the scythe, unsure what was wrong, unsure if I should go to her, unsure if I could help even if I did.

"Your pain's so intense, Cindy, let me help you," she said in a whisper as she reached out her hands towards me.

Puzzled as to why this was about me, I looked around. The swath of destruction around me was incredible. Weeds and small saplings, torn to shreds. Trees, missing chips of bark. I couldn't believe I'd done that. *No way could you have done this, Cindy,* I screamed to myself, *you could never have been that angry!*

I hung my head and looked at my hands; they were ripped to shreds and bleeding, but they didn't even hurt. Not even a tiny bit. With a heavy heart, I knew it had to have been me who created this disaster in this sweet woman's yard. I'd wanted so much to repay her kindness, but I'd only created a mess. Yes, this is what I did on a normal day. I could never do anything good, never do anything right; I only brought disaster and death. People, trees—it made no difference; nothing was safe around me.

Without ever looking at her again, I turned and walked back to the barn. My whole body ached, but not from labor. Rather, from destroying the bond between Annie and I. I bandaged my hands as best I could, then gathered my things and left. Just like that, I left, going the opposite direction of Annie's tiny cabin in the woods. I stumbled around in the forest for what seemed like ages until I found another house with a road and kept on walking. Afraid to get another ride. Afraid to speak to anyone.

Afraid that I was capable of violence towards something other than those weeds. Knowing what harm I'd caused years before, innocent intentions gone wrong.

So very wrong, so very fast. Could I be capable of doing something else? I never wanted to find out...

"So you see, Robert, if your god didn't have a plan for her welfare, then what chance do I have? She was a believer in your god; I think your god is a myth. There can be no hope for me."

This story was a risk to tell, and I knew it. What would he think about me now? Had I completely offended him by trying to prove that this religious stuff was false? Or would he think that I was too far gone into crazy town because of what I'd done on that day? Would this be enough, or was I still going to have to tell him the worst thing I'd done?

Ugh, why do you keep getting back in this car? Why do you keep talking? Will you never learn to just close your mouth? Your daddy was right; you'll never be a good little girl.

Chapter 12

We sat in silence for what seemed like hours but must've been only a few minutes. Not so patiently waiting for a reply, my fingers danced on the seat at my side. On occasion, I would sneak a peek at Robert to try to get a sense of what he might've been thinking. He was completely unreadable; his face was, as usual, a blank slate staring at the highway in front of us. It was starting to drive me crazy how he'd so often sit in silence. He was letting me reflect on something I'd shared, I supposed. I did plenty of reflecting on my own, though, and didn't need anyone else to guide me in that area, thank you very much. Or, maybe he was expecting me to fill every moment with conversation. But, it was exhausting to have me be the only one talking all the time. Besides, you never want to listen to only yourself for hours. Right? Conversation requires two people, two voices, two streams of ideas.

Yet, I was afraid to ask him to tell me more about himself. I was getting enough of the religious talk in the few words he'd imparted. Not only that, but all the memories his presence was bringing up weren't helping matters. No, my stories were more than enough to keep me plenty confused. I should embrace the silence and stop talking, stop spilling my guts. I should sit here in this car until we got to the West Coast and I could tell him, "This is where I'm going." At this point, it didn't even matter where. It was hard for me to remember why I'd felt such a strong longing to go home a few short days ago. No clue at all.

"I need to stop to get gas for the car. Need anything?" Robert finally said, tapping his fingers on the steering wheel in his maddening way. You ever felt like you're going crazy because of something someone else was doing? That tapping of his was driving me 'round the bend.

"Just to use the restroom," I said as I looked out the window at the few houses flying by. I was glad he wasn't going to say a word about the story I'd shared. I might've gotten my biggest break ever. He saw my point, agreed with me, and didn't know how to respond. Well, without looking ridiculous to have believed in his stupid god in the first place, that is.

Could it have been so easy to make him change his mind when it hadn't been simple to change mine? After all, various well-meaning people had been trying to get me to believe in some god or another all the time. In goodness only knows how many soup kitchens, homeless shelters, rest areas, convenience stores, campgrounds and even their own homes, I had heard the spiel. This had been going on for the past ten years. It's happened to you, too, I'm sure. Those religious people are everywhere, trying to push their faith on everyone in their path. But how could I have changed Robert's mind in a few days with a few hard-luck stories? It didn't seem possible. Even remotely.

We pulled off the freeway into a quaint little town; we'd been driving for only an hour or so. As usual, I'd missed all of it. Where were we? Did it matter? Did anything matter? This town seemed like dozens of others I'd passed through over the years—the kind of town that's stuck in a time warp. The kind the world would've completely passed by if the freeway didn't have an exit for it.

Maybe you live in a town like that and like it. Maybe you live in a town like that and wish you could escape to the modern world where the Internet exists. As for me, I was back to feeling like I had before Robert found me in the field—that there was something I was longing for but would never find. *If you've changed Robert's mind, that isn't a good thing*, I decided. A bit of hope was better than the none I'd been living with for years.

Stopping at the first gas station, I saw it had yet another dirty outside restroom for me to use. There had been so many restrooms exactly like this during my time on the road. I don't even wonder anymore why no one bothers to clean them. However, I do still on occasion wonder who uses these dirty bathrooms. Other than homeless people and drug addicts who have no choice, that is. Because, if we're the only people who do, why have them at all? If no one's going to take the time to clean them and make sure the toilets work, why bother? Be honest now, have you ever used one? No, I thought not.

This restroom had toilet paper all over the wet floor. The sink was dripping with a steady plink, plink, plink. The toilet was so stained I don't know what color it was supposed to be—white, pink, mint, take your pick.

Rushing, I did my business and left the nasty room a little better than I found it. With some effort, I managed to get the sink to turn off completely. I picked up some of the paper off the floor as well. Eeww, the room still stank to high heaven though. Nothing I could do about that. Sorry to whoever used it next, not my fault.

Finishing our respective errands, we got back on the road again. The scenery was beautiful as it went zipping by, much different than this morning. Farmland, not forests, was whizzing by much too quickly to be enjoyed. I wished my life had gone past quickly too, because then it would've already been over.

The emptiness would be gone, consumed by the universe—forever part of a vast endless void. Instead, my life had seemed to drag on without end, one misery after another, with a few rare bouts of fleeting happiness sprinkled in, to keep things interesting, I suppose. Guess that's why I'd had no idea what normal was, because that's what normal was for me.

Even if I could see you people who seemed happy all the time, it wasn't real. I had no way to find a place where I could be happy, because I was so fundamentally flawed. Happy was something I was incapable of, for whatever reason. You've got something I can't fully understand and couldn't ever have. Lucky you.

I don't know, maybe part of it was that I'm not a beautiful woman in any way. I've got scars both inside and out. All you other people are always good looking. Or funny. Or charming. Or witty. Or courageous. Or unselfish. Or smart. Or caring. Or something else you find just as wonderful. I'm none of these things, and you always seem to find ways to remind me of that. There's nothing good that I can bring to the table. I'm only a Plain Jane who knows her value is nothing.

Why the encounter with Annie bothered me so much puzzled me to this day; I was so angry by her happiness. No, I take that back. I was jealous of her happiness. I wanted what she had but wasn't going to admit it to anyone, and most definitely not to Robert. But, you shouldn't ever wish for something you know you'll never be able to have. Most definitely shouldn't ever be jealous over it. It's just plain stupid.

"The puzzle pieces are blurry." He broke into my thoughts after about half an hour of silence.

"Huh?" Startled out of my musings, I turned to give him a quizzical look. I had no idea what he meant, but I was afraid that this was going to lead into some kind of lecture. I'd let the silence drag on too long, and now he was going to fill the void.

Maybe I shouldn't have let things hang the way I had. I should've launched into a safe story — not like I could think of one at this point. Even stories I'd thought were safe turned out not to be once I started telling them. Oh well, you live and learn.

"Life's a puzzle, often without a picture to guide us. Sometimes we can't see it clearly enough to put the pieces in the right place. Or, we think we lost a piece and have to go find it. Take your life — you thought you had the puzzle all figured out and were happy with the accomplishment. Or at least satisfied that you'd achieved all the happiness life would ever give you. However, you don't understand the difference between happiness and joy. Annie does, which is why she could be thankful in her circumstances, and that made you angry and confused.

"The Bible says, 'I have learned to be content in whatever circumstances I am in. I know how to get along with humble means, and I also know how to live in prosperity... I have learned the secret of being filled and going hungry, both of having abundance and suffering need. I can do all things through Him who strengthens me.'

"Happiness is fleeting because it's based on circumstances, things you can't control. When things are good, you're happy. When things aren't, you're sad."

He paused for a few moments as his fingers took up their tapping cadence on the steering wheel again, trying to drive his point into my brain. Or, maybe he didn't even realize how nuts it was making me? Then, his fingers stopped all of a sudden. Robert tapped his chest with his right hand while giving me a quick glance.

"Joy comes from within. Only you can create joy in your life by believing in something greater than yourself. You can have joy no matter what happens, good or bad. Because it's always there with you. Because it's part of you. But Cindy, with no joy in your life, something came along. Something blurred your vision and seemed to blow the pieces away. Your life's so confused and blurry, you aren't even sure what pieces are missing. So, now you're trying to rearrange the pieces, picking up those that were lost wherever they may be. That's how you began your current quest, but this journey you're on will not fix the puzzle. Nor could it ever even come close. There is only One who can; are you ready for Him?"

Crud, his silence was because he was trying to frame an answer. Not because you've made him rethink his world view. So yes, this was a lecture. A big fricking lecture about his stupid god. I frowned.

"You're back to that religious thing again. I don't see how you think your god was helping Annie. She shouldn't have to be 'content in whatever circumstances' as you put it. That's a really foolish notion and a rather dangerous one at that. Would you have said the same thing if she was homeless with a child? There was no plan for her welfare, she has no future, and what she hopes in will never happen. Also, I'm not sure that happiness and joy are two different things." I crossed my arms over my chest, glaring at him.

"I would've said the same thing if she was homeless. I'm sure you've meet some homeless people who had joy and were content for that season of their lives. I'm sure even you can see those who are truly content and those who are only happy when things are good. There's a very big difference between joy and happiness."

Well, I could think of several homeless people who seemed content. Sam, whom I'd shared a little bit about on my first day with Robert. The families that'd been part of the baseball outing, and so many others. I guess some would say that I kinda fit in that category. I'd floated along for years not trying to better myself, accepting the situation as is. However, I didn't have a child to think of, and it was pretty definite that I wasn't happy or joyful.

But, were the others I knew of content? Or complacent? Unwilling to change their circumstances? Unwilling to get out of the miserable poverty that'd led to them being homeless in the first place? I, for one, was complacent. I had no desire to change my circumstances, because I'd put myself in them and kept myself in them. In addition, I wasn't in poverty right before I became homeless. Far from it, in fact. So, I was unlike many of the people I'd met since being out on the streets.

Or was I? My poverty may not have been measurable in dollars, but it was in spirit. Do you ever feel that? That you have money but nothing else? I'd felt that my whole life. That there's more to this life than material things, but I'd never have them. My soul would always be empty.

But, the fact remained that I was homeless for a different reason than most homeless people were. Or at least I liked to think I was. Illegal drugs, no. Drinking, no. High school dropout, no. Veteran, no. Illegal immigrant, no. Mentally ill, no. Well, at least I thought not. Criminal, no. Unless you count my petty theft of food. So, you can take your stereotype and shove it. Okay, I'd been a battered woman. But I'd gotten out of the relationship with some money and a job, unlike most of the women I'd met in my travels. Therefore, I wasn't like them either, because I'd put myself out on the streets to prove a point to everyone. Myself included. What that point was exactly, I still hadn't quite figured out, but it's not important to this discussion. You can't judge me for that. There are too many other things you can judge me for. But, I'm not ready to go into that yet.

"That's so unfair. Some people have to be content to be homeless. Yet others get to be content being millionaires.
Annie deserved better; she was working for this god of yours." My arms were starting to hurt where my fingernails were digging into them, so I relaxed my grip some.

"Did you ever stop to think that she wasn't working outside the home so she could be the best mother? The best caregiver to her son that she could be? That she wanted to be the one to raise her son, not some stranger in a daycare center? That the best gifts she could give her son were her time and talents? Not money, a nice house, a better car, or whatever else you think were lacking in their lives? All because she chose to hide away in that holler as you put it. Was she really running and hiding? Or was she living the best life for her and her son?"

He never took his eyes off the road as he said this, but somehow, I felt like he was looking right into my heart and soul. Painfully, in a way that would be impossible to describe, I was being ripped open.

"How can any of that be true? What mother would willingly want her child to live in poverty?" Heat in my chest was building by the second, my voice getting louder, and I almost punched Robert. Instead, I let my clenched fist drop between the seat and the door. I knew it wouldn't solve anything any more than me beating the weeds at Annie's house had.

My face felt hot, beads of sweat were on my forehead, and I could feel them start to slide towards my eyes. *Cindy, calm down, you can't let him get to you like this. This is all talk, just silly talk; maybe you should go back to telling stories.* I looked out the window again, not seeing anything this time, and wiped my brow with a quick swipe.

He left me in silence for a while before asking in a soft voice, "Was she really living in poverty? You said that she had a house and plenty of food."

Taking several deep breaths, I knew I had three options. Keep up this conversation, change the subject, or just shut up for once. But I needed to know more about this god of his. I needed to end some of my confusion. It would be better to get my answers without revealing any more of myself to anyone. Was any of this religious stuff real?

"Yes, but I told you the house was a hovel, and the food was the bare minimum. So, I ask again, what mother would live in poverty like that?" I stared at him as hard as I could. I was hoping for some sign that he wasn't being completely honest with me. But his face was still the soft, kindly face I'd come to know.

Darn him for being so steady and unmoving!

Robert smiled that mystical smile of his, not looking my way at all. "The mother who knows poverty of the mind and soul is worse off than the one who knows poverty of the flesh. Remember the first verse I left for you, that there's more that we need than food and clothes? That there's something else we need? That something is what fills our hearts and our souls. That something gives our lives meaning and purpose. That something gives us the future and hope that are spoken of in the second verse. That something is love, pure and simple as that. After all, you, of all people, should know that love is the greatest gift a parent can give. It's the one thing, above all else, that you wish your parents had given you. Annie was giving that gift to Timmy, giving him more love in his few short years than most people receive in a lifetime. However, there is not only her love, but the love beyond measure, which is the love of God. The wideness of His mercy and grace. The depths of His compassion."

He knew what I'd wanted so much when I was a child, what my parents were incapable of giving me—their love. Which could only mean one thing: I'd been telling more than the basic stories I thought I'd been sticking to.

Darn, how could you have been so stupid as to have been sharing your innermost thoughts? What were you thinking when you were telling Robert these stories?

This is why my rule had always been to never share anything with anyone for any reason. The last time I'd shared anything about me, it had ended in a horrible tragedy. Sure, that time, unlike this time, I wasn't telling the truth and nothing but the truth. Would you? Yeah, you would. You, I'm sure have nothing to hide. No huge skeleton in your closet waiting to come out and destroy you. For me, telling all these stories to Robert would more than likely end the same way as that last time had. Only this time, the tragic ending would be my own, because at this point there seemed to be no other way out.

Could I even face what I'd done and tell someone else the horrifying truth? Once that was out, I knew I couldn't live with the shame of anyone else knowing what I'd done. I'd taken the evidence of my deed then, and I'd stumbled on, knowing that my punishment was living with my failure. Because in my family, failure and flaws were secrets that you always hid—like my dad's alcoholism, like his abusive nature. You tell anyone, and bad things happen, so I never told. Not then, not now. Truth was a dagger pointed straight at my heart, and if I continued to speak, it was going to be the death of me. Now I knew why this was my last trip, the last stop on my journey.

So, *here you are, on this crazy, never-ending ride—which, mind you, Cindy, you kept signing up for each of the last three days. Despite your misgivings, you're still here like the fool that you are. You keep spilling your guts to this guy you know almost nothing about. Somehow, he's opened the floodgates, and you're telling all, the good and the bad.*

I felt like I was going to be sick; I couldn't believe I'd left myself this vulnerable to anyone again. Not only were my walls down, but somehow, Robert seemed to have made them crumble to dust.

I leaned my head on the cool glass of the window and shut my eyes for a moment or two. Truth was, I'd never felt loved, until Annie. Don't you get the wrong idea—not that kind of love. Pure love. She loved me without expecting anything in return. You might ask why. Your guess is as good as mine.

"Parents should give both love and material things—good things, not rags and hand-me-downs," I said it in a hoarse voice just above a whisper, almost hoping that he wouldn't hear me.

It was lame and I knew it, but I couldn't let him score a point for his crackpot theories. Or a hit for his religious nonsense, which was beginning to look less and less meaningless. The longer this went on, the deeper I fell into some kind of hole of which it seemed there was no way out.

But by saying that simple sentence, I was trying to put Annie and my parents on the same level, which was wrong. They each had failed to provide one of the things I was claiming parents should be required to provide. But even I know that love and a nice house aren't equal by a long shot. Annie was a million times better than my parents could ever dream of being. It was like comparing fresh bread with moldy. You knew with only one quick glance which one was better, which one you should eat.

The looks Annie had given Timmy when she kissed him. She touched him. She fed him. She played with him. Heck, when she was anywhere near him. Those looks were so beautiful, they almost brought me to tears. You should know me well enough by now to know that nothing cracks my exterior shell. But that did. You could feel the love she had for her son. It was a real thing; unlike anything I'd ever seen before or since. On the other hand, my parents, especially my father, only looked at me with contempt or pity. Their touch only brought pain. No, you couldn't compare the two sets as being equal.

As a song says, "One is only poor only if you choose to be. It is true we had no money but I was rich as I could be." It was clear that Annie was rich in some sense—I'd felt it. She rejected poverty completely. To her, she lived in a palace. She ate five-course gourmet meals. She wore designer clothes. Life couldn't have been better. Never mind that it was all an illusion; only she saw things that way—that was how everything was. I had tried to destroy her happy little bubble she lived in by showing her that it wasn't real. What would you have done? I know that if I had it to do all over again, I wouldn't have. I'd have left her in peace, not caused her even a moment of unhappiness.

There was also the fact that she'd loved me for the short time I was there, but for the life of me, I had no idea why. I'd given her no reason to care for me. Yet, for some strange reason, I knew that if I showed up at her door again, she'd still accept me. It wouldn't matter to her what I'd done to her yard. She'd wanted to help me then, and I'd rejected her—not the other way around. She was beautiful, inside and out—which is why I could never be anywhere near her ever again. I would only hurt something that lovely, that precious. I was evil; I was worthless; I was beyond redemption. There was never any question about that. But now Robert was here trying to save me, too, in his own way. Why did anyone bother?

"In an ideal world, yes. Love and things are both important. Yet, only love is essential. But the world isn't perfect, life is messy, things happen, and we must adjust to play the hand we are given." With that statement, Robert had won this round. I couldn't hurt Annie any more by my words even though she'd never hear them. "You're wrong about Minnie, also God provided for her needs as well."

"What do you mean? She died." My eyes darted to him as I spat the words out. I was back to feeling almost ready to fight him with more than words at this point. I'd loved Minnie—if I was at all capable of love. You never know; I might be. Hard to say on that score. She might've loved me, too, in her odd way, but unlike with Annie, it was hard to say.

"God sent her you to help her for her last few days. You did a lot of good for her, giving her the peace to rest, sit, and enjoy nature for a while. Then, God spared her from the thing she dreaded the most—losing her freedom. You should understand that." He was tapping on the steering wheel again. It was starting to give me a headache, or maybe it was this conversation. It was a real toss-up on what the cause was—both things were tying me in knots.

As much as I hated to admit it, Robert had won another point. Minnie's feisty personality wouldn't have lasted long in a nursing home. Even I could see that. But it did seem a little cruel for his god to kill the woman rather than find a way for her to continue living at home. Or, at least she could've died at home like she wanted to. So much of her life, her memories, and her very soul was wrapped up in her house. I wish I could've been able to sit beside her bed and watch her die there in peace. You know what I mean? She'd only had those few short hours left anyways.

I closed my eyes again for a few moments to gather my thoughts before moving on to my next issue with what Robert had said. "You're wrong about my finding happiness; I never had any before I left my other life." When I first opened my eyes again, I saw a house that looked eerily similar to the one I'd shared with my husband — the big monstrosity that I was supposed to have filled with the children that I, in the end, never had.

As quickly as I could, I shut my eyes again; I didn't want to see it. My memories were bad enough. I didn't want to let Robert score on this item, either, but yes, for a brief moment, I'd thought I could be happy. With the man I was going to marry, happiness seemed to be within my grasp. We had met in a little coffee shop — one block from his office and two from where I was doing my internship my last semester of college, senior year. He was so nice the few short months when we were dating, giving me presents for no reason, sending me flowers at my dorm, and so many other little things. He was supportive of my wanting to go to grad school, even feeling that I should start in the summer and not wait until fall. He helped me get a job in my field, which not only allowed me the time for my studies but paid for most of the cost. Sweet in so many ways, never pushy about intimacy. On cloud nine, I didn't think twice when he proposed.

But, then, I'd caught him half naked with some girl in the hotel ballroom. Not in a bathroom, no. In the middle of the giant room all decorated in the colors I'd picked out. Right where our reception was to be held, not an hour before our wedding. After she'd fled, he'd yelled at me until I submitted to his will. I agreed to not make a fool of him by standing him up and running far, far away, which I'd had every right to do at that point. He said that he'd lose his job since his boss was there, and he didn't want his colleagues to think less of him. So many of his important clients were there as well, and he could've lost a lot of money.

So, instead, like a trained pet, I followed him out to the hotel garden. I said my vows to the man I knew I'd never loved, who I now knew was no better than my father. A man who would only cause me pain.

Our marriage could only have gone downhill from there. That's exactly what it did, at a breakneck speed. Yet, I hung in there for years to keep his image intact and to be the humble wife he needed. Yeah, you've heard that sob story before. Nothing new here, stop whining, move on...that's what you'd like to tell me. Well, I did—eventually.

Robert reached out for my hand. It now had a death grip on the seat belt. As the feeling of warmth came over me, my eyes popped open. His hand was so much larger than mine but didn't seem to make mine feel lost beneath it. It was more like they'd melded together somehow, like how a husband's and wife's hands should be.

Blushing from my head to my toes at the thought, I was quick to jerk my hand away. I'd never felt so close to my husband or to anyone for that matter. Why did I think that about this man?

"Are you sure about that?" He gave me a quizzical look; it was obvious that he wasn't believing my lie. However, was it a lie when I'd been deceived into believing I was happy for a moment? Or was his look because he'd seen my blush? He needed to stop touching me, because every time he did, something strange happened. That was creeping me out in a way you could never understand unless you'd been there. Felt those sparks. Felt that warmth. Felt that intensity.

I turned away from him and stared at the landscape—pretty little houses, large barns, occasional trees. It all seemed so normal, so safe, so perfect. I wasn't ready to tell this man about my marriage or about any of my past, before this journey. Telling anyone about my journey had been hard enough. But right now, I still had to decide how I was going to deal with Robert.

How much more are you going to tell him? Because there was no hiding from this man. I was in this tiny tin can of a car for hours at a stretch, and there were only the two of us. Even when I wasn't saying anything, he still seemed to see right through me. He knew me in a way that no one else did—I was letting him into my life almost against my will. Has that ever happened to you? Or is Robert the only person in the world with the ability to do this, and you're lucky enough you haven't met him yet?

Fine, on to plan B—change the subject. Well, at least divert it some. "I read some of my journals. Sometimes, fortune does smile on me and my needs are provided for, but I still don't think that's your god. It's random chance, not a plan and not a reason to think I've got a future or any hope that things might change."

I began to rub my hands on my jeans. I still didn't want to look at him, so I shifted my gaze to my fingers as they danced across my thighs. The sun was hitting just right, so my fingers were making interesting shadows. Shapes and patterns began to form.

"How can you be so sure?" His voice was sad, like I was letting him down because I still wasn't seeing things his way.

"Because, I'm not worthy of anyone caring for me." Still not looking up, I watched the shadows.

At that moment, I realized that my whole life had been lived in shadow. Until now, that is, and I didn't think I was ready for my whole life to be brought out into the light of day. I was feeling very exposed, naked, and there was so much more to bring out, so much more of my truth yet to be told.

"Why?" There was a crack in his voice. I think he was about to cry or was crying. There was no way I was going to look at him to find out for sure.

You don't cry for me. Why don't people see that written all over me? When I look in the mirror, I can see it stamped on my face. Why can't you? It's like crying for someone who's been dead for ten years, because that's what I've been. A ghost—that's all that's left. Nothing but a phantom haunting this earth.

This was where things were going to get tough. I mean, how committed to this stuff was he? *If that last story didn't scare him off,* I thought, *he's pretty devoted to this religious cause of his. Worse yet,* I lamented, *what if he was right and this god was real?*

His god would reject me based on what I'd done, and Robert would throw me out of the car. Even he couldn't be so committed to any cause. No, you religious types have your limits. You know it. I know it. Here, I, like a fool, had thought I'd won him over and instead only got him to give me the biggest sermon of my life. But, it still didn't mean his zeal was boundless.

The ugliest truth must come out. Before this went any further, it was time to tell him at least that much. He already knew more than I'd ever intended to share anyway. But, I wasn't sure that I was ready to tell anyone what I'd done. I wasn't ready for the final rejection from Robert that I was so sure would come. What other response could there be when he knew the truth about who exactly he had in his car?

He should never have asked me to tell him stories. He should've known better than to think anything a homeless person had done was important, or even worth knowing more about. Better yet, I should've fallen asleep or at least pretended to, like I usually do when I get in someone's car, not said a word all these miles upon miles. Taken the easy path, not the hard one.

When do you ever take the easy road, Cindy? Never, not even once in your miserable life.

"Because my father told me so." While it was a truth, something was still holding me back from telling the whole truth. No, there was much more behind why I felt that I was good for nothing.

For some reason, I wasn't ready to be alone again, not ready to be out on my own again. Robert was beginning to feel like a friend, and I felt like I needed him, even though the friendship wasn't real. It was based on two giant lies — his false faith and my deception of who I was. Or maybe, there was solely the one — my deception.

"He always said I was worthless, and I know he was right."

"I know you've been told so many untruths over the years. I could sense it from the minute I met you, but that's the biggest one of all." He reached over and took my hand again, and this time, I felt a jolt of electricity pass between us. Snatching my hand free before the sensation could become more intense, I cringed in pain — not from the touch, but from the thought that it might be true and I was worth something to someone.

I looked over at him, ready to lash into him for his statement, but I saw the tears streaming down his face. The front of his pale blue T-shirt was so wet from tears, it was dark blue in large patches. In a flash, his face looked old from the worry lines now etched into it. Misery seeped from every pore of his body, and all because of me.

Fine, no more ducking the issue on my part; he needed to know the truth — well, here goes nothing...

Chapter 13

"Fine, Robert, so you seem pretty sure I was wrong about there being no plan for anyone's welfare. Then let me tell you why I know your god could never care for me personally. Because I did something to make me a permanent outcast, I'm on the road forever as a punishment. When I first started out on this journey, I had a car. Not a great car, because I never got a better one after I finished college. The reasons for that aren't important now." I waved my hand in a gesture of dismissal. "Well, my car lasted about seven months after I left home before I had to dump it. You need to know that story because it'll change your mind about me..." I gritted my teeth; there was no going back from this, and I plunged on.

Early in November of that first year of this new me, I was in Oklahoma, driving on the freeway. Usually, I avoided freeways and crowds, but this morning I was low on funds for the first time. It'd gotten harder and harder to find odd jobs the longer I'd been on the road, and I was now looking a little worse for wear.

Clothes starting to wear out, losing weight—well, you get the idea.

Anyways, I knew that I needed a major city that would have services for homeless people. That's what I now was—I had nowhere else to go. Thus, I was trying to get to Oklahoma City, feeling confident that there one could find a soup kitchen. A homeless shelter. Maybe some better clothes for free. You know, those basics I keep harping on about. At the time, I didn't fully understand how important they were to survival. As I'd started driving that morning, after the briefest of naps, it felt like I'd been playing a game for months—one that had now become all too real.

For the several hours I'd been driving, I'd been alone with my thoughts in the silent car. The rain pouring down was making me feel blue, and I'd been crying off and on for most of the morning.

The visibility was poor as I drove, in part because of my tears and in part because of the rain. It was made worse by the fact that my windshield wipers were shredded. They were flapping in a steady slap-slap beat against the windshield. They were doing next to nothing as far as pushing any water around, yet I kept them on for the company. With the swishing sound and the splash of the tires running through the water on the road, I wasn't alone. It was comforting in a way, sad in another. It was one of those days when people should stay at home and mope, but I no longer had a home to stay at. If you lived in the area that day, I'm sure that you were snuggled up with a nice cup of tea and a good book. Not me—nope, I could only be so lucky. Here I was driving again, an alien in a completely foreign land. As far as I could tell, I was nowhere close to a town. Not like I had any idea, because I'd never been in Oklahoma until the day before. All the towns I'd passed so far were little ones, even before I'd gotten to the freeway. I again wondered if I'd made the right choice to head to Oklahoma City today. Without a map, I was going on gut instinct as to which town would have services for the homeless. Your guess was as good as mine if I'd passed up twenty towns already that could've helped me. I most likely had.

Then disaster struck—the gear stick popped out of fifth and into neutral. The car made this horrible whining sound as it shuddered and the speed dropped all too fast. Terrified, I grabbed the gear stick as quickly as I could and tried to get it back into a gear, any gear, as I slammed on the brakes to pull off the freeway. Sliding on the wet pavement, I almost skidded off the side of the road before coming to a stop.

So Cindy, I said to myself as I tried to catch my breath, *what do you do now?* Nothing like this had ever happened before, and I'd had this car since I was in high school—it was like an old friend. I'd bought it used with the little money I'd hidden from my father from my first job.

He'd stolen most of the money I'd earned, but he didn't know I'd also made tips. My mom helped me register the car, and I kept it around the corner from our house so my dad would never know about it. It was our secret—yet another thing my mom and I never told the world. So many lies, so many secrets, so many reasons I'd left my life behind. No way you'd ever understand.

No idea of what to do came to me, but since whatever happened was a new thing, I was hoping against hope that it was a fluke. Yeah, I know, stupid thought. This was the kinda thing AAA was designed for. You whip out your card, make a call on your cellphone, and a tow truck's there in minutes. Wait, oh yeah, there wasn't ever going to be money for me to pay for things like that ever again. So, I did the only thing I could do— ignored the problem and drove on. Yeah, I know, not a brilliant move on my part.

With trembling hands and a knot in my stomach, I started the car again. Bit by bit, I got the car up to speed, but within a few moments of being in fifth gear, the gear stick popped out again. This time I was ready for it—my hand was poised over the stick, and I immediately grabbed it. I got it put into fourth with only a mild grinding noise. *Way to go girl,* I thought to myself, proud of my quick thinking. You take the wins when you get them.

However, now I was driving on the freeway going well below highway speeds in the pouring rain. What had been rather unsafe before was doubly so now. About twenty minutes later, I'd begun to relax and think I might make it to the town that I'd started to see signs for. Then, that darn gear stick popped out of fourth, leaving me scrambling to get it into a gear again. Now I was driving in third, sure I was going to be a fly on the front of some semi's grill in no time. My not-quite-thirty miles per hour was no match for a semi going seventy.

Only a few minutes later, it happened again. Now, I was driving in second gear. *Just great, how much better could this get?* Quite a lot actually—I was close enough to civilization, and the freeway was getting crowded. I was in pure panic mode. You know the feeling. When your heart's racing. Your hands are gripping some object—in my case, the steering wheel—so tightly your fingers are going to fall off. You're breathing so fast that you're sure you're going to pass out.

Just keep breathing, just keep breathing, I kept saying to myself over and over. Other cars whipped around me in a blurred frenzy from their speed and the rain. Horns blaring as I crept along at fifteen miles per hour. Finally, I could make out an exit sign for the town, only a faint blur. I broke out into sobs at the sight. It was such a huge relief to be out of the pressure cooker that this freeway had become. You could say that the tension washed away in the rain.

Stopping at the first gas station I saw, I went in to ask where a repair shop was. Even though there was no way I could get the car fixed, I still felt that it wouldn't hurt to at least ask how much it would be. One never knows—I might get lucky, and it'd be something simple that I could help around the shop for a few days to pay off. In those days, I didn't look much like I was homeless. Like I was poor, sure. Since I drove a car, no one ever thought twice about helping me—at least, most of the time. Plus, I never carried much with me, and it was always stashed in the trunk, out of sight, away from prying eyes. I even convinced myself that I wasn't homeless then, only someone who traveled an awful lot. You get the idea—permanent vacation. Living the dream. Because it wasn't a nightmare, yet.

With some hesitation, I approached the register, wiggling my fingers, trying to get them to not hurt so much after my tense drive. The clerk was busy with other customers who were, for the most part, buying hot coffee. Lucky them getting to ward off the chill on a damp day. As I waited my turn, I debated about wasting a dollar to buy a cup as well but in the end decided against it. Fresh coffee was a luxury you can't afford when you're in my shoes. After all, I was in need of some new shoes. My tennis shoes had holes in them.

When it was my turn, I stepped up to the counter. "I need to have my car repaired. Do you know where there's a shop nearby?"

"You buying anything here?" The skinny, middle-aged man with an enormous handlebar mustache eyed me with suspicion. You know, back then, those looks bothered me. A lot. What had I ever done to him? Nothing so far.

"No, sorry." I hung my head in shame; maybe I should've broken open the proverbial piggy bank and bought some coffee. You better believe I don't feel like that anymore. One too many of those looks have made me immune—most of the time. Yeah, then there's also the fact of what I would do only a few short hours after this encounter. But we're not there yet.

"Well, how bad is it?" He was looking rather unhappy with me for wasting his precious time. Like working in a gas station was a matter of life and death or something.

"The gear stick keeps popping out."

"Oh, will it go back in, or do you not have that gear anymore?"

"I only have first and second still usable."

"Hank's can take a look at it and tell you what's wrong at least. They're two blocks up and one block over," he said as he pointed in the directions he was describing. "They should be able to fix it no problem from the sound of it."

"Thank you." I smiled at him and exited the store as quickly as I could, before he demanded that I buy something I could've ill afforded. The rain seemed to have let up some; the sky was lighter in the west than the dark gray in the east. I took that to be a sign that my day would get better, because it definitely didn't seem like it could get any worse. Yeah, I know, famous last words and all.

Following the clerk's directions was easy. Before long, I was sitting alone in the tiny waiting lounge, sipping bad coffee and eating their free stale doughnuts for my late lunch, biting my nails as I awaited the verdict, because to me, the car was a matter of life and death. I didn't have a real plan when I'd set out on this crazy trip I was on. Still had no clear plan. I had no distinct idea of what I was doing, where I was going, or even what I was trying to accomplish.

My few clothes were folded, placed nicely and neatly in two shopping bags. My toiletries were in another one. A few odds and ends were in a fourth bag. That's all I'd taken of my old life, all I'd wanted, all I thought I needed. Well, except all the money I'd taken out of the bank account. That money was what I'd been living off of for the past few months with the aid of a few odd jobs here and there. Even living wild and free, you still need some money. Nothing is completely free in this life. You know it, and I know it. Okay, maybe the air we breathe is.

Most of my money had gone for gas. Eating next to nothing, I'd lost a lot of weight. My husband, who'd always said I was too chubby, would've approved. Well, I guess not—he never approved of anything I did, so now he'd say I was too skinny. I'd driven from coast to coast over and over again in those first seven months, putting way too many miles on a car that wasn't in the best of shape to begin with. I hadn't slept much; I kept pushing myself to go further, not noticing how tired I was most days. Do you ever do that? Drive yourself to do something because of a desire deep within? Push yourself beyond what you thought was possible? Force yourself to go on no matter what? I had my reasons, stupid as they may seem now. I'm not sure if you can say that I regret my choice, because I know that any choice I make turns out wrong somehow. Nothing in my life goes as planned.

But, today was different; today, I was about to become homeless in every sense of the word. There would no longer be endless days of driving. Feeling like I was about to lose the cocoon of my car overwhelmed me. Forever, I'd be changed. No more shelter from the cold. No more protection from storms. No more pretending to be a normal tourist by hiding my stuff in the trunk. No more links to the past. Only the here and now, forevermore. You better believe that was scary to think about.

"Miss?" A young man who looked like he could still be in high school in dirty, oil-stained coveralls broke into my musings. As I turned to look at him, it seemed odd that one so young could hold my fate in those dirty hands of his.

"Yes?" *Please let me be wrong,* I thought, *let it be good news. Let my premonition from earlier be right and this day would get better.*

"The transmission's completely shot. We could probably fix it for a couple of thousand with used parts." He gave me a boyish smile, trying to lighten the mood while giving me the bad news. Fat chance.

"Oh." I was determined not to cry; I'd done enough sobbing in the last few months. Heck, I'd done enough today even. It wasn't like this was something I had no way of knowing was bound to happen at some point. While I'd had a considerable larger sum of money to begin with, even then I doubt I would've sunk so much into a car. Given how old this one was, there was no doubt about what to do.

"I hope you don't think I was snooping, but when I checked out the car, I saw what was in the trunk. I'm guessing you don't have the money to fix it." Okay, so he'd seen my threadbare clothing and lack of luggage, then combined those facts with the out-of-state plates and came up with the correct answer somehow. "So, I took the liberty of making a few calls, and Toyotas are worth quite a bit if you sell them to junkyards. I found one that'll pay you over five hundred for it. I can call the guy back, and he'll be here in a few minutes to pick it up. If I'm wrong, I'm sorry." With his hand, he gave a bit of a shrugging motion. The dirty rag in his hand waved in surrender.

This was easy. In truth, there was no choice. "Sell it. The title's in the glove box." I smiled at him. It wasn't his fault he'd pushed me all the way over the edge of the cliff I'd been hanging off of for months. I'd put myself out on the ledge, not him. I was at fault here, and I knew full well I hadn't anyone else to blame. I'd walked as fast as I could away from my old life, and I also knew that I'd done it years too late. I should've left as soon as I learned to crawl, or at least when I learned to walk. I would've saved myself a whole lot of pain, even if I'd had to crawl over broken glass to get out.

"All right, I'll go and make all the arrangements." He turned and walked out of the room, brushing against a cute young woman as she walked in.

Strange, he didn't even acknowledge her at all. Most young men would've lusted after a girl like her—she was what every man wanted. She had short, brown, curly hair and was wearing a cheerleader outfit and an impish smile. You know—the bimbo type, only this one wasn't blond.

"Hi! The name's Sandra. I'm getting a tune-up!" she announced, all perky. All I could think was that it sounded like her brain needed the tune-up, so why was she at a car repair shop? Okay, I know that's rude. "What you in for?"

"Name's Cindy. My car's dead, so I'm selling it to a junk yard," I said through clenched teeth. I couldn't handle perky right now. Not like it was something I was usually good with, but today I was dealing with a death, so it was harder than usual. You ever feel that attached to an inanimate object? Silly, I know.

"Oh, so sorry to hear that. I'd be lost without the car my daddy bought me last year for graduation. Can I give you a lift home?" She continued to smile all happy at me as she fluffed her hair and patted her skirt.

Now, there was the best question anyone could pose to someone like me. I'd given up my home months ago and swore I'd never go back no matter what happened. Huh, I guess I did have a good plan, or at least a goal—stay away from home. Sure, it wasn't what you would call life-affirming, but still, it was something. Better than nothing.

"I don't live around here." I figured it'd be best to keep it simple. Having had little interaction with people in the last few months, I had no idea what she'd say if she knew the truth. The truth at that point was only sad, not horrible. Honest, how many adults do you know who run away from their lives? Only to end up broke and homeless? My guess is that your answer is none.

See, it's sad and rather pathetic.

"Oh, where're you from? You just passing through? Or are you visiting someone?" She hardly took a breath as she flounced onto one of the plastic chairs; it squeaked in protest. Huh, I guess it didn't like perky either.

All were impossible questions; this is why I'd only ventured from my car to buy gas and food, and even then, often only late at night when clerks were too sleepy to care who was in their store—or too lazy to ask complete strangers nosy questions.

"Right now, I'm from nowhere, and I prefer it that way. So, yes, I'm just passing through everywhere I go, and no, I'm never visiting anyone." I sighed. *How do you get out of this stupid conversation, Cindy?*

"Well, where you staying while in town?" She beamed at me, blissful as could be in her little, oblivious bubble.

Oh, my gosh, would this obtuse child never shut up?

Could she not see that I didn't want to talk? Could she not hear all those long pauses before I answered her insipid questions? I almost screamed but managed to hold my tongue for a few moments until I'd calmed down a bit.

"Not sure yet," I said as I got up to get more of the foul-tasting coffee. I figured she'd get the hint if I turned my back on her.

"Well, I live in a community house, and we've got an extra room because a girl dropped out after the semester started. We've let people stay there for a few days, and it's cheaper than a motel. We all kind of agreed that it would be for relatives when they visit, but I could say you're my cousin or something. It'd be fun!" She giggle-snorted. I hoped for her sake that she didn't think it was cute. You know, she was the type that would.

Well, it isn't like you've got a lot of options at this point, and cheaper than a motel sounds way too good to pass up. I was only going to have five hundred dollars, plus the few dollars already in my pocket, to my name. Not exactly flush with money. That money was going to have to last me goodness only knows how long. Definitely not wanting to be stuck in one spot, I was still wishing to move on. But, no longer having my own car was a big problem.

Having no idea what a community house was, I figured it must be some kind of sorority or something. She'd made it sound like she was in college, so it made sense. I turned around with some hesitation and sat down again, taking a slow sip of that vile coffee. As annoying as this girl was, I was going to have to play nice and accept her offer. The idea was as bitter as the coffee and just as hard to swallow. Yuck.

"Okay, I guess for a couple of nights until I figure out how to move on." With as polite a smile as I could muster for a few seconds, I beamed at her. Then, I slurped some more of the coffee quickly, before my face cracked from the effort. You have no idea how much that cost me. I even burned my tongue on the coffee.

"Awesome. I'll text Robyn. She's the adult in charge of the house, so she can make up the room." She then whipped out her pink cell phone and fiddled with it for several minutes. You have no clue how thankful I was that she couldn't text and talk at the same time. Peace entered the room which was in her words "Awesome."

While she was doing that, I tapped my fingers on the side of the Styrofoam cup. Trying to think of what I'd need to move on from this town was not an easy task. First, everything from my four shopping bags would fit with ease into a hiking-style backpack—with room to spare, no doubt about it. I would also be needing a tent, a blanket, and hiking shoes. Oh, and a much better idea of how homeless people lived on the streets.

Would that be something you could look up on the Internet at the public library? I wondered. *Probably not, silly. You should know better than to think that there's a "Homelessness for Dummies" book out there! Yikes.* Yeah, I know. Magical thinking is my specialty.

The guy from the junkyard came with my money, and I, with tears in my eyes, signed over the title to him. Funny how attached to that car I felt. I went outside with the men, only to discover that it had stopped raining. That would've been much more helpful earlier when I was trying to limp my car into this darn town. Knowing I needed to take everything out of my car before it was hauled off, I stood for a few minutes, looking at what was, for all intents and purposes, my home. You'd never look at your car that way, I know. But, you've never slept in it as many nights as I'd slept in mine. Here I was, aching from head to toe over the thought of never seeing my car again, but I'd lost so much already. This was too hard to think about; it was rather stupid of me to be standing here lamenting the death of a car.

The mechanic and the junkyard guy talked while I finally brought myself to comb every inch of the car. I checked two or three times to make sure I hadn't missed anything. It was silly. I had so little that I remembered every item and knew I wasn't forgetting something. Betcha you can't name every item in your house that's crammed full of useless junk.

With love, I patted the roof of the car to say good-bye, not caring what the two guys might be thinking of me at that point. I've been kicking myself for years over how attached to that stupid hunk of metal I was. Still, I miss it every time it's stormy. So much better than a tent.

As I closed the trunk one final time, I gripped my four shopping bags of worldly possessions as tightly as I could. I was beginning to wish that I'd succeeded in taking the other way out of my problems—suicide—rather than running away like the coward that I am. But I'd failed in my last attempt, just as I had in all my earlier ones.

My newly minted ex-husband had found me still alive in what was now his house, and he had been furious. Not mad that I was half-dead, oh goodness, no. He was upset that I was in his house after the date that the court order said I had to be out. *Yet another failure, Cindy. You can't ever do anything right.* And that failure had led me here, to this little town somewhere in the middle of Oklahoma. Without much of a plan of what to do next. Desiring more than anything to be alone so I could sob with wild abandon. Again.

Then, back in the customer lounge, I sat and chatted with Sandra until her car was finished and we could leave. With my bags at my feet, pain in my heart, and almost no money in my pocket. Hoping that a normal conversation would take my mind off my troubles for a while. Yeah, I know, wishful thinking gets you nowhere fast. Just my luck, this chat was in no way normal.

In this case, Sandra turned out to be the most mind-numbingly dull person I'd ever had the misfortune to spend a half an hour with. I now knew a dozen cheers. Who was dating who. Who wanted to date who. Who hated who. What the worst food at the college cafeteria was. Who the heck cares? Would you if you'd been stuck there with this hyperactive brainless twit?

I was almost tempted to go find a cheap motel room. But her promise that the room at her house would cost less kept me hanging in there—that needing-to-make-sure-you-have-the-basics-covered thing I keep going on about. Well, that was when the gravity of those two things was beginning to set in.

I almost wept for joy when the mechanic came in and said her car was finished. It's silly what will make you happy sometimes. Real little things. Pretty rock. Cute squirrel. Being released from the prison of a repair shop waiting room. You know, the real stupid stuff in life. When we exited out to the parking lot, I saw that her car was an almost-new blue Mercedes convertible. It was clear that she was Daddy's spoiled brat who was used to the world revolving around her. Not like I didn't know that already from spending the last half an hour with her. She'd never wound down—like a top that never stopped spinning. Determined to avoid her as much as possible in the next few days, I hardly looked at her. Even if I would be staying in the same house as her, I could hide out. Sure, I may be depressed and suicidal much of the time, but I had no intentions of dying from boredom.

Driving a short distance, I saw a large, yellow, four-story house set back from the road. It was placed in a grove of trees showing off their brilliant golds and reds of fall. It was quite a pretty and peaceful scene, and it didn't seem to fit with Sandra's obnoxiousness at all.

She pulled her car around the back to a small parking area almost full with more luxury cars. Gathering up my bags, I exited her car. My feet made a wonderful crunching sound on the fallen leaves and gravel as I walked, brightening my mood for a moment after such a long, depressing day. I followed her through the back door, and we went down the wide main hallway to the front of the house, landing in what I took to be a lobby or sitting room.

"Have a seat, I'll go find Robyn," Sandra, bold as could be, declared as she swept her arm to show off the room before bouncing away.

The room extended across the whole front of the house. The décor was tasteful, with stiff, almost formal furniture covered in dark, heavy fabrics. Art like Monet and Matisse — the only ones I knew — was hanging in strategic places around the room. Huge windows were covered by lace curtains. It was obvious that these college kids who lived here were all rich like Sandra. They wouldn't put up with a homeless person for long. Even if she was able to convince them that I was a long-lost cousin. You knew that had to be a long shot.

I sank into the deep cushions of a blood red couch and leaned back to relax and close my eyes for a moment. Sandra's endless prattling had given me a serious headache. There was no way I was going to be able to stay here for more than the one night. First thing in the morning, I'd need to find a store that sold camping gear and get the heck out of dodge. This was the kind of place I wouldn't have been welcome in even in my former life, and I was so very far from that now.

"Hello, Cindy." A large matron of a woman had entered the room, with Sandra close behind. Her dark hair was pulled back into a severe bun. She wore a black dress with a white apron over it. "I'm Robyn. As I understand it, you've had some car problems today. Ended up stranded in town and need a room for a few nights, correct?" She crossed her hands over her ample bosom rather than extending one out to me. I took that to mean that I wasn't welcome here no matter what Sandra thought. It was evident that the pretense about being a long-lost cousin had gone out the window. Well, would you have lied for a stranger? No, I thought not. I shouldn't have expected Sandra to do so.

"Yes." Well, one night, anyway. But I decided not to say that in case it was harder or more expensive to get camping gear than I thought it would be. What I'd do if it turned out to be the case, I had no idea, but I'd face it when I came to it. You don't ask for more trouble than what you've already got. It wasn't like I didn't have plenty, or like I wasn't about to have lots more.

"Well, you're in luck. We've got one room available at only five dollars a night." She gave me a giant smile as she clapped her hands together.

That seemed way too good to be true, and as that saying goes—if it sounds too good to be true, it probably is. "What's the catch?" I cocked my head to get a better look at Robyn, to see if she was lying to me and if I could catch her in it. Problem was, I'm terrible at reading people.

"No catch. Just follow the rules." Her smile became a little harder, like she was forcing it. Fine, so I wasn't acting like the grateful guest I should be at this point. No need to get ruder.

"Okay." Standing, I gathered up my things once again. "So what're the rules?" I forced a smile. I needed to play this game for a night or two at least. Was this how it was going to be from now on whenever I needed help? Play the game or else? That had been part of the problem with my marriage. If so, this was going to be so much fun—not.

"Follow me, and I'll tell you on the way to your room." She turned and walked at a brisk pace into the hall, Sandra and I following behind. "Quiet hours begin at 11:00 p.m. The other ladies here go to the local college, so they need their rest, you understand. No men allowed, except in the lobby where we just were. Also, house functions are mandatory. Even for guests, and fortunate for you, we're having one tonight. There's a pizza party at 7:00 p.m., don't be late."

By this time, we'd gone down one hall, up a flight of stairs, and down another hall, and stopped at a door. She opened it and handed me the key.

"Rent is due each Friday, but since today's Tuesday, I'll ask you to pay me tomorrow for three nights. Do you have some form of ID I can look at?" I handed her my driver's license. She glanced at it and handed it back to me. "That'll be all." She dismissed me with a wave then turned her back on us and walked with quick strides down the hall.

"Don't worry, when she warms up to you, she's very sweet," Sandra said as she watched me set my things down on the bed. "I've got to go to class, but I'll see you tonight."

"Later, then. Thanks again for telling me about the room; it's a super cheap option. Oh, by the way, how much is the pizza party?" I frowned. The cheap room was good, but having to pay for a party wasn't.

"It's free, part of the rent." She smiled and waved goodbye as she flounced out of the room.

So, the cheap room was because I was a charity case for these rich people to feel good about—wonderful. I wondered how much they charged real relatives—most likely the same as a motel room.

The room was tiny, with one twin bed, one dresser, one armoire, and one desk. All done in pink and white with lace trim and heart decals on the walls. If you stood in the middle of the room, you could touch everything. This house was a girly girl's dream; definitely not for me.

While putting my few things away, I found pink towels, blankets, and sheets in the armoire. I was glad for that, because, of course, I didn't have any. You've never seen sheets in a store for the back seat of your car, have you? Didn't think so. I didn't even have a blanket then; on chilly nights, I used to wrap up in all my clothes. Or drove all night then slept in the morning when the sun warmed things up a bit. When I cleaned up, I used paper towels. It'd never seemed important to me to spend money on a blanket or towels. A real waste when I'd had a system in place for getting around the need for them. Luxury is relative. You're beginning to see that by now, right?

There was a door leading to a shared bathroom, and there was another door at the other end of it, locked. Figuring it'd be best to take a shower before the party, I dug out what I needed from my shopping bags. I hadn't had one in a few days, quick wash-ups were all. Shopping bags are the worst kind of luggage to have, even if they are matching. They are forever needing to be replaced, because the bags tear with such ease. Now, however, I'd have a heavy pack to put things in. Ugh, I'd have to carry everything I owned with me every second of every day. That wasn't going to be fun.

In the shower, I kept thinking about what this next chapter of my journey would be like. Without the car, I'd no longer be able to stop at campgrounds, take a quick shower, then leave before anyone caught me. Without the car, I wouldn't have shelter on stormy days. The ping of the hail from the last thunderstorm I'd seen filled me with dread.

Without the car, I'd no longer be able to sleep in Walmart parking lots with the other wandering souls. Without the car, I'd no longer have a place to stash my stuff while I was doing other things. This was going to be a rather steep learning curve. Plus, so far in my months of wandering, nothing had seemed to be working out like I'd envisioned with the car. Without the car, this whole insane idea was seeming to be an impossible one.

You should've come up with some kind of a plan for this crazy journey, Cindy, not just a hopeless dream. You took off with this idiotic idea, half-formed and totally unworkable — now look where you are. Flat broke — well, close to it — and still no closer to the dream being fulfilled.

After my shower, I sat on the bed and looked at my tiny journal for a while. I'd gotten it the day I left, at my bank when I closed my account. There'd been this stack of these small promotional notebooks, and I'd asked if I could have one. For some reason, when I saw them, I'd had this childish idea to write down my new story. You see, now things were going to be different. No more being controlled by other people. No more being bullied. I was going to be the master of my fate, and I alone would decide what happened in the end. Yeah, I know it was doomed from the start. You don't need to remind me.

Back then, when I'd first started out, this whole idea had seemed so simple, but now I was in way over my head. I almost didn't want to write in my journal about the loss of my car. For whatever reason, it was more painful than the loss that this trip had begun with. Yet, I'd promised myself that I'd be honest in this journal, no matter what. What had gone before this journey was dead; this was all I had left, and I must make something of what was to come. I jotted a quick note and took a nap, the day having taken its toll on me. Little did I know what the rest of the day would cost me, I would've stayed in the fluffy, soft, pink bed if I had...

I snapped back to the present for a moment, looking at Robert. Should I go on, finish this story, tell the worst of it? Or should I simply leave him hanging, never knowing what I'm capable of? I deserved to be rejected; I deserved my punishment; I'd let him get too close, and I needed to end this now.

"So what did you do, Cindy? So far, none of this sounds like you did anything." Robert had this puzzled look on his face, like for all the world he couldn't see me doing anything wrong.

Why does he keep looking like he thinks the best of me? Hate me! Hate me, like I hate me!

I'd been dragging this story out and had taken so much time to build up to the truth because I'd wanted to chicken out. Being called before the principal is never fun. You don't want to admit what you did. The knot in the pit of your stomach keeps growing, yet you think you can swallow it for a bit longer. The truth must come out sometime, like when you're dead and gone. But now, he's asking for the whole story, so he's gonna get the whole story. Whatever happened when Robert finally knew the truth would be his fault, not mine.

Yeah, you better believe that I could rationalize anything with the best of them. Put the blame on someone else, even if for only a little while. Yeah, to heck with it, I'm finishing this tale of woe.

"Oh, there's more, so much more, unfortunately. Let me tell you what happened later at the party and afterwards..."

Chapter 14

Noise in the hallway woke me up shortly after six. I was glad for that because I'd realized too late that I didn't have an alarm clock. I would've overslept otherwise. You know how it is. You don't want to do something; you find any excuse to miss it.

I dressed in my best outfit, but I was sure it wouldn't be good enough. I looked at myself in the full mirror hung on the back of the bathroom door, unhappy with the reflection. My black blouse was at least one size too large. My jeans were faded and shiny, held up by a belt pulled as tight as it could go. My only shoes other than tennis shoes were these worn-out tan flats so scuffed they should've been thrown away ages ago. Okay, I admit that my wardrobe now is much worse. You've got to expect it would be, since it's been almost nine more years out here. My hair that had always been in a neat, short bob was now a shaggy mop at my shoulders. I had no make-up, no jewelry except my watch, no hair ties, and nothing to put me in a party mood. Not anyone you'd ever put on your guest list.

At a little before seven, I, with a heavy heart, left my room to find the party, wanting to be anywhere but in a crowded room with a bunch of strangers. I've hated parties since I was a little girl. Why guests had to attend at this house was anyone's guess, but at least I'd get free pizza out of the deal. With any luck, after I grabbed a few slices, I could slip away unnoticed, maybe go for a walk under the stars.

I followed several girls downstairs into the lobby area, which was now filled with people, wandering about munching on pizza and drinking sodas, engaged in what could only be more inane talk—like what I'd endured earlier, during my conversation with Sandra. Ugh. They all looked like they were going out for a night on the town, not staying in their house for a party. The scent of a mixture of perfumes was heavy in the air. I looked much worse than I had thought I would compared with everyone else in the room. My cheeks grew hot at the idea, and I almost turned to flee back up the stairs.

"Hi!" Sandra yelled as she waved at me from across the room. At least she'd changed out of the dumb cheerleader outfit. But she was now wearing way-too-skinny jeans. No shoes. A skintight pale lavender sweater that left nothing to the imagination. Well, the fact that she was wearing no bra was no doubt helping the image. She was trying to throw out everything to all those in the packed crowd.

A mind is a terrible thing to waste. Even if you don't genuinely have one, you shouldn't ever let your boobs speak for you.

Making my way to her through the crush of people, I grabbed a slice of pizza from the first box I spotted on an end table. Pepperoni—ick, my least favorite. I grabbed a cola out of a cooler on the floor as well; it would wash down the grease.

"How was class?" I asked—at that point in my life I did care; I wasn't just being polite. I wanted her to learn something. Be something other than this dumb, slutty cheerleader. Become something I could never be. What exactly, I don't know, but something, anything.

You can see the whole wide world from college. Or at least you think you can. Why waste such a great opportunity being stuck in the box you've put yourself in? Or the one that everyone else has put you in because of how you look? Yes, Sandra needed a serious lesson on how to turn on her brain.

"Fantastic! Walt was there, so I got to drool all over him for a whole hour. I told you about him, right?"

Oh, good grief, it was worse than I had thought. Sandra was in college for the ring-by-spring plan, not to get an education. Had I missed that bit of information in our conversation earlier? I guess so; I'd tuned out much of what she'd said because of how brainless it all was.

"Uh, yes." I didn't want to feed into her need to tell me everything, so I felt it best to lie — I had no idea who Walt was.

"I hope he'll show up tonight. Anyway, Cindy, this is Tonya and Trisha."

She pointed to the two girls beside her, tall blonds wearing minuscule, skintight strapless dresses. Their breasts and butts were begging to be set free. The former was skinny in a maroon dress, and the latter was obese in a black one, both wearing too much make-up. Needless to say, it wasn't a pretty picture for either, but they were definitely not out of place in this crowd.

"We're all best buddies, and Trisha's your suitemate."

"Nice to meet you," I managed to say between bites. Even then, a good meal was a rarity, and a hot meal was, for all intents and purposes, non-existent. My goal was to eat pizza until I was sick and then flee to my room. The sooner, the better. Yeah, you're right. Rather rude of me given the circumstances.

"Glad you're here; Sandra said you're a hobo," Tonya said as she stepped towards me, checking me over as if to see if anything weird was in evidence. I had to disappoint her; even now, I don't think I look odd. You may disagree if you feel you must, but a lot of people pay good money for jeans with holes in them. I get mine for free. "Headed any place special?"

Great, Sandra had a big mouth, and it was clear that she'd abandoned the cousin lie completely. Even more reason to eat and run. "No, wandering around is all."

I finished my slice and headed for another pizza box to get more. I grabbed another and was happy to find it was supreme this time. But when I turned, I was unhappy to find that the three girls had followed me like lost puppies.

"Must be nice not to have anywhere to go." Trisha eyed me; there was obvious envy in her eyes. That ugly, you-got-what-I-can't-live-without look. Not good. "My parents have me on this five-year plan. School, marriage, career, kids. I'm not even sure if I get a say in who the husband will be, what my career will be, or how many kids I'll have. What I wouldn't give to be in your shoes, to make my own decision, my own choices, to be free..." Her voice faded.

"Hey, guys, this is a party, you know. Cheer up," Sandra cut in. "Let's go play cards. I think they've started the rummy tournament."

"Oh, great." Trisha seemed less than thrilled by the prospect of spending an evening playing old-fashioned card games. You know, I had to agree with her on that.

"I think I'll have another slice of pizza and head upstairs," I said as I finished my half-eaten piece.

"No way, Cindy. Robyn'll never let you get away with it. You're here 'til the end like everyone else. Trust me, she'll know if you try to sneak out early." Sandra shook her finger at me, giving me a disapproving look. The other girls laughed.

Wonderful. I was stuck in this nightmare with no way out. I guess I was paying for my room in a way much worse than having to pay a lot of money I didn't have. Putting up with a bunch of foolish college students for an evening — oh, the joy.

In the next room, which I gathered was the dining room, there were tables set up. Various games were on them, and both girls and guys were getting settled down to play. That explained the over-dressing on the part of most of the girls I had seen in the other room. Guys will bring out the worst in most girls—like breasts, not brains, were best. Don't even try to pretend it's not true. Like you've never seen it happen.

The only guy I ever dated was my husband, after all. Found out later that he only dated me because he was looking for a wife he could control. Boy, did that work out, for him at least. I'd fit the bill so perfectly. He'd dominated me from the very beginning to the bitter end. I only wish I'd seen it long before my wedding day. The subtle hints about my wardrobe, what I was eating, what I should do after graduation. He was trying to mold me into something he wanted, an image he could show off. Someone he could leave at home while he had his fun on the side. You bet I'd been an ideal match for that man. The weak little mouse who never said "boo" back. Well, it was clear that these girls at this house had a different view of men than I ever had. You never know; maybe they were in control. But it didn't look that way from where I was sitting.

Looking around the room, I figured I was going to have to make the most of the situation. After all, it was this one night of my life. Tomorrow, I'd be gone if all went according to plan. So, the rest of the evening, we played cards and talked. Before they could bore me with more stories like the ones Sandra had shared earlier, I jumped in and shared stories of my adventures on the road. Well, I embellished a great deal, told half-truths and out-and-out lies. My true stories would've been worse than Sandra's. But I was feeding on the energy these girls gave out as I held them captivated with more and more outlandish tales. The guys ignored me, and most left early because I was getting more attention than them. That, I was sure, was a good thing.

Later in the evening, after all the guys had left, us girls moved to the lobby area to be more comfortable. By then, the card games had been long abandoned, the pizza had all been eaten, and most of the soda had been drunk. I again did almost all the talking—they were wrapped around my little finger. It was an odd situation for me to be in; usually I tried to hide in the corner. Unseen, unheard, ignored. Yet, on that night, I became bolder and bolder the later it got. I was the life of the party, and I never wanted it to end. I was even rethinking my intentions to move on the next day. Why should I? These girls idolized me in a way that no one ever had before; I had a power I had never had before, and I was loving every minute of it.

Since I'd never had any alcohol or drugs—except those drugs used in suicide attempts—I wondered if this was what it felt like to be drunk or high. So many people had tried to describe the euphoria to me. Could this be what it was like? I was definitely feeling like I was on something.

"Cindy, don't you miss the stability of a job, a house, family, friends?" Trisha had been hammering me with similar questions all night. This was yet another of her many barrages. I had no idea why she was more curious than the others, but she'd never been far from my side. You'd have thought I had my own personal groupie if you were looking at the scene. She'd brought me soda. She'd brought me snacks. It was fantastic. Usually it was me who was the slave, not the master.

"Not really." I'd never had any real stability; what was there to miss? However, there was no way I was going to tell these girls who were hanging on my every word how bad my life had been. "Freedom's where it's at, the only way to get ahead. At one time, I was on one of those five-year plans like so many of you, but I'm so glad I never completed it."

Waving my hand, I'd thrown that in to goad Trisha. All too well, I remembered what she'd said earlier. I sighed to myself; I'd completed most of my stupid plan. I only wished I'd never done anything on it or even allowed my parents to make one for me in the first place. But again, these girls didn't need to know that and ruin my mystique.

"Why?" They all wanted to know, and they were all leaning closer to me, eager and waiting on bated breath for the answer.

Oh, this answer better be good, Cindy.

"There's too much to see and to do, to taste and to enjoy; why waste life stuck in a job you hate?" I hadn't hated my job; I'd hated what it represented—further proof that I was a failure.

I almost cringed at the memory of my husband beating me when I failed another performance review. Thus, I didn't get the raise he thought I should've had. Or the memory of my husband yelling at me to try harder, to stop being such a waste of space, to not be such a loser. Then hitting me over and over because I was never good enough, for my job or for him. More things they didn't need to know; the lies were so much better than the truth.

As I continued to talk, the girls around me changed with some frequency. I told story after story, lie after lie. They were eating out of the palm of my hand, and it felt good. I was in charge; I was in control; I was important for once. The stories weren't what was important; I was. Or so I thought.

That evening had ended up a whole lot better than I'd ever even dreamed was possible. I was a hero to those empty-headed college girls. All because I'd gotten off the treadmill the rest of the world was on. A bunch of foolish sheep going nowhere. Never mind the fact that none of it was real. That I'd fallen out of my life because I was worthless, and I was now completely aimless. No, little details like that weren't vital right then. You ever feel that kind of power over people? If you have, you'd understand why I couldn't let it go. Couldn't tell the truth and come crashing back into the real world.

It was so amazing how it felt for those few hours to be somebody, to be on top, to be important—to not be me. Usually, I was the one who was on the bottom; I was the one no one wanted, but no, not tonight. For one night, I was a figment of my own imagination—the person I always dreamed I was but knew I could never be. And it was glorious. You have no idea how wonderful it felt.

"Girls, it's time for bed—quiet hours begin in five minutes." Everyone began to scatter when Robyn made this pronouncement, clapping her hands over her head as she did so.

The noise echoed in the room. I couldn't believe that four hours had flown by so quick; the blink of an eye was all I had to be someone else. All of a sudden, I felt drained, like I'd run a marathon but was so very happy.

"Cindy, can I speak with you for a moment?" She turned to me, her face a hard, marble mask and her beady eyes glaring at me.

"Sure." I settled back into the black couch I was on, putting my feet up on the coffee table and crossing my arms behind my head.

I felt like I was in charge of this house after being here only a few hours. No maybe about it anymore, I'd stay for more than a few days. This place was the best thing that had ever happened to me.

"What's up?" I smiled up at her, the smile of a contented person who had the world by the tail. A person who knew everything was only going to be coming up roses from now on. Now I knew why people craved power.

Robyn was still wearing the same black dress as before, only without the apron now. She looked stern and formidable; you could see why she was in charge of all these college girls. One look at her, and you'd step into line in a hurry. "Let's wait a few minutes until everyone's upstairs and out of earshot."

"Fine by me." I continued to survey my new kingdom.

Robyn sat down all prim and proper on the edge of a chair near me. Sitting in silence, she watched like a hawk as the girls gathered up their things. They began to leave the room, wandering down the hall. When everyone was finally gone, she looked at me with a sharp, piercing gaze. Then, she took a deep breath like she was about to begin a big speech.

"I'd appreciate it if you'd stop speaking about how wonderful your lifestyle is. At this house, we try to instill a sense of being grounded in the real world to these students. College is hard enough as a transition from adolescence to adulthood. We don't wish this to be undermined by tales of a wandering gypsy. If you wish to stay here, I will not allow any more of your discussions about such nonsense with my girls. Also, I'll arrange for you to work somewhere for the remainder of your stay.

"I feel that if you were given some discipline, maybe you could stop wasting your life. Then you wouldn't feel the need to lead young, impressionable minds astray." Her frown said it all: *Ungrateful guest, please leave.* You could read it as clear as the giant signs in New York's Times Square.

"Since you're in control here, I know I must obey your rules while I'm under this roof, but I also know how wrong you are. If you don't get attached, you've got nothing to lose. Don't bother about the job; I'm not staying after tomorrow." My arms lowered to my lap really slowly; she'd taken all the fun out of my evening, and I was deflating like a leaking balloon. I was back to being just me; the dream was over—I'd been caught in my lies. You could've seen that coming a mile off, I suppose. But it hit me like a ton of bricks, a total blindside.

"I wish you'd stay; it could be a time for you to mend your hurts. It's clear that you were telling the girls a lot of lies tonight. That could only be because you don't want the truth to be known."

Well, she could state the obvious, but she still didn't wish me to stay. Words lie, but faces don't. Her face was a mix of anger, disgust, and pity—poker face, she was not. Flashing neon signs are easy to read, even for someone like me.

Standing up, I roughly pulled my money out of my pocket, peeled off a five-dollar bill, and extended it out to her. She had no right to say what she did, even if she was right! My hurts were no one's concern but my own.

"Here's the rent; thanks for a real great time." I spit the words at her as I dropped the bill into her lap when she didn't reach out her hand to accept it. "I'll leave first thing in the morning, and don't worry—I won't speak to anyone between now and then. I won't do any more damage to these poor simpletons you've got here." I stormed out of the room, shaking like a leaf over the enormity of what I'd done.

Walking back up to my assigned room, I cursed myself. *How are you going to work around the fact you've got nothing to put your few belongings into? Fool, fool, fool!* There was no way I could waltz out of there with four shopping bags of belongings and expect to get far. You know, like a block or two. Then a bag would break, and I'd be stuck picking my stuff off the sidewalk, trying to carry it in my pockets or something. Or abandoning it there.

I had no idea where to get camping gear, if in fact I could even get it in this town. Plus, there were so many other details I had yet to work out. My temper had dug me a hole yet again, and this one was going to be rather tough to get back out of.

You shouldn't get angry; being a mouse is better. No, I couldn't think that way. This was the new me. Braver, bolder me. The me who had the courage to run. Or the cowardice to run. It was a tossup.

When I first opened my door, I saw that the light was on. Knowing I hadn't left it that way, I entered with caution. Not sure what I might find, afraid it wasn't something good. Trisha was slumped on my bed crying, a soft, moaning sort of lament. I stared at her for a few moments before I closed the door quickly and quietly, unsure what to do. She hadn't seemed very upset earlier, had she? Frustrated at her lot in life, sure. But distressed enough to have broken into my room? That seemed a bit far-fetched. When had she left the party? I hadn't seen her the last half an hour or so, which was odd, since she had been clinging to me like my shadow all night.

"Everything all right?" I said it as softly as I could, almost afraid of the answer. This day was a train wreck, and I couldn't face yet another disaster.

Half-heartedly swiping her eyes with one hand, she succeeded in only smudging her make-up more. Then she looked up at me with raccoon eyes. "Not exactly. I called my mom to ask if I could take more control of my own life, and she totally flew off the handle. I so want to get out of here, but I can't get her to understand..."

I couldn't remember what year she'd said she was in earlier in the evening when I'd asked. Junior? If so, she didn't have long to go. "It's okay. You can wait until you're out of college, and then she can't say anything." My father stopped having a say then, but I'd immediately jumped into a disastrous marriage. Thus, it was too late for me. However, now was not exactly the best time to mention that. Don't judge me for still lying to the poor girl.

"You don't get it either. I thought you, of all people would understand. I can't wait that long. I'm going nuts trying to keep up my grades. I've got no time to do anything but study subjects I've got no interest in. Subjects that I didn't even want to take in the first place and only want to ignore. The only social activities are the horrid required ones around here, and I never have any fun. College is supposed to be about having fun and boys and parties. Take me with you; I'll do anything you say and try not to be much of a bother." Her words seemed to be off, like she was having trouble speaking, and she gave me a weak smile. Even that seemed to take more effort than she could come up with.

"That'd cramp my style." I frowned; this wasn't good. I'd made my life sound way too perfect, and she wanted in on it. My life was sad and pathetic, way worse than hers. But there was no way she had any idea because of all the lies I'd been telling. I was the idiot, not these girls I'd been stringing along all night.

I was starting to sweat. What had I gotten myself into? If I knew nothing about being homeless, then why did I spend the evening pretending I did? *What are you going to do? What are you going to say? Come up with something less lame than what you just said! Don't stand here like a moron, Cindy!* My heart was beginning to pound so hard in my chest that I could swear it was echoing in the room. Foolish, I know.

"Somehow I knew you'd say that." She tried to hold up an empty pill bottle, only getting it a few inches off the bed before shaking it to confirm it was empty. Then she, with great care, pushed a small, empty bottle of booze over the edge of the bed, letting it drop onto the floor with a loud clank, which made me jump. I could see the black label on the bottle as it rolled on the linoleum floor, over and over, like it was taunting me as it winked in and out of focus. "I don't blame you; you've got your freedom, so why take on any responsibility? Shortly, I'll fall asleep, and it'll be forever. It'll be over, and I'll have freedom too..." Her voice was fading, or was I imagining it? *Please let me be imagining it!*

"But that's not the way to gain it, you need to..." I couldn't finish my thought because I had no idea how to gain freedom. I was still standing frozen in place where I'd been since entering the room. The only change was the bottle that had now stopped at my feet as a silent witness against me.

Had she really taken a bunch of pills and drank this alcohol? Did she have more courage than me and was about to succeed at committing suicide when I'd failed so many times?

I was afraid to move closer to her. I was holding my breath, clenching my fists, and fighting for an idea to end this nightmare. Closing my eyes, I kept wishing for this whole scene playing out before me to not be true, but I knew it was all too real. When I opened them, everything was the same. Exactly the same.

"Please let me call for help." I almost choked on the words, but something needed to be done.

"You're way too late. I've been waiting for you for a while now." She tried to push herself up but failed and ended up in a ball, leaning on the headrest.

For a brief second, I had the thought, *I wonder how her skimpy dress is staying in place?*' But it was so inappropriate I couldn't believe I would even go there. "You're still talking to me, so it can't be too late." I tried to smile but failed.

"I want you to have a reminder of me." Her words were becoming weaker and slurred; it wasn't my imagination. "I've got a pack, a tent—you need them. Help me to my room." She tried to wave her arm towards the door, but it was a feeble fish flop on the bed.

I swallowed hard; the pizza I'd eaten earlier was trying to come back up. The taste was vile on my tongue, I'm not gonna lie. With leaden feet I forced myself to move towards her. The closer I got the stronger the alcohol smell got. She reeked from every pore—the bottle had been almost full when she started. I could see the pill bottle clear as day now. Lying on the bed like the evil thing it was—prescription sleeping pills—and I could see whose name was on the label. There was also a single sheet of paper on the bed. I didn't look at it; I didn't need to.

Somehow I got her up, through the bathroom, and onto the edge of her bed. She was completely limp, dead weight—I was simply dragging her along for the ride. Not like it was easy, since she was so much bigger and heavier than me.

"In the armoire," she whispered, not hardly loud enough for me to hear as I laid her down as gently as I could. "Take what you need."

I straightened her out as best I could and covered her with the blanket folded at the foot of her bed. I sat with her for a few moments, trying to decide if I should call someone, but it was obvious to me by that time that she was gone. Her chest wasn't moving. Well, I couldn't see it, anyhow. Her hand that I was holding was growing cold and stiff. Her eyelids were no longer fluttering. Was it that easy? Is that all it takes to end a life? Is death that peaceful? But it shouldn't have been so simple. She had her whole life ahead of her. Nothing she'd told me about her life was so bad that it should've ended this soon.

Odd as it may seem, I felt that I had no choice but to accept her offer of gear, if for no other reason than I could leave in the night and not wait until morning. Sounds horrible, I know. But before you think too badly of me, there was another part of me wanting a reminder of Trisha always. About how her life had been wasted. No, how her life had been wasted by me. Was this what my wandering had gained? I was no better off. I had no idea what I was doing. I, like a fool, told lies to glorify what was a very miserable life. And all for what? I was too much of a coward to take my own life all those times I'd tried. Now I'd succeeded in taking the life of another instead. You've gotta see how that felt. Sucker punches felt better.

Looking over at her still form draped across the bed, I knew there was nothing more to do. So, I ignored my feelings, trying to not let this bother me. There was nothing I could say to make it better, nothing I could do to bring her back. I'd tried to be better than I am. Then I'd been brought back to reality with a slap harder than any my father or husband had ever given me. I knew now, beyond a shadow of a doubt, that I was nothing. I'm no good and could do nothing that would ever be worthwhile with my life. My father was right, my mother was right, my husband was right—I can only be bad; I am evil. In every sense of the word. I felt like I'd been beaten up yet again. Only this time, the wounds were on the inside. The punches were the words coming out of my mouth all night, not someone's fists. I can only hope you've never been in this position, never felt this way. It was lower than low. I almost felt like crawling. I wasn't worthy of even standing upright anymore.

But walk to her armoire I did, on auto pilot, mustering every ounce of ice I could find in my heart to numb the pain like I'd done when I was a little girl and my father would hit me. Way back then, I'd pretend that I was at the beach and playing in the sand. The sun shining on my face. The sound of the ocean waves calming me. The smell of the salt water making me forget my tears. *Nothing bad is happening to me today.* It hadn't worked completely then, and it was clear it wasn't working now. Yet, it was better than letting the pain wash over me, drowning me in sorrow. Because I knew if I'd let even a little of the pain take control, I would've never gotten out of that room. I would've been frozen like a bug in amber.

Turning on her light, I made sure her door was unlocked and ajar a bit, hoping against hope it'd alert someone something was wrong. Horribly wrong. Grabbing Trisha's pack, tent, and sleeping bag, I rushed back into the adjoining room. You know, she hadn't seemed like the camping type. No time to think about that now.

Throwing my few things together with trembling hands, I dropped every other item, wishing things had turned out different, wishing I wasn't who I was, wishing I'd never accepted Sandra's offer. Everything within me was determined to get out of this house as quickly as possible. Yet, I still took the time to make sure there wasn't a single trace of me left in the room.

I left the key in the room assigned to me, the light on, and the door unlocked and ajar as well. As I entered the dim hall, the light from our rooms spilled into it, creating an unnatural glow. Someone would be bound to notice that. Heading down to the now-darkened lobby, haste was my ally. The bile now reached my throat and threatened to spill out. But first I knew I needed to do one last thing, and it was the most important part of my plan. Searching in the dark. Bumping into almost every piece of furniture. Swearing to myself every time I did. When I found the fire alarm, I almost yelled out, "Thank goodness." But I held my tongue, knowing that stealth was my friend right then.

With unsteady fingers, I pulled it before vaulting over a few pieces of furniture. I sprinted out the front door to my escape from the nightmare.

I ran and ran, my sides aching, my breathing coming in quick, loud rasps. Not caring which direction I was running in because the where didn't matter. Anywhere was better than that house, where the body of an innocent girl lay. Where I'd shown the world what I really was. Having broken one of my family's rules — never show our secrets to others — one of mine was now out. Hoping everyone else would forget all the nonsense I'd been spouting all day. That I could then do no further harm. That they'd forget me, like I was sure everyone in my past life had.

Finally, I couldn't run anymore and collapsed in an abandoned lot. My chest heaved as I gasped for breath in the cold night air, and I threw up over and over again, as I sobbed for the life I'd taken, wracked with pain, covered in my own filth. I hoped this was as low as I could go but was afraid that it wasn't. You haven't any clue how much guilt I was feeling at that moment. It felt like it was eating me from the inside out, leaving me just a shell of my former self. A self that was very little to begin with, leaving almost nothing now.

At some point, the cool breeze brought more rain, and it helped clear my tortured mind and soul. As I lay there dripping wet from the rain, I kept wishing it would wash the evil from me. Yet I knew I'd reached a point where it wouldn't ever be possible. *Never, never let people in — look at the pain you caused in one day, Cindy. ONLY ONE DAY! Why'd you lie to her and the others and make everything sound so wonderful in your life?*

What did I know about freedom? I could never be free — pain was within me and was part of who I was. I could never do what she'd done that night all those times I'd tried. I was a hopeless failure. I felt so much remorse that I hadn't told someone to check on Trisha, because maybe I was wrong. Maybe she wasn't dead. Pulling the fire alarm seemed like it wasn't enough. Not by a long shot. What if she was alive and no one found her? But she'd been so still, so cold. There was no way she was anything but dead.

A sorrowful wail from a passing train's horn broke into my thoughts. Even the engineer knew it was a time to weep for one who was lost. The cry rose and fell on the wind as the cold and wet seeped into my bones, and I knew a part of me had died with Trisha. No, not a part. I died with Trisha. I must now face my punishment for my crime.

Now what would a fitting punishment be, Cindy? You took a life, but it is not like you meant to. Hmm. Let's see. So your punishment should be banishment — you can't harm others if you don't get close to them. That means that this journey's now forever — you must wander, endlessly wander. You made her life meaningless, now your life must be even more pointless than it was before.

There seemed to be no other answer. It seemed only fair, justice in a sense.

Sometime later, I got up and started walking towards Oklahoma City, shivering both from the cold and from the realization that nothing had changed. Sure, I'd left my hometown, but I was still me. Evil, through and through. I walked all night; don't even think I acknowledged that in any way. Trisha's pack got heavier and heavier on my back as the night wore on, like I was carrying her, not my meager belongings. A few people stopped and asked if I wanted a ride, but I waved them on. They didn't need me in their lives, and it was now my job to protect others from the evil I could do.

Everyone was right about me; everyone had always been right about me. Nothing could change me, nothing should change me. I was filthy and disgusting. Not only because my clothes were dirty from the vomit and mud I'd lain in for goodness only knows how long. Which I now was hardly noticing as I walked along in the night as the rain continued to fall. No, it was more because I was born who I was always going to be; this was my lot in life.

You're never going to be worth anything. You're never going to be worth anything. I kept saying it as a mantra to myself as I shuffled along, bent from the weight of my burden as my tears mingled with the rain...

"So, now you know why I never tell anyone anything about me, never share who I am. I killed someone!" My words echoed in the tiny car, coming back at me like voices of accusers telling me what I'd done. They were telling me of my guilt and shame, as fresh now as that day nine years ago. "So even if your god is real, he couldn't care about me; he would never provide for me, never give me a future, never want me! My father was right; I'm ugly inside and out. I deserve to be punished; I deserve only this never-ending pain I'm in!

"I thought there would be no harm in telling you a little bit. But I was wrong to start telling you these stories, because it has led me to reveal part of my true self. I was wrong to let you into my world, into my life, into my thoughts! Let me out of this car now!"

Chapter 15

Hot tears streamed down my face. I ripped the seat belt off. It pinged off the door before it took a sharp nip at my arm as it curled back into place. The pain hardly registered as I began pounding on the armrest, trying to get the door open, not caring that the car was still hurtling down the freeway.

My heart felt like it was going to explode; my breath was coming in quick, short gasps. I was a trapped wild animal trying in desperation to get out of the cage this car had become.

"Stop! Stop! Stop!" My voice had turned into a high-pitched squeak even I didn't recognize. For a second, I even thought that it wasn't me yelling like a crazy person.

But no, I was the one yelling; I'd finally gone completely over the edge into full-blown crazy. Well, yes, you saw that one coming, didn't you? It was a rather short hop.

Then, the door flew open as if by magic. The car was still creeping along, and my upper body tumbled to the ground. I was half holding onto the door with my left hand, my body sliding along as the car came to a halt. But my temple hit the ground hard, along with most of my right side. The force of the impact left me in a daze for a moment before I pulled my feet out of the car. I pushed myself to a wobbly standing position, using the car as leverage. I took a few hesitant, weak, baby steps. All that mattered right then was to get away. I was sure I'd forever changed how Robert would view me. I was sure he'd no longer want anything to do with me, and I didn't want to stick around for his rejection. Even though I'd brought it on myself, I had to get away to be alone again—where I was safe.

Robert was behind the car by this point, but I could only look at his feet. I didn't want to see the look in his eyes.

"You're hurt." I was too upset to tell from those few words how he might be feeling at the moment, but I was sure he must be angry at me. What other response could there be to what I'd just shared?

With great care, I pushed away from the car and started to walk eastward like a slowly moving turtle, away from the direction we'd been traveling. I couldn't go down the road Robert was wanting me to go down anymore. I wasn't hurt—I'd hurt someone, and it was something I could never undo. There was no response I could give to him. Nothing I could say could change the past; nothing I could say would make Robert still want me in any way. Shaking my head with regret for what I'd done in the past, I wondered what to do now.

I heard the trunk lid open and slam shut; then Robert was beside me with my pack. "It's not your fault, Cindy. There's nothing you could've done. Even if you're right and she did succeed, you didn't kill her. Here's your pack; you go think about it—I'll be around when you're ready."

It was his same gentle voice, his same calm tone. No emotion, no crazy reaction—nothing was there that shouldn't have been. But there was no way I was hearing him right. He had to have some response, some outburst over what I'd done. I killed someone; he couldn't simply let that pass. You don't let a murderer walk away scot-free like it never happened. No, you punish them. Like I'd done to myself. Maybe I was in too much shock from finally sharing my secret to hear what he was saying. Yes, that must be it. There could be no other explanation at this point.

Without me even slowing down a little bit, he matched my pace. With such tenderness, he placed my pack on my back, sliding the straps over one arm, then the other. I'm not sure why he even bothered; he could've put the darn thing a little bit in front of me and let me pick it up on my own. You don't touch evil. It could rub off. Heck, it had rubbed off. That's why Trisha was dead.

I could hear his footsteps retreating, then the sound of the car doors being closed, and finally, his car pulling away. I never turned around. I couldn't face this man, not now or ever again. What he'd said didn't matter; he'd never find me again—there was no reason for him to. He was a man, nothing more. No matter how odd he'd seemed in the short time I'd known him, he wasn't anything special. There was no reason for him to care about me when he knew nothing about me except that I was homeless. Now he knew the horrible truth, and there was every reason for him not to care.

You're an utter fool, Cindy, I screamed, over and over again to myself as my pace quickened. I began to march along, not caring about all the cars zipping by. Not caring that they were all staring at crazy ol' me. Eventually, I began to wear down like a clock that needed winding. When I brushed my hand against my face to wipe my tears, I was surprised to find blood mixed in. With tender fingers, I felt my forehead where I'd hit the pavement earlier and realized I had quite the bump. *Well, at least now you've got Band-Aids to patch yourself up with,* I thought with bitterness. Rubbing my fingers together to try to remove the blood, I only succeeded in smearing it more.

Knowing I needed rest, I left the freeway I'd been walking along. Setting out across the field beside it, I headed for the grove of trees I could see in the distance. I was back to camping. No more nights of luxury in a motel for me, no more foolishness of thinking I'd ever fit in with people.

This is what you deserve, nothing more and a whole lot less – maybe today will be your last day on earth. Maybe, this stupid bump on the head will finally do the trick.

As I waded through the knee-high grass, I had complete tunnel vision. All I could see were the trees, and they kept getting farther and farther away rather than closer. Nearing exhaustion, I was beginning to panic. I began to think I'd never make it to the shelter of that grove. I never wanted anything more than to reach those beautiful trees that seemed just out of reach. Finally, they seemed within my grasp, and I felt like one of my burdens had been lifted. I'd make it after all. This is why I needed simple. No expectations, nothing to live for but something so basic even a child would want it.

When I reached the trees, I lay down, with my pack as my pillow. I felt hollow like a Halloween pumpkin, like there was nothing left in me. There were so many other stories I could've told Robert, but I'd made the choice to tell him the worst one. Since Robert was so insistent that this god of his cared for me and kept giving me things, then he needed to know the truth. But why I felt that he needed to know everything now seemed silly. I could've kept stringing him along, smiling and nodding when he fed me his religious lines. Rather than me telling him they were false. That's what I'd always done before; I went along or said nothing. Why I'd do something different now was a mystery to me.

My guilt over Trisha's death had always bothered me, but now it felt overwhelming, like I was about to be crushed by it. Worse, what little hope these talks with Robert had begun to give me was now being squashed, destroyed by the heavy weight of my guilt and shame.

This is why I hate spring; things begin to grow and bloom, but in the end they always fade away and die. Over the years, I'd learned to skip the middleman. Where there's no hope, there can be no disappointment—let sadness rule. Simple. You got to love simple.

My jumbled thoughts once again became my companions as I lay there. My mind raced to replay everything that'd happened with Robert. As I watched the leaves of the trees dance in the afternoon breeze, my ideas were as confused as those shapes. At some point, I fell into a troubled sleep in the corpse pose. It was fitting, I suppose.

I awoke with a start. My heart was in overdrive, my hands were shaking, and I was breathing fast—what had caused me to be so panicked? It was twilight now—the shadows were long. I was a lot farther from the freeway than I should've been if I needed help—not good. Headlights from cars were faint dots on the horizon. Traffic noises were lost on the breeze. Darn, I knew better than to go so far. But earlier I hadn't been in a state of mind to care about something as important as that. As I sat up real slow, I was careful to scan the area. I realized that Robert was sitting in his car a few feet from where I'd been sleeping.

How in the world did he find me?

So now I had a stalker. It was creepy and weird. I lay back, hoping in the half-light that he hadn't noticed I was now awake and had sat up. He had complete control over me if he wanted it. Every woman's worst nightmare is to be in such a vulnerable position.

All your instincts told you this ride would only lead to trouble; you should've listened to them. You are such an idiot! How could you have been so stupid!!

So, Cindy, what're you going to do now, I thought. *Because if that last story didn't scare him away, then it's obvious nothing will. Could you sneak away in the night? Probably not; you didn't get a good look at the area when you took off from the freeway earlier.*

I lay there for a while, trying to slow my breathing, and was only a little bit successful. Usually, the birds chirping had a calming effect on me, often lulling me to sleep. Now, their noise was as grating as nails on a chalkboard, and it was making me cringe. The wind sounded like someone moaning, and the tree leaves sounded like shuffling a deck of cards. Trying to tune out everything again, I couldn't, and calm was becoming a relative term. Like you're living in a scary movie and there's no way to end it. This, somehow, had become your life.

My head was pounding, both from where I'd banged it the night before on the headboard and from earlier on the pavement. Maybe I was seeing things; maybe Robert wasn't there after all. I mean, wouldn't I have heard a car driving up and parking right next to me while I was sleeping?

I turned my head somewhat to see if I could spot the car in my peripheral vision. When I saw no glint of metal, I sat up again, and the car was gone. Poof, just like that. Yeah, I'd imagined the whole thing.

Darn, I must've hit my head harder than I thought, or I really and truly had gone insane. Well, isn't that what everyone thinks all homeless people are—nuts? I guess I was ending up a sad, pathetic cliché. You better believe I saw the irony in that.

Sitting there looking out into the gathering darkness, I nestled my head in my hands. My thoughts again turned to what had happened on this latest chapter of my journey. In three days of traveling with Robert, I'd gone about three hundred miles. That is if I was where I thought I was right at that moment. Which, given my present state of confusion, was unlikely. Not like it mattered much. However, I'd gone a million miles in terms of what I'd said, what I'd told, what I'd shared, and what I'd learned. He now knew things I'd never told anyone. He knew me in a way no one else did. No one else could. Yet, he still didn't know the whole story. I guess that was a good thing; what he knew was bad enough. The problem was that I was seeing things in a different light, and I, all of a sudden, cared what Robert thought about me. I regretted horribly the fact that I'd had to destroy his idea that he could help me, save me, that I was even worth saving.

Day had now turned to night, not just in the real world but in my life as well. The light of hope that for a brief moment had been lit by Robert was snuffed out forever. Hope is cruel to someone like me, someone who knows nothing can change the past, that because of the past, there can be no future. Why had I thought that Robert, with his crazy religious ideas and his crazy verses, was the answer? Even for a brief moment? Why, when I'd all but given up, had I thought he was what I was seeking?

It was clear I was grasping at straws because of the deep emotional hole I was in. You know that feeling? That any answer was better than none? But what did that leave me with? Nothing, same as before. So was the urge to go home still within me? I didn't know; I was so confused at this point that south was north and west was east. I wasn't even sure anymore that home was a real place I could point my feet towards. It may have been another of my illusions, a hope that I shouldn't have ever dared to have. It wasn't like going home was a reason to have any hope in the first place. It was an ending place.

I lay back against my pack, not caring that the night was turning cool fast now that the sun had set. Not caring that it was too early in the spring to sleep without a blanket or a tent. Not caring that I had a lot of money tucked in my pack. I could've walked to the freeway, hitched another ride, and found a motel, then lived content for a little while. If tomorrow came, it was another day when I could worry about such things. Or, I could ignore them and continue to lay here in this grove of trees, staring at the sky for the rest of eternity...

My eyes hurt. Rolling over, I realized I wasn't sleeping in a soft, warm bed but on hard ground near some trees. The sun was high in the sky; it must be noon or later, and the day was warm by spring standards. My clothes were dusty in places and damp in others where I'd been sweating in the sun.

Wishing that I'd bothered to lay down in the grass, I grunted in disgust at myself. My face was sunburned and raw. My mouth was sandy and rough. My hands were clammy. My stomach was queasy. Overall, I'm sure it wasn't a pretty morning-after picture. You know what I'm talking about—homeless drunk, minus the drunk part.

Sliding myself and my pack over into the shade, I pulled my coat and shirt off—thankful that I was now wearing a bra under it all. Not that it mattered anymore, not like anything mattered anymore.

Twisting myself up to a sitting position against a tree, I debated about removing my pants as well. In the end, I figured it'd be too uncomfortable to sit in the dirt in my underwear. Plus, I didn't have the energy to pull the blanket out of my pack and then roll myself onto it. Sorry, your image of me not being a lazy bum has turned out to be false. I'm as lazy as they come; well, at least that morning I was.

Rummaging in my pack for something to slake my thirst, I figured that most of what I was feeling was a mild case of dehydration. Having not had anything to eat or drink since my breakfast the day before, I should've been hungry. But I wasn't. Feeling something cool, I pulled out a can of tuna in triumph. The tuna was packed with fishy water; better than nothing at this point. I slurped down the rather nasty-tasting water, then ate the tuna with my fingers, not caring that I was back to being nothing better than an animal. That I didn't have the manners to wash my hands before eating. There was no one here but me. I wasn't sure if I was ever going to leave this spot, and I most definitely didn't care how dirty I was anymore.

This is silly, Cindy, you're better than this; have a little pride. You can care about yourself, even if no one else should. I fished out a few wet wipes and cleaned up after my rather odd breakfast or lunch.

Who knows what time it was exactly, but since it was my first meal of the day, I guess that made it breakfast.

I sat watching the butterflies float on the breeze for a few moments. Their bright yellow and black bodies shone brightly in the sun. The bark of the tree bit into my bare back. The wind rustled my now loose hair — had I lost my new bow? The smell of the dirt, the leaves, and nature in general was as intoxicating to me as it had ever been. Maybe spring wasn't such a bad time of year. This felt good; this felt right somehow to be out here with new beginnings all around me. Perhaps it was my time for a new beginning too, but was that too much to wish for? Most likely it was...

On the spur of the moment, I decided to come up with a list of things to do — if I made a plan, then I'd have to stick with it. I had things in my pack that others could use if I was determined to take that one final step to have today be my last. If not, then I needed to make a decision about whether to go home or not and what to do with Robert's money.

Since I'd left him with such abruptness, I'd failed to sneak the envelope into the glove box — another of my plans that I had failed at. After all, no matter what he'd said, there was nothing for me to think about as far as he was concerned. There was no way he was coming back for me. Last night had been an unhinged delusion on my part, nothing more. Even you can see that. It didn't matter what I wanted or that I was starting to care about what Robert might think about me. The simple fact was I was alone again, as I should be. I knew better than to accept a ride that lasted longer than a day.

He was wrong about Trisha's death not being my fault. My guilt over the whole affair had been eating at me for over nine years. There were lots of things I could've done differently. Sure, you can tell me that hindsight is 20/20 and I'm only seeing things now because of that. But I know better, because I knew then that I shouldn't have been doing those things. Most of them were little things that most people would've done in the situation. But the biggest thing was what I hadn't told Robert, what I couldn't bring myself to tell him—where she'd gotten the pills and the alcohol.

They were mine.

They were my escape hatch. I'd left my old life with them in case this new life hadn't worked out. After all, I'd had a string of failures under my belt long before I left that old life. The odds that I'd left all that behind weren't great. The whole idea of my new life being a success was doomed from the start. You see the wisdom in that, I'm sure.

When I'd left home, I'd given myself one year to find a place to land that would be my paradise—somewhere no one knew me and where at last I would be away from the misery that had always been part of my life, part of me. If I couldn't find a place like that, I was going to commit suicide. Not another half-ass attempt at suicide like before. No, I was finally going to do it right and succeed. I'd done all the research after my last stupid failed attempt at my house when my ex-husband had found me. Now I knew what I'd done wrong; there would be no failure this time. That was why my pace was so frantic those first few months on the road. My time was short; I had an expiration date; I had to find a safe harbor soon before I lost my nerve again. You've got no idea how much pressure I'd put myself under by thinking thoughts like those.

But, instead, I'd killed an innocent college girl who was mixed up, not abused like me. She'd gone through my things, found my notes, and knew what to do. When I'd found her that fateful night, she had the page with my handwritten directions with her on the bed. My bottle of alcohol was what she'd pushed on the floor. My bottle of prescription meds was next to her. They were given to me under the guise that it was hard to sleep because of the divorce. The doctor had bought that lie hook, line, and sinker.

Trisha could've been helped. She could've been saved. She should've been here talking with Robert. Not me, not the very damaged, unlovable, unsalvageable me. No, my punishment was to wander, forever wander with no end, knowing full well what the cost of freedom was, knowing that I'd lost everything, including the life of someone else. Freedom comes at a higher price than you'd ever want to pay. If I'd known the cost, I know I'd never have wanted it in the first place.

So, whatever plans this god of Robert's may have had for me were gone—I wasn't worth anything anymore. I was so damaged from my childhood that I'd dragged scars into my adulthood like an anchor weighing me down. I was pure evil, down to my very core. All the times my father had beaten me hadn't produced the desired result. I never became good, never did things right, never learned from my mistakes. But, the abused person I was didn't seem like it was me anymore. Yet if it wasn't, I didn't have an identity any more—I was only a chameleon trying to hide in plain sight. When I'd tried to not hide, tried to stand out in the crowd for one brief moment in time, it had been a disaster.

I was better off when I was one of the millions of nameless, faceless homeless people on the streets—someone whom everyone ignored and pretended didn't exist. Yes, you don't see me. Do you? Be honest now. You only notice the homeless when they're in your way. When they're shouting at you because they're drunk. When they're blocking the entrance to where you work. But me? No, you don't see me because I don't do any of those things. Because I don't want you to see me. Hiding is simple. Simple is good.

So, here I now was, sitting in a grove of trees in the middle-of-nowhere, Ohio like a dunce, wishing I'd never made all those mistakes, never caused any harm. But I am me, and causing harm is all I can do. Maybe if I'd tried a whole lot harder, maybe if I'd learned something along the way...but it wasn't to be. I was the failure everyone always said I'd be, that I'd always known I'd be.

So yes, I had to accept my punishment of being forever a nomad who had to keep others at arm's length for their safety. Either that or end it all today. There was no longer any middle ground. Robert was wrong: There was no god; there was no hope; there was no future; there was no love for me. There never was, there never could be, and I couldn't for the life of me figure out why he couldn't see that as clearly as I did.

Shaking my head, I reached into my pack to pull out another can of tuna but found the bag with my journals in it instead. Pulling them out, I thought, *Cindy, you might as well look through them one more time. Then you should throw them out for all the good they're doing you. Why must you keep rehashing past mistakes? Reliving the horror that is your life when you know it never leads anywhere?*

I reached into the bag and yanked one out, cursing myself for indulging in this charade about knowing where I'd been. About finding an impossible answer to a question that never even existed in the first place.

Just one last time! The cover caught on the back of another journal and gave way with a loud rip. Cradling the wounded journal in my hands, I was sorry I'd hurt such an old, dear friend. With gentle strokes on the first page, I began to cry. A few drops at first, but the tears were all too quick to turn into a flood that stopped as quickly as it had begun.

"You have been told so many lies," Robert had said on the first day, and he was sorry about that. What had he meant by that?

Oh, good grief, are you getting sucked into this religious nonsense again? He's gone, out of your life forever — move on or give up; there are no other options anymore.

The salt in my tears was making my sunburn sting, so I roughly brushed the moisture lingering on my face away, willing myself to stop being so oversensitive and melancholy. I flipped the journal open to a page at random, and a small, white index card fell out. I watched as it floated to the ground on the mild breeze but didn't immediately reach out for it. Instead, I looked at the page I'd opened.

"July 29: Dave, Old Faithful, hiking around geyser basins"

That was our second day together, an easier day after hiking Uncle Tom's trail the day before. I can almost still smell the sharp sting of the sulfur, the whoosh of water when geysers erupted. The crowds, the animals, the sun beating down on us as we walked around the hot pools. Casually, I picked up the card, wondering what it could be since I didn't remember ever putting anything in my journals. Written on it was Dave's address, and below it was the second verse Robert had given me.

As the sunlight filtered through the trees, it cast odd, misshapen shadows on my lap. Not that I noticed; everything had stopped. I stopped breathing. I no longer heard the birds. I no longer felt the breeze. This wasn't possible; there was no way it was possible. My hand was trembling so hard, I was sure I hadn't read it right. It's not conceivable for two men who'd never met to both give me a card with the same verse written on it— years apart, no less.

I closed my eyes; the card was not real. I'd left it in a Bible I'd abandoned years ago. *It's just your imagination, like Robert in his car yesterday; it's just your imagination. Nothing you dream is real. Only nature is real. The bark of the tree on your back, the wind in your hair, the scent of grass in the air – those were real. This god thing wasn't real; religion wasn't real; nothing that Robert tried to tell you was real.*

With my heart racing and my head pounding, I opened my eyes to see that I was still holding the card. It hadn't disappeared. It was still plain as day that Dave's name and address were on it, and what's more, the verse was still there:

'For I know the plans that I have for you,' declares the Lord, 'plans for welfare and not for calamity to give you a future and a hope.'

I turned the card over and over and over with quivering fingers, but that verse was there, glaring at me, daring me to believe. *How could this be happening? How could this be real?*

The only way this made sense was if God was real and had used both men to tell me that. Then, this god did have a plan for my life, he did care for me, and somehow he had been trying to tell me for years. But how could I tell God what I'd done? Or did this god somehow know all along? After all, I'd met Dave months after the incident in Oklahoma and Robert all these years later.

This couldn't be some strange coincidence. I didn't understand this whole religion thing, but even I could see there had to be some kind of a link. This wasn't only my craziness talking; there was something here that I couldn't explain, something I couldn't ignore. Unless you want to be stupid and say your nose isn't there anymore. That's how real this now seemed to me.

Great, Cindy, you didn't even wait to find out what Robert's exact reaction was to what you did. You bailed, plain and simple as that. You're the one who was upset and screaming, not him. You need to find him and show him this card, get him to explain it.

But how could I find him again? If only it was as easy as dreaming him up like I had last night. I needed a plan, so to start, I had to think about all the things I knew about Robert. Unfortunately, that wasn't much. I hadn't wanted to ask him questions because I hadn't wanted to know the answers. And now that I did, I hadn't any way of finding him to ask them — so typical of my life.

Think, Cindy, think. So, I knew he spoke at churches — well, maybe not. Okay, correction, I knew he spoke to people about his god. I knew he ate at diners that most of the rest of the world just passes by. I knew he stayed at cheap motels. I knew what car he drove and what state the license plate was from. I knew he was headed to the West Coast but not exactly where.

Well, that was a start anyway. Yeah, I know, not much of one. Next course of action based on these scant facts? Fine, I'd get up, go to the freeway, and either hitchhike or walk to the next town. Then, I'd start looking for him at dive diners since he seemed to like to make friends with waitresses. Not a great plan, not even a good plan, but it was the only plan I could come up with. You know me and plans. I haven't met a good one yet.

I pulled out my last remaining clean shirt and put it on. Then, I shoved everything else into my pack. *This is really, really crazy. You're now going to go searching for Robert? What in the world are you thinking?* But that was just it; I was no longer thinking. I was acting on emotions alone. Slinging my pack onto my shoulders, yet again, I headed towards the freeway, fearing that I'd lost Robert and that my chance for finding answers was gone for good this time. My stomach was in knots; everything ached. Sure, it could be from wolfing down tuna plain, but I didn't think so.

In the end, I didn't want to talk to anyone else; only Robert would do. So, I ended up walking. The day was pleasant enough, and I hadn't been for a good walk in days. Maybe it'd clear my head. But then again, most likely not; I'd allowed Robert to twist me around so much at this point. Yesterday, I had no intention of continuing to go westward. Yet today I had, of my own volition, set my feet on this path — Robert's path. I still had doubts; I still was unsure if all this was real. Most important of all — what if I couldn't find Robert to help me understand? What would I do then? I'd face it when I came to it, I guess.

Each step gave me a sense of accomplishment; I was finally getting closer to my goal. Yes, there was also a sense of dread; I could be getting farther from ever finding it. A big part of me felt sure that I'd walked away from the one person with my answer.

I had no idea if I was headed in the right direction by going the way I'd last seen Robert driving.

He could've pulled off the freeway and turned around or gone north or south for all I knew. But he said he'd be there; I was clinging to the hope he'd meant it somehow, that he was only in the next town waiting for me. Everything within me seemed to be swinging on a pendulum. Answer to no answer. Hope to no hope. Home to no home. Robert to alone again. The wild ride was making me sick. So no, it wasn't the tuna.

After who knows how long of this back and forth in my head and heart, I began to see signs of a town. What had been a few scattered homes and farms was now homes in small clusters. The cars on the freeway were much more numerous. I realized that my feet hurt; I was beyond hungry, and the sun was low in the sky. I must've walked farther than I thought. My thoughts doing cartwheels in my head had been such a distraction.

Okay, this is it, where do you start looking? No, first things first, have something to eat. You don't want to wander into every café in town hungry. I left the side of the freeway to walk across the field, or what was more likely someone's very large backyard, trying to find a quiet place to rest for a while. You know me and solitude.

Shortly, I stumbled onto a residential street lined with neat cookie cutter homes. They were all the same, except a few had beige rather than white siding. Walking up the street, I spotted a small park. It should've been filled with families enjoying the warm spring evening. But instead, it was empty. Ghost towns are sad because they're a reminder of days gone by when things didn't work out like they should've. However, ghost parks are even sadder. They're a reminder that people can't be bothered to stop looking at their screens long enough to enjoy the things that matter—things like family, friendship, nature, and quiet. Whatever happened to simple? You need simple as much as I do, even if you refuse to acknowledge it.

Sitting down on a bench at a picnic table, I found my wet wipes and washed my hands. Pulling the crackers out of my pack, I crunched a few onto the table top before beginning to eat a few myself. I was rewarded with a few cautious robins joining me at my feast, singing to me as I ate.

Next, I pulled out a can of tuna, since the crackers had made me thirsty. Satisfying my thirst with the rather disgusting tuna water for the second time that day, I then ate the tuna. I could hear a squirrel chattering nearby, so I crunched a few more crackers. Putting them on the ground a few feet from me near the base of the tree, I hoped he would join me too. That squirrel finally did while I was enjoying my dessert of a granola bar. He was handsome too—a shiny silver back with a bright, white tummy. He kept waving his tail at me to say hello as he poked around looking for something to eat. Unfortunately, I didn't have any nuts for him. I knew he wouldn't want the crackers; they were only to get him curious enough to come out of the tree. The birds would get them later.

Dining al fresco was always my favorite now that I was homeless. I could sit and watch the animals for hours; they were better than any TV show. I wish we could've done it when I was a child—there's no way to be mad at someone when such beauty was all around you. Well, probably not; my dad could get mad at me for the most simplistic of reasons. One day, I was smacked for not tying my shoes with the right knot. I still can't tell the difference between the two.

Darn, here you are daydreaming while the light is fading. Instead you need to be finding Robert, so snap out of it!

I picked up my trash, removed my trash from earlier out of my pack, and put it all in a wastebasket as I walked out of the park. People who litter bug me. They're throwing their junk in what now amounted to the middle of my living room. The whole wide world was my house, after all. Betcha you never thought of it like that. I know a lot of homeless people don't feel that way.

They seem to be the worst offenders when it comes to leaving trash everywhere. But, get real, why make a mess where you sleep, eat, play, live? You don't do that in your house, right?

This, I'm sure, was another holdout from my super strict upbringing. I could no more create disorder outside than inside—unless it was in my own head and heart. Of course, that was also a product of my father's heavy hand. It's hard to think clearly when you're being beaten for not putting the fork on the left side of the plate at the age of four. Abuse messes you up in so many ways. I hope you don't know what I mean from firsthand knowledge the way I do.

I shook my head. *How foolish to let yourself get so sidetracked from the mission.*

I headed down the street. I was determined to find Robert in this town, if in fact he was here, even if it took me all night. No stone unturned, well, no café not peeked into, I was going to not be a failure for once in my miserable life. This was something I had to succeed at no matter what; there was no going back. So, once again, I was doing what I do best—putting one foot in front of the other, marching on towards the unknown looking for something I was sure to never find...

Chapter 16

To be honest, this whole idea of finding Robert was one of my more insane ones. Over the years there had been a lot of rather batty plots coming out of my dopey brain. It was especially insane given the fact that I was trying to find him to ask him questions about this god of his. Who would've ever believed that I, of all people, was wanting answers about religion.

I was the one at all the soup kitchens and shelters with sermons who was the loudest mocker among the crowd. I'd heckle those do-gooders who were always there when I needed a hand. Not always did I scoff at them behind their backs, either; no, I wasn't that kind. Now, it seemed like the joke was on me. I'm sorry if you were one of those I'd been mocking all these years. You deserved better. I see that now. Forgive me.

Boy, is that hard to say.

My thoughts moved to the verse again. Come to think of it, I'd missed a big part of the second verse. I'd been focused so much on the welfare, future, and hope part that the rest of it had seemed so unimportant. But, it had also said something about seeking someone and finding that someone. I could only guess it meant god.

So, was I now seeking Robert or this god of his? Well, in truth, I should say, Robert's and Dave's god. If I was seeking their god, that was a rather scary thought because that meant that I'd now have to change who I was. Yes, I still felt there was no way that this god of theirs could accept me as is, even if he might know what I had done.

Robert and Dave had both seemed not only normal but good — no, good was not a strong enough word. They were both men of excellent character, something rare and wonderful, like — I don't know — maybe Mother Teresa. You'd never put yourself on that level, even if you have volunteered for a day or two at a kitchen or shelter. But beyond that, Robert seemed to be almost not human. He could do things that no one else could.

Okay, I know this sounds nuts, but I think he could read my mind. He knew things he shouldn't. He found me that first day and made it sound like it was no big deal.

However, if I was seeking god as the verse said, which was a big *if*, mind you, I wasn't doing it with all my heart. Thus, would it work? I mean, it's not like I was completely convinced at this point that there was a god or even if god was what I was looking for. What I was seeking was answers.

Yes, it did seem like there may be something to this whole god thing. But was I ready to go so far as to say that the myth was busted? That god was real? No, there were too many things not adding up in my fuzzy brain, and I needed to make some sense out of it all. Maybe coincidences were real and this god wasn't. You never could tell. Well, you might be able to. You might've had the key to this whole puzzle and been sitting there laughing at me this whole time. I'm moving on before I make a bigger fool of myself if that's the case.

The first café I spotted didn't appear to be the right type for Robert — it was a chain place and almost brand new, whereas he seemed to favor mom-and-pop places with a lived-in look, to put it as generously as I can. I could have said "dump," you know. In addition to that, his car wasn't out front, but I went in anyway. After all, we'd seemed to always walk, not drive when we went out to eat.

Taking a deep breath, I did a quick scan of the place, desperate for a friendly face. The few paying any attention to me were scowling—you had to see that coming. Unfortunately, I didn't see Robert, but this was as I expected. *Don't be disappointed—you knew he wouldn't be in the first place you looked.* Nodding to myself, I turned to go, my heart sinking beneath the floor as I did so, my feet dragging a little bit.

"Hey, you looking for someone?" I turned back around to see the speaker, a chubby, short, unsmiling waiter who was about my age. His dark hair framed his dark face, and I knew that no matter what I said, he wouldn't have been willing to be helpful. But I had to try; I had to find Robert at all costs.

"Um, yes. My friend—his name's Robert. He drives a small, red sports car, speaks at some kind of meetings in towns all over. Well, he's tall, um, dark hair, um, a little younger than me. Seen him around?" Geez, why had I blurted all that out? Crazy alert.

"Sorry, no. Anything else I can help you with?" His eyes darted toward the door and I knew he just wanted me to leave. I shook my head no and slunk out in shame. Did you expect me to do anything else? It wouldn't have made a difference if I had.

And that's how the rest of my night went. Café after café, restaurant after restaurant, convenience store after convenience store, motel after motel. I'd look for his car outside, never seeing it. Then, I'd go inside to look for him and was always turned away. Always I felt like I wasn't welcome in no uncertain terms. I wonder if they would have changed their tune if they'd known about the brand new clothes and money in my pack. I doubt it; I screamed homeless to them. In fact, it might've made things worse—people would've thought I'd stolen the money.

Several times during the evening, I sat on some curb, dejected. I watched people go by as I munched on some crackers or a granola bar. I guess I was hoping that Robert would happen to be walking or driving by, but of course that never happened.

Yeah, I know what you're thinking. This plan was even crazier in practice than in theory. No argument from me. I even got so desperate at one point that I started to look for churches as I walked up and down the streets of the town. None of them had any lights on, so I kept walking and walking. Or, rather, dragging my tired feet and body from place to place. My hope in my futile attempt at finding Robert was fading fast. Don't judge; you'd never even have tried to find Robert in the first place. You've got what you need. Desperation isn't your friend. Options for me were slim—no, make that none. Religion was his thing; going to churches seemed to make some sense.

Then, at one church, a dim light was on in the way back, and when I tried the door, it opened with a loud squeak. Hesitating, I looked around to see if anyone was watching me; it was quite late at that point, but no one was around.

As I slunk into the quiet building, I saw that the light was a simple one hitting on a single spot. It was highlighting only a wooden cross hung on the wall in the front of the main room. There were chairs placed in several rows in semicircles facing the cross, but no one was there.

Creeping towards the front, I, with care, sank onto a soft padded chair in the far back row. Church had never helped me before when people were there, but maybe it'd be better now. A place of solitude for a few moments, where I could gather my thoughts and reflect on what to do next. You know, that feeling like being in the forest? Peace? Quiet? Being completely alone? What better place in a city than an empty building? Simple enough.

Slipping my pack to the floor, I pulled my feet up under me and curled into a ball. *Are you there, God? Are you real? Can you help me? I need Robert; do you know where he is?*

My heart was beating so hard it hurt, tears were flowing yet again, and I didn't care if they were ever going to stop. All I ever seemed to do was cry; there seemed no point in the constant fighting of the feeling to weep anymore. I couldn't believe I'd gone so far that I was now sitting here in this lonely church thinking that I could talk to this god. Nothing happened, nothing changed, no one was there. There was only me and the single beam of light on a silly piece of wood. Someone had forgotten to lock the door and flip a switch. Thus, I'd been able to enter this church without permission after seeing the light had been left on.

No, I couldn't be seeking this god. After all, if what people said was true, that church was god's house, then there couldn't be a god. This church was cold and empty; God wasn't here. It wasn't a home, it wasn't a place where someone living and real could dwell. Your home is warm and welcoming, right? Your guests feel at ease, like they've been there before. Like they could come anytime they wanted and it'd never be a problem or a bother. That's not how this church felt. It was only an empty shell, like no one had ever been here before and wouldn't ever be here again.

Shivering with the chill that passed over me with the thought, I knew I was in real trouble. If god wasn't real, then I was as good as lost forever. Lost in the endless void of homelessness and despair that I'd forced myself to be exiled in. There was no going back, there was no hope, there was no future. But, what about all the things Robert had shown me? What about the two cards with the same verse on them? What about all that I'd learned by the simple act of telling Robert some of my stories? There had to be something more; this couldn't be all there was. Life has to have some meaning, or what's the point?

"Where are you?!" I screamed at the top of my lungs as I jumped up, my hands balled into fists as I shook them at the sky in vain.

To be honest, I don't know if I wanted to know where this god was or where Robert was. At that moment, it didn't seem to matter; I needed someone—anyone who could start to clear my muddled thinking and end the torment, even if but for a moment.

My words echoed back at me in the empty room, and I realized that I needed to ask myself that question. Who I was had been lost; maybe I never knew who I was because I was always trying to hide from something. Or someone. Was I still a frightened girl hiding in the corner so my father wouldn't find me and beat me again? Only now I was in adult clothing and hiding from the whole world, who I now felt was out to get me for my evil deeds? Yes, more than likely, I still was just that scared, lonely child. How do you come out of hiding after so much time? How do you learn who you are? Who you could be? Maybe there was a way past evil.

Every step I took now seemed to lead me to more questions and no answers. I'd thought I had everything figured out a few short days ago; now I knew that I'd never even been close. *Cindy, you need Robert. Stop wasting time in this empty building; you need to get back out there and keep looking. He isn't here; move on.*

I'd lost my way for a while, been sidetracked in what I'd intended to do, but never again. You've been there, I'm sure. As quickly as I could, I snatched my pack up, and stomped out of that church without even a look back. If god is real, I don't know where he lives, but people are wrong—he doesn't live in a church. Next time you tell me that, I'll tell you you're wrong and why. Trust me.

With renewed strength, I marched up the street to the first gas station and walked in like I owned the place. No hesitation on my part this time, I went right up to the clerk. I slapped the counter so hard my hand hurt. "I'm looking for my friend. He drives a red sports car and is tall, dark, a little younger than me. Can you help me?"

"No. What's your problem? I don't want any kind of trouble here." He didn't even get a good look at me but thought he had me pegged regardless. Boy, was he wrong. But I'd been getting this kind of attitude all night, and now I wasn't going to let it get to me.

"Fine, thanks anyway." Waving as I left, I knew I had to keep trying.

Yeah, I'm sure I ended up in some of the same places twice; I wasn't paying much attention. Frantic desperation was the only thing keeping me going. I kept looking, but defeat was beginning to look like it would win despite my half-time pep rally. Like those perpetual underdog teams who never win. You root for them because you believe at some point their luck will change. It never does, no matter what.

That was me. This night was no exception to that rule. Robert was nowhere to be found. This town wasn't very big and, unfortunately, he'd had a rather large head start on me. My pity party from yesterday had taken too long. Regardless of what Robert had said the last time I'd seen him, he hadn't hung around for me, and I'd lost my chance. So stupid of me to think he'd be waiting for me when I was ready. That my once-in-a-lifetime chance meeting with him could happen twice, and that I wasn't stranded on my own again.

Who knows what time I finally gave up and admitted defeat. The moon had been up for what seemed like hours by then. Between the faint light of the street lamps and the distant glow of the moon, it was hard to see much of anything. My search was becoming harder with each passing minute. Red cars were hard to tell apart from blue ones unless they were parked well away from the shadows. Everything now seemed black or gray, you know how it is. My heart was telling me to continue on, but my head was telling me to find a place to sleep for a while. Maybe try again in the morning. My head won. No surprise there.

As I was making one more round in the last two motel parking lots, I spied a person huddled in the alley, tucked between the two motels sleeping without a blanket or even a coat. The night was chilly after such a warm day, and I felt sorry for this person who had no blanket while I had two now. My day had been a complete waste of time, but this was something I could do to redeem my time.

As quietly as I could, I lowered my pack to the ground. I dug out my old blanket and bent to lay it over what I discovered was an old man and paused for a moment. His white hair glowed in the moonlight. His skin was the color of dark-stained mahogany and blended into the shadows so well that he was almost invisible. His tattered shirt exposed most of his arms and a long strip of his back, revealing white scars from a life that was quite likely harder than mine. Sad that a life would end like this, alone in a dirty alley, cold and hungry.

I reached out to touch his hand for a second, and I could feel the iciness of his skin on mine. Concerned that he might not make it through the night, my breath caught in my throat. With care, I pulled the blanket as tightly as I could around him, tucking in the edges. Giving him a slight pat on the shoulder, I wished him goodnight without a word. He didn't stir, only kept up his loud snoring in his spot between a dumpster and the brick of the building wall.

From experience, I knew that this was a good spot when you didn't have a tent. The brick would hold a little residual heat, and so was a bit warmer than anywhere else. The buildings and dumpster provided some shelter if it should rain. You could find worse spots, but then again, you could find better ones. Better yet, you could not send your life into such a downward spiral that you ended up in this pickle in the first place. But, I digress.

Next, I pulled out my last box of crackers, my last two cans of tuna, and a couple of granola bars and placed them beside him. Tomorrow, he'd wake up and think it was Christmas. Even you'd have known to do that. Give him one of the basics he didn't have—food. Okay, maybe not. But by hearing my tale, maybe now you will. Yes? No? Maybe? Please?

I'd have left a few dollars as well, but I could smell the booze on his breath and knew it wouldn't do any good. I didn't want to be responsible for enabling him to go out and buy more alcohol; it was the last thing he needed.

If it hadn't been the middle of the night in a strange town, I would've found a shelter. Yes, that's basic number two. I wanted to report his whereabouts to someone, let them figure out what to do for him. Unfortunately, I had no idea where to go for help in this town, so what little I'd done was going to have to be enough for now.

Maybe tomorrow you can do something more, I thought with a sigh. As I stood watching him, almost like a mother would watch an infant, I saw him snuggle into the blanket. It was unconscious, as he tried to get more comfortable and warm. Do you do that too in your nice, cozy bed at night? I know I do with my worn blanket.

"'For I was hungry, and you gave Me something to eat; I was thirsty, and you gave Me something to drink...to the extent that you did it to one of these brothers of Mine, even the least of them, you did it to Me'."

Spinning around to see who was speaking, I was surprised to find Robert standing behind me in the alley.

"That's what the Bible says—giving to the poor is actually giving to God. See, you're part of His plan—you're good, not evil."

Concerned that I was dreaming this whole scene, I was afraid to look away. I didn't want Robert to disappear again; I needed him. My heartbeat quickened, and I could hear my pulse pounding in my ears. It was so loud that I was afraid it would drown out anything more that Robert had to say.

"How can you say that after what I've done?" I said.

"Because, even after that unfortunate incident in Oklahoma, here you are, being kind. A simple act in an alley, giving what little you've got to a complete stranger. You're doing what Annie did, even though you faulted her for giving away what little she had. Yet, here you are, doing the same. Only someone who is good deep down would help another. Plus, I know God's still been helping you, protecting you in every step you've taken since the event that you think was so awful."

He held his hand out to me, a gesture of acceptance, of love. Though his face held no discernible expression, I felt that he was smiling at me, smiling with all the warmth and love he could send.

Picking up my pack, I felt tears begin a slow slide down my cheeks. I was afraid to speak, afraid to go to him, afraid that none of this was real.

"I'm glad you found me. I've been looking for you all night." I was hesitating; this seemed too easy. He was acting like what I'd done to Trisha was nothing, no big deal. Not the vile act it was. I couldn't be good; sharing was part of the code of being homeless, something I did without even thinking about it. When you can only carry so much, you can't hoard. When you know if you try to hoard it'll be stolen, you see the value in sharing. It's easy when you think about it. True, not all of us share, but not all of you do either.

"I know, but you needed to finally come to the point where you wanted to learn more about God and seek Him with all your heart. I waited until you were ready before I approached you." He was now holding both hands out to me, willing me to join him.

"How'd you know when I was ready?" Tilting my head, I squinted, trying to get a better look at him in the faint light. No help there—his face was, as it often was, completely blank and unreadable. Yet somehow, there was this sense that if I would only go to him, then everything would be fine. That feeling was getting stronger by the second.

My hands began to sweat despite the chill in the air, and my pack was becoming hard to hold. I knew I'd have to make a decision soon—to move or stay frozen. Was this real or not? My head didn't hurt so much anymore; maybe I didn't have a concussion and yesterday was a fluke.

What to do? What to do? What to do? And why do you have to keep asking yourself that? Damn it—make a choice!

"You passed this same sleeping man several times tonight but didn't stop to help him until now." He waved to the man now nestled in my old, worn blanket. All of a sudden, I was ashamed that I'd given him the ratty one and not the brand new one.

"Oh." Frowning, I began to have doubts about Robert's intentions again.

How could he have known that I'd walked by this guy several times tonight? Not unless he'd been watching me the whole time. My premonition from yesterday about how he was stalking me must've been right, which was a rather scary and uncomfortable thought. But how would he have seen me without me seeing him? Plus, what Robert had said made no sense at all. What difference did it make when I helped this guy? The fact was that I'd never noticed this homeless man until now, so I couldn't have helped him earlier. There simply was no way I could've been so blind as to miss another homeless person. But, then again, this whole day had been rather surreal, so maybe I had missed him.

"There's something else on your mind. What is it?" He still hadn't moved, but then again, neither had I.

"I found the card from Dave, and it's got one of the verses you gave me on it. Why?" Kicking myself for asking this now, when I was beginning to doubt him again, I almost told him to forget it.

"Why did God try twice to give you the same message?" He smiled at me as gently as someone would at a child who's being slow to grasp something new in school.

Despite how I was feeling, I gave an eager nod in reply. I could feel my cheeks grow hot. I was being pretty foolish to trust someone who'd been watching me, waiting for the right time to pounce. But it's clear that I'm not one to learn lessons well. Somehow, I still wanted him to help me understand this god and religion thing—to help me understand myself. After all, he'd said he'd be there when I was ready, and now I was. I should've expected him to have a way to find me; this shouldn't have been a surprise, and I shouldn't be so upset. Like asking a snake not to eat the mouse in its cage.

Okay, you're right, bad analogy.

"Because you didn't get it the first time; if you'd read the card then, we might not have ever met. There wouldn't have been a need for us to."

"Huh." He had me there. So, this god was watching me and was using people like Dave and Robert to do it. It still seemed a little weird that something so powerful as a god needed spies. Then again, god wasn't here, and people were. How else was he supposed to know what was going on?

My other questions were even more important, but I wasn't ready to ask them yet. It was enough right now to know that this god all of a sudden seemed very real. My heartfelt cry hadn't gone unanswered; I'd found Robert. Well, as a point of fact, for those of you keeping track, Robert had found me. Now everything would be all right. Not perfect, not great, but good enough for me to be able to go on. For at least a few seconds more.

My feet finally became unglued from the pavement, and we began walking up the alley. Then up the street until I noticed his car a short distance away. Had it been there in that space all along? Because, I swear, I'd walked by the same spot I-don't-know-how-many times that night. Never once had I seen any car that had even sort of looked like his.

He unlocked the car door and opened it for me after taking my pack from me yet again. It felt comfortable to lean on him. I know it shouldn't have. But I had the sense that I only needed to trust him enough to not freak out again and then I would have my answer. That trusting part wasn't going to be easy. Settling into the car, I didn't know where we were going. But I knew we would go down my memory lane as far as I was willing to go.

Robert said, "If it's okay with you, we can sit in the car; that way we'll have some privacy since it's almost midnight."

"That's fine." I leaned my head back against the seat, thankful to be off my aching feet for a while. I was a dead man walking — well, sitting. But my brain was nowhere near ready to shut down; I had too many unanswered questions

He reached into the backseat and grabbed a small cooler. "I've got snacks and drinks if you'd like anything." He placed the cooler on my lap, the ever considerate host — even if we were only sitting in his car.

Opening the cooler, I pulled out an apple juice and gulped it down like someone who was dying of thirst, oh-so-glad for something to drink other than tuna water. I should've gotten something to drink in one of the many places I'd asked for Robert during the night, rather than letting them all run me off, like the spineless worm that I so often am.

"So, first off, I need to finish the last story..."

"There's no need, Cindy. I can guess what you left out that made you so upset. Trisha was in your room; she went through your things and found your alcohol and pills. Enough said." He gave me a sad, all-knowing kind of smile and gave my shoulder a soft pat.

Fighting back the tears I was afraid I'd never have been able to stop if I'd let them start again, I closed my eyes. I no longer wanted to wallow in self-pity and tears forever, I wanted the peace that Robert had. He was always so calm, and I needed that with such desperation in my life. Here, I'd been berating myself since yesterday for even starting to tell him the story. Then, I hated myself for not finishing it, and here he already knew the whole story about me — well, that one anyway. How he knew so many things without them being said was a complete mystery to me. He had a wisdom I couldn't comprehend.

"Why do you care so much about me?" I asked in a soft whisper. To Robert, to his god, it didn't matter.

"Because you are a life worth saving. Even you're beginning to think that there's something left in you worth saving. That's why you came looking for me today, to find out more about God and how He can help you. The thing is, God saw your value long before you did, so He's been providing for you and protecting you for years. Through all your heartache and pain, He's been there for you even when you didn't see it."

"But how, after all I've done? Does your god even know what I've done?" This was the most important question — well that, and did he know I was evil. My voice was a shout, loud enough to split ear drums in the confined space. Robert didn't even wince, didn't seemed concerned in the least.

"Yes, God knows everything, but God gives gifts based on what He's done, not on what we've done. The Bible says that 'every good thing given and every perfect gift is from above, coming down from the Father of lights.' He's given you many gifts over the years, some more obvious than others." He took my hand and that now comforting feeling of electricity warmed my body from head to toe. He gave me a reassuring look, and somehow I knew what he was telling me was true, but I didn't want to believe it. I never get gifts. Not from my parents, not from anyone. Gifts are for good girls. "Cindy, you've been stuck. All you are, all you see, all you want to be is a victim. Wanting nothing more than to wallow in your guilt. Choose something more. Choose what God has been trying to give you."

All I could do was pull my hand away, tuck it between my legs and look at the floor. *Was he right? Had I put myself in this role? Not my circumstances like I'd always thought?*

With a distinct catch in his voice, Robert said, "It's very late; let's go to the motel and get some sleep. We'll talk more tomorrow."

I followed him out of the car and walked in a daze to the motel across the street, where he directed me to the room that was mine. I never turned on the light, only put my pack down near the door and flopped onto the bed, still dressed.

It was only after I'd laid down that I realized he had at some point earlier checked into this motel. He had gotten two rooms, all the while having no idea when or if I'd reappear.

Then, something else hit me. At the diner with the flamboyant waitress, Robert had said something about her seeing 'the light.' Now he'd said something about gifts coming from the father of 'lights.' Was that the same thing? If so, what was this 'light'? I'd dismissed it earlier and now was wishing I hadn't. But, as my thoughts were chasing each other around my head, sleep overcame me.

Chapter 17

As was his apparent habit, Robert woke me at the crack of dawn with a rap on the door. "I'm leaving in ten minutes; I hope you'll join me. Meet me at the car."

"Okay, but I may need a few more minutes than that!" I replied as I groggily got out of bed and, in a dreamlike state, took a quick shower.

My eyes were opened in slits, and I was only going through the motions, trying to be as presentable as possible without ever looking at myself. You ever done that? It's not the easiest way to get ready for the day. I had no idea where we were going so early or if Robert had any kind of plan, but at this point it didn't matter. I needed to know more about this god of his. I was sticking to him like glue until I could make more sense of a few things. Or until I was at least satisfied that I'd learned all I could from him. Yeah, I know that sounds rather selfish of me. I don't care. Nothing else in my life has been about me getting something I needed — until now. This was my new basic need — it was more important than those other things I've been harping to you about.

As soon as we got in the car, I ignored the bag of what I took to be pastries on my seat and put it on the floor. I took a few sips of the coffee to settle my nerves. You're right again, not the best idea. The caffeine hit my empty stomach like a lightning bolt making me more on edge than ever. Don't know why I was on edge, other than massive lack of sleep the past few days.

"So where do you want to go, Cindy?" He gave me a brief look before returning his eyes to the road. A look that said so much. Pain. Love. Confusion. Hope. Anger. Happiness. Don't ask me to explain it.

But Robert's question was the proverbial ten- thousand-dollar question, one that I'd asked myself only moments ago as well. But I didn't know. Going home seemed like a stupid idea. There was nothing for me there. All I'd remembered about my parents, my husband, and my old life made me see that. Things I'd been stuffing for years now were out. Home was no place for me. No, I needed to find god. Oh yes, you heard me right. Not a church. Not religion. Not a person who knows god. But this thing, this entity, this being. This God. Yes, I was willing to jump off that cliff, take the leap of faith I'd heard about. It was now a hunger as strong as any I'd ever felt when my stomach had been empty for days.

"Away from the pain." I whimpered in a pain filled cry.

"As the Bible says, 'Whoever seeks to keep his life will lose it, and whoever loses his life will preserve it'." Robert looked at me for a moment. It seemed like fire was coming from his eyes, his gaze was so intense.

"Are you saying that I have to lose my life before I can gain what I've always wanted? That's insane. Especially since I'm not sure even now what I want. A few days ago, I thought that I might finally want to go home, but now I'm sure that I don't even want that." Was he now pushing me towards suicide? Now that I was off that path?

"Not exactly, it means surrendering your life to something greater than yourself. Then you will see greater things. Because the Bible also says, 'Give, and it will be given to you. They will pour into your lap a good measure—pressed down, shaken together, and running over.' God's blessings are endless."

"Well, then what about Annie? If what you're saying is right, she was giving until it hurt but was getting nothing in return." Annie had seemed happy. Was that the difference? God wouldn't help her because she was satisfied with having nothing?

"What if you hadn't gotten so angry over Annie's situation? What if you'd stayed and helped her build something good? Or, for that matter, how do you know that the day after you left, someone didn't come in with a work crew to fix up her house? Or clear her property? Or give her a new car? Either way, Annie needed nothing more than what little she had. She already had everything she needed. She had God. The blessing from both of those scenarios would've been to the people trying to help her, not to Annie. You know that to be true and have seen it—I know you have because you've seen God's blessings work in so many ways. Yet you've continued to run from Him."

Tap, tap, tap went his fingers on the steering wheel again, drilling into my brain like so many times before. He needed me to see this.

"The Bible says 'And we know that God causes all things to work together for good to those who love God, to those who are called according to His purpose.' You could have that in your life as well, if you'd only begin to believe in God." His face had the grimmest expression I'd ever seen on anyone. It was like he was asking me at that moment if I wanted to live or die because there was a gun pointed at my temple.

But I was sure it wasn't a simple choice at all. There had to be so much more to life than this faith of his acting like magic and making everything good. His attempt to show me I was good had begun to soften me somewhat, but he didn't know all there was to that. He didn't know the seed that had been planted when I was a child, the seed that had been nurtured by my father and finally bloomed when I met Trisha.

Without thinking, I began to gnaw on my fingernails, destroying the even lines that I'd cut the other day with my new nail clippers. Looking at the raw edges, all I could think was that this was another wasted effort on my part. But pretty nails weren't a major concern in my life. I needed so much more to bring stability into what was becoming a teeter-totter of an emotional life. Maybe it was better when I was lying face down in the proverbial mud pit of life. But when I was under a tree yesterday — Was it only yesterday? — I'd gotten up, determined to find something more. I wanted something more.

And Robert had found me. Yes, I'd cracked open a doorway in my mind to let this god in. Now here I was entertaining the notion, no, I was starting to believe that all this was real. That somehow this god was interested in me. Yeah, I'm sure he'd be more interested in me if I'd start reading the Bible stuffed into my pack. But there hadn't been anytime to do that yet, now that I was wanting this god.

Everything had been laid out for me. So many people had been pointing in god's direction, but still I hesitated. If god cared for me, there still was the problem of my parents. Robert's answer from earlier wasn't sitting well with me, but maybe there was more than he'd said.

That verse he'd quoted moments before said you had to be called for things to work out. No way was I called by this god as a child, at least I don't think I was. Was it fair to expect that kind of pressure to be put on a child? To think that it was the child's responsibility to turn to this god for help? Long years of experience had taught me that life wasn't fair. But even to me, it seemed to be beyond the limits of what anyone could accept. You don't expect a five-year-old to pay the mortgage. So why expect someone so young to find something as important as god?

"Where's god?" My whisper echoed in the car. I hadn't meant to say it out loud, but my cry came back to me as a haunting voice floating on a distant wind.

"What do you mean?" His voice was like a soothing salve for my troubled soul. I started to feel ashamed that I was having such conflicting thoughts again.

"When I couldn't find you last night, I went to a church, but your god wasn't there. It was a cold, empty building, and I felt more lost than I'd ever been before. People say it's god's house, but they're wrong. So, if this god is real, where is he?" I looked at Robert for the longest time.

I actually looked at him, as he sat in the driver's seat of not only the car but of my life. I assessed this man I was placing so much trust and faith in. His face was smooth and unlined one moment, then worn and wrinkled by the cares of the world the next.

His fingers glided across the steering wheel, hardly controlling the car, then gripping it tightly with his fists turning into hard knots the next. The tension flowed through his hands before they flew without effort again. His chest hardly moved under his T-shirt. Then, his breathing became quick to the point that he was almost hyperventilating. Finally, he relaxed once more. He was ageless, timeless, felt emotions in nanoseconds. It should've scared the heck out of me but didn't.

"The Bible says that if we believe in Jesus then 'God abides in him, and he in God.' So yes, the church is empty of God if you're the only one there because you don't believe yet. However, God's here in this car because I believe. God has been with you throughout this journey because you were often with believers. And God was with you as a child because all children are given the grace to be believers. When you went to church with your grandmother, you felt a sense of wonder and awe, correct?"

"Yes, but that wasn't faith. That was fairy tales, lights glowing, and magic." I frowned. He always seemed to know so much about me and what I was thinking. Even things I was thinking before we met. I had no idea how he did it, but he was the best psychic I'd ever run across.

"No, childlike wonder is God's greatest gift to children — natural faith. When it's nurtured and allowed to grow, people turn into adults who know and understand God and his word. When it's abused and put down, people turn into cynics. Or worse, depressed, angry, vengeful riffraff, only out to hurt everyone and anyone who comes across their path. You fell somewhere in the middle, unsure of yourself and the world around you. But, instead of finding out how to solve your problems, you ran and ran and ran. That seed of natural faith's still in you, Cindy. Or else you wouldn't be questioning this now. You wouldn't have been questioning things for years."

"Oh." If he was right, it explained so much. But if he was right, it also meant that I'd been running from my answer for years instead of towards it. Feeling so stupid, I almost laughed.

"So why did your father tell you that you were worthless?" His face was back to a frown.

There were many little reasons. And one big reason was burned into my brain because my father had kept reminding me of it. *Hmm, should you go there, Cindy?* Didn't seem to be any reason not to. Robert more than likely knew anyways. He knew everything else without me telling him.

"When I was five or six, a man came to our house for one of my father's many drinking parties. He ended up in my room. He was big and scary to my little eyes, like the boogeyman monsters in books. My door didn't have a doorknob because I'd, like a fool, tried to lock my dad out once after a rather vicious beating. So anyone could walk right in on me.

"Anyways, he stood there staring at me, his fingers still stuck in the hole in the door where the knob should've been. Called me pretty. Then he came into my room. He sat on the edge of my bed and put a huge hand on the bedspread where my left knee was. Even with the layer of bedding between him and me, I could feel the heat of his hand burning my leg. Despite the warmth, I shivered. I could smell smoke and beer; I didn't like that scent on my father, and I definitely didn't like it on whoever this was.

"Desperate to make myself smaller, I curled into a ball. Stopping me, he gripped my knee tight enough to hurt. He began to slide the covers off the bed, revealing my blue PJs and leaving me hugging myself on a corner of my now-naked bed. He slid his hand under my PJ top and rubbed my chest. I remember wetting my pants, feeling so cold and alone. He was starting to uncurl me, trying to get one hand in my PJ shorts, when my father came in my room.

"My father yelled, his face purple with anger, veins popping out all over his neck and forehead. At the time, I had no idea what was going on. I only remember wanting this scary guy to go away, and now I was getting yelled at — again — which meant I was going to get a good whipping for whatever this guy was doing even though I had nothing to do with it."

Stopping my narrative, I realized that I'd curled into a ball in the car. Tangled up in the seatbelt, I was wedged against the door. Even now, all these years later, I felt like I was there. The terrified little girl who had no idea she was moments away from being molested by a drunk.

Robert didn't reach out to me, but I felt a wave of peace flooding over me. "You were only a little girl. You've got to let go of that shame. That hurt, that pain. You don't have to tell me the rest if you don't want to."

Resting my face on the cool glass of the window, I closed my eyes. Strength filled me, why I don't know. But now I knew I had to face what had been done to me. If I didn't, it would continue to haunt me. If I did, then I'd be free from it.

"Well, the man looked happy when he jumped up and left, seconds after my father burst onto the scene. Of course he was happy, he wouldn't have to face my father's wrath. That was mine to face alone—again.

"I jumped up to change the sheets, on the far side of the bed, hoping that just this once I'd escape punishment. Knowing it was always best to never look right at my father, I looked down at my feet. Striding to me, he bunched the fabric of my PJ top in his hand, picked me up like I was a rag doll, and shook me hard. My teeth rattled, my whole body hurt, and I knew it was only the beginning.

"My father smelled like smoke and beer same as the other man, my stomach heaved, and I tried hard not to be sick. My father hated it when I threw up on him when he was shaking me. He blamed me for the man in my room; I think he said I'd lured him in. I don't know how long he hit me that night, but as he did so, he kept repeating over and over, 'You're worthless. You're evil.' He started with his fists, moved on to a big book." My eyes were still closed, but for once they were dry. Images of my father hadn't moved me to tears.

My childhood had taught me that people who went to church wore two faces. The man who'd felt me up was one. I saw him the next Christmas at mass, greeting people at the door. The priest at the church was another. How he could have ever ignored what was obviously going on in my home, I'll never understand. So, yes, Robert was right, if children have natural faith, mine was never nurtured. But a new faith within me was being nurtured now. I'd be the one to feed and grow it. I wanted this God more than anything else. No more sitting on the fence, waving about in the wind. I was picking a side.

"I think you now see that your father doesn't have power over you anymore," Robert stated the obvious. When I peeped at him, you would've thought I'd given him the greatest gift he'd ever been given.

"Yes. Now don't get too excited. I'm not sure that means your god is real." It was hard for me to say this with a straight face. But I wasn't ready to admit to Robert that I wanted to know his god. Even you've got to see how wrong I am most of the time. It was probable that I was wrong now thinking that God was real.

"Okay, so how did your quest start?" His grin hadn't diminished at all by my last remark. You betcha he knew which way I was leaning.

How did this journey start? Did it have a set beginning, or had I always wanted to run away from my life? The wanting to wander off and start anew, everything luring me to the unknown? The genuine need to begin again with a new identity, a new soul? I wanted more than anything to be without the emptiness deep within. To be found and no longer lost among the sea of misery, to be whole and not feeling like I was shattered all the time.

No, the journey had always been within me, from the moment I was born. Because abuse leaves you in so many pieces, half of them missing, that you know you can't ever be complete. Because abuse leaves you in a shell so thick you can't ever get out to get those missing pieces. You're frozen, never to be whole again. So, I guess I was destined to be a stranger who didn't have a place, to always be alone and without a connection to others.

Even this journey to "find" myself was bound to fail because I could never fill the hole that was me—I was only a void. Thus my feelings of emptiness were always there; it was who I was, and it felt like nothing could change it. For a brief moment, I had thought that maybe having a child of my own might change things, but I couldn't get pregnant. Therefore, when my husband, Bill, sent me the divorce papers, there was nothing left for me to cling to. What little I had was gone. He'd left me for someone younger, prettier, and pregnant—he was getting everything he wanted.

The day those papers came, I sat alone in our house; it'd never felt like a home. It was too large and had been decorated by a designer rather than me. Everything was uncomfortable, formal, not my style. We'd hosted parties there while I played the dutiful hostess, knowing that if anything went wrong, there'd be heck to pay later in the form of another of my husband's rages. At least he, unlike my father, was careful to never hit me where it'd show. Thus I never had to hide the evidence of the beatings afterward.

I'd spent so many hours alone in the house I hated so much, but there was little choice — it was my personal prison. Bill knew when I should leave for work and when I should be home. If I didn't set the alarm for the house within a certain time frame of that, he would accuse me of sneaking around. Like I'd ever invite another man into my life. Between my father and my husband, I knew men were bad news; best to be avoided.

So the day the papers came, I knew I'd earned my way out. Every blow landed had gotten me an inch closer to freedom. If I went along with everything, there was nothing more Bill could do to me. The divorce was inevitable once I learned I couldn't have children. Thanks to all the abuse I'd endured as a child, I was sterile. Not like Bill's forever kicking and punching my abdomen had helped matters. I was the shy Plain Jane accountant who was supposed to have been the baby-making factory. Once I'd failed, it'd been pointless to keep me around for only a punching bag.

Of course, he waited to divorce me until one of his many bimbos was knocked up. No reason he should make the same mistake twice. No, he wasn't going to marry someone else who couldn't produce an heir to his kingdom. I almost pitied the poor woman. Wondered if she'd already been slapped around. If she knew she was marrying a drunk. If she knew she wasn't the only tart my husband had on the side. Faithfulness wasn't something he was ever going to be capable of.

When that last suicide attempt failed, I knew I had to find meaning somehow or find a way to succeed in suicide. When I got out of the hospital, I had nowhere to go. I'd made no plans for living as a divorced woman. That's when I marched into the bank, closed my account, put a few things in my car, and left. After, of course, going to another doctor. One who without knowing had helped me with my escape hatch for what was to be my last suicide attempt. Somewhere, there had to be an answer, even if I was unsure of the question. It seemed certain that other people didn't feel the pain I felt all the time, and I needed to find out why. I needed to understand 'happy'.

But so much fed into my sense of needing to escape. The needing to find freedom. Needing something to change who I was on a fundamental level. All the times my father had beat me. All the times my mother ignored me. All of the times various people in my life had told me I was a bad little girl. All of the times my husband abused me emotionally and physically. Added to that was the fact that I was scarred, flawed, imperfect on the outside as well as the inside. There were scars on my wrists and arms from suicide attempts. There were scars on my heart from all the emotional trauma. So how do I answer Robert's question?

"I wanted something more. Needed something more. Longed for something more." I thought it summed it up in a nice little package with a bow. Yeah, it was the easy way out. But Robert seemed to know my thoughts anyways, so what was the point in rehashing it?

"I understand that. I think you're beginning to believe God is real. You can see how you've been trading truth for lies. You don't want the lies anymore. You want only the truth. So, you're ready to start seeking Him. Run to Him not from Him," Robert said.

I wish I'd known to run to Jesus all those years ago. I wish I hadn't thought flawed believers and God were one and the same. I wish I'd known what truth was.

Chapter 18

Waking with a start, I realized that I was no longer in Robert's car. Looking around, I sat up, brushing my tousled hair out of my eyes, trying to get a handle on what was going on. I couldn't find him or his car. I was alone, sitting on a park bench in the middle of what might've been a town square. I had no idea what town or even what state.

Why do you never know where you are anymore? How did you even get here?

The dawn was starting to break, and making out the license plates on the few cars parked on the street with the aid of the dim light from the street lamps was like trying to see underwater. Missouri, huh; I didn't think we'd gone that far or even in that direction. We must've taken a major detour south somewhere. Yet, for some reason, I'd completely missed that fact.

How long had I been asleep in the car? Ten, twelve hours? How was that even possible?

My pack was at my feet, with a grocery bag beside it and a travel mug of what I took to be coffee. *At least he provided breakfast and maybe lunch before he ditched me,* I thought with some remorse. Why did he change his mind about taking me anywhere I wanted to go? This wouldn't have been my pick for a place to dump me in, but hey, what difference did it make in the long run? By this stage of the game, I knew that I'd been wrong to set my feet towards my hometown. Gotta know how glad I was that I was still thousands of miles from there. You avoid monsters; you don't run towards them. Well, unless you have a death wish. But I no longer wanted to die.

"So what have you learned, Cindy?" I could hear Robert's voice clear as a bell. I could smell his faint muskiness. I could feel the warmth of his touch as if he was holding my hand. It was if he was right there with me. For once, I didn't mind the jolt of electricity I was feeling. It was just like I'd felt so many times before when he'd taken my hand.

My fingers tingled, and my heart began to beat faster. I watched as the sun began its climb into the sky. The darkness was being chased away. The cool was being replaced with warmth. Everything was signaling the beginning of a new day. I was finally starting my new beginning too. There was a fire in my soul, burning as bright as this new sun was. I'd been so very wrong before. Running away hadn't started a new life for me; rather, it'd only made my tragic life a moving target. Hard to hit with disaster, sure, but not impossible. Today was different; I now knew things I never did before. I knew where I went wrong, and it had nothing to do with what I had thought it did. Today a switch had been flipped and the whole world was now plain for me to see. I was no longer stuck. I was no longer helpless. I was no longer a victim of my past.

I sat like a statue for a long time, soaking in the energy, feeding off of it. With each new breath I was taking, I was gaining more strength. For the first time in my life, I felt like I had a source of power, and I never wanted to let go of it.

You're right, I'm sounding all crazy again. Robert wasn't really there anymore, and he wasn't the source of this power. We couldn't have stayed connected forever, and thus we'd needed to go our separate ways. Yet, for now, this felt so incredible to pretend he was still there. I missed him so much that every part of me ached, even though he couldn't have been gone more than a few hours. He was my only friend, and his strength had helped me come to terms with my past, both what I'd done and what had been done to me. But God was where I needed to be focusing, where the power must've been coming from. It was the only way this made sense. Okay, even then, ending up in a town almost a thousand miles from where I last remembered being was a little weird.

Shaking my head, I almost laughed at how foolish I'd been only a few short days ago when Robert and I first met. I had thought that the strange feelings when he touched me was lust on his part, but I knew better now. No, these feelings were the power I'd been needing to move on. The jump start I needed to get out of the rut, because, after all, ruts are only very long graves. I was so glad that I had never told him what my initial thoughts about him were. However, I'm sure he suspected based on what he'd said about "all men not being the same." Well, that and some of my funny reactions to him on occasion. I was sure I'd hurt him, but he never showed much of a response. I don't know how he had so much restraint in the face of my manic behavior.

And now I'd lost him; he'd put me out of the car in this town without a word. Did he feel that I'd shared enough? Did he feel that I'd shared too much? Did he think that he couldn't help me anymore? Did he no longer want to help me? Once again, I was faced with being on my own without a plan. Wanting Robert to reappear like a genie I could call at will, I almost started calling out his name. I stopped myself before I did—no need to sound like an idiot crying out for a shadow in the night.

But with Robert gone, what would I do now? Thanks to him, I had the seed money to take care of my physical needs for a while. However, I now knew that those weren't the basics I'd always thought they were. No, food and shelter weren't important when it came right down to it. It explained why they'd never satisfied me in all these years. There had been so many others who, like Robert, had tried to show me what was of utmost importance all this time. Show me what would satisfy the deepest hunger within me—God and God alone. I'd ignored them, pretending I couldn't see any of it.

Would Robert leave you here, Cindy, if there wasn't someone you could turn to? Would he be so cruel as to take you only so far and then abandon you before you're able to make it on your own? No, he must've felt you're ready for this next step, whatever that may be.

There had always been someone who'd been wanting to help. Wanting to tell me about their faith, about their god—that was evident in all the stories I'd shared with Robert. There were so many other examples I hadn't shared, so many other good people who must've had some understanding of the love of God. Who knew what Robert had been trying to teach me, trying to remind me of what others had already taught me. This town, then, must be what I'd felt drawn to a few short days ago when I had felt the unmistakable urge to go "home"—when I'd had the false belief that home meant my hometown, the place of so much ugliness and pain. No, home wasn't what I had thought it was.

So, what makes this place special? Have you been here before, Cindy? Does anything about it seem familiar? Could this be your "home" that you've been seeking?

Looking around again, I could see a statue of a man and a sign as proud as could be stating, "Welcome to Liberty." Nope, I'd never been here before, I'd have remembered a name like that. Well, either Robert had a rather interesting sense of humor, or this town was just well named. This could be where I'd begin again, if I could let go of the past, the pain, the failures. My liberty from pain would be found in the town of Liberty, if I could only believe that what Robert had said was true. Yes, I believed. For now. No, not for now. No more being tossed about on the waves of unstable emotions. No victims allowed here.

But I needed to build a new foundation, a strong one, one that wouldn't crumble when times got hard. Because the hard times would always come. That was one thing I'd learned through all my years of wondering. Faith didn't make you immune. You see that too, right? However, I needed what Phillip had. What Annie had. What Minnie had. What Robert had. What so many others I'd met along the way had. I could see that now; freedom was nice, but running wild could only get me so far. I needed the peace that had led Annie to know that all would be well no matter the despair. I needed the wisdom that had led Minnie to know when to help others. I needed the compassion that had led Philip to eat among the homeless. I needed the grace that had led Robert to forgive me. He also had given me the gift of love when I thought I didn't deserve it. Well, to be honest, they all did in their own way. But most of all, I needed a relationship with God like they all had—a deep, personal friendship on a level that I'd never known before with a being that I couldn't even see. But I could feel Him, and I thought I could now hear Him.

No, I know now that home isn't a physical place you can go to. It's having the joy, the peace, the love, the mercy, and everything else I'd been shown. If I could find those things, then I'd finally be home. I was well on my way. At least, I really wanted to be. I so hoped I was getting close. I so needed my heart to have a home, a place of safety, of rest, of security— something I'd never even been close to having because when it was offered to me I had shoved it away with all my might, not understanding what I was turning down. You see, that was one more legacy from my parents—I had a twisted view of love. So, I believed my husband loved me also—with his fists. When I left, I thought love was something I never wanted again. Therefore, I'd rejected it every time it was offered, thinking that love was something bad. But love shouldn't hurt. That's not real love. No, love is good. I could see that now.

Sitting there in the middle of some small town might have been the oddest place to find myself at the end of my very long journey. Yet, this was where I'd landed. Many times before, I'd thought my life was over, but I'd always been wrong. But now, I'd actually ended it all—the previous night had been Cindy's last on earth. Robert was right—I had to lose my life to gain it. Today, I was genuinely a new woman, and it was an exhilarating feeling and a terrifying one at the same time. What if I messed up again, became the same royal failure that I'd always been? But I couldn't think that way, not anymore. No, this was the new me. I was a survivor. Maybe I'd even give myself a new name. No longer was I the wounded outcast, running scared, afraid of my own shadow. I didn't quite have joy yet—confidence was building fast, but there was so much to learn about God, so much to learn about His love.

I felt like a weight had been lifted off of me; a burden I'd been carrying was gone. The world truly was now in beautiful shades of every color you've ever heard of. How could you deny a creator when looking at such wonders as a tree? The new flowers? As me? If even I was lovable, then there must be a God.

My journey had turned out to be a failure in one regard, I hadn't found what I'd thought I wanted. There was no paradise, no place free from pain. Pain was part of life. But I had found something, as the song says: you can't always get what you want, but sometimes you get what you need. It is indeed true. I wanted freedom, but what I needed was so much more important. Lucky for me, I'd gotten that in spades when I opened my heart. I needed a Savior, simple as that. Me, who had always felt I could take care of myself, couldn't.

Betcha didn't see that coming, did you? No, having heard it said all these years that Jesus had died to save the lost, now I understood. Yeah, no one could've been more lost than I. Both in a physical and spiritual sense, I had been nowhere to be found.

But how exactly does one become found? Well, in my case, by sheer luck. But I needed more than luck now. I needed a guide, and mine had flown the coop on me. Robert had said God was in church when believers were there. So, I'd have to find a church filled with people.

Church bells began to ring in the distance. *It must be Sunday — find that church! Then listen to what they have to say. Don't be snarky and rude, Cindy.* There was still a longing within so deep it hurt, but it was because I wanted God so much now.

Leaning over to pick up my belongings, I spotted Robert's neat handwriting on the paper bag.

"For where your treasure is, there your heart will be also." Matthew 6:21

You're ready to begin a new life. You've taken the longest, hardest journey of all — from your head to your heart.

"So if the Son make you free, you will be free indeed." John 8:36

You're forgiven, free from the past, free to begin again. I've done all I can for you.

Robert.

My treasure was finding the pot of gold at the end of the rainbow I'd been chasing and finding a "who," not a "what." Okay, you're so right. That's super corny. But I'd been chasing God without even knowing it. Thus, finding God was better than anything else I could've ever done in my mixed-up life. Yet, did I know enough about God to start this new life? Yes, I now knew that I needed something greater than myself. I knew that He'd been there all along, trying to teach me what I needed to know about Him.

Putting lots of people in my path with lessons along the way. God just needed me to start seeking Him before anything else, but I had never seen the signs.

You know, those giant neon signs pointing you where to go, flashing brightly in your face. Like a blind beggar, I'd missed them all. Somehow, Robert had pointed them out to me in a way that I could see them for the first time, teaching me many lessons about myself and God, lessons I'd kinda remembered hearing over the years. Then I guess he felt I'd learned enough to stand on my own.

But had I learned enough? Have you?

Thanks for reading! If you enjoyed this book, please leave a review. If you spotted an error, or just want to send me a note please email me at:

leighlincolnauthor@gmail.com

Made in the USA
Lexington, KY
15 March 2017